Acclaim for Dorothy Love

"Dorothy Love writes with such rhythm and grace. Her attention to historical detail creates the perfect setting for characters we swiftly grow to love and cheer for. *The Bracelet* is a jewel of a story."

—Tamera Alexander, *USA Today* bestselling author of *To Whisper Her Name* and *A Lasting Impression*

"*The Bracelet* by Dorothy Love was a fascinating and exciting antebellum novel that kept me flipping pages way into the night. I loved the insight into events that triggered the war, and Love's writing is beautiful and evocative. Highly recommended!"

—Colleen Coble, author of *Seagrass Pier* and the Hope Beach series

"*The Bracelet* is the perfect blend of mystery, history, and the quest for love and truth. A great read for not only lovers of period fiction, but for anyone who hungers for a well-told story."

—Susan Meissner, author of *A Fall of Marigolds*

"With a country on the brink of war and her own future uncertain, Celia Browning's faith will be tested and her very life put in jeopardy by the mystery of the bracelet. In a novel inspired by actual events, Dorothy Love artfully recreates the lavish world of power and prestige in 1850s Savannah with unforgettable characters and the attention to historical detail her readers have come to expect. Vivid and entrancing . . . I was swept away!"

—Kristy Cambron, author of *The Butterfly and the Violin* and *A Sparrow in Terezin*

"Subtle and suspenseful with exquisite descriptions of antebellum Savannah, Georgia, and a tender love-story to boot. D[illegible]rothy Love's *The Bracelet* takes the reader on a chilling jo[illegible] mysteries surrounding one of Savannah's m[illegible]ring the days before the Civil War. I[illegible]rose provide a story that will deligh[illegible]

—[illegible]owan House, *The* *Sw*[illegible]rets of the Cross Trilogy

"Vivid and romantic . . . recommended for fans of *Gone With the Wind*."

—LIBRARY JOURNAL ON *CAROLINA GOLD*

"Beautifully portrays an independent Southern woman . . . Pitch perfect . . . A memorable book."

—HISTORICAL NOVELS REVIEW ON *CAROLINA GOLD*

"A beautifully written Southern historical that should appeal equally to Christian and secular readers alike."

—READING THE PAST ON *CAROLINA GOLD*

"*Every Perfect Gift* is certainly a gift to readers."

—PUBLISHERS WEEKLY

"Romance and a strong sense of place recommend Love's delightful Southern-flavored historical."

—LIBRARY JOURNAL ON *EVERY PERFECT GIFT*

"Romance, mystery, and intrigue . . . Love gives readers even more than they expect . . ."

—ROMANTIC TIMES REVIEWS ON *EVERY PERFECT GIFT*

"Love's amazing historical has all the elements readers expect . . . Romance, mystery, and characters who want more out of their lives."

—ROMANTIC TIMES REVIEWS ON *BEAUTY FOR ASHES*

"With well-drawn characters and just enough suspense to keep the pages turning, this winning debut will be a hit . . ."

—LIBRARY JOURNAL, STARRED REVIEW FOR *BEYOND ALL MEASURE*

THE BRACELET

OTHER BOOKS BY DOROTHY LOVE

A Proper Marriage (e-novella only)
Carolina Gold

THE HICKORY RIDGE NOVELS

Beyond All Measure
Beauty for Ashes
Every Perfect Gift

THE BRACELET

DOROTHY LOVE

THOMAS NELSON
Since 1798

NASHVILLE MEXICO CITY RIO DE JANEIRO

Published in Nashville, Tennessee, by Thomas Nelson. Thomas Nelson is a registered trademark of HarperCollins Christian Publishing, Inc.

Thomas Nelson titles may be purchased in bulk for educational, business, fund-raising, or sales promotional use. For information, please e-mail SpecialMarkets@ThomasNelson.com.

Publisher's Note: This novel is a work of fiction. Names, characters, places, and incidents are either products of the author's imagination or used fictitiously. All characters are fictional, and any similarity to people living or dead is purely coincidental.

Library of Congress Cataloging-in-Publication Data

Love, Dorothy, 1949–
The bracelet / Dorothy Love.
pages ; cm
ISBN 978-1-4016-8760-1 (softcover)
1. Family secrets—Fiction. 2. Savannah (Ga.)—History—19th century—Fiction.
I. Title.
PS3562.O8387B73 2014
813'.54—dc23 2014024002

Printed in the United States of America

HB 04.11.2019

For Daisy Hutton

"There are no secrets that time does not reveal."

JEAN-BAPTISTE RACINE

Prologue

September 27, 1843

INSIDE THE CARRIAGE HOUSE THE AIR WAS DAMP AND STILL, thick with the smell of leather and horses. She shook the rain from her hair and eased the door closed. In the dim light coming through the high windows she could discern the shapes of two carriages, one an open surrey with three rows of seats, the other closed and more commodious—and beaded with rain. Beneath the window: two metal buckets, a buggy whip, a squat wooden table with peeling paint and coated with dust.

She had not seen him since the accident, but she had waited for him in the garden behind the house, just as he'd asked, until the storm broke. Maybe he loved her as he claimed. But in his world, love was easily won and just as easily tossed aside.

For months she had known this day was coming, and she'd waited for her heart to be free. But longing was a sickness that wouldn't leave her. She couldn't explain even to herself why such feelings bound her to him despite the torment of parting, the fear of discovery, and the price they now would have to pay.

She sank to the floor, the brick pavers rough against her bare feet, and her foot hit a coil of rope lying in the corner. She looked up to the cobwebbed rafters, and something broke inside her. Who would miss her if she were gone? Certainly not the child, too young to know its mother. Maybe Phoebe from the kitchen would shed a tear. Maybe Primus and Fanny, who had covered for her when he sent word and she slipped away. Otherwise she would be forgotten. Erased. A stone beneath rushing water.

She uncoiled the rope, and the weight of it gave her courage. It would be easy enough to form a knot. Climb onto the table, toss the rope over the rafters. Slip the noose over her head and kick the table away. A simple end to a complicated life.

She dragged the table to the center of the room and with trembling fingers fashioned the noose. She swung it over the rafters. On the third try, it caught. She slipped the noose over her head, the scratchy rope pressing heavily against her throat.

She closed her eyes, the sound of her pulse rushing in her ears, tears scalding her cheeks. Phoebe said it was a sin to die by one's own hand and such an end would lock the gates of heaven against the sinner. But maybe she deserved whatever fate waited for her on the other side. She could see no other way for this story to end. Desperation had overtaken her and now exerted its own logic.

The storm intensified, jagged lightning cracking open the sky, the roll of thunder swallowing the sound of her sobs. She longed for a swift end to her suffering. But still she hesitated. What of the child? Who would care for her little one with the same affection its own mother would? A mental image of the helpless babe sent another wave of guilt washing over her, weakening her resolve. If she stayed in this world, a life of longing and regret would be her penance. But if she died here, and in this way, the child would have an even heavier cross to bear. Grief upon grief.

The table beneath her feet cracked and abruptly tilted, one leg splaying out at a precarious angle. The rope tightened, and black spots danced before her eyes. She teetered, both arms outstretched, and regained her balance, then stood motionless—afraid to move, afraid not to move, every muscle aching with the strain.

The carriage house door slid open. A flash of lightning briefly illuminated a dark figure silhouetted against the rain-swollen sky. In the garden beyond, the gazebo stood out in sharp relief, the roses and jessamine bent and sodden.

"Please." Her throat felt raw. Her tongue stuck to the roof of her mouth. "Please help me."

1

Savannah, Georgia, September 15, 1858

AT THE SOUND OF MALE VOICES IN THE ENTRY HALL BELOW, Celia Browning left her window overlooking the garden and the redbrick carriage house. She set aside her book and opened her bedroom door just wide enough to afford a view of the door to her father's study down below. The house was quiet, the entry hall now empty. Dust motes swirled like snowflakes in the late afternoon sunshine, pouring through the fanlight above the front door and reflecting in the ornate gilt mirror on the wall. She cocked an ear to listen, but the conversation taking place behind the massive mahogany doors was lost in the vast space.

"Oh, fiddlesticks!" Frowning, she leaned against the polished mahogany banister and wondered what she was missing.

Papa often included her in discussions of the shipping company that had made him the fourth richest man in Savannah, behind Mr. Low, Mr. Green, and their neighbor on the square, Mr. Sorrel. She relished the lively discussions regarding Browning Shipping Company's fleet of snows and schooners that transported cargo to ports around the world. She liked keeping up with the prices of timber, cotton, and turpentine and the news of markets that might soon admit ships from Savannah. Most of all she loved that her father treated her as an equal, allowing her the occasional visit to his counting house on Commerce Row, overlooking the river.

"Eavesdropping, Cousin?"

Celia jumped at the sound of Ivy's voice. Ivy grinned, one brow raised.

"I'm not eavesdropping. Even if I wanted to, I can't hear a thing."

Ivy eyed Celia's bare toes peeking from beneath the pink bell of her skirt. "You'd better not let Mrs. Maguire catch you running about without your shoes."

Celia waved one hand. "She won't care. She secretly likes looking after us."

"She likes looking after you and Uncle David. I'm only the poor relation who causes more trouble than she's worth."

Celia studied her tall, sharp-faced cousin. Ivy had come to live with the Brownings when Celia was eight and Ivy ten. After fifteen years it was hard to remember a time when Ivy had not occupied the bedroom across the hall from Celia's in the terra-cotta-colored mansion on Madison Square. Papa had done everything possible to make Ivy feel welcome, but lately Ivy's usual determined cheerfulness had been replaced by periods of dark abstraction that lacked an apparent cause. It seemed she looked for opportunities to remind the Brownings that she didn't really belong to them. Or to Savannah, a city Celia and her father loved almost as much as they loved each other.

"What's the matter?" Celia placed a hand on her cousin's arm. "It isn't like you to feel sorry for yourself."

"Oh, don't mind me." Ivy lifted one shoulder in a tiny shrug. "I'm out of sorts today. I don't feel sorry for myself, and I don't want anyone else to, either." She tucked the book she'd been reading beneath her arm. "I've been an orphan for so long that I actually find it quite liberating."

"You're certainly in an odd mood today."

A burst of laughter escaped from below. Celia peeked down and saw that the door to Papa's study had opened. Now he stood in the foyer with his clerk. Elliott Shaw was a slight, thin-shouldered man of uncertain years whose generous mouth and thick eyelashes gave an almost feminine cast to his pale features. Celia had met him a few times at Papa's office. Mr. Shaw was always courtly, if a bit shy, but his movements, so awkward and constrained, made her feel ill at ease. Still, nobody knew accountancy and maritime law better than he.

Mr. Shaw retrieved his hat and took his leave. Papa returned to his study. Celia padded silently along the upper hallway, passing portraits of generations of Brownings and Butlers, and ran lightly down the carpeted stairs, one hand trailing along the polished banister that gave off the pleasant scent of lemons and beeswax.

"Papa? Do you have a moment?"

He looked up from the stack of papers on his desk, a smile creasing his handsome face. "Always have time for you, darling. Give me a moment to finish signing these."

Celia plopped into her chair and tucked her bare feet under her. A sultry breeze stirred the curtains at the open windows and carried with it the sounds of horses' hooves plodding along the unpaved street, the voices of children playing in the tree-shaded square. The rustle of Papa's papers mingled with the faint ticking of the clock on the mantel above the fireplace. Celia watched a woman and a small boy hurrying along the street, the child clinging like a barnacle to her voluminous skirts. A flock of sparrows rose and fell along the rooftops.

Celia released a contented sigh. She loved every room of this house—the drawing room where she entertained her friends, the spacious dining room with its massive mahogany table and a marble-topped sideboard that held the family silver. The library, bursting with books and filled with warm Georgia sunlight that poured through the tall windows facing the street. But Papa's study was her favorite. Dark-green walls were adorned with paintings depicting ships at sea. Books on maritime law sat side by side with novels by Mr. Thackeray, Mr. Scott, and Mr. Dickens. A glass-fronted secretary held her father's cherished mementoes: medals for his service to the army, a framed drawing of Celia's that had won a prize at school, a pair of silver-handled antique dueling pistols purchased on a trip to France, and a miniature portrait of her mother, painted shortly before she was lost in the *Pulaski* steamship disaster.

Papa set down his pen and pushed his papers aside. "Now then, Celia. What's on your mind? I hope you aren't cross at having missed my talk with Mr. Shaw just now."

"Well, I am disappointed. But I can never stay cross with you, Papa."

He smiled. "You didn't miss a thing. Shaw only wanted to bring by these papers before he leaves for Cassville to spend a few days with his sister. She hasn't been well these past months. We discussed nothing of consequence." Papa removed his gold-rimmed spectacles and folded them carefully. "How is your work for the asylum coming along?"

"Very well. Mother's friends are happy I've decided to finish the work she started all those years ago. I only wish I could have taken up the cause much sooner."

"Your schooling had to come first."

Papa had paid two hundred dollars a year for her and Ivy to attend the female academy in Atlanta. They had spent six years learning French and astronomy, science and mathematics, needlework and music. Celia loved science especially, but marriage, motherhood, and charity work were the only permitted aspirations for a woman of her station. In the five years since graduation, she'd devoted herself to various causes, including improving the lives of the girls at the Savannah's Female Orphan Asylum.

"I wish Mother could know how much progress we've made with the girls. But there's still so much to be done, and all of it takes a good deal of money."

Papa nodded. "I saw Alexander Lawton at the club last week. He said Mrs. Lawton intends to make a generous contribution."

"I thought she might. She's working hard to gather more support for the indigents at the hospital too. She feels as I do, that improving the lives of the least fortunate will benefit all of Savannah." A thick dark curl escaped its pins, and Celia tucked it behind her ear. "I wish you could see how much progress Annie Wilcox has made. She has been at the asylum less than a year and already she reads as well as I do. And she's a genius at trimming hats. Mrs. Clayton thinks Annie might one day find a position at Miss Garrett's."

Her father's brows rose in a silent question.

"Miss Garrett owns one of the finest millinery shops in Charleston. Wouldn't it be wonderful if Annie could work there and one day open a shop of her own?"

His expression grew tender. "Seeing those girls succeed is terribly important to you, isn't it?"

"Yes, and not only for the sake of Mother's memory. Most of the girls are working so hard to learn something that will allow them to live a respectable life. I can't help hoping they will succeed. But we need more books and perhaps one of those new sewing machines everybody is talking about for those who want to learn dressmaking. And a piano for Iris Welborn. She's a musical genius who plays much better than I do, even though she has never had a lesson in her life. If she learns to read music, she might one day earn a good living as a music teacher."

"Savannahians are generous people. I can't imagine that you won't raise enough for those things."

"Oh, I think we will. Several of the ladies have already pledged their support. But we need to expand the building too. Just last week three new girls arrived. That place is bursting at the seams."

Papa took off his spectacles and polished them on his sleeve. "A building expansion is quite an ambitious undertaking."

"I know it. But if men like you and Mr. Green and Mr. Low will help, I'm sure we can do it."

"Of course you can count on me, but you must remember most of Savannah is still recovering from last year's financial crisis." Papa raised an eyebrow as if to remind her of the importance of tact. "Many of our friends fared much worse than we did."

"I'll be circumspect, Papa. I'm planning a quiet reception later this fall where people can come to socialize and contribute to the fund anonymously. That way everyone can preserve appearances without feeling compelled to give more than they can really afford."

He glanced out the window. "I'm pleased things are going so well, but something tells me you didn't come here to give me a progress report on the Female Asylum."

She shifted in her chair and dug her bare toes into the thick carpet. "Alicia Thayer called here this morning with the most exciting news. I hope it's true."

"Ah. Is this about Sutton Mackay?"

"Then it is true! He's on his way home?"

"I haven't spoken to Burke Mackay about it yet, but I saw Mr. Stiles this morning, and he says Sutton left Kingston last week. I imagine young Mr. Mackay will turn up here any day now—just in time for the start of the social season."

"May we host an entertainment for him, Papa? Nothing too elaborate."

"The last time you said that, we wound up with fifty guests for Christmas dinner."

She laughed. "I will admit it. That one got a bit out of hand. But people still talk about how much they loved the food. And the Mysterious Fantasticals."

"And well they should. Do you have any idea what that dinner cost me?"

"Mrs. Stiles says one never should discuss the cost of hosting guests. Or of anything else for that matter."

"And she is right, of course. Forget I said anything." Papa rose and retrieved his pipe from its stand on the corner of his desk. He took his time filling it while he stared absently out the window at the leafy, parklike square.

"Were you and Mr. Stiles talking business this morning? Or politics? If the former, I am quite piqued at being left out."

He puffed on his pipe to get it going and sat down heavily behind his desk. "William prefers not to discuss business with women present."

"Too bad. He could learn a lot from us. We women know much more than most men think."

Papa smiled. "You didn't miss any news from Commerce Row. William is concerned about the next presidential election."

"Already?"

"He says there's some talk Mr. Lincoln from Illinois might run. Lincoln says he has no wish to meddle in our affairs despite his opposition to slavery. But William is certain his election would spell doom for the South."

Celia plumped the needlepoint pillow behind her back. "Last week at tea, Mrs. Quarterman said the Dred Scott decision should have settled the entire issue. She says the court has decided that a slave is the property of his owner no matter where he goes. But if we secede, I don't think the Northerners will care what the judges say."

Her father nodded, his expression thoughtful. "I'm proud that you're so well informed, Celia. But I regret that the ladies of Savannah find it necessary to spend so much time worrying about politics." He gestured with his pipe. "The election is nearly two years away. There's no sense worrying about it today."

"I agree. But Mrs. Quarterman said some of the Negroes are starting to talk politics in the streets, and not just in Currytown and Old Fort. She says they're becoming outspoken right here in our own neighborhoods too."

"There have been some noisy discussions in the streets of late. I do want you and Ivy to be careful when you leave the house. If you need to go farther than Reynolds Square, please have Joseph drive you." He set down his pipe. "Now, what type of entertainment are you contemplating for the esteemed Mr. Mackay?"

"I haven't had much time to consider it, but in the carriage on the way home this afternoon, I was thinking that a masked ball might be just the thing. Nobody has given one in quite some time, and I know Sutton would enjoy it. I'm sure people don't host masquerades in Jamaica."

"Perhaps not." Papa opened his leather appointment book. "I must make a trip to Charleston at the end of the month, but we could arrange something for early October. The weather should permit us to serve a buffet on the rear terrace."

"I suppose that's enough time for us to send the invitations and for our guests to assemble their costumes."

He ran his finger down the page. "Does Saturday the ninth of October suit you, my dear? Assuming of course that Sutton is home by then. Sea voyages can be unpredictable this time of year."

"Perfect. Thank you, Papa. Will you ask Sutton the moment he arrives home?"

"I shall inform him of your intent at the first opportunity. And I'll see his father at the club tomorrow. I'll mention it to him then." Papa took another draw on his pipe and sought her gaze. "I'm glad to see your happy anticipation, darling. I know how fond you are of Sutton. But I must caution you not to wear your heart on your sleeve."

She laughed. "I'm afraid it's entirely too late for that. Everybody in Savannah knows how Sutton and I feel about each other."

"A childhood friendship is not the same as marriage. People change with time."

"He hasn't been away that long."

"Two years is a long time in my book. You are not the same young woman you were when he left the city."

"I hope not. I hope I'm wiser now. Certainly I'm old enough to marry, and there is no one on earth I'd rather marry than Sutton Mackay."

"All the same, I don't want you to fix your affections too hastily, Celia. Take your time getting to know Sutton again, to be certain his habits and principles are still a good match for your own."

"Of course, Papa." But deep down she couldn't imagine any fault of Sutton's that would dampen her affection for him. He possessed all the qualities of an ideal suitor—good blood ties, a fine education, solid economic prospects, and impeccable manners. He was quick to laugh, slow to anger, quick to forgive. And he was the handsomest member of the Chatham Artillery, the most prestigious of all the city's volunteer companies. His letters from the Mackays' shipping port on Jamaica's Black River, though infrequent due to distance, were full of lively observations of local life and news of his thriving business, and they left little doubt about his intentions regarding their future. That suited Celia perfectly.

She hated the whole tiresome notion that a girl must wait to be chosen. With any luck, her wait was almost at an end.

A carriage rolled past the window, the horses' hooves kicking up clouds of sand. A fire bell sounded in the distance. Papa knocked the ash from his pipe. "Now you must excuse me, my dear. I must attend to some correspondence before dinner."

"All right." Celia rose, her silk skirts rustling, and planted a kiss on the top of his head. "Don't work too late. Mrs. Maguire has made a beef roast for dinner and syllabub for dessert, and you know how she fusses if she has to wait to serve it."

"Hmmm."

She frowned. "You are worried, Papa. And not only about politics. What's troubling you?"

He tapped the copy of the *Daily Morning News* folded neatly on his desk. Celia glanced at the headline. "The house of love and grief: New mystery surrounds Browning mansion on Madison Square. New mystery? What new mystery?"

"There is no new mystery. It's only the wild imaginings of a journalist who apparently has come to town for the sole purpose of writing about us and reviving the tragedy that befell this house all those years ago. There is no purpose in it apart from selling more newspapers." Papa released a heavy sigh. "I'm quite disappointed in William Thompson. I've known him ever since he became the editor at the paper, and I can't say I understand at all what is to be gained by resurrecting such painful memories."

Celia had been only a child then, but fragments of memory still lay like shards of glass in her heart: A black wreath on the door. The parlor mirror draped in black. Mrs. Maguire's grim, pale face, the furtive whisperings of the mourners, and Ivy's heart-wrenching wails as the coffin was lowered into the ground. Then the dark, tragic coda to a story she still didn't understand.

Now she worried that the whole scandalous story would play

out in the newspapers all over again, just when Sutton Mackay was returning home. Even the best people were endlessly fascinated by tragedy so long as it was not their own, even in a city such as Savannah, which prided itself on observing propriety above all else. She frowned. "Isn't there anything we can do?"

"I intend to speak to Thompson tomorrow. But frankly, I'm not too hopeful he'll quash the story. He's in the business of selling papers after all." Papa jabbed a finger at the folded newspaper. "If this Channing fellow can find even one new half-truth to splash across the headlines, I'm sure some people in town will be unable to resist reading about it."

"Miss Celia?" Mrs. Maguire's voice preceded her into the room. The Irish housekeeper bustled in carrying a stack of clean linens and bobbed her head at Papa. "Good afternoon, sir."

"Mrs. Maguire."

"Miss Celia, I've been callin' you for the last ten minutes and here you sit, daft as stone."

"I'm sorry. What is it you wanted?" Celia regarded the housekeeper fondly. Though Mrs. Maguire had arrived in Savannah aboard a ship from County Waterford nearly thirty years earlier and had worked for the Brownings ever since, her speech still held strong traces of her native country. Especially when her feathers were ruffled.

Mrs. Maguire thrust the linens into Celia's arms. "These are the things you wanted to donate to the asylum. Sure and you'll be wantin' them for your meeting tomorra mornin'. They're old, but serviceable. I'm sure the girls will be happy to have them." With another bob of her head, she hurried toward the kitchen.

Papa cleared his throat and stared pointedly at the papers on his desk. Celia took the hint and hurried up the stairs to her room with her stack of linens, determined not to let politics or the specter of a scandalous newspaper story spoil Sutton's homecoming.

If all went as she hoped, she and Sutton would be engaged by Christmas.

"Listen to this." Celia set down her pen and held her sheet of writing paper to the gray light coming through the parlor window. A thick layer of fog had come in with the tide, painting the city a somber shade of gray and bringing with it a steady rain that thwarted her plans to deliver clothing and linens to the Female Asylum.

Ivy set down the scarf she was knitting. "I'm all ears."

Celia read aloud:

The dark Peruvian and the Naples maid
Fly through the waltz or down the gallopade.
Spain's haughty grandee seeks the gypsy girl,
And Greek and Frenchman join the airy whirl.

Ivy nodded. "Very clever."

"I'm thinking of putting it on the cover of our invitation to the ball. I know Mrs. Naughton will be pleased. Remember the year she came to Mrs. Sorrel's party dressed as a gypsy girl?"

"Vaguely." Ivy resumed her knitting.

Celia let out a sigh. "You might be a little more enthusiastic."

"Yes, I might be, but this blowout has little to do with me." Ivy's needles made a faint clicking sound in the large room. "I know it's important to you, but I've never been one for dances and such."

Celia regarded her cousin with a mixture of sympathy and exasperation. Though Papa saw to Ivy's every creature comfort, she had grown up knowing little of the carefree gaiety most young women of her social class enjoyed. "You'd like them more if you'd learn to waltz. Papa would teach you or hire an instructor."

"I know, and I'm grateful. But really, I'd rather stay home with a good book and a cozy fire than spend an evening pretending to like people I can barely tolerate."

Celia set down her pen and paper. "You've been like this ever since we learned of Sutton's return. What's the matter? Our friends are the nicest people in Savannah. I should think you'd be pleased at the prospect of an evening with them."

"Some of them are all right. But Fanny Ward sets my teeth on edge." Ivy finished off a row of stitches and unwound more scarlet-colored yarn from the basket at her feet. "She doesn't do anything except spend her father's money and gossip. And Rose Shaw is too clever by half, if you ask me."

"Rose is brilliant. Mrs. Mackay says Rose is to have her poetry book published next summer."

"Nobody likes a woman who is too clever. And Rose simply tries too hard."

"Well, I think she's remarkable. I wouldn't mind publishing a book someday."

"Sutton Mackay might have other ideas about that."

"Sutton will want whatever makes me happy. That's one reason he's so wonderful."

Ivy frowned. "May we please speak of something else? It seems he's the only topic of conversation in this house these days. I find it tiresome."

Celia stared. "I thought you adored Sutton. Besides, you're the one who brought him up."

"I do like him. Very much. But too much talk of any one subject is like having pudding three times a day. Eventually one becomes sated."

"Then how about helping me with the guest list. I must finish it soon and get the invitations to the printer's." Celia read off a list of names that included the Stileses and the Mackays, plus the Frasers, Butlers, Greens, and Wards. "Too bad the Lows have left for England. I'll miss having Mary here. Have I forgotten anyone?"

"What about the Sorrels?"

The Sorrels were their neighbors on Madison Square, having built a magnificent home that rivaled her own. The dapper and engaging Mr. Sorrel, who was said to be half Haitian and half French, was the third richest man in Savannah and excellent company. But his poor wife, Matilda, was plagued by fits of melancholy and wildness that made her an unpredictable guest.

Celia scribbled their name and added a question mark beside it before glancing at her cousin. "I'm inviting Alicia Thayer."

"I assumed you would. Despite my feelings about it."

"How can I not? She's my dearest friend. And she never meant to embarrass you by inquiring about an engagement that never happened. She thought you were quite serious in your intentions toward Mr. Carlisle. We all thought so."

"I can't help it. I'm still mortified every time I think of it."

"Heavens, Ivy. That was more than a year ago. And Alicia has apologized more than once."

Ivy kept her eyes on her knitting. "If you loved me as a cousin ought, you would never invite her."

Celia doodled on her notepaper. Allowances must be made, Mrs. Maguire always said, because Ivy had no parents. Celia knew being an orphan was difficult. She had grown up without her mother after all, and she knew how lonely it could be. But all their lives, Ivy had wanted whatever was Celia's, whether it was a doll or a hat or a new dress, and Celia had acquiesced rather than disappoint Papa. Now that they were adults, she had grown weary of being the one who was always expected to give in.

"What about the Gordons?" Ivy said. "You know how everyone in Savannah has taken to Nellie Gordon." She shook her head. "Who would have thought that with all the lovely girls right here in Savannah, William Gordon would up and marry someone from Chicago?" Ivy laughed. "They say Mrs. Gordon has a habit of sliding down stairway banisters. Do you suppose it's true?"

"I haven't any idea. But I'm sure she isn't sliding down banisters these days, and she won't be here for the masquerade. Mrs. Mackay says Nellie's baby is due any day now."

Downstairs the doorbell chimed, and a moment later Mrs. Maguire appeared in the doorway. "Miss Celia, you have a caller."

"At this hour? In this disagreeable weather?" Celia patted her hair and smoothed her blue gabardine day dress. "I'm not prepared for callers, Mrs. Maguire. Please ask whoever it is to leave her card."

"'Tis no lady, my girl, but a gentleman. From the newspaper, he says."

"The newspaper? You mean the one bent upon stirring up trouble for us?"

"I can't say. Here's his card."

Celia glanced at the name printed on flimsy paper rather than engraved on heavy stock as a proper gentleman's card should be. "Tell Mr. Channing I am not at home."

"Ah, but you are." The man strode into the entry hall and peered into the parlor.

Celia whirled and scowled at him, taking in his cheap wool suit, the jacket patched at the elbows and brown boots desperately in need of a proper polishing. "Mr. Channing, it is highly impolite to barge into a home when you have not been invited."

Hat in hand, he sauntered into the room. "I realize that, and I do apologize for my lack of propriety, but I don't imagine you would have invited me inside under any circumstances."

"You are correct. Mrs. Maguire will show you out."

His eyes caught hers and held. "You won't grant me even a single question, Miss Browning? After coming all the way across town in this messy weather?"

"I'm not responsible for the weather, nor for your poor judgment."

Ivy set down her knitting. "What is it you wish to know, sir?"

Celia glared at her cousin. "Surely you are not thinking of—"

"I saw the newspaper yesterday." Ivy looked up at the interloper, who stood just inside the door, his hat tucked beneath his arm. "I am Ivy Lorens. It's my parents' story that has captured your imagination, I believe."

"So I understand. But the, um, tragic events occurred here. Or, more precisely, in the carriage house." He shrugged. "One of them did anyway."

Celia waved one hand. "None of which is in dispute. I cannot see the point of this conversation at all."

"Doesn't it seem odd that two such terrible events, occurring within weeks of each other in the same house, should both be attributed to bad luck?"

It was not the first time Celia had heard the question, but it was the first time it had been spoken so boldly in her presence. "Everything that happened here was thoroughly investigated. My father saw to it personally."

"And through his friendships at the newspaper, he controlled the reportage." Mr. Channing surveyed the spacious room. Celia watched him taking in the fine carpets, the mahogany tables and silk draperies, the Egyptian marble fireplace anchoring the far wall. "I haven't been in Savannah too long, but long enough to know that David Browning is a man of means. And men of means in this city can do as they please."

"That is quite enough, Mr. Channing. I won't stand here and listen to you accuse my father of covering up the facts."

His lips lifted in a sardonic smile. "Whatever gave you that idea?"

"What possible reason is there for bringing up such unpleasantness now and reminding my family of such terrible twists of fate?"

The reporter raised a brow. "How can I resist? Such intrigue will make quite an interesting book. And I intend to write one because, my dear Miss—"

"I am not your dear anything. Now please, leave us in peace."

"Because," he repeated, leaning languidly against the door frame, "I don't believe it was accidental at all."

2

"HONESTLY," CELIA FUMED AS THEIR CARRIAGE ROCKED ALONG toward the asylum the following morning, "I have never met a more unpleasant character than Leo Channing."

Beside her on the tufted red leather seat, Ivy shrugged. "True, his manners could use some refinement. But beneath those rough clothes he's really quite handsome."

Celia laughed. "You're joking. I thought he looked rather like a Methodist parson."

"Only because he didn't smile very much. But you must admit it took courage to barge his way into the house."

"Courage? By that measure any common burglar might be elevated to the status of a hero."

"I don't know why you're letting his visit upset you so. If I was not offended, I can't see why you should be."

Celia kept her eyes on the passing scene. Behind banks of palmetto, Spanish dagger, and pride-of-India trees stood fine houses of pink stucco, gray brick, and brownstone, all of them graced with marble steps, copper finials, and cast-iron balconies. "You should be offended by anyone who calls our family liars."

"He never said that."

"Not in so many words, but everyone in Savannah knows

that what happened was an accident. To imply otherwise is to impugn our veracity and our good name. I should think you'd be insulted for Papa's sake, if not for your own. After everything he's done for you."

The carriage drew up at the imposing building that housed the orphaned girls. Joseph, the freedman who had worked for the Brownings all of Celia's life, opened the door and handed her out of the carriage. "Want me to wait for you, Miss Celia?"

"Yes, please. We won't be long." Celia gathered the parcel of linens and shirtwaists for donation and looped her reticule over her arm. "Ready, Ivy?"

"I'm coming." Ivy retrieved another parcel and straightened her ostrich-plumed hat.

They walked through the wrought-iron gate and up the steps to the front door. Ivy rang the bell. Faces appeared briefly in the second-floor windows before Annie Wilcox, the red-haired would-be milliner, opened the door. "Miss Browning and Miss Lorens. Please come in. I'll fetch Mrs. Clayton for you."

"Hello, Annie." Celia smiled at the girl. "No need to disturb her if she's busy. We only wanted to drop off these things for you girls."

"Very kind of you, I'm sure." The girl took the parcels. "Some of the other ladies have been by this week. Mrs. Fondren and Mrs. Sorrel were here just yesterday. Brought some new bed linens and not a moment too soon either." The girl frowned. "'Course, what we need most is a sewing machine and a piano for Iris, and—"

"Annie?" The asylum director hurried into the foyer, patting her silver curls into place. She adjusted her spectacles and squinted at Celia. "Who . . . oh, Miss Lorens. And Miss Browning."

Celia inclined her head. "Good morning, Mrs. Clayton."

The woman smiled and dismissed Annie with a curt nod. "May I offer you some tea? I'd like to discuss something with you if you have a moment."

Celia hid her surprise. Though she was in charge of fund-raising, the older ladies in her circle—Mrs. Mackay, Mrs. Low, Mrs. Green, and Mrs. Lawton—were equally devoted to the aims of the asylum: to ensure that orphaned or abandoned girls grew up to lead moral, disciplined, and productive lives. Mrs. Mackay and Mrs. Lawton were usually the ones to whom Mrs. Clayton turned for advice.

"It won't take long," the director said.

Ivy stepped forward and smiled. "Of course we are happy to help in any way we can, Mrs. Clayton."

The older woman led the way into her small parlor and rang a bell for tea. Celia took a chair by the open window that afforded a view of the carriages and buggies crowding the street and of a small garden filled with jessamine and magnolias. Palmettos rustled and clacked in the warm September wind.

A plump young woman in a faded calico dress brought the tea things. The director poured, passed the milk and sugar, and dismissed the girl. When the door closed, Mrs. Clayton leaned forward in her chair. "You probably don't know Captain Stevens. He's hardly a member of your circle. But he's well known on the waterfront."

Celia sipped her tea, recalling glimpses of a beefy, broad-shouldered man who commanded three cargo vessels. "I can't say I've met him, but my father pointed him out to me several times. The captain is Danish, I believe. He makes quite a good living transporting produce from the plantations. He consigns his cargo to one of Papa's colleagues on Commerce Row. Mr. Habersham."

"That's the one," Mrs. Clayton said. "Well, last week Captain Stevens turned up here with a girl in tow. Apparently she hid herself away on one of his vessels, and he didn't find her until he docked in Savannah. Of course he didn't know what to do with her, so he brought her here. In rags and half starved she was, but she refuses to say where she came from. Captain Stevens will make inquiries on his next trip to the island, but for the moment we can't be sure whether she is without a family or merely ran away."

"But in any case, she must be looked after," Ivy said, stirring more sugar into her tea.

"Precisely." Mrs. Clayton turned her faded blue eyes on Celia. "That's where you come in, my dear. So long as she is here, we must do our best to mold her mind and her character. She has shown some interest in books, but she is so far behind the other girls that Miss Ransom despairs of catching her up. I remember how much the girls enjoyed your reading to them on your visits last spring, and I hoped you might find time to read with Louisa. She seems bright enough."

The director paused for breath. "I know it's presumptuous of me to ask, especially when you're working so hard to raise money for us, but everyone else has declined. All for very good reasons, but still . . ." She smiled. "I'm sure we will see great progress even if you can spare only a few hours each week."

Celia set down her cup. She wanted to do as much as possible for the girls, and she was curious about the runaway. But in addition to the fund-raising reception, she had the masquerade ball to plan. And dinner tomorrow night with her father at the Greens'. And Sutton might arrive home any moment. "Mrs. Clayton, I would love to help but—"

"We'll both help," Ivy said. "With the two of us taking turns, the girl will progress even faster." She set down her cup and smiled at Celia. "It's always a privilege to help those less fortunate. Isn't it, Cousin?"

Mrs. Clayton beamed. "Splendid. Miss Ransom will be so relieved. When can you start?"

Celia stifled the impulse to do Ivy bodily harm. Nothing to cause permanent disfigurement. That would be wrong. But a good hard pinch on the arm or a swift kick in the shins . . .

She forced a smile. "May I consult my calendar and let you know?"

"Of course." Mrs. Clayton rose. "I must speak to the cook, and I imagine you have much to do as well."

"Yes," Celia said. "We really must go."

"I'll look forward to seeing you soon." Mrs. Clayton patted Celia's arm. "You, too, Miss Lorens. I cannot thank you enough."

Celia and Ivy left the asylum and descended the steps to the street, where Joseph waited with the carriage. He doffed his hat and helped them inside.

Celia tamped down her anger and stared out the window as Joseph turned the carriage for home.

"Don't be cross with me," Ivy said minutes later as they approached Madison Square.

"Why shouldn't I be?" Celia let out an exasperated sigh. "First you defend that awful Leo Channing, and then you volunteer my services to the asylum when you know perfectly well I have a million things to do. Whatever is the matter with you?"

"Be honest, Celia." Ivy reached up to corral a wayward blond curl that had escaped the confines of her veiled hat. "Aren't you the least bit intrigued by the notion of a runaway? I haven't met Louisa yet, but I must say I admire her for striking out and pursuing what she wants. It couldn't have been easy to sneak aboard a cargo vessel and remain in hiding for days."

As the carriage made a wide turn onto Bull Street, Celia spotted a familiar horse and rig standing outside her gate, and her anger dissipated like morning fog. The instant Joseph halted the carriage, Celia wrenched open the door and raced up the steps, Louisa and the masquerade and Leo Channing fading from her thoughts.

Sutton was home.

She found him in Papa's library and stood stock still, drinking in the sight of him. He was every bit as attractive as she remembered—tall and broad-shouldered, dark hair curling over his forehead, his skin deeply tanned from two years beneath the harsh Jamaican sun.

"Celia!" He set aside the magazine he'd been reading and strode toward her, both hands outstretched, his gaze warming her like a fire.

Breathless with joy, she dropped her hat and reticule onto a settee and rushed into his arms. The long separation, the desperate silences between their letters, the powerful yearning to be with him every single minute were instantly forgotten. "You're really here."

"At last." His gray eyes lingered on her face. "My dear Miss Browning. Just as beautiful as I remembered."

"My dear Mr. Mackay. Just as silver-tongued as I remembered." She laughed. "Not that the compliment is unappreciated."

He stepped back and bowed, his expression grave. Their eyes met, and they dissolved into the helpless laughter of their childhood.

Mrs. Maguire came in with a tea tray and set it down with more force than was necessary. Celia sobered and inclined her head toward the housekeeper. "Thank you, Mrs. Maguire."

"Sure and you're welcome, Miss." Arms akimbo, the housekeeper frowned at Sutton. "So here you are at last."

"Yes, and very happy to be home." Sutton grinned. "You're looking exceedingly well, Mrs. Maguire. I do believe you are even more beautiful than when I left, if such a thing is possible."

Mrs. Maguire blushed. "Humph. Had you given me decent notice, boyo, I might have made that almond cake you're so fond of. Instead, you'll have to settle for yesterday's tea cake."

Sutton winked at her. "I'm sure whatever you've brought will be just fine, and I thank you for it. You're perfectly right. I should have given you more warning of my imminent arrival, but I was so eager to see you all that I couldn't wait any longer."

Ivy appeared in the doorway, her hands clasped at her waist. "Hello, Mr. Mackay."

"Miss Lorens. You're looking very well."

Ivy lowered her gaze. "I am well. And happy to see you."

"I'm delighted to be home. Jamaica was an interesting place to do business, but there is no substitute for Savannah." Sutton motioned them to be seated on the settee. He took a chair opposite them while Mrs. Maguire poured tea.

"I cannot believe how the city has grown." He waved one hand. "Waterworks, mills, more railroads, half a dozen new stores. It's quite amazing in light of last year's crisis." He bit into a tea cake and closed his eyes in appreciation. "This is delicious, Mrs. Maguire. I think I like it every bit as much as your almond cake."

A brief smile lit the housekeeper's weathered face. She smoothed her apron. "Will there be anything else, Miss Celia?"

"No, thank you."

"Let me know if you change your mind."

Mrs. Maguire left, closing the door behind her.

Celia couldn't stop looking at Sutton. She longed to throw herself into his arms and never let go, to have him all to herself for a private conversation, but of course propriety dictated that she not be alone with him until they were officially engaged. She nibbled at the tea cake, but she was too excited to taste a single bite. "When did you get home, Sutton? Have you seen Papa?"

"I arrived night before last."

"Night before last? And you waited till now to visit me?"

"Trust me, I was in no shape to call upon a lady. We hit some rough water just off Kingston, and I was awake for twenty hours straight. I went directly to Mother's and slept like the dead. Then I needed a trip to the barber's. And the haberdasher's."

"I forgive you then," she said, smiling. "And you do look quite fetching."

He laughed. "Is that a word applied to gentlemen? What do you say, Miss Lorens?"

"I'm sure I don't know." Ivy set her cup down. "But it is very good to see you. I hope you'll come to dinner soon and tell us all about your adventures in Jamaica. I've heard it's quite primitive."

"Parts of it are. But there are some fine homes there too. And some fine horse breeders, in among the crocodile-infested mangroves."

He turned to face Celia. "I saw your father this morning. He told me about the ball you're planning for next month."

"Did he tell you it's to be a masquerade? They are always such splendid fun, and nobody has hosted one since the last bad fever epidemic. At least this year's outbreak was relatively mild. The Irish neighborhoods took the worst of it." She studied his face, hardly able to believe that he was home at last. "You are pleased with my plans, I hope."

"I am delighted but undeserving of so much attention. The Lawtons are hosting a dinner at the end of the week, and Mother is planning a reception for me at the Pulaski Hotel next Saturday. I'm sure you'll all be invited to both." He grinned. "I feel like a prospective bride."

"Speaking of brides," Ivy began. "Lacy Fondren is engaged to William Sikes." She brushed a crumb from her green silk skirt. "But I'm sure you knew that already since she was such a good friend of yours."

"Yes, Celia and Mother mentioned it in letters that arrived just before I left Jamaica." Sutton helped himself to more tea and another tea cake. "I'm delighted for them. Celia and I both feel they are quite suited to one another."

"Oh." Ivy folded her hands in her lap and looked at the ceiling as if she expected to see another topic of conversation written there. "Celia and I visited the Female Asylum this morning and discovered there is a stowaway in residence. We're to make a project of her, catching her up on her studies."

"I'm sure you'll do splendidly." Sutton smiled at Ivy. "Miss Lorens, I wonder if I might ask a great favor of you."

"A favor?"

"I'd like to escort Celia on a walk around Madison Square. I know you must be busy with your own pursuits, but I would certainly appreciate your coming along, if you can spare the time."

"Of course." Ivy smiled at Celia. "I know how eager she has been for your return."

"Well, then, shall we go?"

He offered an arm to each of them, and they left the house. The scent of the last of the summer flowers mingled with the smells of the sea, horses, and food cooking. Sutton chose a bench near a row of low green hedges.

Celia sat down, but Ivy stood, hands to her sides. "I'm sure you'd rather be alone. I'll sit over there." She indicated a white wrought-iron bench next to the small fountain.

"You're welcome to join us," Sutton said, but Celia read the longing in his eyes. He was as eager for time alone as she, but much too well-mannered to exclude Ivy.

"Well—" Ivy glanced away and fussed with her hat.

"You might enjoy all the catching up we have to do," Sutton went on. "The business situation in Jamaica is quite interesting. I've always thought that a lady with such a broad and serious brow must surely have a lively mind."

Ivy's smile evaporated. Her expression went hard. "An attempt to console me for my plainness, Mr. Mackay?"

"Ivy!" Celia rose, frowning. Ivy had always been moody, and Celia usually felt protective of her prickly cousin. Right now, however, she wanted to strangle Ivy.

Sutton looked surprised but not angry. "Why, I've always

thought you quite a lovely and charming lady, Miss Lorens. I'm sorry if my compliment missed the mark."

Ivy gave him a grudging nod and whirled away.

Sutton watched her go. "Your cousin seems to be in high dudgeon about something."

Celia plopped down next to him. "I know it. She's been this way for days, and I haven't a clue as to why."

"Well, I am sorry to have said the wrong thing." Sutton relaxed on the bench, his long legs crossed at the ankles.

"She'll get past it." Celia glanced at her cousin, who had perched on a bench beneath a moss-draped oak tree. "Her moods usually don't last long." She paused. "We had an uninvited visitor yesterday."

Briefly she told him about Leo Channing and his determination to resurrect the events that had taken place fifteen years before. "Ivy claimed it didn't bother her, but now I'm not so sure. Perhaps Mr. Channing has upset her more than she's willing to admit."

"What does your father say?"

"He was furious when he learned Mr. Channing had barged into the house and announced his ridiculous notion of writing a book. Papa intends to talk to the *Morning News* editor, but of course Mr. Thompson will do whatever he thinks will sell the most newspapers."

Sutton nodded.

"But I don't want to talk about that anymore." Celia faced him and took his hands. "I missed you terribly, and I'm dying to hear all about Jamaica."

"I wrote you most of it. Jamaica is not the same place it was when I first went there with my father. I was just a boy, of course, but I remember the talk about how the slaves had received emancipation and the speculation about how that would affect the sugar crop." Sutton waved away a bee buzzing about their heads. "Sugar was practically the only export back then. Now the colony is much more diversified. The last two years we shipped more bananas and coffee than anything else."

"Papa says the South Coast is still prospering, even without slave labor."

"Yes. The port at Black River is still growing."

"Doesn't that prove we could survive here, too, if the slaves are freed?"

"I doubt it. Most of the Jamaican farms are much smaller than ours, and their crops require much less labor than our rice and cotton plantations. The end of slavery here will mean the end of life as we know it."

"Some people think war is inevitable. Especially if that man from Illinois is elected president."

"Yes. My father thinks so, too, as do most of our friends at the club."

"I pray they're wrong, Sutton." The mere possibility of sending him off to fight with the Chatham Artillery was too much to bear.

Sutton tipped her face to his and smiled into her eyes. "Let's not think about that now. The election is still two years away. Anything might happen before then."

"Such as?"

"Some kind of compromise."

"That seems unlikely now that the court has declared a slave to be a slave wherever he goes. From what I've read in the papers, it seems people's attitudes are more unbending than ever."

Sutton was still smiling at her.

"You're amused?"

"No, enchanted. Delighted that you've grown into a woman who is not only beautiful and gracious, but smart too. And not afraid to express an opinion."

"Papa thinks I should be more circumspect." Celia sighed. "I know he's right, but sometimes I wish I didn't have to observe so many rules."

"Well, you can break all the rules you want with me." He clasped her hand. "Celia?"

She caught her breath. Was this the moment she had been waiting for?

"Yes, Sutton?"

"I've been thinking it's time we—"

"Sutton!"

Celia looked up to see her father hurrying across the square, his coattail flapping behind him, his face pink with exertion.

She and Sutton rose.

"What is it, Papa?"

Papa kissed her cheek. "Hello, my dear. I'm sorry for this interruption, but I'm afraid a crisis has arisen. We're meeting at the club in half an hour." He glanced at Sutton. "Your presence is required, my boy."

"What's happened, sir?" Sutton retrieved his hat from the bench and buttoned his jacket.

"My driver is waiting. I'll explain on the way."

3

Midnight. The little French chime clock on the fireplace mantel in her bedroom marked the hour. Wide awake, Celia slipped from the bed and parted the curtains. Flickering gaslights illuminated the empty street and the dark shapes of the houses on the square, the globes of orange light suspended in the inky darkness. A stray cat crossed the street and disappeared into the shadows.

What could possibly be taking Papa so long? A thousand imagined horrors crossed her mind. Some problem with his business. More political unrest. A killer on the loose.

After her father came for Sutton, she and Ivy had returned to the house, Ivy to resume her knitting, Celia to choose the books she would take to the Female Asylum for Louisa's first reading session tomorrow. Mrs. Maguire had served supper in the parlor before retiring to her own room. Much later the Mackays' driver had arrived to retrieve Sutton's horse and buggy. And still Papa had not returned.

The sound of a horse and carriage echoed in the empty street, and the Brownings' carriage halted at the gate below. Finally! Celia grabbed her dressing gown and hurried barefoot down the darkened staircase just as the door opened.

"Papa?"

"Heavens, girl, you startled me."

Celia folded her arms across her chest. "Where on earth have you been? I've been awake half the night, imagining all sorts of dire calamities."

"Forgive me, my dear. I intended to send word that the meeting would run late but nobody wanted to leave the proceedings." He headed for his study.

She followed and waited while he lit the lamp. "Is Sutton all right?"

Papa fell into his chair and managed a tired smile. "Yes, but perturbed at me for taking him away from you so soon."

"I should be perturbed too. I think he was about to propose just when you arrived."

"Oh, my dear, I do apologize. But you can be sure he won't let this interruption derail his intentions. If I know Sutton, he will declare himself soon enough."

She settled into the chair across from his. "What was so important that it took all night?"

He sighed and pressed his fingers to his eyes. When he looked up again, his expression was grave. "I'd rather you didn't repeat this to anyone. The situation is volatile enough without the weight of too much discussion."

"Of course." There had been only the two of them since her mother had died at sea. In the seventeen years since, whether the topic was business or politics, her father had treated her as an equal. He was the only person besides Sutton in whom she had complete faith and trust. "What's happened?"

"I barely know where to begin. You know about the articles William Thompson published in his newspaper this summer, calling for a reopening of the slave trade."

"Yes, Sutton mentioned it in his last letters from Jamaica. He says Mr. Thompson isn't the only one. Some of the planters feel that way too."

"Charlie Lamar is in the middle of it. Apparently he spent this year up in New York state secretly building a new slave ship. He's already made a trial run to New Orleans, and he's outfitted the ship with enough water for a long voyage. It seems he intends to defy federal restrictions and bring more slaves into Georgia."

"Won't the authorities stop him?"

"They will try."

"But, Papa, who would purchase his cargo and risk having federal marshals at their doors?"

"That's what tonight's meeting was about. We hoped to band together to convince Lamar not to pursue such an undertaking, but it appears we're too late. We think the *Wanderer* has already sailed for Africa."

A wave of revulsion washed over her. Just last spring, on an outing with the Mackays to Isle of Hope, Sutton's father had spoken at length about the early days of the African trade and the unspeakable cruelties that had taken place aboard the British slaver ships. It was unlikely that conditions had improved much since then. Celia balled her fists in her lap. "I cannot abide Mr. Thompson and his newspaper. It seems he's always stirring up trouble. First the slave trade and now that disgusting Leo Channing prying into our family's past."

Footsteps sounded in the hallway. The door opened and Mrs. Maguire, in a blue dressing gown, her iron-gray hair in a thick plait, came in carrying a supper tray. "I heard your voices and thought you might be hungry."

"Thank you," Papa said. "I am a bit peckish, but you should not have disturbed your rest on my account."

"'Tis no trouble." The housekeeper set down the tray and poured coffee. "I was awake anyway. I don't sleep well until all my chickens are safely under the roof. And that includes you, Mr. Browning."

He laughed, blue eyes twinkling, and picked up his cup. "I don't know what we'd do without you, Mrs. Maguire."

Mrs. Maguire pointed a finger at Celia. "You'd best be gettin' your sleep, my girl."

"In a minute." Celia helped herself to a sandwich. "I want to say good night to Papa."

"Then don't be blaming me when you wake up tomorra all out o' sorts and with circles under your eyes."

Mrs. Maguire left, the hem of her dressing gown whispering on the carpet. Celia bit into her sandwich, chewed, and swallowed. "So, Papa, if Mr. Lamar has already left for Africa, what is to be done?"

"Nothing. As nearly as we can calculate, he should be returning sometime in November." He drained his cup and set it on the tray. "Until then, the less said about it the better."

"Was Mr. Thompson at the meeting tonight?"

"He was—to try to convince us we're wrong about Charlie Lamar."

"Did you ask him about Leo Channing?"

"I stated my objections to Mr. Channing's intentions in the strongest possible terms."

"And?"

"He has assured me that Channing will stay away from this house and from you and Ivy."

"But he won't order Channing not to write about us?"

"He made no promises beyond assuring me that anything that is printed in the paper will be fair. But of course if Channing decides to write a book, Thompson can't stop him."

"Do you believe him?"

"Thompson's articles have been fairly evenhanded, though I

don't always agree with his point of view." Papa leaned forward to pat her shoulder. "I know you're worried about Channing stirring up all those old stories again, especially now that Sutton is home. But Sutton knows us, Celia. He knows your heart. Nothing Channing can write will change that."

"It won't change the truth either, but you know how people love to gossip." Celia finished her sandwich and wiped her fingers on her napkin. "I didn't care much for Uncle Magnus, but I hated the things that were said about him after Aunt Eugenia died. And now Mr. Channing has said he doesn't believe her death was an accident."

She folded her napkin and placed it carefully on her plate. "It was an accident, wasn't it, Papa?"

Papa rose and briefly embraced her. "It's late, Celia. Go to bed."

Celia followed Mrs. Clayton down the quiet hallway of the Female Asylum. The girls had gathered in the spacious parlor on the first floor with Miss Ransom, leaving their bedrooms empty, the narrow beds neatly made, curtains fluttering in the languid September breeze. Through an open window Celia spotted three young women hurrying across the lawn, the hems of their skirts flipping up behind them to revealing glimpses of white petticoats.

Mrs. Clayton stopped before a closed door near the end of the hallway, knocked once, and motioned Celia to follow her inside.

"Louisa," she said softly. "I've brought Miss Browning to read with you."

The girl was a study in contrasts: coffee-colored skin, bright-blue eyes, a penumbra of curly hair that was neither blond nor brown. She was older than Celia had imagined, though it was hard to guess her true age. She might have been as young as twelve, as old as seventeen. Certainly she was as tall as Celia herself, whip-thin and all sharp angles.

The girl set aside her needlework and folded her hands, waiting.

"Hello, Louisa." Celia crossed the narrow room and held out both hands. "Mrs. Clayton has told me about your—about how you came to Savannah. I must say I admire your bravery."

Ignoring Celia's outstretched hands, the girl shrugged.

"Well," Mrs. Clayton said, "I'll leave you two to get acquainted." She left, pulling the door closed behind her.

Celia perched on the edge of the bed and opened the small travel satchel she'd used for transporting the books. "I wasn't sure what kind of stories you might like. I brought—"

"Don't matter."

"But surely you'd like to catch up to the others so you can study with Miss Ransom. I understand she plans to—"

"Listen. You're trying to do a good thing. It's what rich ladies are supposed to do—got nothing else to occupy their time. But I have my own plans, and they don't include staying at a place like this any longer than I've got to. It's a waste of time, teaching me to read better than I already do."

"Learning is never wasted." Celia glanced around the room. With whitewashed plaster walls, dusty windows, and plain furniture, it lacked a feminine touch, but it was clean and safe. The girl's embroidery hoop lay on the narrow bed. The half finished piece was exquisite, featuring birds and butterflies and entwined flowers, each tiny jewel-colored stitch neat and perfectly matched to the others. "Someone spent a lot of time teaching you to do such beautiful needlework."

Silence.

Celia tried a different tack. "I imagine Captain Stevens was quite surprised to find you aboard his boat."

The girl chewed off a ragged fingernail and spat it onto the braided cotton rug covering the pine floor. "Said I could get him in a peck of trouble. But I'm not a slave." Louisa's expression was one of steely determination. "I can go wherever I please. I told the captain I was born in freedom, but it didn't matter. He was real mad."

"Because you might have made trouble for him. But he was still concerned enough to bring you to Mrs. Clayton. He could have turned you over to the authorities. There are penalties for stowing away."

Downstairs, the front door opened. Through the window Celia saw Miss Ransom and her charges spilling onto the narrow lawn bordering the street.

Following Celia's gaze, the girl unfolded her long legs, her movements fluid as smoke, and got to her feet. "Looks like reading time is over."

The girl's lack of cooperation rankled. Most of the young women at the asylum were grateful for the chance to better their lives, but Louisa seemed not to care at all.

Celia took a couple of books from her satchel and handed them to Louisa. "Perhaps you'd enjoy reading *Jane Eyre* on your own. Or *Vanity Fair.* The author, Mr. Thackeray, visited Savannah a few years ago. He stayed at the home of a friend of ours. Mr. Low. I was so excited to meet him that when we finally were face-to-face I could barely speak a word."

The girl set the books aside and glanced at Celia's satchel. "What else you got in there?"

"Let's see. How about *Indiana*, by George Sand. It's a love story that takes place partly in a castle and partly in Paris. But it was written almost thirty years ago. Perhaps you've already read it."

Louisa shrugged.

"I brought a few magazines too." Celia offered the girl the latest issues of *Peterson's Magazine* and the *Home Journal.* Louisa flipped through the *Peterson's*, not bothering to read anything, but pausing here and there to study illustrations of lavish ball gowns and plumed hats.

Perhaps fashion was a way into this girl's guarded heart. "I must go, but I'll leave these with you. When I come again we can discuss the ones you've read, and I can help you with any words you don't know. Would that be all right?"

"Suit yourself."

"Good. In the meantime, perhaps you shouldn't mention to Mrs. Clayton that we didn't read today. She seems very determined that you should catch up to everyone else, and I don't want to disappoint her."

"I'm not stupid."

"Of course not. I only meant—"

"I have to go. Mrs. Clayton gets her drawers in a knot if we're late to chores."

Celia stifled a laugh. "I'll walk down with you."

4

PAPA SET DOWN HIS GLASS AND SMILED AT HIS DINNER GUEST across the dining-room table. "We're delighted you could finally join us, my boy. I'm afraid Celia has not quite forgiven me for interrupting your walk in the park last week."

Celia took a sip of water from her cut-glass tumbler. "I forgive you, Papa. It wouldn't be fair not to, considering everything you've done to help with the masquerade party for Sutton next month."

"I'm honored that you've all gone to such lengths to welcome me home." Sutton ate another bite of roast beef. "There's nothing more welcoming than a dinner under your roof, Mr. Browning. But I will admit a costume ball is more excitement than I've had these past years."

Ivy caught Sutton's eye. "Have you chosen your costume yet? Or will it be a surprise?"

"To be honest, I haven't had much time to think about it." Sutton's expression clouded. "Father has not seemed quite himself of late, and then there was that worrisome business about the *Wanderer.*"

"Has there been any more news?" Celia asked.

"Nothing," Papa said. "I ran into Captain Stevens a couple

of days ago. He's just back from a trip to St. Simons and hasn't seen anything of the *Wanderer.* We are in for some difficult days if Charlie Lamar does return with human cargo."

Celia buttered a slice of bread. "I suppose you saw Mr. Thompson's piece in the paper yesterday. He's all for importing more slaves, and yet he seems to think the poor whites here in town might decide they have more in common with the blacks, economically speaking, and side with them against the slaveholders. Thus we must guard against an excess of democracy, or so he says. It's quite contradictory. I didn't know there was such a thing as too much democracy."

"Blacks and whites can work together," Sutton said. "In Jamaica it's the only way to get things done. Of course, slavery has been outlawed down there for twenty years." He set down his fork. "I don't like the idea of bringing in more slaves. Lamar is putting all of the Lowcountry at risk."

Papa nodded. "Mr. Sneed said as much in his piece in the *Republican*. I can see his point. If Georgia experiences another flood of Negro labor, the poor white men will have no chance to adequately support themselves, and the divide between rich and poor will only grow wider. That won't be good for Savannah or for the rest of Georgia." He sighed. "The whole situation is worrisome."

"Worrying about it won't change anything, Uncle David," Ivy said.

"You're right about that. No sense in borrowing trouble."

Sutton smiled and changed the subject. "So what about you, Ivy? Have you chosen your costume for my party yet? It's only two weeks away."

"I'm not sure I will attend." Ivy pushed her plate away.

"Oh, but you must," Sutton said. "I'll be terribly disappointed if you don't."

Ivy brightened. "You will?"

"Yes, indeed. The whole evening will be much more enjoyable if you're there. Won't it, Celia?"

"Of course." Celia sent her cousin an encouraging smile. "Besides, Ivy has been so much help with the planning, it would be a shame for her not to see how everything turns out."

Brows raised, Papa helped himself to another glass of Madeira. "Dare I ask how many guests we are expecting?"

"Fewer than a hundred," Celia said. "Only our closest friends—and Sutton's, of course. We've arranged for the flowers and the musicians, and several of Mrs. Maguire's friends are helping with the food. It will be simple fare that can be served on the terrace. That way we can keep the ballroom clear for the dancing and the promenade. And—"

Celia stopped, suddenly aware of Sutton's intense gaze. "What's the matter? Have I forgotten something? Do I have gravy on my nose?"

"Not a thing, I was just marveling at what an accomplished hostess you've become."

"Losing my mother so soon, I've had lots of practice." Celia looked up at the life-size portrait of her mother hanging above the fireplace. With her dark hair and violet eyes and her stylish entertainments, Francesca Butler Browning had been widely admired as the most beautiful woman and the most accomplished hostess in the Georgia Lowcountry. Celia had inherited her mother's sense of style and her unusual coloring. As she grew into womanhood, people had often remarked upon the close resemblance.

Mrs. Maguire came in with the coffee service and a coconut cake. "I've brought your afters."

The four waited while the housekeeper cleared the dishes and served the dessert. At last she draped a linen towel over the tray of dishes and lifted it.

"This looks wonderful, Mrs. Maguire." Papa picked up his silver dessert fork. "Thank you. Dinner was delicious."

"Indeed," Sutton said. "I enjoyed every bite, Mrs. Maguire."

"'Twas my pleasure, I'm sure."

When she had gone, Sutton sipped his coffee and regarded Celia over the top of his cup. "What about you, our esteemed hostess? What kind of costume do you have in mind for the masquerade?"

Celia hesitated. She had meant to broach the subject with Papa in private, but perhaps this was as good a time as any. She turned to him now. "Do you remember the gold silk costume Mama wore to the Christmas ball the year you and she went as Antony and Cleopatra?"

"I do indeed. Your mother looked every inch the queen. I wish now I'd had her portrait painted in that gown. It was quite remarkable." He smiled. "Though I also recall her complaining about the weight of it."

"I was thinking I might wear it." Celia watched Papa's face. He was unlikely to deny her wishes, but she would attend the party in rags before hurting him. "But I won't if it would make you sad."

"On the contrary." Papa set down his fork. "I would enjoy the sight of a beautiful girl in a beautiful gown. Remind me, and I'll fetch your mother's diamond necklace from the bank vault."

Celia pushed back her chair and rounded the massive table to embrace her father. Sutton rose with her.

"Thank you, Papa. I'll be careful with it. I know how much it means to you."

"The necklace was my gift to my wife upon our engagement," Papa told Sutton. "One day it will be Celia's, of course."

"And Celia will look like a queen as well," Sutton said, his eyes warm with affection.

"So long as she doesn't confuse the role with reality." Ivy

spoke lightly, but Celia detected a veiled barb in her cousin's voice. "Anyway, I'm sure the two of you will make a splendid pair."

"I'll have a hard time coming up with a costume worthy of her," Sutton said.

"I don't care if you come dressed as a rag picker." Celia looped an arm through his. "I'm simply glad to have you home."

Papa rose. "Would you care for a cheroot and a brandy in the library, Sutton?"

"Thank you, but I promised Mother I'd be home early. She's worried about Father."

"He did seem a bit under the weather when I saw him at the club yesterday. Perhaps he needs a few days away from Commerce Row to rest."

"Mother and I have both suggested as much, but he won't hear of it. After so many business failures last year, he's afraid to take his eyes off our interests for even a day."

Celia felt a stab of sympathy for Mr. Mackay. Last year's financial crisis had dried up many sources of credit for the cotton trade, forcing nearly a hundred Savannah businesses—including factors' houses, insurance companies, even the main branch of the Bank of Georgia—to fail. Papa had been terribly worried about Browning Shipping Company too. She didn't blame Mr. Mackay for his diligence. But she worried about him for Sutton's sake.

The four of them moved from the dining room to the entry hall, where Sutton retrieved his hat and thanked them again for dinner.

"Sutton, can you wait a moment?" Ivy asked. "I have a present for you."

He laughed. "I always have time for a present, but what's the occasion?"

"Just a little something to welcome you home. I won't take a moment." Ivy hurried up the stairs and soon returned with the red woolen scarf she'd spent the last weeks knitting. "Sorry I didn't have time to wrap it up. I finished it only this afternoon."

Sutton's brow furrowed as he ran his fingers over the wool. "Well, it's wonderful, and I sincerely appreciate it. But I . . ."

Her face fell. "You don't like it. I can tell."

"I do like it, and it was very kind of you to go to so much trouble." He lifted Ivy's hand and kissed it. "I've always thought of you as the sister I never had. Sweet and generous. And now, every time I wear this scarf, I'll think of you."

He turned to Celia. "Will I see you tomorrow at church?"

"Of course."

"Celia wants to ride her horse tomorrow," Papa said. "Perhaps you'd like to join us at the track after church?"

"I'd love to. Poseidon and I need to get to know each other again after all this time. And I've been looking forward to meeting your Zeus."

"I can't wait for you to see him," Celia said. "He's quite wonderful, but more spirited than I expected. He gets hard to handle if he's idle for too long. The boys at the track take him out every day, but I'd rather do it myself. And lately I've neglected him."

"We'll give him a good long workout tomorrow," Sutton promised.

They said their farewells. Celia watched from the front door as Sutton set off toward his home on Lafayette Square, the red scarf draped jauntily about his shoulders.

Sitting between her father and Ivy the next morning in their pew at St. John's Church, Celia turned to look over her shoulder. Where was Sutton? All night she had tossed and turned, too excited about the prospect of an afternoon ride with him to sleep. Since his return they had had only a few moments alone. It seemed something always happened to keep them apart.

The service continued, and she forced herself to concentrate on the familiar prayers and the hymns, made all the more beautiful by the sound of her father's rich baritone. Beside her, Ivy mouthed the words, but no sound came out. No doubt her thoughts were on other things as well. Maybe she had decided to attend the ball after all and was mulling over her costume choices. Or was she disappointed that Sutton had not seemed more excited about her gift?

Celia rose with the other worshipers for the final hymn and stole a glance at her cousin. Ivy had taken particular care with her hair this morning, fashioning her shining blond locks into a mass of ringlets that brushed her shoulders and set off the black lace shawl pinned with the cameo brooch Papa had given her for Christmas last year. At twenty-five, Ivy was an attractive woman, well-read and with a fine education. There was no reason, apart from her prickly nature, why she could not find a suitable match.

Celia gathered her own shawl and reticule and followed her father up the aisle and into the church yard, Ivy trailing behind them.

"Celia, there you are. I was hoping to see you this morning." Sarah Lawton made her way to Celia's side and clasped her hand. "I don't have but a moment, my dear. Alexander is waiting in the carriage, and I must get home to the baby, but I desperately need a favor."

"Anything." Celia regarded the older woman with affection. Mrs. Lawton was everything Celia herself hoped to be—gracious, compassionate, and beautiful even in maturity. With her copper-colored curls and bright blue eyes, Mrs. Lawton looked far younger than her thirty-odd years.

"You remember, of course, that Nellie Gordon is about to become a mother," Mrs. Lawton said.

"Yes. Any day now, or so Mrs. Wade said just before the service this morning."

"I had so counted on Mrs. Gordon to finish collecting for the Christmas drive for the Poor House and Hospital, but with both of us confined these past months, I'm afraid we've fallen behind."

Celia nodded absently and peered over Mrs. Lawton's shoulder, hoping to spot Sutton. Clouds were building, promising rain, and she wanted to finish working Zeus before the weather changed.

"Nellie has done much of the preliminary work," Mrs. Lawton continued. "It's mostly a matter of collecting the promised donations and delivering them to the hospital in time for Christmas. I know you're working on the fund-raising for the Female Asylum and helping Mrs. Clayton with that new young woman too. But could you possibly take on one more thing?"

Though Celia dreaded the prospect of anything that would take more of her time away from Sutton, she couldn't disappoint a woman she so ardently admired. "Of course," she said.

"Oh, my dear, I am so relieved." Mrs. Lawton's eyes shone. "Sometimes it seems we will never catch up after being away all summer. I'll bring the list by in a day or two. Perhaps Ivy will lend a hand."

"Doing what?" Ivy halted beside them and bobbed her head at Mrs. Lawton. "Good morning."

"Good morning, Ivy. Your cousin has just agreed to deliver Christmas to the poor unfortunates at the hospital." Mrs. Lawton patted Celia's gloved hand. "I wonder whether Savannah fully appreciates what a dedicated young woman she is."

"Well, Uncle David and I are certainly proud of her," Ivy said. "I can't begin to keep up with her." She inclined her head to indicate the older woman's colorful jeweled necklace. "What a beautiful piece. I don't think I've seen anything quite like it."

"It was an anniversary gift from Alexander." Mrs. Lawton

unfastened it and draped it over her gloved palm. Six square-cut jewels in a variety of colors glittered in the light. "The first letter in the name of each jewel spells out a message. Amethyst, diamond, opal, ruby, emerald, diamond. A-d-o-r-e-d." She blushed like a schoolgirl. "His way of telling me he loves me."

"How very clever," Ivy said.

"Isn't it just? They say it's becoming quite the custom these days. I read an article about it in the *Lady's Book* this summer. 'The Secret Language of Jewels'—perhaps you saw it?" Mrs. Lawton refastened her necklace and planted a swift kiss on Celia's cheek. "I must go before Alexander sends out the police to search for me. Thank you again, my dear. You have taken quite a load off my mind."

Celia waved as Mrs. Lawton crossed the church yard. Most everyone else had gone, save a young couple with two small children in tow, Papa, and his banker, Mr. Waring.

Ivy looked around. "I wonder what happened to Sutton."

"I don't know. It isn't like him to break an engagement. I'm worried that perhaps his father has fallen ill."

Ivy's expression grew serious. "That thought crossed my mind too. But surely Sutton would have sent word to us if that were the case."

"Maybe he was too late for church and is waiting for me at home." Celia gathered her skirts, and they crossed the yard to the carriage, where Joseph waited to drive them the short distance home. "Even if he isn't there, I still want to ride Zeus. I've missed him."

Ivy grinned. "You and that horse. What a pair."

"You should come with us." For some reason Ivy's mood had turned sunny, and Celia wanted to make the most of it.

"Thank you, but no. It's my turn to read with Louisa this week, and I want to choose a book for her."

"Maybe you'll have better luck than I did. The girl seems to have arrived here with an agenda that does not include improving her mind."

Papa concluded his conversation with the banker and helped the cousins into the carriage before climbing in and settling on the seat opposite them. One look at his face told Celia the conversation had not been a pleasant one.

"Something the matter, Papa?"

"Nothing that can't be remedied." He smiled, but she was not convinced. "Would you mind terribly if I begged off from the trip to the track this afternoon? I promised to meet with Mr. Waring again tomorrow, and I need some time to prepare."

"Of course not. Are you sure there's nothing wrong? Sutton didn't come to church as promised, and now this—I can't help but feel you're both keeping bad news from me."

Papa sighed. "This discussion is to remain within the confines of this carriage."

"Of course, Uncle David." Ivy reached across to pat his hand. "What's the matter?"

"One of the Mackays' ships is overdue and feared lost."

Celia's stomach lurched. "Maybe it encountered bad weather and put into port somewhere. Sutton said one of their ships had to wait out a bad storm last year that put him almost a week behind schedule."

"Even if that were the case, it should have been here by now. Cyrus Wheaton's captain brought in his brig last night and reported sighting debris off the North Carolina coast."

Ivy smoothed her skirt. "I can see why the Mackays would be worried. But what has this to do with you, Uncle David?"

"I guaranteed the loan Burke Mackay took out for that shipment. Or a good part of it, anyway."

"Through the safe fund?" Celia asked. Some time ago Papa had told her of the money the elite men of Savannah kept aside to lend out when one of their number encountered financial difficulties.

"No. Burke refused to ask for help from the fund. He came to me privately and asked me to guarantee his loan at the bank. He didn't want Sutton to know the company is in trouble. But the cat is out of the bag now, of course."

"Won't the insurance company pay for the loss?" Celia asked.

"The company went bankrupt last fall. Burke intended to buy a new policy, but so many insurance companies failed last year that the few that are left are charging outrageous premiums. Burke decided to take a chance on this one shipment. Now it looks as if both the schooner and the cargo are lost."

"And the bank is looking to you to absorb the loss," Celia said.

"I'm afraid so."

"Can we weather such a loss, Papa?"

"That's for me to worry about."

"Poor Sutton," Ivy murmured. "No wonder he didn't feel like showing up for church."

The carriage drew up at the door.

"Remember," Papa said, handing Celia and Ivy out of the carriage. "Not a word of this to anyone."

"Of course not." Celia kissed his cheek.

Papa's blue eyes held hers. "You are not to let this news spoil your day, darling. Joseph will drive you out to the track when you're ready. The Warings' daughter is going riding too. The groom is there now, taking care of the horses. He'll help you tack up Zeus if Sutton doesn't make it."

"All right." She tried to smile as she mounted the steps to the front door, but the joy had gone out of the day. Anything that worried Papa worried her. And now she was concerned for Sutton too.

Mackay Shipping Company was his life. His passion. His hope for their future. What would happen if it all fell away?

5

CELIA CHANGED INTO HER RIDING CLOTHES AND HURRIED downstairs. The house was quiet. Mrs. Maguire had left early for mass and now was off on her usual Sunday afternoon visit with friends. Ivy had retired to her room. The door to Papa's library was firmly closed.

Joseph was waiting at the gate. He handed her into the carriage and fixed her with a baleful stare. "Not a fit day to go riding, Miss Celia. We gon' have rain 'fore this day is done."

"I'm afraid you're right, but I haven't had a chance to ride in days. Maybe the rain will hold off for a while."

"Maybe so." The driver climbed up, spoke to the horses, and they began the three-mile drive to the track. The Ten Broeck Race Course had opened last year to much fanfare. The track formed a large oval anchored on one side by a long, low grandstand. On the upper level a sheltered platform provided a viewing stand and a judges' booth. Down below were sheds where horses were stabled or readied for races. The Brownings had attended a few races, but Celia preferred solitude to the noisy confusion of race day. The deep woods surrounding the track provided a tranquil place for riding.

The stables were roomy enough, and clean, but Celia disliked having Zeus kept so far from home. After they'd acquired her beloved gelding, Papa had mentioned razing the boarded-up carriage house behind their house to build a proper stable for Zeus and for the family's carriage and horses. But so far that hadn't happened. Papa paid Joseph to look into the carriage horses at Mr. Sweeney's livery. But Mr. Sweeney, who ran the best livery in town, didn't have room for Zeus.

She chewed on her lower lip as the carriage approached the race course. That Sutton's father had needed a loan was worrisome. Perhaps Papa was in financial trouble, too, and waiting until his situation improved before undertaking construction of a new carriage house. How much money had he lent to Mr. Mackay anyway?

Moments later, Joseph halted the carriage. Celia stepped out and looked around, hoping to spot Sutton's big bay, Poseidon. But only the Warings' chestnut mare, her thick tail swishing, waited in the enclosure next to the grandstand. Finn O'Grady, the red-haired groom, lifted one hand in a little wave as she neared the enclosure.

"If you're here to ride with Miss Waring, she ain't got here yet." Finn blew out an exasperated breath. "That woman's never on time."

A rumble of thunder rolled across the track, and he frowned. "If she don't get here soon it'll be too late."

"I'll ride alone, then. I need you to tack up—"

"Zeus. Yes, Miss, I know that gelding of yours. Just about the finest horse in Georgia, I reckon."

She laughed. "Well, I think so anyway."

"A man come here the day before yesterday, asking if I thought you'd sell Zeus. I told him no, sir, not at any price."

"You're right about that. Now, if we could please hurry . . ."

Finn turned toward the stables. "I'll get him ready. Won't take me but a minute."

Joseph stood nearby holding the carriage horses' reins, one

eye on the darkening sky. "Reckon I might as well wait right here till you're ready to go back, Miss Celia."

"Oh, Joseph, I hate to make you wait. Besides, Papa might need to go out this afternoon, and he'll need the carriage. I wouldn't want him walking about getting wet and chilled."

"If you don't hurry yourself up, you gon' get wet and chilled your own self."

"If it starts to rain, I'll shelter under the grandstand."

"Well, all right then. But I don't like it. Not one bit."

Joseph vaulted onto the seat and turned the carriage for home just as Finn came out leading Zeus. The black gelding shied and danced behind the groom, but when he saw Celia he blew out a greeting and nuzzled her hand. She laughed and reached up to scratch behind his ears. "Hello, my darling. Did you miss me?"

Zeus shook his head and pawed the track. She laughed. "I thought so. Let's go."

Finn boosted her onto the saddle and handed her the reins. Zeus tried another little dance, but she gathered him in and urged him into a smart trot toward the track. She let him take one lap at his own pace, then bent low, and with subtle pressure to his sides, asked him to canter. Zeus responded, hooves flying, and they circled the oval, churning red dirt in their wake. Once he settled she'd take him down the wooded trail to the pretty little pond nestled at the back of the property—if the rain held off long enough. She glanced up just as the first drops plopped onto the ground.

Celia sighed and took a firm hold on the reins. "All right, then. Just one more lap before the storm hits."

Zeus lengthened his stride as they approached the far turn. From the corner of her eye, Celia glimpsed movement in the thick stand of trees bordering the track.

A dark-clad figure rose from the undergrowth and lobbed an empty whisky bottle onto the track. Celia wheeled Zeus just in time to keep him from tripping. But the sudden movement startled the gelding, and he bolted into the woods. Celia felt him stumble beneath her as he threw a shoe.

The rain intensified. She slid from the saddle and checked his feet. Zeus's left rear shoe was gone. She wiped rain from her face and chastised herself for not checking the horse herself instead of relying on the young groom.

Zeus, his sides heaving, shook his head and snuffled. "It's all right," she said. "We'll walk back."

The undergrowth rustled, and her breath caught.

"Celia?" Sutton appeared on a weedy path through the woods leading Poseidon, his hat dripping rain.

"Sutton! Where were you? I waited for you at church and then—"

"I know. I'm sorry. I've spoiled the whole day. And I will explain, but I think we ought to get out of this weather. What happened to Zeus?"

She explained about the thrown shoe. "I'd rather not ride him back, even if it is only a short way."

"Come on."

In the pouring rain they hastened through the woods, skirted the muddy track, and headed for the stables. Finn appeared at the door of Zeus's stall. Sutton walked Poseidon into an empty stall and began drying him off.

"My horse has thrown a shoe." Celia removed her sodden hat and handed Finn the reins. "You should have checked the shoes when you tacked him up."

"Sorry, Miss." The groom picked up a heavy towel and began drying the horse's flank. "It was careless of me, sure enough. It won't happen again."

Celia nodded. "All right then. Please see that he is ready to ride again at ten on Thursday."

"I will." Finn plucked another towel off a stack. "Looks like you could use this."

She squeezed water from her hair and blotted her face, keeping an eye on the groom as he removed Zeus's tack and filled the water trough. Finn fished a key from his pocket. "This opens the grandstand office. You might want to go in there and dry off, wait out the storm."

Sutton appeared, beads of water dripping from his hair. She handed him the towel and the key.

"We look like a pair of drowned rats," he said. "Do you suppose Finn left any coffee in the office?"

They hurried along the grandstand to the office, a small, plain room fitted with a desk and chair, a bookshelf, and a filing cabinet. A single window afforded a watery view of the track. Sutton started to close the door.

"Please leave it open," Celia said quickly.

"Oh yes, I remember. Of course." Leaving the door ajar, Sutton pulled out the chair for her, and then perched on the corner of the desk while she related the story of the thrown bottle, shivering more from the memory of the danger to her horse than from the dampness.

"If I hadn't turned Zeus when I did, he might have fallen and snapped a leg. Why would anyone want to hurt him?"

"It was probably some thoughtless child making mischief. It's what children do—make decisions before they're old enough to understand the consequences."

She looked up, surprised by the edge in his voice. "You're talking about that night at the Screven's Ferry Landing."

He nodded. "A couple of men rowed over yesterday to ask about working for me. They mentioned they'd been hunting over that direction—and I was reminded of that night yet again. Even after all these years, I still feel guilty for what I did."

Celia frowned. "That was a long time ago. We were just children, Sutton. There was no way you could know about—"

"No, but my father taught me to be better than that." He shrugged. "The only good thing that came out of that night was meeting you."

She smiled at the memory. "I wonder if our tree is still there."

"One of these days we should go look for it." He released a gusty sigh and peered out the window. Rain pattered on the roof. "Celia, what would you say if I told you that I've come to a decision? That I've changed my mind?"

She felt the blood drain from her face, felt her body folding in upon itself.

"Miss Celia?" Joseph loomed in the doorway holding a huge umbrella. "Your daddy's worried 'bout you being out in this storm. I've come to take you home."

Celia looked up at Sutton, her heart hammering. "You've changed your mind?"

"We can't talk now." He clasped both her hands. "May I call on you tomorrow?"

"Of course. But—"

"I'll be there at ten sharp."

There was nothing to do but to follow Joseph to the waiting carriage.

Overnight the weather turned chilly. Celia rose to the sound of a fire crackling merrily in the grate and the smell of Mrs. Maguire's soda bread wafting up the stairs. She dressed carefully in a salmon-colored silk dress, pinned up her hair, and went down to breakfast. Her father had already left; his empty coffee cup still sat at his place at the table along with a copy of the *Daily Morning News*.

Ivy looked up from her plate of eggs. "Good morning, Cousin. Did you sleep well?"

Celia sighed and slipped into her chair just as Mrs. Maguire appeared with another plate and the coffee pot.

"Here you go, my girl." Mrs. Maguire studied Celia over her spectacles. "You're looking pale as rain this morn. I hope you're not getting sick from spending all afternoon yesterday in the damp."

"I'm all right. I didn't sleep well last night."

Mrs. Maguire clucked her tongue. "If you're askin' me, Mr. Browning should *niver* have let you go to the track with a storm brewing. But I reckon he knows better than to try to keep you away from that horse." She turned to go.

"Mrs. Maguire?" Celia said. "Mr. Mackay is coming at ten this morning. I wonder if you'd make some tea and some of your benne seed cookies he's so fond of."

"Aye, I will. Go on now and eat your eggs before they get cold."

When the housekeeper had gone, Ivy slid the newspaper across the table. "Mr. Channing has written another article about us."

Celia frowned as she scanned the headline and the brief story beneath.

> The Curious Case of the Laundress: Was It Suicide . . . or Cold-blooded Murder?
>
> Rumors persist that the death of the beautiful young mulatto fifteen years ago at the Browning mansion on Madison Square was not what it seemed. For some time, talk had swirled that the young woman, a resident of St. Simons Island, was involved in a romantic liaison with a member of the Browning family. Such a thing seems plausible to this reporter in light of the other death that took place in the same house only two weeks earlier. It was rumored . . .

Celia tossed the paper aside. "If I weren't so angry, this would be laughable. Is this what passes for journalism these days? Listen to him: 'rumors persist . . . talk had swirled . . . it was rumored.' Mr. Thompson should be ashamed of himself for printing such drivel. There is not one fact in the entire piece."

"Well, hardly any, anyway," Ivy said.

"How can you sit there so calmly when our name is being dragged through the mud for no reason? I should think you of all people would be outraged."

Ivy shrugged. "You forget that I was subjected to years of whispers and rumors at school." She set her cup aside. "Of course no one will say so, but I'm quite sure it's the reason I've had no marriage proposal. Or at least not one I cared to accept. And time is running out."

Celia felt a pang of sympathy for Ivy. Every young woman felt the pressure to find a suitable match before the window of opportunity closed, dooming her to spinsterhood.

"Oh, Ivy, I didn't—"

"Mr. Channing's silly newspaper article pales in comparison to the humiliations I've already suffered." Ivy refilled her cup and flashed a smile that didn't quite reach her eyes. "I refuse to let it upset me. Plenty of women live fulfilling lives without the benefit of marriage, and I fully intend to become one of them. Now tell me. What was it that disturbed your dreams?"

"At the racetrack yesterday, Sutton told me he has had a change of heart."

"A change of heart? About what?"

"I don't know. Joseph arrived to bring me home before we had time to discuss it." Celia tried to eat a bite of bread and jam, but it stuck in her throat.

"You don't suppose that after keeping you waiting all these years, Sutton has decided not to marry?"

"I thought I knew his heart, but I admit I'm afraid he—"

"Has he said anything to make you doubt his intentions?"

"Not at all. But then we've hardly had a moment alone since he got home. And now, with the loss of his father's ship, I expect I'll see even less of him, at least until it's sorted out."

"Well, then, I would advise you to follow Sutton's own advice and not borrow trouble." Ivy placed her damask napkin beside her empty plate. "Now, I must go. I'm expected at the asylum to read with Louisa this morning."

"What book are you taking?"

"*Ravenscliffe*, by Anne Caldwell. It's an older book, but I doubt Louisa has read it."

"Perhaps it will hold more appeal for her than my choices. She showed no interest at all in either Emily Brontë's work or Mr. Thackeray's."

"Thackeray can be a challenge, even for an accomplished reader." Ivy touched Celia's shoulder as she turned toward the library. "Please don't worry. I'm sure your fears regarding Sutton's intentions are ill-founded."

"I hope you're right." Celia glanced at the mantel clock. "In any case I'll know soon enough."

"Everything will work out just as you wish it. You'll see." Ivy hurried up the stairs for her cloak and hat and returned moments later, just as the Brownings' carriage drew up at the door.

She peered into the dining room on her way out. "I'm off. Remember me to Sutton."

6

CELIA RETRIEVED HER WRITING BOX FROM HER ROOM AND settled into the library to wait. She rested her feet on a small footstool and began a letter, but her thoughts wouldn't settle. For weeks she had looked forward to Sutton's homecoming, but everything had gone wrong.

First, there was Leo Channing and his nonsense. Was Channing the reason Sutton had changed his mind? The Mackays were one of the best families in Savannah. Perhaps Sutton wouldn't want a wife whose family was mired in a salacious story even if the events that had precipitated it lay years in the past. Then there was the Mackays' missing ship and Papa's worrisome obligation for it.

She closed her eyes and replayed yesterday's brief conversation with Sutton, recalling the childhood escapade that had brought them together but nearly ended in tragedy. It had happened on All Hallows' Eve thirteen years ago. Sutton had just turned fourteen and Celia was barely twelve.

All of Savannah, eager for diversion after a summer marked by fears of yellow fever, had turned out in costume to promenade through the squares. Celia was with a group of girls from her school, laughing and teasing one another as they ran along Bull Street. It was dark as pitch, save for the flickering torches people had placed at the street corners. Firecrackers popped, scattering a group of smaller children playing in the park.

A small boy tossed a ball into the air, and it lodged in the tree branches. He began to wail, and nothing would distract him. Setting her basket of goodies on the ground, Celia hiked her skirts and shinnied up the tree to rescue the ball. When she dropped to the ground, a very attractive young boy stood there, grinning down at her. "Bravo."

"Brava." She tossed the ball to its grateful owner as the revelers headed toward the river to watch a fireworks display.

"Come again?" He braced himself against the tree, one arm outstretched.

"Bravo is masculine. Brava is feminine. I'm a girl."

He laughed. "You don't say? You sound just like my teacher."

"Goodness, I hope I'm not as stuffy as all that. But it's important to get things right, don't you think?"

"I do." He handed her the basket of chocolates and oranges she'd been carrying. "Going to the fireworks?"

"Of course."

"Want me to walk with you? Keep the haints away?"

"No such thing."

"'Course there is. They're everywhere." He fell into step beside her. "The worst of 'em isn't here in town though. The worst one lives in the woods out by Screven's Landing. They say she knows how to mix a poison that will turn you into stone if you so much as get it on your skin. And if she catches you messing around her special tree, she ties you up and makes you drink the poison so you can never leave and tell anyone where she lives."

A delicious trickle of fear skittered along her spine. "That's the silliest thing I ever heard." Celia looked up at him as they passed beneath a flickering torch, the grass brittle beneath their feet. "What's your name anyway?"

"Sutton Mackay. I know you. You're Mr. Browning's daughter."

"Yes. How did you know?"

"I saw you coming out of church with him on Sunday. And with your sister, I guess.

"My cousin Ivy. She lives with us because she has no parents anymore."

They cut across Reynolds Square and headed for the river, where the crowd had gathered for the fireworks.

Celia shifted her basket to her other arm. "I should know you, too, but I don't."

"Our fathers know each other from Commerce Row. I've been away at school every year since I was seven, and my family spends most summers in Europe. I like traveling around and seeing new places, but my mother complains that we are hardly ever at home in Savannah."

They stood together on the crowded wharf as the first fireworks exploded above the dark waters of the river and the onlookers broke into applause.

"I can prove it, you know," he said.

"Prove what?" She glanced up at the gray-eyed, curly-haired boy who stood a head taller than she.

"That the Screven's Landing haint is real."

"Sutton Mackay, are you trying to scare me? Because it won't work."

"Good. If you aren't afraid, then you won't mind coming with me."

She sucked in a breath. "You're going over there now? In the dark?"

"Of course. That's when the haints come out." He stepped back and grinned down at her. "Come on. I'll row us over."

"I can't. My father will expect me home soon."

"We can get there and back in an hour."

Celia hesitated for only a moment. Something about this boy spoke to her girlish heart. He was courteous. Smart too. And he would be an extraordinarily handsome man one day, if his muscles ever filled out his skinny frame. Her father knew his, so it wasn't as if she were heading off with a total stranger. And for some reason she found it important to impress him. "All right. But we can't stay long."

"Come on." The boy grabbed her hand, and they wove through the crowd to a short wooden pier near the offices on Commerce Row. Instinctively Celia glanced up at the darkened windows of her father's office overlooking the Port of Savannah. From time to time he allowed her to visit to watch the activity on the wharves, where the noise of men loading cotton and timber onto snows and schooners and the screech of railway cars mingled with the piercing whistles of steamships coming up the river from Boston, New York, and New Orleans.

"Here we are," Sutton said above the pop-pop-pop of fireworks still raining red and green sparkles into the water. He jumped into a small skiff tethered to a wooden piling and helped her into the boat. He cast off and began to row toward the landing on the South Carolina side of the river. An autumn breeze ruffled the surface of the water awash in moonlight.

"You ever been to the landing before?" he asked.

"Once or twice with my father." She remembered the narrow corduroy road that led through the swampy Carolina lowlands, the slaves working in vast rice fields separated by a network of dikes and ditches. The smell of pluff mud in the tidal creek. The unrelenting sun.

"But not at night, I bet."

"No." Now that they were in the middle of the river in the dead of night, she was frightened, sorry she had agreed to such a silly adventure. To quell her nerves she took a chocolate bonbon from her basket and popped it into her mouth.

Sutton pulled smoothly on the oars. "You got any more chocolate?"

She proffered the basket and he chose a piece. "Thanks."

Celia looked up as a muted roar rose from the wharf. The last of the fireworks shot into the darkness. Now the crowd would disperse. Her friends would wonder what had happened to her. Papa and Mrs. Maguire would expect her home. "Sutton, we have to go back."

"Why? Getting scared?"

"No. It was wrong of me to go running off without getting Papa's permission. He will be worried if I'm not home on time."

"We're almost there. We'll wait five minutes, and if we don't see the haint, we'll start straight home."

Moments later she felt the boat bumping the landing. Sutton tied off the skiff and helped her onto the bank. Moonlight illuminated the deserted road. Insects trilled in the marsh grasses. The air smelled of sulfur and salt.

"See that tree over there?" Sutton pointed to a spot just off the road where the dark shape of an ancient oak tree loomed, its mossy beard moving in the slight breeze coming off the sea. "That's where the Screven's haint lives."

"She lives in a tree?"

"No. She lives in back of it, farther in the woods. But that tree is her special one. It's the one she'll kill to protect. We have to get closer to it to coax her out of her hiding place."

"I've seen enough."

"We haven't seen anything yet. Come on." He took her hand, and they approached the tree. Celia shivered.

"Listen," he whispered. "Someone's coming."

Celia strained her ears. "I don't hear anything."

They waited for what seemed to Celia like hours. She imagined the worried faces of her father and Mrs. Maguire. Papa might punish her, or he might be so happy to find her alive that he would let her off with a stern reprimand. Right now either was more appealing than standing here waiting for something that did not even exist outside this boy's wild imagination.

"I know how to make her come out." Sutton took a penknife from his pocket.

"What are you doing?"

"Carving our initials into her special tree."

"No! She might—"

"Oh, so you do admit she's real." He began carving a small *S* into the tree.

"No. Yes. I don't know." She stamped her foot. "Sutton Mackay, I demand that you take me home this instant."

He finished the *S* and began a *C*.

She stood by, tapping her foot and swatting at insects that darted through the chilly night air.

"There." He gave a quick nod of satisfaction and put his knife away. "Now spit on your hand."

"What?"

"Spit on your hand."

"I will not. That's disgusting."

He laughed. "Come on. Just one dainty little spit bubble?"

She spat into her palm. "There. Satisfied?"

He followed suit, then pressed his palm against hers. "Yep. Now we're friends for life."

"Fine. May we please go home now? I—"

She was interrupted by a low growl and the sound of rushing feet. Weak light from a small torch glimmered through the trees. She screamed.

"Run!" Sutton shoved her onto the path in front of him.

A dark figure emerged from the undergrowth. Sutton stuck out his booted foot, and the haint went down with such force that Celia heard a bone snap.

An animal-like howl filled the air. Then the plaintive cry of a human voice. "Help me!"

Sutton was shaking, breathing so hard Celia could hear every intake of air.

"This isn't a haint," she said.

"No." He retrieved the torch and knelt. "It's a live person. And she's hurt."

Celia knelt on the other side of a thin, elderly woman. "Are you all right?"

"My arm. It's broke, I think." The old woman tried to move but then winced and lay still.

"If you can make it to the skiff, we'll take you to the doctor," Sutton said. "My father is Burke Mackay. He will take care of—"

"Just leave me alone." The old woman sat up and cradled her injured arm. "Just git on outta here. I don't need you. I got my own remedies."

"We're sorry," Sutton said. "You scared us, coming out of the dark like that."

"Wasn't that what you wanted? To be scared witless on All Hallows' Eve so's you could go back and boast to your friends how you saw the Screven's haint?"

"It was only a silly dare," Celia said. "I'm sorry I took it. And I'm sorry you got hurt."

"Sorry won't fix nothin' now, will it? Help me up."

Sutton complied. "At least let us help you get home."

"So's you can tell all them other ruffians where I live? I'd never hear the end of it then, would I?"

Sutton handed her the sputtering torch, and she disappeared into the trees.

"Let's go." Shame laced Sutton's voice.

Celia felt let down too. What had begun as a lark had ended in regret. Wordlessly they entered the boat and started back across the river. When they landed at the dock on East Broad Street, the streets were nearly empty.

"Are you going to tell anyone what happened?" Sutton asked as they hurried through the velvety darkness toward Madison Square.

"If Papa asks where I've been, I won't lie."

"That's what I thought." They reached Bull Street. Sutton paused.

"What?"

"I have to take her some money or some food or something. To make up for what I did."

When they reached her gate, he handed her the basket. "I'm sorry, Celia. I never should have taken you over there." He shrugged. "I guess I wanted you to like me."

"And you thought the best way to accomplish that was to scare me half to—"

"Miss Celia?" Mrs. Maguire was standing above her, shaking her shoulder. "Miss Celia, wake up. Mr. Mackay is here."

Celia jerked awake. Cups rattled in their saucers as Mrs. Maguire set a tea tray onto the table beside her chair. Sutton stood in the doorway, half hidden behind an enormous bouquet of late-season roses. He crossed the room, handed her the roses, and planted a kiss on her cheek. "Did we wake you?"

"I didn't sleep much last night." Celia inhaled the faint, sweet scent of the copper-colored roses. "These are beautiful. Thank you." She caught the housekeeper's eye. "Mrs. Maguire, could you find a vase for these?"

"I'll put them on the table in your room." The housekeeper swept one hand toward the tea tray. "I brought the cookies and extra milk for the tea."

She took the roses and pulled the door closed behind her.

Celia motioned Sutton to the chair beside hers and picked up the teapot to pour.

"I'm sorry if our conversation yesterday was the cause of your restless night." Sutton reached out to take the cup she offered him. "I shouldn't have brought it up then, but it has been weighing on me ever since I got back, and it came out before I meant it to."

Celia wrapped both hands around her own cup, her calm exterior concealing unspeakable anguish. Sutton had changed his mind about something important. About her? About their future? She had loved him half her life. How could she bear it if her tender feelings were no longer returned?

Maybe Papa was right and two years in Jamaica had changed Sutton's heart. It was possible she no longer knew him at all.

Sutton ate a couple of Mrs. Maguire's cookies, chewing with apparent relish. Celia set down her cup and twisted her fingers into a hard ball. How could he even think of eating at a time like this?

She shifted in her chair, and her napkin slid to the floor. Sutton retrieved it and brushed a curl from her forehead. "You were sleeping so peacefully when I came in, I hated to wake you."

"I was dreaming. About the first time we met."

"All Hallows' Eve?"

"Yes. I suppose it was on my mind since you mentioned it yesterday." She managed a smile. "It seems so long ago now."

"I still feel terrible about it."

"I've always thought it was wrong of your father to punish you for trying to protect me from the frightful haint."

"He punished me for hurting that poor old woman, for taking the boat without permission. For endangering you." He shrugged. "In some ways I was much more sure of myself at fourteen than I am now."

Her heart beat wildly in her chest. Her mouth went dry. However dire the news, it was best to get it over with. "Perhaps you should tell me why you've come."

"All right." He set down his cup and hitched his chair closer to hers until their knees bumped together. "You know that my plan was to spend this year helping Father and then return to expand our operation in Jamaica."

"Yes. But I thought . . . that is . . . in your letters you implied I might be accompanying you. You said—"

"That was the plan." He clasped both her hands and held them to his chest. "I love you, Celia. I've loved you since that first night at Screven's Landing. From that night on, I intended we'd marry someday."

"But?"

"But things at the company are much worse than I thought. And we just got word that *Electra* is lost at sea with all her cargo and—"

"It's confirmed then. Papa said—"

"You knew?" He blew out a long breath. "I suppose half of Savannah knows by now."

She reached for his hand. "I'm so sorry. I know how much your father was counting on that shipment to turn things around."

"It's a devastating blow. I don't know how much longer Mackay and Son can survive."

"The safe fund—"

"It would take much more than that to get the company back on its feet."

"Then what will you do?"

"Father is cashing in some railway stock and selling our farm in Cassville. He and Mother will be secure for a while. I'm consigning some of our shipments to Wheaton's company. If we have a good season, we might break even this year."

"Then it makes sense to return to Jamaica next year as planned and try to recoup your losses."

"By next summer, we might be close to war."

"Surely not." She pressed a hand to her midsection. "I know there's been some talk, but—"

"It's more than just idle talk. The Negroes have been openly discussing the Scott decision ever since it came down last year, and the men at the club are debating the merits of seceding from the Union. And it isn't only here in Georgia. Did you see this morning's paper? Secession is the number-one topic of debate in South Carolina too. If South Carolina leaves the Union, you can be sure that Georgia will follow."

"But that's ridiculous. People don't solve their differences by running out. Surely there's room for compromise."

"I don't think so, Celia. An entire way of life is at stake, and that way of life depends upon the continuation of slavery." Sutton leaned back in his chair. "Our country is rapidly dividing into two camps. And eventually both sides will be forced to fight for their principles."

Her stomach dropped. "You're telling me you're prepared to fight?"

"I'm a member of the Chatham Artillery."

"Of course. But—"

"I don't expect you to understand the feelings men in uniform have for one another. It's a kind of brotherhood. I can't let them down."

"I see." Celia blinked back hot tears. "Your loyalties to them are stronger than your feelings for me."

"That is neither fair nor true. One has nothing to do with the other."

"But we aren't going to be married this year, are we, Sutton?"

He got up and paced the room. "I've been thinking of going to England."

"To England?"

"When we go to war, the first thing the North will do is blockade our ports. Everything from Virginia to Florida will be bottled up, and our cotton, rice, and lumber will rot on the wharves. What is worse, we won't be able to import even the barest of necessities—food, medicine, clothing, ammunition. The Northerners won't have to beat us on the battlefield. They can simply starve us out."

Sutton leaned over to pick up the pen and ink that lay atop her writing box. Returning to his chair, he sketched on the back of his calling card. "I'm thinking of going to Liverpool, to the shipbuilders there. If they can build a boat that sits low enough in the water, it might be able to slip past a blockade. Get some of our shipments in and out."

"But wouldn't that be terribly dangerous?"

"No more dangerous than manning an artillery rifle. And in the long run, it might be more useful to Savannah." He tapped his drawing. "We can burn anthracite coal, so there won't be any smoke to give us away."

"It seems you've thought of everything."

"Not by myself. One of my classmates from Harvard wrote to me last week, proposing the same idea. Wilkerson has contacts in Nassau that might take our cotton shipments and provide us with medicines and munitions for the return. Of course, we'll need financial backing to get the ship built, but I hear the British are eager to invest in American shipping."

"I see."

"Do you, darling? I hope so. Of course I'm thinking of your welfare, but I'm thinking of our city, too, and of the entire South. I'm not certain secession is the wisest course either, but whatever comes, I must do all I can to help." He tipped her face up to his. "It's my duty as a soldier and a Southerner. Please tell me you understand."

She sighed. At least his feelings for her hadn't waned. But what good did it do to love one another if they were destined always to be apart? Wasn't being together the entire point of loving someone? Being together and building a home and a family?

"I do understand." She chose her words carefully. "But I wish you weren't the one to be—"

"Oh, I won't be the only one. Wilkerson says several other men in Virginia and South Carolina are interested in building runners too. But I'm the one with the connections to the shipyard in Liverpool and to the bankers."

She fought her rising tears. "When will you leave?"

"Not until the new year. Father needs my help in settling his affairs, and of course I'll need to gather enough investors to convince the shipyard to go ahead and build."

She rose, willing herself to be calm. "At least we'll have Christmas together."

"Yes, and many more Christmases, my love, once the coming unpleasantness is behind us." His arms went around her, and she leaned into his strong, warm embrace. Sutton's bravery and concern for others were among the many reasons she loved him. He was one of the most unselfish people she knew. And everything he said made sense—but how could she bear to give him up again so soon? She drew back to look up at him. "Why do you have to be so virtuous?"

"Pardon me?"

"You came back here to face all these problems when you could have stayed in Jamaica playing poker and drinking rum."

He arched a brow. "You've met my cousin Hugh?"

Despite her sadness, she laughed. "And now you're off to England."

He smiled into her eyes. "Let's not talk any more about it right now. Tell me, how are the plans for my party progressing?"

"I've sent out the invitations and ordered the things Mrs. Maguire will need for the centerpieces. And you know I plan to wear Mama's gold dress."

"I can't wait to see you coming down the stairs in it."

The mantel clock chimed the hour.

"Will you stay for dinner?" Celia asked. "Mrs. Maguire baked soda bread this morning."

"I'd love to, but I'm meeting Mr. Stiles at the club. He's promised to fill me in on last year's Commercial Congress. And then I must meet with Father's clerk to go over the shipping manifests for the lost cargo."

"Oh."

"How about Saturday? If you're free, we'll tack up Zeus and Poseidon and give them a good workout."

She had planned to call at Mrs. Lawton's to see the new baby, but a morning with Sutton was a luxury too rare to pass up. "I'd like that."

Celia moved to the window to draw the blinds and gave an involuntary gasp. Ivy stood in the shady park across the street, her golden hair glittering like a new coin, chatting with Leo Channing.

Sutton frowned. "What's the matter?"

"My cousin is talking to that shameless newspaper writer."

Sutton joined her at the window. "He's shameless all right. That piece he wrote is full of nothing but fabrication and innuendo."

"Exactly. But his articles still worry me, not to mention his ridiculous plan to write a book about us. You know how people here detest any hint of scandal. Papa already has enough on his mind without worrying about how Mr. Channing's writings will be received. I cannot imagine why Ivy is standing there with him in broad daylight."

She yanked on the tasseled cord to draw the blinds. "Mr. Thompson promised Papa that Leo Channing would stay away from us. It looks as if he forgot to tell Mr. Channing."

"Say the word, and I'll go out there and give the fool a good drubbing."

"Thank you. But he isn't worth it."

Arm in arm they quit the library and walked out to the entry hall, where Sutton retrieved his hat. "I'll see you tomorrow," he said. "And in the meantime, try not to worry about Channing—or my trip to England, for that matter. Who knows? By the new year circumstances might well have changed and a trip won't be necessary."

"Sutton Mackay, you know perfectly well you will go. You're only trying to make me feel better."

Sutton planted a kiss on her cheek. "Good-bye, darling. Don't be too hard on Ivy. I'm sure she must have a reason for her behavior."

He opened the door just as Ivy came through the wrought-iron gate, swinging her book satchel like a schoolgirl. "Good morning, Sutton."

He tipped his hat. "Miss Lorens. You seem particularly happy today."

He waved and let himself out through the gate.

"Yes, Cousin." Celia folded her arms and glared at Ivy as they walked inside. "Tell me, what has put you in such an agreeable mood? Was it the drive from the asylum in this brisk weather? Your reading lesson with Louisa? Or your cozy talk with the heinous Mr. Channing? How you can even speak to him after that piece in the paper this morning is surely beyond my ken."

Ivy swept into the library, set her satchel onto a chair, and unpinned her hat. "I saw him in the park when Joseph drove me back from the asylum. I thought if I talked to him he might temper his future writings. I don't care, of course, but it's important to you." She turned to face Celia, her eyes bright. "I did it for you."

"Oh, Ivy. I didn't mean . . . I don't know what to say."

"You could start with thank you." Ivy leaned in to study her own reflection in the gilt mirror near the door.

"I'm sorry I spoke so harshly. It's just that Papa has so much on his mind these days, he doesn't need the distraction. And I do want Sutton's party to be perfect. Now more than ever."

"Oh? Why is that?" Ivy patted a blond ringlet into place.

"He's leaving again. After Christmas."

Ivy spun away from the mirror, her pink dress swirling. "Leaving? Oh, dear. I know how you had counted on marrying him, but perhaps it simply isn't meant to be."

Celia was too tired to explain. And perhaps it was best to guard Sutton's plans, at least for now.

The doorbell rang and Celia went to answer it. Leo Channing stood there in his rumpled, disreputable suit, hat in hand. "Miss Browning. I've just spoken with your cousin, and I was wondering whether you'd care to comment on—"

"I would not. And what is more, I intend to report you to the police. Your employer has instructed you to stay away from this house, yet here you are again."

"True enough. But since Miss Lorens has been so accommodating, I thought perhaps you, too, might have had a change of heart."

Celia made to close the door, but he wedged one booted foot into the opening. "Did you see this morning's piece?"

"Half-truths and sensationalism. Exactly what I expected from someone of your caliber."

Channing narrowed his eyes. "No need to get nasty. You might do well to remember that two can play that game. And I have a public forum for my comments."

"Please remove your foot from my door."

"Did you ever meet her—the laundress who met her sad demise here?"

Celia drew herself up and met his gaze. "The mills of God grind slowly, Mr. Channing. But they grind exceedingly small."

The reporter stepped back. "Don't threaten me. Get in my way, and you will regret it."

He turned and hurried through the gate and onto the street. Celia slammed the door with such force that Mrs. Maguire came running from the kitchen, her hands covered in flour, apron strings flying out behind her. "By all the saints, Celia Browning. What the *divil* is going on?"

Beyond the river, a storm was brewing.

7

THE NOTES BEGAN ARRIVING EARLY ON SATURDAY AFTERnoon, delivered by messenger or by household servants, all of them pleading an excuse—the arrival of an unexpected guest, a sick child, a prior engagement suddenly remembered, the onset of a ragged cough. By early evening, thirty-seven guests had canceled.

"What are we going to do, Papa?" Celia's voice trembled as she dropped the latest one, a note from Mrs. Fanning, onto the silver tray in the entry hall. "This party is ruined."

"Carry on as best we can." He drew her into an embrace and planted a kiss on the top of her head, just as he had when she was a child and scared of the dark or complaining of a skinned knee. "We mustn't spoil the evening for those guests who do attend. Besides, a smaller party might actually be more enjoyable because we'll have more time to chat with everyone. And the size of the crowd makes no difference to Sutton. He'd be just as happy to be spending this day swimming and fishing or attending the boat races with you over on Isle of Hope."

"I wish now I'd thought of that." She stepped back and searched her father's face. "It's because of those ridiculous newspaper articles that so many have canceled."

"I'm afraid so. But the best way to combat Channing is to pretend indifference. He isn't invited, so he won't know how many guests have decided not to come. As far as he's concerned, your masquerade ball is a smashing success."

"I suppose. But Mrs. Maguire and her friends have been cooking for days. There will be so much food left over. I hate to see it all go to waste."

"We'll send some home with the servers, and the rest we'll deliver to the indigents at the Poor House and Hospital. They'll be glad of it." Papa managed a tired smile. "Why don't you lie down for a while before you get dressed? Ivy can answer the door."

"Ivy is locked in her room, working feverishly on her costume."

"She's decided to come down for the party?"

"Yes. She decided it just this morning. I'm glad. I feel guilty when I'm down here having a good time and she is all alone with her nose in a book."

"I'm glad of it too. I'd like to see her socializing more." Papa tapped the ash from his favorite pipe and returned the pipe to its wooden chest on his desk. "I do wish she hadn't encouraged Mr. Channing, though. The less said to that reprobate, the better."

"Ivy says she and Mr. Channing have a great deal in common. That he lost his parents at an early age, too, though not under such dramatic circumstances. But I can't help thinking he's lying to gain her sympathy and ensure her cooperation."

"Well, Ivy is a grown woman," Papa said as the doorbell rang again. "She must make her own judgments about him."

Celia pressed her fingers to her temples to quell the headache that had been building all afternoon. "Perhaps I will lie down for a little while."

"I'll have Mrs. Maguire bring you some chamomile tea. And please don't fret about this evening. The important thing is that Sutton will be here."

"Thank you, Papa. You always know what to say to make me feel better." She started up the stairs.

"Celia?"

She turned, one hand resting on the polished mahogany banister.

"I'm sorry I forgot to get your mother's necklace from the bank. With everything else going on these days, it slipped my mind."

"It doesn't matter."

She went upstairs, unpinned her hair, removed her pink dressing gown, and slid beneath the lavender-scented covers. Soon Mrs. Maguire arrived with the tea, her faded eyes full of sympathy. The housekeeper drew the curtains, poured a cup of tea, and stood beside the bed, hands clasped at her waist, while Celia sipped the warm infusion. "There now, and you'll be feelin' better after a good nap."

"Can you stay with me a moment?"

"Sure. Nothin' more to do downstairs until it's time to set up the table." Mrs. Maguire moved a chair closer to the edge of the bed. "Now there is no use in worryin' any longer about that Channing fellow. He's a thorn in the side of this household all right, but—"

"It's so unfair." Celia raked her hair away from her face. "Tormenting us, turning our friends against us, all because he wants to write about a crime that didn't even happen."

Mrs. Maguire patted Celia's hand. "My *mam* used to say if everything in the world was fair, there would be no need for courage. I'm thinkin' she was right about that. But you mustn't let this man upset you. 'Tis only a lot of blather that will be forgot soon enough."

The tea and Mrs. Maguire's company had the desired effect. Celia grew sleepy as the housekeeper chattered on about the new store that had just opened downtown, plans for an autumn festival at her church, a letter recently received from a niece in Ireland.

When Celia woke, darkness was descending, and the gaslights

along Bull Street were just coming on. She lit her lamp and splashed cold water on her face, drew on her dressing gown, and went across the hall to knock on Ivy's door.

"Come in."

Celia peeked in. "Is your costume ready?"

"Yes, but I want it to be a surprise." Ivy's eyes glittered with a feverish excitement Celia had seldom seen. "Shall I help you into your Cleopatra gown?"

"Would you?"

Together they returned to Celia's room. Celia took the dress from the wardrobe where it had hung since she'd retrieved it from the room that had once been her mother's. She removed her dressing gown and stood before the mirror as Ivy slid the heavy column of gold silk over her head. The dress shimmered with every movement, catching and reflecting the light.

"Hold still while I do up the buttons." Ivy's eyes sought Celia's in the mirror. "Uncle David was right. In this gown you do look exactly like Aunt Francesca. As much as I can recall of her anyway."

"I wish I remembered more about her." The buttons finished, Celia picked up her hairbrush and began fashioning her long hair into a cascade of ringlets held in place by two small diamond-studded combs. Her memories were few and fleeting. But judging from her mother's portrait, Francesca, with her dark hair and violet eyes, had looked nothing like her auburn-haired, light-eyed sister. "Sometimes it feels as if our family is a string of broken pearls, with people going in all directions, getting lost and never found."

"I remember my mother talking about how she and Aunt Francesca were such good friends growing up. She said they played endless games of old maid and smoot and never fought at all." Ivy sighed. "I wish the two of us got along as well. But we are too different."

That much was true. There had been a time when Celia looked up to her older cousin. She'd admired Ivy's practicality and fearlessness, her sheer inventiveness when it came to devising games and adventures Celia wouldn't have dared undertake on her own. But admiration had turned to wariness the day Ivy lured Celia into the garden shed and locked her inside. To this day, the prospect of confinement in a small space made Celia's heart pound, though Ivy had long since apologized, and Celia had long since forgiven her for the prank.

"I suppose we are different." Celia smiled at her cousin as she applied a bit of pomade to her lips and dabbed rosewater behind each ear. "But we are still family." With a final glance at her reflection, she rose. "I must check with Mrs. Maguire and see whether the musicians have arrived yet."

"I'll be down in a while." Ivy picked up Celia's gold-trimmed half-mask from the dressing table. "Don't forget this."

Celia went downstairs, through the ballroom, and onto the rear terrace, where the serving table had been set up. Candles in clear glass globes and pots of ivy and copper roses lined the perimeter of the terrace, which opened to the lawn and the ivy-covered outbuildings beyond. A white linen tablecloth had been laid on the long table, each end anchored with pyramids of oranges encased in spun sugar.

The centerpiece was a miniature tree three feet high and made entirely of ground-pea candy. Each of the tiny branches was loaded with crystallized fruit. A bird's nest fashioned from chocolate held three blue eggs.

It had taken Mrs. Maguire and Mrs. Hemphill from the bakery downtown three days to complete. And now there would be so few to appreciate the whimsy and artistry of it.

The terrace doors opened, and Mrs. Maguire and her helpers began laying out the buffet—plates of ham and beaten biscuits, trays of roast beef and parsnips, iced cakes and bowls of pudding for dessert.

The musicians arrived and began tuning up. Soon carriages and buggies would be making their way to the door. It was time to begin. Celia took a deep breath and headed inside to greet her guests.

"Celia, there you are." Papa, dressed as a sultan with gold turban and matching slippers, caught her by the hand and twirled her around. "You are just as beautiful as I imagined. I'm glad now that I forgot the necklace. No need to paint the lily, as they say."

"Thank you, Papa. And may I say you make a dashing sultan?"

He laughed and offered her his arm. "Let's go."

They took up their places as the guests entered. Behind the traditional half-masks her friends were recognizable. Several of the men, including Mr. Mackay, wore sailor costumes. Others came dressed as shepherds, oracles, and French noblemen in tight white breeches and powdered wigs. Mr. and Mrs. Stiles arrived costumed as King Ferdinand and Queen Isabella. Mrs. Stiles's bright laughter rose above the hum of conversations and the music coming from the terrace.

Mrs. Harding arrived costumed as a Scottish lass, Mrs. Green as a Swiss maid. Sutton's mother, Cornelia Mackay, arrived in an alpaca riding skirt with a black velvet basque, linen collar, and a smart feathered hat. Celia grinned. "Diana Vernon, if I'm not mistaken."

Mrs. Mackay laughed. "And I thought I was being so clever, choosing one of Mr. Scott's characters." She kissed Celia's cheek. "I so enjoyed reading *Rob Roy*."

"Me too. And you are Diana in the flesh."

"Thank you, my dear. And you—you look simply magnificent."

Celia smiled. "The dress was my mother's."

"I well remember. And I must say you do it justice. Sutton will be stunned."

Celia looked around at the guests clustered in twos and threes, their small number lost in a space meant for a much larger crowd—and tamped down another rush of anger at Leo Channing. "Where is Sutton?"

"He was getting dressed when we left. He'll be along momentarily, I'm sure."

"Miss Browning?" Celia turned to see her father's clerk, Elliott Shaw, bearing down upon her, a plain domino mask his only concession to the party.

She felt a momentary stab of panic, fearing more bad news from Commerce Row. "Mr. Shaw?"

"I . . . hello." Behind his mask, his eyes were unusually bright. "I'm sorry for barging in when I wasn't invited, but I must speak to you for a moment."

She discreetly fanned away the faint smell of spirits coming off him. "About what?"

"In private?" He waved a hand toward the terrace.

Mrs. Mackay touched Celia's arm. "Go ahead, darling. I'll keep an eye out for Sutton."

Frowning, Celia led the way to a shadowed corner of the terrace. "What's this all about, Mr. Shaw? What can I do for you?"

"I don't want a favor, Miss Browning." He removed his mask and heaved a sigh. "Unless accepting a gift from an admirer constitutes a favor."

He produced a small box from his pocket and pressed it into her hands. "I'd be honored if you'd accept this."

"But why?"

"Why?" He wiped his palms on the sides of his trousers. "Surely my admiration for you hasn't escaped your notice."

She tried to remember whether she had ever said anything he might have construed as encouragement, but nothing came to mind. "We barely know each other."

"I know a lot about you. I admire you for all the work you do for the orphan girls and for the interest you take in your father's business. I can't afford a real fancy present, but this is a heartfelt one, and I only wish—"

"It's very kind of you, Mr. Shaw, but I cannot possibly accept this." She returned the box.

"How do you know? You haven't even opened it."

"I don't wish to offend, but it simply isn't proper. We're practically strangers, and besides, you are Papa's employee. And, well, I simply cannot. Now, if you'll excuse me, I really must return to my guests. Shall I ask my father to show you out?"

"No need, Miss High and Mighty. I know the way out." He turned on his heel and stalked away.

Moments later Sutton came through the door dressed as a pirate, a black eye patch substituting for the customary half-mask. He hurried over to Celia and stopped short, one hand clapped to his heart. "Cleopatra!"

She laughed, the unsettling episode with the clerk instantly forgotten. "Jean Lafitte? Or Blackbeard? Whichever, I like the eye patch." She took his arm, nodding at the heavy coin necklace draped over his blue jacket. "The pieces of eight are a nice touch too."

In the ballroom, the musicians had begun a lively waltz, and the guests paired off for the first dance. Celia danced first with Sutton, then with his father, then with Papa. As they twirled around the floor, she kept one eye on the hallway, looking for Ivy. What was taking her so long? Celia hoped her cousin hadn't lost her nerve and decided not to come downstairs after all. It wasn't natural for a woman of Ivy's age to spend so much time alone.

After another half hour, Papa rang a small crystal bell to get everyone's attention. Celia bowed to Mr. Lawton, who had been her partner for the last dance, and went to join her father.

"Welcome to our home," he said. "We hope you're enjoying

yourselves. By now most of you have had a chance to welcome home our guest of honor, Sutton Mackay."

Smiling, Sutton stepped forward and nodded.

"We're proud of you, Sutton, and proud to welcome you home to Savannah."

"Thank you, sir. It's good to be home," Sutton said, "and an honor to be received in a home where I have spent so many happy hours." He crossed the floor and took Celia's hand, drawing her to the middle of the room. She looked up at him, a question in her eyes. Sutton glanced around the room at the costumed guests. "Most of you in this room have known Miss Browning and me for our whole lives. You've watched us grow up together. You have encouraged us and prayed for us, and I am sure some of you have wondered when we intended to wed."

"Amen to that!" Mr. Mackay said, and everyone laughed.

Celia's knees went weak. Surely Sutton wasn't about to propose now, in front of all these people.

"We're not yet sure of the date," Sutton said, his eyes never leaving her face. "But this is the time to remove all doubt as to our plans for the future. That is, if Celia will have me."

He removed a ring from his pocket and held it out to her. "This belongs to my grandmother Manigault, but she's given it to me for my engagement. I've been hoping to marry you since you were twelve years old. I think you're old enough now to accept my proposal. If you want to."

Her throat constricted, shutting off her words. She could only nod as Sutton slipped the ring with its cluster of nine diamonds onto her finger. The guests broke into applause. The music started again, and Sutton swept her into a dizzying waltz.

When it ended, the ladies crowded around offering kisses and congratulations, but Celia moved in a fog of happy disbelief. The evening that had begun in humiliation had turned to triumph. She couldn't help feeling a small surge of satisfaction that those who had made excuses to avoid attending the party had missed an event that would keep their social circle buzzing for weeks.

Papa sent for champagne, and the guests moved outdoors to the buffet table. Sutton filled their plates, and they sat on a wrought-iron bench in the garden. He bit into a ham biscuit, chewed, and swallowed. "Lovely party, wouldn't you say?"

She lifted her hand and watched the play of candlelight on the diamonds. "Sutton Mackay, you leave me speechless."

He laughed. "I very much doubt that, my darling, but that's all right. You've been speaking your mind since the night we met. I don't expect you to go mute just because we're betrothed."

She nibbled on a bit of cheese and set her plate aside. "I'm sure you noticed that more than a few of our friends are missing."

"I noticed, but I don't care." He touched his glass to hers. "As much as I love Savannah, I'm ashamed when people let their fear of impropriety overwhelm common sense. But you mustn't worry. Channing can't keep the story going forever."

"I hope not."

"And just imagine tomorrow morning, when the no-shows wake up to the news that they missed the most romantic marriage proposal in the history of Georgia. They will be green with envy."

She laughed. "Is it wrong of me to hope you're right?"

He shook his head. "One of the things I've always loved about you is that you don't try to cover up what you feel. You are not afraid of emotion. I hope you won't ever fear to share with me whatever you're thinking. Even if we disagree."

"Which I am sure we will. For instance, this scheme of yours to build a—"

He stopped her with a brief kiss and drew her to her feet. "That is a topic for another day. I have another surprise."

She eyed him warily. "Am I going to like it?"

"I can almost guarantee it. I was hoping to have it in time for the party, but it's been delayed."

"Give me a hint?'

"No. You're too good at guessing, and I want you to be as astonished as you were this evening. Come on. We should join the others."

"In a moment. There's Alicia Thayer. I haven't seen her since she got back from Philadelphia."

"Don't be long." Sutton eyed the buffet table. "In the meantime I think I'll have another sandwich."

Celia crossed the terrace to where her friend stood sipping a glass of punch.

"Celia." Alicia planted a kiss on Celia's cheek. "Let me see that ring."

Celia held out her hand.

"It's stunning," Alicia said. "And I'm thrilled to pieces with your news. You and Sutton are the perfect match. Everybody says so."

"I hope so." Celia smiled at her dearest friend. "I only wish my mother were here to share in the excitement."

"I know. I can't imagine growing up without a mother, even though my own drives me to distraction sometimes. Anyway, I'm happy to have made it home in time for this party."

"Mrs. Stiles told me you've been up north."

Alicia sipped her punch. "Yes. Visiting Mother's cousins. It was billed as a relaxing holiday, but all they wanted to talk about was abolition and Mr. Lincoln." Alicia shook her head. "Can you think of anything more rude than to invite people to visit and then insult them at every turn? They look down on Southerners and call us ignorant, but they are the ones whose assumptions are completely false. They think everyone south of the Mason Dixon is a slaveholder. It came as a big surprise when I told them most of us make our livings as merchants and lawyers and such."

A serving girl came by, and Alicia set her empty glass on the tray. "And then we got home only to see that ridiculous article in the paper. It makes me sick that some of our friends are wallowing in gossip."

Celia pulled her friend into the shadows. "Tell me. What are they saying?"

Alicia shook her head. "I shouldn't like to repeat such things."

"I want to know. Perhaps then I can refute them."

"I know how you feel, but maybe it's better not to say anything. To protest will only fan the flames and keep the story alive longer."

"I'm sure you're right, but I still want to know what's being said."

Alicia sighed. "All right. They say your Uncle Magnus had something to do with what happened, and that's why he disappeared. They say your father knows and is covering everything up to spare your cousin—and to save the Browning name as well. They say your Aunt Eugenia's accident was not an accident at all."

Anger burned like acid in Celia's veins. She fought the urge to hurl a glass to the floor. Leo Channing was not reporting the facts. Instead he was inventing facts to create a more provocative story. And the cost to her family could be enormous. Her father's business, her charity work, social calls, teas, and receptions were the scaffolding upon which her entire life was built. Without them, everything would collapse.

"What else?"

"What else?" Alicia shook her head, and her sapphire earbobs caught the candlelight. "Goodness, I think that's quite enough, don't you?"

Alicia linked her arm through Celia's. "Please don't let mean gossip spoil your happiness. This is a night you will remember for the rest of your life. And when we are two old ladies having tea on the front porch, the memories of it should be only sweet ones."

Celia let out a ragged breath. "Of course you're right. It's no secret I've loved Sutton my whole life. This is a very happy evening."

"As it should be. Now, let's join the others. It's almost time for the promenade, and I haven't had a chance to see all the costumes."

As midnight drew near, the guests assembled in the ballroom. One by one they twirled around, showing off their costumes before removing their masks and bowing to applause. The guests voted for best costume, a distinction that went to Mr. and Mrs. Stiles as Ferdinand and Isabella. After another round of chocolates and champagne, Mrs. Maguire brought out baskets filled with party favors—small jeweled boxes for the ladies and fine cigars for the gentlemen.

Celia stood between Sutton and Papa as the guests departed, Sutton holding tightly to her hand. She wished that more of her friends had been there to share her big moment. But the uncertainty about her future was over. Her wedding might have to wait, but Sutton was hers. That was all that mattered.

At last Sutton shook Papa's hand and thanked him again for the party. Then he bent to kiss her cheek. "I suppose I ought to go. Good night, my queen."

He left, whistling as he pushed through the gate to the street.

On the terrace, Mrs. Maguire and Mrs. Hemphill were boxing up the food and the elaborate centerpiece for delivery to the hospital. The musicians had packed up their instruments and left by the side gate.

Papa placed an arm around her shoulder. "Quite a night, my dear."

"Yes."

"Your future husband has a talent for surprise."

"To say the least." Celia threw both arms around him. "Thank you for this party, Papa. Despite Leo Channing, despite Sutton's troubles and ours, I am supremely happy."

"I'm glad to know your future is settled. Especially in these unsettling times."

She released him. "Has something else happened?"

Papa huffed out a sigh. "Abolitionists are coming through the plantations over on St. Simons, talking up freedom to the slaves. There's talk that some of the Irish in town are siding with them." He stifled a yawn. "But this is not the time for a political discussion, darling. It's time for your old, gray-haired papa to be in bed."

"Me too." She frowned. "I didn't see Ivy all night. Did you?"

"Come to think of it, no. Maybe she changed her mind again." They climbed the stairs together, and she went down the hall to her room.

A thread of yellow light showed beneath Ivy's closed door. Celia put her ear to the door and knocked softly. "Ivy?"

"Come in."

Celia opened the door. Ivy lay on the bed, her skin flushed, eyes bright.

"What happened? Are you ill?"

"I was getting ready to go downstairs when I felt faint. I lay down for a moment and started feeling worse." Ivy pressed a hand to her midsection. "My stomach feels unwell."

"I'll be right back."

Celia retrieved the camphor and flannel cloths from the cupboard and helped Ivy bathe her stomach. "Better?"

"A little. I'm sorry I missed the party. Who won the promenade?"

"Mr. and Mrs. Stiles. Ferdinand and Isabella."

"Was it too awful, having so many people absent?"

Outside, carriage wheels squeaked. A dog barked. Celia dabbed more camphor on the flannel rag and handed it to her cousin. Such moments of harmony and closeness were much too rare. Why couldn't she and Ivy be as close as their mothers had been?

"It was awkward at first," Celia said. "We had too much food by far. But then—" Celia held out her hand to show Ivy her ring. "Sutton proposed marriage to me tonight. In front of everyone."

Ivy blinked. "He proposed? But I thought . . . you said he'd changed his mind."

"And so he has. But luckily for me, about something else entirely." Celia waggled her fingers, watching the diamonds refract the light. "We won't be going to Jamaica next year as we planned. But I don't care. As long as I have Sutton, I can be happy anywhere." She sighed. "I can't believe it's really happened, and I'm going to be Mrs. Sutton Mackay."

Ivy pressed the camphor flannel to her stomach. "Congratulations."

"Oh, Ivy, I do want you to be happy for us."

"I know you do, and I truly am sorry I missed your big moment." Ivy sat up, and a dark-brown velvet cloak and matching breeches tumbled to the floor. "My costume. I was planning to come as Robin Hood." She was seized with a coughing fit that went on until Celia took up a magazine lying on the table and fanned her cousin's face.

"I'll get you some water."

"Would you?"

Celia ran down to the kitchen. Mrs. Maguire had gone to bed too. The dishes were drying on the counter. A white dish towel was folded neatly on the table. Tomorrow's yeast rolls were rising in a yellow crockery bowl beside the hearth.

Celia filled a pitcher, set it and a glass on a small tray, and started back upstairs. A single sheet of paper folded into quarters lay on the floor just inside the front door. Had it been there all evening? She hadn't noticed. Undoubtedly a guest had dropped it during the flurry of good-byes. Frowning, she set down the tray and unfolded the paper.

8

CELIA DREW HER SHAWL ABOUT HER SHOULDERS AND LOOKED out the window as the carriage rolled along the street clogged with people, carriages, and buggies. The weather had turned chilly, but the sky was a brilliant blue and a fresh breeze blew in off the river. A perfect October afternoon in Savannah. If people chose not to come to her engagement reception at Mrs. Mackay's this afternoon, their absence certainly would not be in consequence of the weather.

"Why the frown?" Ivy shifted on the leather seat and smoothed the folds of her dress.

"I'm worried that nobody will come today and Mrs. Mackay will be terribly embarrassed. I don't want her hurt on our account."

Ivy leaned over to pat Celia's hand. "Don't worry. Uncle David might be one of the richest men in Savannah, but there's no family more important than the Mackays. People wouldn't dare ignore her invitation for fear of being banished from her guest list forever." She paused, her head tilted. "Something else is bothering you."

Celia hadn't told anyone about the anonymous message she'd discovered the night of the masquerade ball, and the secret had finally become too heavy a burden. She opened her bag and withdrew the folded paper. "I found this in the foyer the night of the ball."

Ivy unfolded the paper and read aloud. "Foul deeds will rise, though all the earth o'erwhelm them, to men's eyes." She looked up, her face suddenly pale. "What does it mean? Who would send us such a thing?"

Celia shook her head. The words seemed vaguely familiar, but she couldn't readily remember where she'd heard them. "I don't know."

"I don't understand. What did Uncle David say about this?" Ivy handed the paper back to Celia, who put it away.

"I haven't told him. He's been preoccupied with politics and the Mackays' lost ship. He doesn't seem quite himself these days. He skipped his usual lunch at the club last week. I'm worried about him."

"Is he ill?"

"He hasn't had much of an appetite lately. Nor his usual energy, either."

Ivy sighed. "Maybe Mr. Channing left the note. I wish now I hadn't talked to him. But at least he hasn't published any more stories in the paper. I think he's grown tired of the chase."

"I hope so." Celia toyed with the clasp on her reticule. Leo Channing's stories had stirred up an unsettling mix of unsavory secrets that left her with a nagging fear of impending disaster.

"Promise me you will tell Uncle David about that note," Ivy said as their carriage drew up outside the Mackays' mansion on Lafayette Square. "Surely there must be something else he can do."

"I doubt it. He has already spoken to Mr. Thompson, and I don't think the editor is trying very hard to protect us from Mr. Channing." Celia opened her gold compact and dabbed rice powder onto her nose. "I don't want to worry Papa needlessly."

"Well, don't think about it just now." Ivy patted Celia's gloved hand. "Today is a day for celebration."

Joseph opened the carriage door and handed them out. Celia smoothed the ruffles on her dark-blue dress. Ivy was right. She ought not give another thought to Leo Channing. She should think only of her future with Sutton. But even as they mounted the marble steps and pressed the bell, she couldn't stop thinking about the rumors Alicia Thayer had shared the night of the ball. Had Uncle Magnus left town because he knew more than he admitted? Had there been something between him and the laundress? Was that the reason Aunt Eugenia had left the plantation on St. Simons and shown up at the Brownings' house in the middle of the night all those years ago?

Mrs. Mackay's housekeeper, Mrs. Johns, opened the door, a smile brightening her round, careworn face. "Miss Celia. Mrs. Mackay told me the wonderful news, and I couldn't be one bit happier if you were my own daughter."

At the housekeeper's warm welcome, Celia felt her anxieties melting away. "Thank you, Mrs. Johns."

The housekeeper stepped back to let them enter. "Good afternoon, Miss Lorens."

"Mrs. Johns." Ivy's tone was brisk as she handed the housekeeper her wrap.

"Mrs. Mackay is waiting for you in the parlor," Mrs. Johns said. "The guests will be arriving in a few minutes."

As Mrs. Johns motioned them into the Mackays' parlor, Celia let out a contented sigh. All her life, just being inside Sutton's house had made her happy. It wasn't the expansive, flower-filled foyer, the well-proportioned rooms with their tall ceilings and ornate furnishings, or the thick carpets that muffled her steps as she crossed the room. It was the sense of peace. The Mackays' house seemed always to be relaxed and filled with love. Not that she felt unloved at home on Madison Square. Far from it. But her mother's death had left an empty space, an aching loneliness that never completely disappeared.

Cornelia Mackay stood, both arms outstretched, a gentle smile on her face. "Ivy. Welcome, my dear."

"Thank you, Mrs. Mackay."

"And darling Celia. My daughter-to-be."

Celia kissed the older woman's cheek. "Thank you for planning this tea. I've been looking forward to it all week."

"So have I. We haven't had as much time to visit lately as I would like." Cornelia motioned them to the settee facing the fireplace. "Of course, it won't be as elaborate as your masquerade ball. Everyone is still talking about that centerpiece. How did you ever think of it?"

"A classmate of mine told me her Aunt Ella in Augusta made something similar for a party back in the forties. I thought it might be nice to try something different. But all the credit for the actual execution belongs to Mrs. Maguire and Mrs. Hemphill."

"Well, it certainly was clever. Don't you think so, Ivy?"

Ivy fussed with her gloves. "Yes, very clever."

The bell rang, signaling the guests' arrival. Within half an hour, the Mackays' parlor brimmed with Savannah's elite, eager for a glimpse of Celia's ring and for the details of the proposal. A small fire warmed their faces as Mrs. Johns moved among the guests with trays of sandwiches, small iced cakes, and glasses of cider.

Mrs. Lawton praised a story she was reading in a magazine and reported on the health of her baby son. "Alexander thinks the baby is smiling at him already." Her blue eyes shone with merriment. "Of course any mother knows better, but why spoil my husband's happiness?"

Mrs. Stiles had something weightier on her mind. "My cousin Martha says the abolitionists are still on St. Simons, inciting the Negroes to revolt, and are no longer making any pretense of their purpose."

"Well, I can't imagine any of our servants rising up against us," Mrs. Dickson said. "My husband is just back from Wayland Hall, and he says everything is business as usual."

"Of course. They wouldn't dare give him any hint that they are thinking of rebelling." Mrs. Stiles dabbed at her lips with a napkin. "William says secession is certain should Mr. Lincoln be elected. And then we shall all be called upon to support it."

"But secession is so impractical," Nellie Gordon said from her chair near the fire. "Would I need a pass of some kind to visit my family in Chicago? Would we be permitted to travel to Saratoga or Ohio or New England for the summers, or would the Northerners force us to remain here and face the possibility of death by yellow fever?"

"But if we don't support it, everything we have achieved, everything we hope for our children's futures will be lost." Mrs. Lawton's cup rattled in its saucer. "Personally I wish every last slave in Georgia had gone back to Liberia two years ago when they had the chance."

"But, Sarah," Mrs. Dickson said. "How would my plantation operate without them?"

"Perhaps you could hire them," Mrs. Stiles said. "Sooner or later they all will be free, and that will be the only course of action available to us."

"Sutton says the system of hiring free blacks works in Jamaica," Ivy said. "Growing bananas and coffee is not the same as cultivating rice or cotton, but still—"

"You're quite right, Ivy," Mrs. Mackay said. "But this is not the time to worry about such things. We're here to celebrate with my future daughter, and I for one am ready to discuss less serious subjects."

Celia nibbled on a cucumber sandwich, relieved that politics had been set aside. Even better, her failed masquerade ball and Mr. Channing's stories seemed forgotten. If any of the ladies felt uncomfortable in her presence, they hid it well. Perhaps Ivy was right and none of them dared offending their hostess.

Near the end of the afternoon, an old woman appeared in the doorway. Celia's heart leapt at the sight of Sutton's grandmother. Caroline Manigault was nearly eighty, but her dark eyes were still bright with curiosity, her white hair still thick and glossy and gathered in a low bun at the nape of her neck. Today she wore a russet silk dress with a white lace collar and a rope of pearls that hung nearly to her waist. Leaning on her ebony cane, she made her way across the room. Celia moved closer to Ivy to make room for her on the settee.

"Mrs. Manigault." Celia kissed the woman's withered cheek. "I have no words to express how pleased I am to have your ring. It's generous of you, and I promise to take care of it."

"Let me see how it looks on your finger, child."

Celia held out her left hand, and Mrs. Manigault nodded. "Looks better on you than it did on me. My fingers are too stubby for such a big ring, though I won't deny it brought me much pleasure through the years." She patted Celia's hand. "But it's time to pass it on now. I'd like to think that when you are my age, you'll hand it down to your eldest grandson as well."

Celia's heart brimmed with love for this sweet and generous woman. "Of course I will. And I'll be sure to tell him the story of how his Grandpa Sutton was dressed like a pirate the night he proposed."

Mrs. Manigault laughed. "Sutton came to my room to say good night before he left for your party, and I must say that for a moment he gave me quite a turn."

"He has been fascinated with pirates and the sea since he was a boy," Mrs. Mackay said. "He's always been happiest on the water."

"Tell us, Celia, will you marry in the spring?" Mrs. Gordon set down her cup. "I've always thought May is the loveliest time for a wedding in Savannah."

"We . . . aren't certain yet. But we will fix the date very soon, I hope."

"Good," Mrs. Manigault said. "Because I need something to think about besides the unpleasantness the abolitionists are stirring up. I don't like the atmosphere it's creating here in Savannah. It makes everybody feel uncertain. People are afraid to plan anything for fear of what might happen next month. Or next year."

"Speaking of plans," Mrs. Lawton said to Mrs. Stiles, "Have you heard from that daughter of yours? I wonder whether she and Andrew intend to return home in time for the holidays."

"I had a letter from England last week," Mrs. Stiles said. "Mary writes that Andrew is eager to return to his business interests here, but they haven't any firm plans yet." She sighed. "I do miss them terribly."

After another round of cider and sandwiches, the ladies gathered their things and said their good-byes. Ivy stepped outside to wait for Joseph to bring the carriage around. Celia joined Mrs. Mackay and Mrs. Manigault at the door and thanked each of the ladies for coming.

When the door closed behind the last guest, Mrs. Mackay nodded with satisfaction. "There. All that ridiculousness from your ball is dead and buried."

Celia chewed her bottom lip. "I hope you're right. But . . . Mrs. Mackay? Did Mr. Mackay attend a meeting with the mayor at the gentlemen's club last week?"

"I think he mentioned it in passing, but I'm afraid I didn't pay much attention. It seems our menfolk are always running from one critical event to the next these days. Why do you ask?"

"Papa wasn't invited. He only heard about it later, from Mr. Lawton. I can't help but think he was excluded on purpose because of the gossip that newspaperman is stirring up."

"I'm sure it was just an oversight. I'll ask my husband about it. He will see that it doesn't happen again."

"I'm grateful." Celia let out a long sigh. "I'm glad everyone came to tea today, and not only for my sake. I have the girls at the asylum and their various needs to consider. I must have a good turnout for my reception if we're to raise the necessary funds."

"Don't you fret about that, my dear," Sutton's grandmother said. "I'm not above twisting a few arms if I have to. But you'll see. This unpleasantness will be old news soon enough."

"I hope so."

"Now," Mrs. Mackay continued, "I thought we might go shopping next week to choose a few things for your house."

"I'd love that, but we have no idea whether we'll be living here or . . . elsewhere."

Mrs. Mackay waved one hand. "Oh, that Liverpool business. Sutton will get it sorted out quickly. He won't stay away too long."

"Quite right, Cornelia." Mrs. Manigault leaned in toward Celia. "And I think it wise to choose your things now, my dear, in case the situation worsens sooner than we think. With everything so topsy-turvy these days, who knows how much longer we'll be able to buy good china and linens? Make hay while the sun shines, my girl. That's my advice."

"Perhaps you're right. Would next Wednesday be agreeable, Mrs. Mackay?"

"Perfect." Mrs. Mackay walked out onto the porch with Celia. "We'll start early and have lunch at the Pulaski Hotel. Their onion soup is heavenly. Ah, here's your carriage."

With a final wave, Celia descended the front steps and joined her cousin in the carriage.

"Well," Ivy said as Joseph flicked the reins and turned for home, "that went very well."

"Yes. Thanks to Mrs. Mackay, I feel much better. I'm lucky to be marrying into such a wonderful family." Celia straightened her hat and settled into the seat. "Mrs. Mackay and I are going shopping next Wednesday. She and Grandmother Manigault think I ought to start collecting things for my home. She's taking me to lunch at the Pulaski."

"Nothing but the best for our golden girl."

"Why don't you come with us? It'll be fun. We can visit that new millinery shop that just opened. I overheard Mrs. Stiles telling Mrs. Lawton that the prices are very reasonable. And you and I both need new hats for winter."

"I'm afraid I don't know much about choosing a trousseau," Ivy said. "I'd only be in the way. Besides, I want to look for some of my old books for Louisa, the ones I loved as a child. I haven't seen them in years."

"Louisa!" Celia clapped a hand to her chest. "I completely forgot. It's my turn to read with her next Wednesday. I shall have to postpone my trip with Mrs. Mackay."

"I can go in your place," Ivy said. "I don't mind."

"Oh, Ivy, would you? I do think it's important to keep our lessons going. Last week Louisa seemed a little more interested in reading, so perhaps we are making some progress. What do you think?"

Ivy shrugged. "She's compliant enough. But the last time I was there, she told me she hadn't come to Savannah to learn to read."

Celia frowned. "Did she say why she's here?"

"No but I believe she is hoping to live in Savannah permanently. She complains all the time about plantation life."

Another few minutes brought them home, where an unfamiliar horse and buggy stood near the gate.

"Were you expecting anyone?" Celia gathered her bag and shawl.

Ivy shook her head. "The rig must belong to one of Uncle David's associates."

The door flew open as they mounted the steps. Mrs. Maguire stood there, pale-faced and trembling. "Miss Celia, thank goodness you're home. Your papa has taken a bad turn. Dr. Dearing is with him now."

9

CELIA SLOWED ZEUS TO A WALK AND GLANCED OVER HER shoulder. Behind her, Sutton reined in on Poseidon and drew up beside her on the narrow path through the woods. After church this morning they had driven to the racetrack in Sutton's rig to exercise the horses. Now their mounts were tired and cooling down on the return to their stalls.

Sutton leaned over to stroke Poseidon's sleek neck. The horse blew out and nodded his head. Sutton laughed. "That's my boy."

Celia watched man and horse and felt a surge of love for both. She was lucky that she and Sutton shared a common interest in horses. His letters from Jamaica had been filled with descriptions of the blooded horses being bred there, and she had looked forward to seeing them. But now their future was clouded by the prospect of war and another long separation, not to mention the uncertainty regarding Papa's health.

Celia let Zeus set his own pace as they neared the oval racetrack and tried to focus on the more pleasant aspects of the past few days. After four days in bed, Papa was feeling much better and eager to return to business on Commerce Row. Speaking to her in the parlor after his examination of her father, Dr. Dearing had cautioned Celia to refrain from discussions that might upset her father. In the meantime, plenty of rest, Mrs. Maguire's Irish stew, and some fresh air would do her father a world of good.

Celia also had her upcoming shopping trip with Mrs. Mackay to anticipate. She caught Sutton's eye. "Your mother and I are shopping for our china this week. If you have a preference as to the color of the cup that holds your morning coffee, speak now or forever hold your peace."

He laughed. "It makes no difference to me. Choose whatever appeals to you."

They entered the track and walked their mounts to the stables. Sutton was lifting Celia from the saddle when Finn O'Grady came out and took Zeus's reins. "Bet he didn't throw a shoe today, did he, Miss?"

"Thankfully, no."

"That's 'cause I checked him out extra careful when I tacked him up." Finn nodded to Sutton. "Did the same for Poseidon, Mr. Mackay."

Sutton fished an apple from his pocket and fed it to his horse. "We appreciate that, Finn."

"Yes, sir." The groom took the reins of both horses and led them toward the stalls. "I'll take good care of 'em. Don't you worry."

Celia linked her arm through Sutton's. "We should be getting home. Mrs. Maguire gets cross if I'm later than she thinks I ought to be." He helped her into the buggy, and they set off on the three-mile trip to Madison Square.

"Can you stay for tea this afternoon?" Celia asked. "I know Papa would love it."

"Oh, so the invitation is for his sake, is it?" Sutton teased. He guided the horse around a deep rut in the road.

"Perhaps I would enjoy your company too." She sent him a sideways glance. "To some degree."

He laughed. "I'd love to come, but I ought to head home. My Uncle Arthur arrived from Charleston last night and Mother will expect me for an early supper." He caught her eye. "I'm going back with him on Tuesday."

"To Charleston?"

"Only for a few days. He's offered to introduce me to a friend of his. Griffin Rutledge."

A carriage bearing three ladies in their Sunday finery approached. The driver tipped his hat as they passed on the sun-dappled road.

"Mr. Rutledge is interested in building a boat too," Sutton said.

"To thwart the blockade."

"If it becomes necessary. Uncle Arthur believes South Carolina will secede, maybe as soon as next year."

"Yes, that's what everyone says."

Sutton reached over to squeeze her hand. "I know it's worrisome, but it's better to be prepared for the worst."

They reached the city, and Sutton turned onto Bull Street. "At any rate, I won't be gone long. I should be back from Charleston by Friday, and you can show me everything you and Mother have bought for our home."

She smiled ruefully. "If only we knew where that home will be."

Sutton drew up at the house. "I don't care where we live as long as we're together." He glanced at the Sunday crowd milling about in the verdant little park opposite the house and sighed. "I want to kiss you, but with all these people about, I suppose I'd better not."

He handed her down from the buggy and walked her through the gate and up to the veranda. "Don't worry. Whatever comes, I'll take care of you."

"I know you will." Standing on tiptoe, Celia planted a swift kiss on his cheek. "I love you, Sutton Mackay."

"That's what all the girls say."

She gaped at him in mock horror. He grinned and headed for his rig before she could think of a retort.

She waited until he turned the corner before going inside. She crossed the entry hall and peeked into the library.

Papa looked up from his book, one finger marking his place. "How was your ride with Sutton? How is your mighty steed these days?"

"The ride was lovely, thank you. And Zeus is in fine form. It's hard to say who enjoyed it more, Sutton and me or the horses." Celia removed her hat. Despite her refreshing outing with Sutton, she felt weary, burdened by secrets. She wanted to tell Papa about the anonymous message she'd discovered in the foyer the night of the masquerade and about Sutton's plans for his ship, but Papa didn't need more worries. "What are you reading?"

"Mr. Emerson's essays." Papa rolled his eyes. "The writing is fine, but overall the book lacks dramatic tension."

She grinned, relieved that he could still joke with her.

"Dr. Dearing says I am to avoid reading anything that might cause me distress and tax my old heart."

She bent to kiss his cheek. "Then no newspapers for you, Papa."

He frowned. "Where is Ivy?"

"Off with Lucy Chase. Lucy invited her to a picnic after church this morning." Celia settled onto the chair and arranged her skirt.

"Humph. " He set his book on the table, facedown. "How was church?"

"Fine. Though Alicia Thayer nearly fainted during the general confession."

"Miss Thayer isn't ill, I hope."

"No, I think her corset was laced too tightly."

Papa laughed. "I wish I'd felt well enough to attend."

"Perhaps next week. Mrs. Lawton brought her new baby, who was very much admired. And she reminded me of my promise to collect the Christmas donations for the hospital." Celia sighed. "I suppose I should see to that next week since November is practically here. Mrs. Lawton does not believe in leaving things until the last minute. And I still have to plan the fund-raiser for the Female Asylum."

The door opened, and Ivy stuck her head into the room. "I'm home."

Papa motioned her into the library. "Celia tells me you had an outing with Miss Chase."

Ivy removed her hat, unwound herself from her shawl, and checked her reflection in the mirror.

"I'm happy to know the Chases are back in Savannah," Papa continued. "I understood they were away until the Christmas holidays. When did they return?"

"Oh, did I say it was Lucy Chase?" Ivy turned from the mirror, two red spots staining her cheeks. "I misspoke. Mary Quarterman invited me. We were discussing the Chases after services this morning, and I guess Lucy was on my mind. A silly slip of the tongue." She smiled at Papa. "I do hope I haven't missed tea."

Celia glanced at the clock and rose. "It should be ready any moment. Papa, if you will excuse me, I'd like to change out of these riding clothes."

He waved her away. "I'm not going anywhere. Take your time."

Celia picked up her hat and climbed the stairs to her room. She shed her alpaca riding skirt and blue bodice and left them on the back of a chair to air, changed her shoes, and donned a simple rose-colored day dress. She leaned toward the mirror to check her hair and saw a small wrapped package lying on her dressing table. When had it arrived? And who had put it there?

She untied the string, unwrapped a small white box, and lifted the lid. A gold bracelet set with a quartet of square-cut jewels lay in a nest of cotton.

She laughed. This must be the other surprise Sutton had mentioned the night of the masquerade. But how had he managed to get it into her room without her noticing? Perhaps he had conspired with Ivy or Mrs. Maguire to leave it where she would be sure to find it.

She draped the bracelet over her arm. The jewels glittered in the afternoon light streaming through the window. Diamond. Emerald. Amethyst. Diamond.

"Oh!" The bracelet slid to the floor. Cold fear spurted through her arteries.

It was possible this was merely a harmless coincidence, that Sutton had sent it, unaware of the so-called language of the jewels. But if the bracelet was indeed the surprise he'd been planning for her, why would he not have enclosed a note?

The room spun before her eyes. She pressed a hand to her midsection.

If Sutton hadn't sent it, who had?

Who wanted to see her dead?

10

"CELIA?" IVY RAPPED SHARPLY ON THE BEDROOM DOOR.

"Just . . . just a minute!" Celia quickly retrieved the bracelet and swept it with its box and wrapping paper into the drawer of her dressing table.

Ivy hurried into the room. "Mrs. Maguire says to tell you tea is—oh, my goodness, what's the matter? You're pale as a fish. Shall I fetch the ammonia wine?"

"No, I'm all right. I didn't eat much for breakfast this morning, and I feel a bit faint." Celia opened the window and gulped the cool October air, taking in the flower beds below and the gnarled tree that grew well past the second-floor balcony. Had someone climbed the tree and entered her room through the window?

Ivy joined her at the window and put an arm around Celia's waist. "Considering everything that has happened these past weeks, Mr. Channing's antics and the masquerade ball and that silly note you found, plus Sutton's proposal and the reception at his mother's, it's little wonder you're overwrought." She squeezed Celia's hand. "A cup of Mrs. Maguire's tea will set you to rights. Come on. Let's go down."

Celia allowed her cousin to lead her down the stairs and into her father's library, where he waited with a tea trolley laden with a silver service and platters of sandwiches, cake, and fruits.

The Irish housekeeper looked up when they came in. "There you are, Miss."

Celia blew out a long breath and pasted on a smile. "I'm sorry to have kept you waiting."

Papa closed his book and waved her into a chair. "I don't mind, but Mrs. Maguire is eager to be away."

"Of course." Celia perched on the deep-green velvet chair next to Papa. Ivy chose the settee. "Do forgive me, Mrs. Maguire. I know how much you look forward to your Sunday afternoons."

Mrs. Maguire poured tea and passed the platters. "Mrs. Reilly and I are off to a concert this afternoon. Haydn, I think she said. And an ice-cream party afterward—the last one until next spring, I expect."

Papa picked up the silver tongs and added sugar to his tea. "Enjoy yourself. You've earned it after caring for me these past days."

"No trouble at all lookin' after you, sir." Mrs. Maguire rearranged the blue-plaid blanket covering his knees. "Sure and it does my heart good to see you lookin' better." She straightened and surveyed the room with apparent satisfaction. "If there's nothing else you'll be needin' . . ."

"We don't need a thing." Ivy made a shooing motion with her hands. "Have a lovely time."

Mrs. Maguire sailed out of the room. Moments later the door closed behind her.

Ivy's spoon clinked against her saucer. "Uncle David, did Celia tell you Cornelia Mackay is taking her shopping this week?"

"She did. It's generous of the Mackays, but unnecessary since I intend to provide Celia with a handsome dowry. And considering their present circumstances." He smiled at Celia over the top of his china cup. "I know you'll keep those circumstances in mind and refrain from choosing anything too extravagant."

"Of course." Celia took a long sip of tea, willing the queasiness in her stomach to settle. She moved in a fog, removed from herself, like an actress in a play. She wanted nothing more than to escape to the privacy of her room to examine the bracelet more closely and to figure out what she should do about it. But if she left the room now, Papa would surely suspect something was wrong, and she didn't want to worry him. "I asked Sutton this afternoon whether he had a preference, but he left it up to me."

"As he should." Papa helped himself to another slice of sponge cake and refilled his tea cup. "China and such are a woman's domain. So tell me, Ivy, what goes on with the Quartermans these days? I haven't seen them in a while."

"Oh, you know, Uncle David. The usual." Ivy laughed. "Nothing much changes in Savannah from one day to the next."

He smiled. "I suppose you're right. I can imagine you young people long for less predictability to your days and more excitement. But when one reaches my age, one longs for peace and quiet."

"Well, there's something to look forward to." Ivy drained her cup, blotted her lips with her napkin, and rose. "If you will excuse me, I have some letters to write."

Papa nodded. "Of course. I suppose I should look over the report Mr. Shaw dropped off here on Friday. He'll need my instructions first thing tomorrow."

Celia looked up with a start. Had Elliott Shaw sent the bracelet? He had been offended that she'd refused his gift unopened on the night of the ball. He had called her Miss High and Mighty. Maybe the bracelet was meant to bring her down a notch or two.

Ivy patted her uncle's cheek. "Don't work too hard, and don't upset yourself. You know what Dr. Dearing said."

"Bah. If he had his way, he'd wrap me in a bale of cotton and lock me in a padded room."

Ivy grinned. "We only want what's best for you."

"What's best for me is to get on with my work."

Celia stacked their cups and saucers onto the tea trolley. "Do you want anything else, Papa? Shall I leave this here?"

He waved it away. "I'm full as a tick. Won't need another bite till morning."

Ivy left the room and ran lightly up the stairs. Celia gathered their soiled napkins and folded the white damask cloth over everything.

"Celia?" Papa placed a hand on her arm. "You've been preoccupied ever since you came down for tea. What's troubling you?"

Tears sprang to her eyes. What a relief it would be to unburden herself and seek his wise counsel. But she wouldn't risk his well-being. "Nothing, Papa. I'm all right."

His gray brows rose. "No trouble between you and Sutton?"

"Oh, no. He's wonderful. He's off to Charleston on Tuesday, but only for a few days. I expect him back by week's end."

"I hope you aren't still stewing about that Channing fellow."

"I do wish he'd leave Savannah, but I'm relieved he hasn't written any more newspaper stories of late. I sincerely hope he's realized there's really nothing to tell."

"What is it then?"

"You worry too much."

"When it comes to my only daughter, I plead guilty."

"I got overtired at the racetrack this afternoon. Sutton and I rode for almost two hours. I'm not used to such long rides anymore. I'll admit I've had much to think about lately. But truly, I'm all right."

"If you say so." He motioned toward his desk. "Could you bring that file? And my pen and ink?"

She brought his things and lit the lamp beside his chair. "I'll be in my room if you need anything."

He nodded absently, already absorbed in his work.

Celia returned to her room and locked the door. She closed the window, lit the lamp, and took the bracelet and its packaging from the drawer. Again, she checked inside the box for a note, for any clue as to who had sent it. She smoothed the plain, brown wrapping paper, matching the two sides of the tear she'd made in opening the package and discovered a handwritten message she'd previously overlooked: "Foul whisperings are abroad. Unnatural deeds do breed unnatural troubles."

Hands shaking, she fished the other note from her bag and compared the handwriting, but it was impossible to tell whether the same person had also written this one. Was it Leo Channing? He had warned her not to get in his way. But did he hate her enough to want her dead?

Celia woke with a start. Since Sunday she'd slept fitfully, the old nightmares of her childhood invading her dreams. Downstairs the back door opened and closed as the hired laundress delivered her usual Wednesday load of cleaned and pressed linens.

Wednesday. Celia sat up in bed. Today was the day of her shopping trip with Mrs. Mackay. But instead of a bride's happy anticipation she felt nothing but dread. The bracelet and the two anonymous notes sat like loaded weapons in the bottom of her bag, ready to blow her world to smithereens.

She rose, drew on her dressing gown, and went downstairs. Mrs. Maguire met her in the dining room.

"I thought I heard you a-stirring." The housekeeper poured coffee and set down a plate of sausages and eggs. "Is Miss Ivy awake?"

"I don't know. Her door is still closed." Celia sipped her coffee. "Where is Papa?"

"Gone to Commerce Row, against all my advice."

"I knew he couldn't stay away from his office for long, no matter what the doctor says. He is the most headstrong person I know."

Mrs. Maguire smiled, one brow raised. "The acorn falls not far from the tree."

"I suppose so. Has the paper come?"

"It has, but your father took it with him."

Celia frowned. Usually he left it for her.

Ivy's footfalls sounded along the upper hallway. In a moment she swept into the room, her hair perfectly dressed, her cheeks pink.

"Going somewhere?" Mrs. Maguire asked, pouring Ivy's coffee.

"Calling on Mrs. Dillon. She promised to lend me a book I've been dying to read." Ivy dug into her eggs and chewed with gusto. "And then I'm off to the asylum to read with Louisa. Though I think the girl would be just as happy to abandon her studies altogether."

Mrs. Maguire began collecting the breakfast dishes. "Will either of you ladies be back for lunch?"

"I won't." Ivy set her napkin on her plate. "Mrs. Clayton will give me tea after Louisa's lesson."

"And I'm to have lunch with Mrs. Mackay," Celia said. "If there's time afterward, I want to call on the ladies who are donating Christmas things for the hospital. Mrs. Lawton is keen to have everything done as soon as possible."

An hour later Celia was dressed and ready to go. She knocked on Ivy's door, then peered into the room. Two dresses and two pairs of shoes lay in a heap on the unmade bed. Ivy sat at her dressing table, fiddling with her hair. She set down her brush and smiled at Celia in the mirror. "I can't decide what to wear today."

"Louisa won't notice," Celia said.

Ivy rose and picked up a deep-green dress with lace-trimmed sleeves and a ruffled hem. "This one will do. Can you hand me that lace handkerchief on the table?"

Celia retrieved the handkerchief and handed it to her cousin.

"Help me with the buttons." Ivy stepped into the voluminous skirt and slipped her arms into the sleeves.

Celia obliged, and Ivy tucked the handkerchief into her sleeve and bent to fasten her shoes. She pirouetted before the mirror. "How do I look?"

"Much too elegant to be giving a reading lesson at the asylum."

"Mrs. Clayton says we are to be an example to the young women in all things." Ivy retrieved her reticule and shawl. "Ready?"

Together they descended the staircase. Joseph delivered Ivy to Mrs. Dillon's house on Reynolds Square, and soon Celia was on her way to the Mackays, determined to put aside her worries and enjoy the day.

"There you are, my dear," Cornelia Mackay said when Celia was ushered into the Mackays' parlor. "I've sent for our carriage. It won't be a moment. Oh, I am excited about today. This is so much more enjoyable than shopping for myself."

"It's very generous of you. And quite unexpected."

"I realize your father will provide you with whatever you need, and no doubt you'll have your mother's lovely things, but I want to contribute something too. After all, Sutton is my only living child." Mrs. Mackay laughed, her cheeks pinking. "At my age I'm not likely ever to be a mother of the bride. And I wanted to do something for Francesca. Your mother would dearly have loved being a part of such happy preparations."

"Yes. When I was very young my mother and I once held a pretend wedding in the garden. With an imaginary groom." Celia smiled at the bittersweet memory. Neither of them could have known that the make-believe ceremony would be the only one they would ever share. She shook off her melancholy and smiled at her hostess. "I assume Sutton is still in Charleston."

"He is," Mrs. Mackay said. "I don't mind telling you, my dear, that I am not at all in favor of this blockade-running scheme he is so intent upon. But once that young man gets something into his head, he's stubborn as a dog with a bone." Mrs. Mackay peered out the window. "Here's the carriage."

A short drive brought them downtown. At midmorning the streets teemed with people headed to the markets, with shoppers darting in and out of stores, policemen on horseback, and groups of children and stray dogs dodging the rigs and carriage wheels.

Inside the china shop, Celia pored over delicate translucent cups trimmed with bands of gold, platters decorated with turkeys and landscape scenes, ivory plates rimmed with borders of deepest blue. After much discussion—and a discreet inquiry as to price—she decided upon a blue and gold pattern embellished with tiny red flowers. Mrs. Mackay added a graceful little chocolate pot and eight matching cups, a silver coffee urn, and a dozen pairs of ivory-handled grape scissors.

Leaving their purchases to be boxed and delivered later, they crossed the street to Mrs. Haverford's linen shop where Celia chose sheets and duvets of warm ivory and left instructions for monogramming. Then she and Mrs. Mackay walked to the Pulaski Hotel for lunch.

"Mrs. Mackay." The head waiter's mouth formed a tight line. "It has been awhile since you and Mr. Mackay joined us for dinner."

"Yes, it has been longer than we like. I'm afraid business has taken up so much of my husband's time, and we've been busy since our son returned from Jamaica."

"His reception here certainly was well attended. It seems all of

Savannah is happy to have him home. You and Mr. Mackay most of all."

"We are indeed. I'm sure you know his intended, Miss Browning."

The waiter's eyes flickered briefly before he bowed. "Of course. Miss Browning. We at the Pulaski wish you every happiness."

"Thank you."

Mrs. Mackay surveyed the room. "We'd like our usual table by the window, please."

"That table is spoken for, Mrs. Mackay."

"But how can that be? I reserved it two days ago."

He shrugged. "An unfortunate misunderstanding, I'm afraid. The only table I have open at the moment is this way. Please follow me." He led them across the busy dining room and seated them at a table partially hidden behind an enormous potted palm. "Perhaps you will be more comfortable here anyway. This table is much more private."

Celia's face burned. She knew exactly why he had seated them out of sight of the other patrons. She was about to protest when Sutton's mother slid smoothly into her chair and met the waiter's haughty gaze. "What do you recommend today?"

"The soup is very good today, ma'am."

They ordered and he disappeared. Mrs. Mackay pulled off her gloves and set them on a vacant chair. "Well, my dear," she said with a determined smile, "I think we acquitted ourselves quite well this morning."

Celia toyed with her heavy silver spoon. How like Mrs. Mackay to ignore the unpleasantness to spare her future daughter-in-law embarrassment. "I'm sorry about this—"

"It isn't important. Small-minded people always need someone else to look down upon, whether or not it's warranted. Now, let's speak no more about it. Didn't you think the linens at Mrs.

Haverford's were exquisite? I think the ivory you chose is just right."

"Yes. I hope Sutton approves."

"He's much like his father. Easy to please in such matters." Mrs. Mackay's blue eyes were full of affection. "Sutton loves you so. I doubt any decision you make will meet with his displeasure."

"Oh, I hope you're right. I couldn't bear it if I disappointed him."

"Tell me. Have you two discussed a date for the wedding? I can't get a word out of him about that."

"No. Everything has happened so quickly, and he has been so intent upon his boatbuilding venture that we've had little time to consider it."

The soup came, steaming and redolent with sweet onions and melted cheese. Celia picked up her spoon and broke the crusty top. "I pray we can avoid war. But Sutton has made it plain that if war comes, he will do whatever it takes to defend Savannah and the South."

"Men are such idealistic dreamers," Mrs. Mackay said. "They dwell too much upon the glories of war without counting the cost. Sometimes I think the country would be better off if women were in charge. We look at things with a more practical eye."

"Yes, but the suffrage movement isn't making much progress," Celia said. "I doubt women will get the vote in my lifetime, much less achieve elected office."

A carriage rumbled past the hotel. Mrs. Mackay peered around the potted palm and through the window opposite. "I believe that is Mrs. Lawton's rig. Which reminds me, I promised to call on her this afternoon. I suppose we should be going soon."

They gathered their things, and half an hour later, Celia was returned to her father's house. Ivy was still out, but Joseph was waiting patiently beside the gate. He tipped his hat. "Miss Ivy said you wanted to go calling this afternoon."

"Yes. To the Stileses' and then to the Quartermans'."

They set off in the carriage. Celia called on Mrs. Stiles, where she collected a box of warm winter coats and six scarves knit from the softest wool. As Celia prepared to leave, the older woman proffered a check. "I find cash is always appreciated at the hospital."

"Yes." Celia tucked the check into her bag. "Mrs. Lawton will be delighted."

"Give her my regards and tell her I'll call soon. I want to see the baby."

Celia waved and returned to the carriage.

"You goin' to the Quartermans' now?" Joseph asked.

"Yes, please."

"You planning on staying long?"

"Not long. Why? Is there some place you need to go?"

"Got to fetch Miss Ivy from the Female Asylum. I expect she's waitin' on me by now." Joseph climbed up and flicked the reins, and the carriage lurched along the dirt road. At the Quartermans' handsome house on Abercorn Street, he halted and helped her down.

"No need to wait for me," Celia told him. "According to Mrs. Lawton's list, I've only to collect a check from the Quartermans—no heavy boxes to carry. I can walk home."

"You sure?"

"Positive. It's a beautiful afternoon. I'll enjoy the chance to spend a few minutes outside. Besides, Ivy took my turn at the asylum today. I don't want to make her wait too long."

Joseph frowned. "Well, if you're sure. Mr. Browning tol' me I was s'posed to carry you and your cousin wherever you want to go. Keep you safe from the troublemakers on the street."

"Go ahead. I won't be long."

The driver waited beside the carriage until she had rung the bell and the Quartermans' butler had answered the door.

"Please follow me," the butler said. He led her into the parlor and disappeared.

Celia perched on the edge of the velvet settee. She had been so busy all day that she hadn't had time to think about the bracelet or to decide what to do about it. Now, in the silence of the Quartermans' elegant parlor, her fears came roaring back. Who had sent it and the cryptic messages? What did it all mean? Was this some sick game, or was someone out to harm her?

Mary Quarterman hurried into the parlor. "Celia, forgive me for making you wait. Mother was in the middle of one of her lectures, and I had no choice but to hear her out." Mary laughed. "She thinks she can simply harangue me into getting married. If only it were that simple!"

Celia smiled. She and Mary were the same age and moved in the same social circle. Celia was not as close to Mary as to Alicia Thayer, but she and Mary liked each other. And today, at least, it seemed Mary didn't intend to hold Mr. Channing's scurrilous writings against her.

"I imagine you will be engaged before Christmas," Celia said. "Alicia says Miles Frost is quite taken with you."

"So says my brother, who has his own romantic prospects to think about." Mary glanced toward the door she had left ajar, and lowered her voice. "He's sweet on Alicia, but don't you dare breathe a word of it."

"I won't tell a living soul." Celia grinned. "Maybe the four of you will have a double wedding. Remember when the Sinclair sisters married on the same day?"

"I remember." Mary sighed. "If Miles does care for me, he has yet to declare himself."

"Oh, I know you'll make a good match one of these days."

"Spoken with the confidence of one who is safely engaged. But I do appreciate the encouragement. But enough chat—you're here for the check for the hospital. Come on in to Pa's study."

Celia followed Mary down the hallway and into a book-lined

room overlooking the street. Mary crossed the room to a walnut desk piled high with papers, drawings, newspaper clippings, and magazines and began tossing things aside. "I know he left that check here somewhere."

She paused in her search to show Celia a large sketch of the waterfront. "Pa's latest idea. He wants to dredge the river so larger ships can access the Port of Savannah. He's corresponding with Mr. Lee in Virginia about it. Mr. Lee supposedly has experience with such things."

More books and papers went flying. Desk drawers opened and closed. Mary frowned and burrowed farther into the pile. "Aha!"

She emerged at last, triumphant. "Here it is." She glanced at it and whistled. "Generous too. Don't tell Mother. She worries about money all the time."

"I won't. But it is for a good cause. Without the hospital, the sick and the indigent would have no place to go."

Mary's gray eyes hinted at mischief. "Pa says the hospital is more for the sake of the city than for those poor unfortunates. He says we must keep them off the streets to protect Savannah's reputation among the Northern investors."

"Whatever the true reason, the funds will be put to good use." Celia folded the check and put it away. "I suppose I should go. Our driver has gone to collect Ivy from the Female Asylum, and they'll be home soon."

"How is Ivy?" Mary plopped into her father's chair. "I haven't seen her in ages."

Celia frowned. "I thought she went on an outing with you on Sunday."

"No. Mother wasn't feeling well after church, so we came straight home."

"That's odd. I could have sworn . . . but maybe I misunderstood." Celia started for the door.

Mary walked her out. "Give your cousin my regards. An outing would be wonderful. We should plan one soon before the weather turns cold."

Mary waved as Celia went through the gate and headed for Bull Street. The afternoon was waning. A cool breeze blew in from the river, and the low sun cast long shadows across her path. Celia tucked her bag securely beneath her arm and headed home. She was exhausted after a day of shopping and visiting and eager to reach the safety of her room to ponder Mary's assertion that she and Ivy hadn't spent Sunday together. If Ivy had not been with the Quartermans on Sunday as she claimed, where had she been? And why had she lied about it?

Celia hurried past a group of children playing beneath the trees on Abercorn Street. Here the shadows grew longer, and she felt a sudden, inexplicable chill, as if something unseen waited for her behind the tall brick walls surrounding the houses. She glanced around, but nothing moved save the thick ropes of Spanish moss undulating in the breeze.

Holding tighter to her reticule, she hastened toward home. But as she turned the corner a man stepped through a short iron gate and blocked her path. "Miss Browning."

Leo Channing wore the same suit and battered felt hat that he'd worn on his visit to her home. His ink-smudged collar sat slightly askew. The smell of spirits came off him in waves.

She attempted to step around him but he put out an arm, blocking her path. "What's your hurry?"

"Please let me pass, Mr. Channing. I have nothing to say to you."

"Well, that's too bad," he said. "What I can't know for sure, I'll have to make up."

"Isn't that what you do anyway?"

"I worked hard on those newspaper pieces."

"That doesn't mean you should have written them."

"I was working on another one," he said, shrugging. "Before I got the sack."

She blinked. "Mr. Thompson dismissed you?"

"This morning. Your daddy went by there complaining about my latest piece, and the next thing I knew, Thompson had given me the old heave-ho." Channing drew a dented flask from his pocket and took a swig from it. "But it's what you might call a silver lining because now I have time to write the book I intended to write in the first place. I've always thought your family's story would do well in book form. Mystery, romance, scandal—it would put a novel to shame, don't you think?"

Relief turned to despair. The longer Leo Channing kept the story alive, the harder it would become to remain above it all. Celia didn't want the old, sad story to be the thing that defined the Brownings. And for all their professed loyalties, even the Mackays and her closest friends would tolerate only so much.

But she would not allow Channing to see her weakness. "You've heard of slander, I presume."

"Of course."

"Write even one word about my family that is not a matter of public record, and my father will have you in court faster than you can count to ten. Now get out of my way."

The reporter laughed. "Why certainly, your highness. Far be it from me to hinder you on your royal rounds."

"Since you are so determined to destroy my family's reputation and peace of mind, may I at least know the reason why?"

He pressed his fingers to his mouth to suppress a fetid, noisy belch. "It has nothing to do with you. Back in Baltimore I've got a wife and four young'uns to feed, two of 'em sickly most of the time, and newspapering hardly covers the bills. I need a big story, one that will get readers' attention. And yours was one of the biggest stories ever to hit Savannah."

"So you are willing to invent a scandalous, sordid tale and to destroy my family in order to save your own."

"Well, parts of it I had to invent—or hint at, anyway." Channing leaned against the gate and sent her a bleary stare. "But other parts of what I have written are true. People know things, Miss Browning. Things that would shock you if you knew. Things they're too polite to say to you because your family is richer than Croesus himself."

Celia's heart constricted. She and Ivy had been so young when the accidents occurred. Undoubtedly they both had been shielded from circumstances they were too young to understand. The explanations she'd been given as she grew older had been hurried and vague. Were there details she didn't know?

She met his unfocused gaze. "Then perhaps you'd enlighten me."

Channing shook his head. "Not yet. Because what you say about slander is true, and I don't intend to get myself thrown in jail. That wouldn't help the missus and the young'uns at all, would it? I am looking for proof. And I believe it exists."

In the distance Celia spotted her father coming along the street, headed for home. It was bad enough that he refused to let Joseph drive him to Commerce Row. The last thing he needed was to see her talking to the despicable newspaperman. Without another word, she darted into the street.

"The red diary. That's the key," Channing whispered as she hurried past. "Mark my words. Sooner or later every secret comes to light."

11

CELIA REACHED HOME JUST AHEAD OF HER FATHER AND HURried up the stairs, her mind whirling. *People know things.* Was Leo Channing trying to scare her into divulging facts that she really didn't have? Was it true that behind her back all of Savannah was buzzing about the house of love and grief? Two horrid accidents within two weeks was unusual and certainly a regrettable spate of bad luck, but that is all they were. Accidents.

Weren't they?

In her room, she tossed her shawl and reticule onto the bed, removed her hat, and sank into her chair beside the window. The street and the garden were in shadow. The distant, boarded-up carriage house brooded in the stippled light. Closing her eyes, she tried to summon the memory of the night in late spring when Ivy and Aunt Eugenia had arrived unexpectedly from their St. Simons Island plantation.

Aunt Eugenia had told Papa she had quit the island out of fear for Ivy's health, that an outbreak of fever had taken the lives of several slaves already. Listening at the parlor door, Celia had wondered about Uncle Magnus. Wasn't his life in danger too? But he'd stayed behind for three days before showing up in Savannah.

Celia vaguely remembered late-night discussions between her father and her uncle, discussions that had sometimes become heated. But in the mornings, peace had seemingly been restored, and the household had fallen into a new routine that accommodated Ivy and her parents.

"Celia?" Ivy's knock at her door dispelled the memory. "Dinner is almost ready."

"Coming."

Celia checked her appearance in the pier glass and joined Ivy in the dining room. Soon Papa appeared, looking tired but also inordinately pleased about something. The three of them sat down to Mrs. Maguire's roast beef, gravy, and roasted potatoes.

Papa offered a blessing and passed a platter to Celia. "How was your day, my dear?"

Avoiding the topic of Mr. Channing, Celia told him about her shopping trip with Mrs. Mackay and described the china and linens she had chosen. "Mrs. Haverford at the linen shop had some very pretty things." She paused to eat a bite of potatoes. "I thought of Louisa from the Female Asylum when I saw the fine embroidery. She may well find a good position for herself in such a shop when she leaves."

"That may happen sooner than we think," Ivy said. "Mrs. Clayton told me today that Mrs. Foyle is looking for an assistant. Mrs. Clayton intends to recommend Louisa."

Papa chewed and swallowed. "Mrs. Foyle? Do we know her?"

"She's Mrs. Stiles's modiste," Ivy explained. "Very talented. She made the dress Mrs. Stiles wore to last year's Christmas ball. It was quite the talk of the evening."

"I see." Papa's eyes twinkled. "I suppose I ought to pay more attention to such things, now that Celia is in need of a wedding gown."

"Well, I don't think you can do better than Mrs. Foyle." Ivy spooned gravy onto her roast beef. "But I wouldn't wait too long to engage her services. Mrs. Stiles says Mrs. Foyle stays quite busy."

Papa turned to Celia. "Tell me. Were you able to finish collecting for the hospital Christmas drive? I saw Alexander Lawton at the club this afternoon, and he said his wife has been anxious about it."

"All finished," Celia said. "I'll take everything to the hospital tomorrow." She caught Ivy's eye across the polished mahogany dining table. "I called on Mary Quarterman. We had quite an interesting conversation."

"Oh?" Ivy paled, but her gaze was steady. "What about?"

"This and that." Celia intended to get to the bottom of her cousin's deception, but not in front of Papa. Though he claimed to be quite recovered, she didn't want to upset him. "Mary says that her father has been corresponding with Mr. Robert Lee in Virginia. Something about a scheme to deepen the river."

Papa nodded. "People have talked about it for years, but dredging the river will be terribly expensive and will require investments from many on the waterfront. Mr. Quarterman may well be onto something, but now is not the time. Too many people are still trying to recover from last year's financial setbacks." He helped himself to more coffee. "But at least we have some personal good news on that front."

That explained his unusually cheerful mood. "What is that, Papa?"

"Sutton returned from Charleston this afternoon with news that he has secured a new investor in Mackay Shipping. One that will make it possible to replace the *Electra* and hire a new captain—and repay the loan I secured on their behalf."

"That is wonderful news," Celia said. "I'm relieved, as I'm sure you are. Though I should be cross with Sutton for not letting me know he's home."

"He's only just arrived, darling. I'm certain he's eager to see you."

Mrs. Maguire came in carrying a lemon pie. "'Tis the last one of the season; there'll be no more till we can get some decent lemons again. Will you be wantin' a piece just now, Mr. Browning?"

"I never pass up a chance for your lemon pie, Mrs. Maguire."

Mrs. Maguire served the dessert, collected their dinner plates, and returned to the kitchen.

Celia took a bite of pie. Cold and tart, just the way she liked it. "Did Sutton say how his shipbuilding proposal went?"

"There wasn't time," Papa said. "Just before I headed for the club, I had a visit from Mr. Thompson at the paper."

"Oh?"

"He came by to let me know he has dismissed Leo Channing. And good riddance, I say. That piece in this morning's paper was far beyond the pale."

So that was why Papa had taken the *Daily Morning News* with him today. To shield her from its contents.

"Even Mr. Thompson was dismayed that Channing would go so far as to accuse a member of this family of murder," Papa continued.

Celia's breath caught.

"Who?" Ivy breathed.

"Channing wouldn't say outright. It's only more innuendo, aimed at selling papers and generating talk. Thompson feared, and rightly so, that I would suspend advertising in his paper and sue him for slander in the bargain. He's prepared to print a retraction in tomorrow's edition along with a notice that Mr. Channing has been discharged." Papa pushed away his empty plate. "I sincerely hope this is the end of Mr. Channing."

For a moment Celia was tempted to tell him about her encounter with the drunken newspaperman and to ask what the man had meant by his reference to a red diary. But Papa looked better tonight than he had in some time. Clearly he was buoyed by the news of Channing's dismissal and of the new investor for the Mackays' firm that would absolve him of the burdensome loan he'd made. Besides, Channing was such a liar, who knew what to believe?

The faint chiming of the doorbell drew her attention back to the table. Papa was enjoying another cup of coffee, but Ivy seemed distracted. Lost in thought.

Mrs. Maguire came in, her cheeks pink. "Miss Celia. Mr. Mackay is waiting for you in the library."

Celia shot to her feet. "I'll be right there. Papa, will you excuse me?"

He laughed. "Would it make a difference if I refused? Go on. Ivy and I will adjourn to the parlor, perhaps for a game of chess."

"Oh, Uncle David, would you mind terribly if I excused myself?" Ivy set down her cup. "The trip to the asylum today tired me out more than I realized. I think I'll read in bed for a while if that's all right."

"Of course, my dear. I suppose I can entertain myself."

Celia rushed to the library to find Sutton standing beside the fireplace. He turned as she entered and crossed the room, arms open in greeting. "Hello, my love."

She relaxed into his strong embrace. "I didn't expect you back so soon."

"Mr. Rutledge had another appointment for tomorrow that he had forgotten. We had to conclude our business rather hurriedly, but conclude it we did."

"Papa told us you found a new investor for Mackay Shipping too."

They moved to the settee by the window. Sutton sat down beside her and took her hands in his. "Yes. Mr. Rutledge is investing in a new ship for us. It's the answer to prayer, really."

"Your father must be relieved."

"We all are. Ever since the *Electra* was lost, Mother has tried to keep up a brave front, but she's been terribly worried. I'm glad she had her shopping expedition with you to take her mind off Father's troubles." Sutton kissed her temple. "Mother says you have exquisite taste."

"That is true. I chose you, didn't I?"

He laughed. "I can't wait to make a home with you."

She drew back to meet his eyes. "Will it be soon, Sutton?"

"I hope so. Mr. Rutledge wants to invest in my ship and to build one of his own. He's going to England next month to talk to shipbuilders. Once we make a choice, I shall have to go, too, to see that construction is started."

"Yes," she said slowly, "so you've said."

Recent incidents had awakened in her the desire for distance. If only it were possible to leave at once for Jamaica. To sail with Sutton among the sun-shot mangroves, the ship rocking on the waters of the Black River, the pink myrtle bushes baking in the heat. She longed for someplace where everything was foreign, where their future would unfold before them, unsullied and unfettered. But now, that dream would have to wait. Unless . . .

Sutton folded his arms and grinned at her. "What are you thinking, Celia Browning?"

"Let's get married right after the new year, and I'll go with you to England."

"Liverpool is hardly the kind of place for a honeymoon, darling."

"I don't care. What if war breaks out while you're gone, and you can't get back to Savannah? I couldn't stand it."

"It could happen, I suppose. But I plan to be safely home from England long before the next election."

"You promise?"

"Wild horses can't keep me in Liverpool one second longer than is necessary."

The mantel clock chimed. Sutton rose. "It's getting late. I should go."

"But you just got here."

"I know. But I promised Father I'd go over the terms of our agreement with Mr. Rutledge this evening. He wants to get everything signed as soon as possible."

Together they walked to the door. Sutton took her hands again. "Mother told me what happened at the hotel this morning. She said you were upset."

"I tried not to show it, but I really wanted to kick that unctuous waiter's shins."

Sutton grinned. "He deserved it. But don't let it bother you. People like him are always looking for someone they can look down upon, and when that someone is a Browning or a Mackay, the urge can be too powerful to resist."

"That's just what your mother said. Anyway, Papa says Mr. Channing has been dismissed from the paper and tomorrow there will be a retraction of today's story. That's something, I suppose."

"Well, there you are then. The end of this whole silly business." Sutton glanced down the hallway and then looked toward the gallery. "Are we alone?"

"Ivy and Mrs. Maguire have retired for the evening. Papa is probably still in the parlor, pretending to read."

"Then we are as alone as we'll ever be."

Sutton bent his head and kissed her. She closed her eyes and clung to him, lost in his arms. When the kiss ended, she looked up at him, shaken, her heart brimming with love for him. All her life, Sutton Mackay had left her breathless.

"There's a new play opening at the theater a week from Friday," he said, his voice husky with emotion. "Would you like to go?"

"Of course."

"I'll come for you at seven. Wear something pretty."

She pretended to consider. "I was actually thinking of wearing my old fishing costume. The one with the patched skirt and the distinct odor of trout."

"And you will look splendid in it." He kissed her forehead. "Go to sleep, my love. And don't give this Channing fellow another thought."

He left, whistling, as usual. She lifted the curtain and watched his rig moving down the gas-lit street.

If only she could let go of her worries about Leo Channing. He'd been dismissed from the newspaper, but he'd made it clear that he wasn't finished with her family's story. Not by a long shot. He would continue probing every nook and cranny for something to put into his book. Unless she could prove his theories were false, the cloud of suspicion would continue to hang over their lives, tainting their good name and harming their livelihood. Threatening the success of her work on behalf of the orphaned girls and diminishing her mother's legacy. She couldn't allow that to happen.

"The red diary," the man had told her. *"That's the key."* Was there really a diary somewhere that would explain everything?

Celia let the curtain fall and headed to the parlor to say good night to Papa. He and Sutton and this house were everything to her. She would not allow any of them to be sullied. However difficult and painful it might be, she would find a way to stop Leo Channing.

She peered into the parlor, but Papa had already retired, leaving his book lying open on the chair. Celia doused the light and headed upstairs. Ivy sat on the landing. In her pale-green dressing gown, her blond hair falling loose around her shoulders, she looked young and vulnerable.

"You're still up?" Celia said.

"It isn't terribly late. Besides, I wanted to talk to you."

"What about?"

"Don't be coy. I saw the look you gave me at dinner tonight when you mentioned your visit to the Quartermans'." Ivy pushed her hair off her face and got to her feet. "No doubt you know I wasn't out with them last weekend."

"I wasn't deliberately trying to catch you out. Mary asked how you were and said she hadn't seen you in a while." Celia opened the door to her room and motioned Ivy inside. She slipped off her shoes and sat on her bed, tucking her legs beneath her.

Ivy perched on the edge of the little velvet-covered chair beside the window like a bird poised for flight. "I met someone," she said.

"A man?"

Ivy rolled her eyes. "Am I so unattractive you can't imagine anyone being interested in me?"

"Don't be silly. You don't need me to tell you that you're quite pretty. Who is he?"

"Michael Gleason."

"Do we know his family?"

"See? This is exactly why I didn't tell you and Uncle David about him. The only thing you care about is whether someone is from the right part of town." Ivy fidgeted in her chair. "You don't know him. He's Irish. And a drayman."

"A drayman?"

"He has his own horse and wagon, and he makes deliveries all over town. I met him at the asylum the first day I went to tutor Louisa. He was delivering kitchen supplies for the cook."

"I see."

"He's very smart and kind, and he has a wonderful sense of humor. He asked me to walk out with him after church last week. I knew you and Uncle David wouldn't approve, so I made up the story about visiting with Lucy Chase. Only it turned out Uncle David knew they weren't in town, so then I said I was with Mary."

Ivy gave a brittle little laugh. "I have the worst luck in the world. I can't even tell a lie and make it stick."

"Papa doesn't harbor ill will toward anyone just because of their social class. And he wants only the best for you. Surely you know that."

"Yes, but his idea of what is best for me isn't always the same as mine."

"Well, you're twenty-five years old, capable of making your own choices. If your affections are settled upon this Mr. Gleason, then—"

"I do feel something for Michael, though we haven't spent much time together. We think alike. We laugh at the same things. It's as if we've known each other forever. But then I worry that he might turn out like my father."

"In what way?"

Ivy waved one hand. "Don't tell me you have forgotten the gossip when we were at school about how Father courted Mother only to prove that he could win the heart of a woman far above his own social standing."

"But that's all it was, Ivy. Just silly schoolgirl gossip. I don't remember very much about Uncle Magnus, but I am sure he and Aunt Eugenia loved each other."

Ivy's face clouded. "Maybe he loved her at first. But later—" She shook her head. "Anyway, I hope Michael's motives are pure. You won't mention this to Uncle David, will you?"

"Just be careful to guard your heart and your reputation."

"My reputation? What am I saving it for? I am officially an old maid, the spinster cousin of the beautiful and soon-to-be-wed Celia Browning. I doubt very much if anyone else in Savannah cares what I do." Ivy got to her feet. "That's all I wanted to say. Good night."

12

SUTTON HANDED CELIA INTO THE CARRIAGE, THEN SETTLED himself on the seat across from her and knocked on the door to signal his driver. As the carriage rolled down the street, Celia was filled with a sense of happy anticipation. She had always loved the theater. Stepping inside, settling into the darkness, was akin to entering another world, a world that allowed her to temporarily set aside her fears and worries. She snuggled into the warmth of her blue woolen cloak and watched the gaslights coming on. Tonight she would forget about Leo Channing, the anonymous notes, and the jeweled bracelet with its sinister message hidden in the bottom drawer of her dressing table.

"Warm enough?" Sutton smiled into her eyes and she felt the tension draining from her shoulders.

"Yes. It's a bit chilly tonight, but I love November in Savannah."

"Have I told you how lovely you look in that gown?" Sutton sniffed the air. "I can hardly smell the dead trout at all."

She laughed. "Have you seen the program for tonight's performance? I hope Mrs. Cushman reprises her role as Meg Merrilies."

"*Guy Mannering* is one of my favorite plays too," he said. "If only because it's less complicated than Mr. Scott's novel. I got bogged down in that book more than once, trying to keep all the characters straight."

"Mrs. Lawton told me that Mrs. Cushman's singing voice failed and she had to quit her opera career."

"Opera's loss is theater's gain." Sutton fished his watch from his vest pocket and peered out the carriage window. "We're going to miss the curtain if Steven doesn't speed things up. Wonder what's taking so—"

The sound of breaking glass startled them both. "What was that?"

Sutton peered out into the growing darkness. "There's a group of men on the corner. Maybe one of them dropped his bottle of spirits."

Then came the pop-pop of gunfire. The carriage wheels ground to a stop. Before Sutton could open the door, the driver jumped down and rapped on the glass. "Mr. Mackay?"

"What's the trouble, Steven?"

"I don't know, sir, but the street is blocked off up ahead. Looks to me like a mob, with they shotguns and such. What do you want to do?"

"Take Miss Browning home. I'll go see what this is about."

The driver shook his head. "Mr. Mackay, I been workin' for your fambly since you was in short pants, and I ain't leaving you to no mob. No, sir."

Shouts erupted behind them in the street. Celia turned to look and saw another group of men, some white, some Negro, moving along Bull Street, their torches blazing in the darkness. Another carriage drew alongside Sutton's. A man got out and rapped on the window.

"Alexander!" Sutton opened the door and moved over to make room for Mr. Lawton, a husky man with a neatly trimmed beard and kind eyes that just now were filled with worry.

"What the devil is happening here?" Sutton asked.

"Word just came that Charlie Lamar has returned from Africa in the *Wanderer* with his load of slaves. More than four hundred of them, if the report is accurate." Mr. Lawton glanced uneasily out of the carriage's back window. "He is to blame for this unrest."

"Surely he hasn't brought the Negroes here to Savannah."

A brick sailed through the air and shattered the window of Mr. Lawton's carriage. Sutton's horse shied in its traces, and the carriage lurched.

"No, he's put them ashore on Jekyll Island." Mr. Lawton let out a gusty breath. "The Irish and the free Negroes have joined in protest. The police are out to restore order, but we ought to get off the street as soon as we can."

"Agreed."

Celia peered out the window. The crowd seemed to be growing larger by the minute. Men stood five and six abreast in the street, packed as densely as cordwood, their voices like a chorus of angry bees. Bull Street was rapidly becoming impassable.

Sutton turned to Celia. "We'll have to walk home. Can you manage?"

She nodded. "I think so."

"I'll go with you," Mr. Lawton said. "My carriage can't move either." He shook his head. "Sarah was disappointed at the thought of missing the theater tonight. But our boy is sick, and she didn't want to leave him with the nurse. I'm thankful now that she is home and safe."

Mr. Lawton pushed open the carriage door, got out, and held his hand out to Celia. The drivers abandoned the carriages and pushed through the crowd.

Celia stepped into the packed street, Sutton close behind. Walking between the two men, she concentrated on taking one step, then another. Shouts, sporadic gunfire, and the sound of breaking glass erupted around her. The mob surged, their faces in the torchlight glowing with fervor and excitement. Sutton drew her close and pressed on through the crowd.

At last they reached her gate. Sutton and Mr. Lawton hustled

Celia up to the door, and the three of them rushed inside. Lights blazed in the library where Papa and Mrs. Maguire sat, their expressions anxious, their cups of tea untouched.

"Sutton—thank God!" Papa rose to greet them. "Are you all right, Celia?"

"Fine, Papa. Sutton and Mr. Lawton kept me safe."

Papa nodded. "Hello, Alexander."

"David." Mr. Lawton removed his hat.

"What's happened?" Papa asked. "I heard gunfire on the street."

Briefly, Mr. Lawton recounted the news of the *Wanderer*'s return and the resulting unrest.

Behind his gold-rimmed spectacles, Papa's blue eyes were worried. "Our old city is in deep trouble, my friend."

"I fear so, yes, though I don't expect Georgia planters will buy Lamar's slaves. He'll have to sell them farther north if he can find buyers at all."

"Well, the whole enterprise was ill-advised from the beginning." Papa's shoulders drooped. "I suppose Thompson over at the newspaper is happy. He was all for Lamar's scheme."

"I've known Mr. Thompson for years," Mr. Lawton said, "and I always thought he was a reasonable man. But lately he has been on the wrong side of several issues. I don't—"

"Where is Ivy?" Mrs. Maguire shot to her feet." I thought she was with you, Celia."

Celia shook her head. "I haven't seen her since this afternoon."

"I thought she was goin' with you to the theater. But it seems I'm mistaken."

"Are you certain she isn't in her room?"

"I'm sure. Unless she's just come in through the window."

Well, that was a possibility, since more than likely Ivy had sneaked away with Michael Gleason. "Perhaps she's with a friend, waiting out this disturbance."

Mrs. Maguire rolled her eyes. "That Ivy Lorens will be the death o' me, sure as I'm standin'." She motioned Sutton and Mr. Lawton to sit. "I'll just go get some more cups. You gentlemen are bound to be here for a while longer."

"No tea for me, Mrs. Maguire, thank you." Mr. Lawton caught Papa's eye. "I wouldn't mind a bit of spirits though, if the ladies will indulge us."

Papa went to the side table and poured a bit of bourbon into a cut crystal glass. "How about you, Sutton?"

"Yes, thanks."

The three men clinked glasses and sipped. Celia helped herself to a cup of lukewarm tea and stared into the fire cracking in the grate. Another hour passed. A police wagon clattered along the street, setting off a chorus of barking dogs.

A short time later, the doorbell sounded. Mrs. Maguire hurried to the door, Sutton and Mr. Lawton in her wake. Sutton's driver, Steven, stood at the door. Beyond the gate stood Sutton's carriage and Mr. Lawton's.

Steven snatched his cap off his head and nodded to Mrs. Maguire. "Evening, ma'am. Is Mr. Mackay still here?"

"I'm here, Steven," Sutton said, "and so is Mr. Lawton. Are you all right?"

"Yessir, we fine. The horses is kinda spooked, and the carriages are a little the worse for wear, but I expect I can fix yours up good as new. Mr. Lawton's going to need hisself some new glass, though." The carriage driver paused. "The po-lice done got everything under control. Took some folks to jail, I reckon. Anyway, the streets is all clear now, Mr. Mackay, if you and Mr. Lawton want to go home."

"We do," Sutton said. "It has been quite a night."

Sutton and Mr. Lawton said their good-byes and soon were on their way.

And still Ivy had not appeared.

"I suppose I should go look for her," Papa said.

Celia shook her head. If Ivy wanted to risk her good name and her very life, that was her business, but it wasn't Papa's responsibility to save her cousin from her own poor choices. "Where would you look, Papa? She could be anywhere."

"True. But still I—"

"I'm sure she's safe with one of our friends. I'll wait up for her if you like, but I won't have you going out in the dark to search for her. She should have told us where she was going."

He sighed and set his empty glass on the table. "I suppose you're right. But I still can't help worrying." He removed his spectacles and briefly closed his eyes. "I am tired."

Celia squeezed his hand. "Go to bed."

She followed him up the winding staircase. In her room she lit the lamp, removed her garnet silk gown, hung it in the clothespress, and pulled on her dressing gown. She unpinned her hair and lit a small fire to ward off the evening chill.

Down below, the floor creaked as Mrs. Maguire headed up the servants' staircase to her quarters off the kitchen. Celia peered out the window. At the far end of the street, a few torches still flickered, silhouetting a lone police wagon and an abandoned carriage. A dog barked.

A dark shape at the rear of the garden drew her attention. At first she thought it was only the shadow of the old trees near her window. But as she watched, the shape—barely illuminated by the gaslights along the street—began to move, slowly at first and then faster until it disappeared near the abandoned carriage house.

Celia found her slippers and opened her door. The house was silent. No light showed beneath Papa's door. She descended the staircase, crossed the foyer, and headed for the back door.

The kitchen door creaked when she opened it. Keeping to the far side of the garden path, she hurried toward the carriage house.

The garden, though well past its summer prime, still held enough cover to conceal her movements.

When her eyes adjusted to the darkness, she walked around the back side of the old structure, the remnants of broken brick pressing through the thin soles of her slippers. She paused and held her breath, listening.

The next thing she knew, she was lying face down in the dirt, and someone was sitting on top of her.

"Who's there?" With a loud grunt, Celia reared and threw off her attacker. She scrambled to her feet, but the person had fled, disappearing into the shadowed garden. Her palms stung. Her cheek throbbed. She looked around again and hurried back to the house.

In the kitchen, Ivy and Mrs. Maguire sat in the circle of pale lamplight, two glasses of milk on the table before them. "Lord preserve us." Mrs. Maguire got to her feet and hurried to Celia. "What in the world happened to you, my darlin'? You're hurt."

She drew Celia to the fire and held the lamp to inspect Celia's face. "'Tis nothing but a scratch. But saints in a sock, whatever were you doin' out there in the middle o' the night?"

The housekeeper poured warm water from the teakettle onto a clean towel and cleaned Celia's cheek.

"I saw someone sneaking around in the garden. I went out to investigate, but whoever it was knocked me to the ground and ran off."

Ivy set down her cup. "You shouldn't have been outside with everything's that's been going on. All sorts of people are on the streets."

Celia frowned at her cousin. "I might say the same to you. Where on earth were you?"

"With Mrs. Clayton. I was late leaving the Female Asylum this evening, and when I saw the mob in the street, I asked her driver to take me back. He brought me home just now. I'm sorry you were worried, but I had no way to send word."

"I suppose all's well that ends well." Mrs. Maguire trained her steady gaze on Celia. "Methinks you ought to leave the investigatin' of prowlers to the authorities. And don't you be worryin' your father with this either."

"I won't mention it to Papa. But I intend to find out who is sneaking around our house."

Mrs. Maguire sniffed. "Curiosity killed the cat."

"Come on, Celia." Ivy linked her arm through Celia's. "Let's go upstairs so Mrs. Maguire can get some sleep."

They went up the stairs. At the door to her room, Ivy paused. "I know what you're thinking. And I know I haven't been exactly truthful with you of late. But I am not the one who was in the garden tonight."

"I know that. You couldn't have knocked me down and returned to the kitchen before I got back inside. There wasn't time." Celia shrugged. "Maybe it was one of the rioters, too drunk to know his way home."

"I'm sure it was Leo Channing," Ivy said. Her bottom lip trembled. "Anyway, I won't be seeing Michael Gleason anymore."

Celia felt an unexpected stab of sympathy for her cousin. Ivy wanted so desperately to fall in love, and love always eluded her. Celia ushered Ivy into her bedroom and closed the door. "Tell me. What happened?"

"He asked for money. To help organize the Irish workers and the Negroes."

"Mr. Gleason was part of this riot tonight?"

"I suspect so. He told me last week they knew the *Wanderer* might be returning, and they wanted to show the planters around here that any more slaves wouldn't be tolerated. When I told him that I had no money of my own, that I am dependent upon Uncle

David, he got angry. He said if I loved him I would find a way to help him. This afternoon he came to Mrs. Clayton's, and when I told him I had nothing for him except my affections, he laughed." Her voice broke. "And then he left."

"Oh, Ivy."

"He cared nothing for me. He only wanted to use me." Tears streamed down Ivy's face. "Oh, why can't I have someone like Sutton, who is kind and smart, and—"

"Mrs. Maguire says God moves in mysterious ways."

"God? If God were paying any attention to me at all, my entire life would be different. Better. But who knows? Maybe I deserve everything that has happened to me. I suppose I ought to be grateful I haven't been struck by lightning."

"Misfortune is rarely deserved."

Ivy shrugged. "In any event, Mr. Gleason is gone for good."

"You will meet someone else," Celia said gently. "Someone wonderful. Someone who deserves your affections. You'll see."

Ivy sniffled and shook her head. "I'm thinking of leaving Savannah."

"But where would you go?"

Ivy brushed at her sleeve. "The night my father left, I begged him to take me with him, but he said it was better for me here, and I believed him. Now I wish I had fought harder to stay with him."

"You were a child."

"I was old enough. But maybe it's too late now." Ivy headed for the door. "We should try to get some sleep."

Celia stoked the fire and checked her reflection in the mirror. The scratch on her cheek would fade much more quickly than her questions about who had put it there, and why.

13

Celia peered out the window as the carriage headed for the dressmaker's. She felt slightly silly at having to take the carriage on such a beautiful, crisp November morning. The weather was just right for a brisk walk from Madison Square to Rosie Foyle's dressmaking shop on Drayton Street. But less than a week had passed since the disturbance that had shuttered the theater and sent the residents scurrying for cover, and Papa had insisted that Joseph drive her to the appointment.

As they turned onto Jones Street, Celia noted that every vestige of the riot had been cleared away. All the broken glass had been swept away and every broken shop window replaced. The charred torches that had been left smoldering in the streets were gone. The trampled shrubs lining the little park had been removed and replaced with even nicer ones. Like the women in her circle, who kept any unpleasantness to themselves, the city of Savannah also presented her best face to the world. Beautiful, charming, and serene, as if nothing had ever disturbed her perfect façade.

According to Papa, Charlie Lamar still was struggling to sell his human cargo to planters farther north. As predicted, the Georgia planters had no wish to call down more wrath upon their heads and so had refused to purchase slaves from the *Wanderer* at any price. There was talk that Mr. Lamar had so thoroughly displeased the members of his Northern yacht club that they were considering throwing him out. He was the talk of the Savannah Gentleman's Club too. It was a relief to Celia that, at least for now, Savannah had found a topic of conversation other than her family.

This morning at breakfast, Papa had mentioned that he and Sutton would be spending the afternoon at the club with a group of fellow businessmen, including Mr. Thompson of the *Daily Morning News*. Celia intended to take advantage of the newspaperman's absence from his office to pay the newspaper a visit. Determined to get to the bottom of Leo Channing's insinuations, she'd decided the best place to start was to read the old newspaper accounts of the deaths of Aunt Eugenia and the laundress—if the newspaper's records went back that far. But first there was the meeting with the modiste to choose a pattern for her wedding dress.

Sutton's mother had planned to accompany her this morning but had begged off with a headache. Ivy claimed a prior commitment, though Celia suspected her cousin couldn't bear to be part of such a happy errand when her own marriage prospects seemed so dim. Sutton's grandmother was coming, however, and the prospect of seeing Mrs. Manigault again lifted Celia's spirits. Caroline Manigault was everything Celia hoped to be one day. The years had not dimmed her intellect, nor had her losses dampened her spirit. That she had given Celia her own ring and welcomed her with such openhearted joy made Celia all the more determined not to let gossip and lies tarnish her own name and that of her future kin. Perhaps the newspapers would help her set the record straight.

The carriage creaked to a halt outside the dressmaker's small, tidy studio. Joseph helped Celia out and watched until her knock at the door was answered.

"Come on in." Mrs. Foyle, her gray-streaked hair in a messy

bun, her ample bosom buttoned tightly into a plain green bodice adorned with straight pins, led Celia to a small room in the back of the studio. A rainbow of satins, velvets, and watered silks lay unfurled across a wooden table. A small, round stool stood in front of a full-length mirror affixed to the wall.

Through a narrow doorway, Celia glimpsed two young girls at work appliquéing a bridal train. Yards of pale-pink satin studded with seed pearls spilled across their laps and onto a sheet of clean muslin covering the floor. The younger of the two whispered to her companion, and they shared a laugh.

Celia watched as their fingers plied the expensive fabric. Where did they live, and how did they spend their free time? What would it be like to be a young woman on her own? Not that she aspired to a lower rung of the social ladder. But she couldn't help envying the girls their freedom from rules and expectations, from worrying about other people's judgments and opinions.

" . . . right behind that screen."

Celia started. "I'm sorry. What did you say?"

"Caroline Manigault isn't here yet," Mrs. Foyle said. "But I do have a schedule to keep, and what I said was, would you mind removing your dress so I can get your measurements? We might as well do that while we wait."

Celia shimmied out of her skirts and bodice. In her chemise and linen drawers, she stepped onto the little stool. Like a bee buzzing around a hibiscus blossom, Mrs. Foyle moved around Celia, measuring and muttering and jotting down numbers on a little tablet. The bell above the door jangled. Mrs. Manigault arrived.

"Celia, dear, there you are." Sutton's grandmother peered around the screen, then plopped into a chair and propped her cane next to it. "I am late, and I have no excuse other than these old bones of mine take longer to get going nowadays."

Celia longed to sweep the older woman into a happy embrace,

but she settled for a smile. "I'm glad you came, and I'm sorry Mrs. Mackay is not well."

"So am I. Cornelia sends her regrets." Mrs. Manigault drew her black lace shawl more tightly around her shoulders. "We both wanted to be here in place of dear Francesca." Her dark eyes glittered. "How she would have relished this day."

Celia fingered the small gold locket she always wore beneath the collar of her dress. It held a miniature portrait of her mother and a lock of glossy black hair that matched her own. In the years since her mother's death, Celia had come to terms with her loss, but it had never stopped hurting. Not completely.

Mrs. Foyle brought out a length of new muslin and began pinning it to Celia's frame, forming a pattern for the lining of the gown. She draped and tucked and pleated and secured it into place while Celia stood on the stool obeying commands to turn first one way and then the other. At last the modiste was satisfied. While Celia dressed, Mrs. Foyle selected several fabrics and trims and spread them on the table.

"Have you chosen a fabric yet?" she asked. "Perhaps you should tell me when the wedding is to be and I can offer some recommendations."

Sutton's grandmother sent the dressmaker a rueful smile. "That's just it. My grandson is waiting for the perfect time, and I have told that boy a million times there is no such thing. If war comes, it comes. If the business improves or not, there's nothing Celia can do about it." She leaned forward and patted Celia's hand. "Sutton is my grandson, and I love him more than my own life, but he's being silly not to set a date to make this girl his own."

"I'm hoping for early spring," Celia told the modiste. "April perhaps. May at the latest."

The dressmaker nodded. "May is the perfect time for a Savannah wedding. In that case, I'd suggest this white satin." She cocked her head and studied Celia. "A beautiful girl like you can get away with anything, but I think an off-the-shoulder style with pagoda sleeves might be especially becoming. A full skirt, of course. And then a train attached at the waist, something simple, with a single appliqué surrounded by pearls."

Celia chewed her bottom lip. "You don't think such a style would be too immodest for a bride?"

"Not at all." Mrs. Foyle took out a pad and sketched the gown she had in mind.

Celia studied it. "Mrs. Manigault, what do you think?"

"It sounds perfectly lovely."

Mrs. Foyle seemed relieved at having the decision made without too much haggling. "You'll need a veil, too, Miss Browning. I could—"

"I have my mother's veil," Celia said.

The modiste frowned. "Oh, dear."

"What's the matter?"

"Sometimes sentiment can ruin a perfect creation. A veil should complement the overall style of the dress. If it's the wrong fabric or the wrong length . . ." Mrs. Foyle sighed and shrugged.

"It's made of needlepoint lace," Celia said. "My grandfather got it for her in Paris."

"Well, I'm sure it's very nice, but I don't know whether it will work with what you've chosen."

"Can't you use a similar lace for the undersleeves?" Mrs. Manigault asked.

Another sigh from the dressmaker. "It would not be my first choice, but if you are determined—"

"We are," Mrs. Manigault said firmly. "Celia and I are most determined."

"Very well." The dressmaker gathered her fabrics and her sketchpad and carefully folded the pieces of the muslin pattern she'd made. "Bring the veil to me, and I'll see what I can do. And come by next week for your first fitting, Miss Browning. I should have the lining basted together by then."

Together Celia and Mrs. Manigault left the dressmaker's shop. Both their carriages waited near the door.

"Will you come back to the house for tea?" Mrs. Manigault clapped a hand on her white-plumed hat as a wind gust blew between the buildings. "Despite her headache, Cornelia would enjoy seeing you and hearing about the dress you've chosen."

Celia would have loved spending more time with the Mackay women, but this might be her only chance to visit the newspaper offices without having to dodge Mr. Thompson. She laid a hand on the older woman's arm. "I'm afraid I can't today. But I promise to visit early next week, and we can tell her all about it then."

"All right. I suppose I should be getting on home then. Cornelia worries if I'm out later than she thinks I ought to be." Mrs. Manigault waved to her driver, and he ran around to help her into the carriage. Once settled, she leaned out the open window and caught Celia's eye. "The next time you see my grandson, you tell him what I told the dressmaker today. He's foolish for putting off such an important thing. We have no guarantees in this life, and I personally detest the thought of you two unnecessarily spending even one day apart."

"So do I." Celia couldn't hold back her smile. "I'll tell him."

Mrs. Manigault waved as the carriage rolled away.

Joseph jogged over from the bench across the street, where he had apparently been enjoying a slice of caramel cake from the bakery. Sugar crystals clung to his gray beard. "Where to now, Miss Celia?"

"The newspaper office, please. I may be there for quite some time."

"Yes'm." He dusted off his hands and wrenched open the

carriage door. "Don't make no difference to me. I got my instructions from your daddy to carry you wherever you decide to go. You go ahead and take your time."

Minutes later the carriage drew up at the newspaper office, and Celia hurried inside. The room smelled of ink and hot lead. The building hummed as the press churned out tomorrow's edition. A copy boy scurried among several desks carrying pages of newsprint. A bald man in an ink-stained apron sat at a desk near the dusty windows, marking up copy with his pencil. Celia approached his desk and waited until he lifted his head, pencil poised, a question in his eyes.

"Begging your pardon."

He waved one pudgy, ink-stained hand. "The advertising department is up the stairs. To your left."

"I'm not here to place a notice. I'd like to see your archives, please."

He tossed his pencil onto the desk. "Come again?"

"Back issues of the newspaper."

"I know what archives are, girl. What I don't know is what you want with them."

"I'm in charge of raising funds for the Female Orphan Asylum, and I want to compile a list of charitable activities benefiting the various organizations here in town."

"So's you can figure out who's got the deepest pockets."

She laughed. "And the softest hearts."

He picked up his pencil again, rolling it between his fingers as he squinted up at her. "From what I hear, the director out at the asylum's not too popular with the board of managers these days. They say there's no point in encouraging those girls to ambitions above their station."

"There are some who think that the girls should be trained only for domestic service and that reading, writing, and arithmetic are a waste of time. But I agree with Mrs. Clayton that each girl should be literate and encouraged to employ whatever gifts she possesses—whether for music or teaching or needlework." Celia fussed with the ribbons on her hat. "Not everyone is cut out for household tasks."

"I thought there was already an organization that supported women who can sew."

Celia nodded. "The Needle Woman's Friend Society. But I hope some of the girls can establish their own enterprises some day, and for that they need more than a basic education. My aim is to see that their ambitions are not hampered by a lack of funds. Now, if you could show me where the archives are . . ."

The man shrugged and pushed back from his chair. "Far be it from me to stand in the way of female progress. Follow me."

He wove among the desks, stacks of newsprint, and buckets of broken type waiting to be melted and recast and led her toward a cramped, airless room in the back. A desk and a single cane-backed chair were the only furnishings. Tall shelves were stacked with newspapers organized by month and year. Autumn light filtered into the room from a single window above the desk. Celia tensed and looked around for an exit—as she always did when entering a confined space. She relaxed when she saw another door on the outside wall.

The man pulled a stack of papers from a high shelf and plopped them onto the desk, sending up a puff of gray dust. "We put out a special edition back in '55, when the Union Society reopened that orphanage for boys. I remember the year because it was around the time my wife died."

He flipped more pages. "Here's a story about the Female Seamen's Friend Society keeping the drunk sailors off the streets. And one we published last spring about Mrs. Lawton's appeal for donations for the Poor House and Hospital." He scratched his head.

"Savannah's got so many charities and societies I can't keep track of 'em all. But I reckon the muckety-mucks in this town always have more money to devote to a good cause. I'm sure they'll support your project at the Female Asylum, despite the complaints from the managers."

"Thank you, Mr.—"

"Just leave the papers there when you're finished, and I'll put 'em back." He headed for the door. "Mr. Thompson is particular 'bout the way we keep things here."

Celia pulled off her gloves and sat at the desk, glancing at the stories he'd mentioned though there was little about the ladies' charity work that she didn't already know. When the door closed behind him, she stood and shuffled through the stacks until she found the papers dated 1843—the year of the accidents that had so interested Leo Channing.

Movement outside the window caught Celia's attention. Two young girls, their arms wound around each other's waists, made their way along the street. Celia thought of her years at school, when the other girls had formed tight little groups that did not include her. She hadn't been an outcast exactly, but not having a mother had set her apart. She'd been respected for her high marks and tolerated on field trips and outings. But she had never been included in their intimate little circles, never been privy to their shared secrets. Perhaps they'd feared her misfortune was contagious.

Whatever the reason, the memory of being on the outside looking in still stung. And it made her more determined than ever to quell Leo Channing's threat to her family's reputation and her future happiness.

She flipped through the issues for March, April, and May of 1843, her eyes moving quickly down each column of smudged and faded print. The big stories on May 29 were the departure of John C. Fremont's second expedition to Oregon and an announcement that Mr. Thompson's sketches of daily life in Georgia were to be compiled into a book. A rowing team had been established at Harvard, and someone named Albert Brisbane was forming a Utopian community in New Jersey.

She thumbed through several more papers, expecting to find some mention of Aunt Eugenia's death and funeral. But every issue from August and September was missing. The next paper in the stack was dated October 25, 1843.

Obviously Leo Channing had taken the August and September papers. It seemed that he had thought of everything and would stop at nothing. But she couldn't report the newspapers missing and still keep her investigation a secret.

She heard the front door of the office open and close, then voices. The bald man's and then another, deeper voice. Mr. Thompson.

Celia scrambled to return the 1843 papers to the shelves, leaving the others on the desk. She grabbed her reticule and gloves and hurried to the outside door. She yanked on the metal doorknob, but the door wouldn't budge. Her heart sped up. She would have to go back through the newsroom and risk running into Mr. Thompson. At least she had the story about the charities as her reason for being here and the bald man to corroborate it.

"Who left this door unlocked?" Thompson's voice reverberated in the adjacent hallway, just outside the door where she stood. "I thought I told you to keep the archives locked up."

She heard the sound of a key being inserted into the lock and then a faint click as the lock engaged. She bit her hand to keep from screaming.

"Hello?" She knocked on the door. "Hello, Mr. Thompson." But her voice was swallowed by the incessant clacking of the typesetter's composing sticks and the muted street noises coming through the windows at the front of the building.

She looked around the room wildly, beads of perspiration popping onto her forehead as the old childhood panic overtook her. She leaned over the desk to open the window, but it was stuck. Painted shut. She returned to the outside door, grasped the knob with both hands, and pulled. At last it yielded.

Weak with relief, Celia leaned for a moment against the doorjamb and then stepped onto an unfamiliar street, weaving her way around loaded drays, horse droppings, a vendor's cart. The squeak and clang of an iron gate slamming shut behind her sent a prickle of fear through her bones. She had the feeling that someone was watching her from the shadows of the buildings, but when she turned to look, no one was there.

She hurried past a row of shops and emerged at last onto the street where Joseph waited with the carriage. He jumped off the driver's seat at her approach, a frown creasing his face. "Something the matter, Miss Celia? You pale as rain."

"What? Oh, no—nothing." She forced a smile and took a shaky breath. "I've a lot on my mind these days."

"Yes'm, reckon that's so. You ready to go home?"

"I had hoped to stop by Mr. Loyer's jewelry store."

He pulled his watch from his pocket. "You got time, I reckon."

The jewelry store was just down the street, sandwiched between the bakery and a milliner's shop.

"Wait here, please. I won't be long."

"That's what you said this morning."

She couldn't help smiling. Joseph was the soul of patience, and she had sorely tried it today. "This time I mean it. I only need to speak to Mr. Loyer for a moment."

He heaved a sigh. "Moment mos' likely be a hour, but you the boss, Miss."

"Oh, Joseph, I know it's a nuisance having to escort me everywhere, but you know how Papa is these days."

"Yes'm, I surely do. You go on now. The sooner you get your business done, the sooner we'll both get home."

Celia hurried along the sidewalk to the jewelry store and ducked inside. Mr. Loyer sat behind a row of glass cases displaying jeweled necklaces, pins and gold watches, ropes of pearls, and rings sparkling with sapphires and diamonds. He looked up from his work as the door closed behind her.

"Good afternoon. It's Miss Browning, isn't it?"

"Yes. Good afternoon."

He swept a hand above the display cases. "What may I show you today?"

She opened her bag, took out the bracelet, and laid it on the counter. "I received this recently but I don't know who sent it. I'm hoping you can tell me who purchased it."

He shook his head. "I can tell you right now it didn't come from my shop."

Another dead end. She swallowed. "You're sure."

"Positive." He picked it up and turned it over. "The settings are"—he paused, obviously deciding how to frame his comments without causing offense—"not as well-made as mine. See here? The underside is still a bit rough. I always smooth mine out so they are equally finished on both sides."

He picked up his jeweler's loupe and fitted it to his eye before running his fingers over each of the stones. "The diamonds on either side appear to be genuine, but not of the highest quality, I'm afraid. As for the emerald and the amethyst, I believe those to be made of paste."

"I see."

He removed his loupe. "I heard you and Mr. Mackay were recently betrothed."

"Yes."

"You're wondering whether he sent this."

"I know he didn't."

"Well, that's something anyway." He handed her the bracelet. "I wish I could be of more help."

"Can you tell me who might have made it? Someone else here in Savannah? Or perhaps in Charleston?"

"I couldn't say." Impatience flickered in his eyes." I don't wish to be rude, but I am expecting a customer in a few minutes, and I promised to choose a few pieces for her inspection."

Desperate to solve the mystery, Celia decided to trust him. "Mr. Loyer, are you familiar with the current custom known among the ladies as the language of the jewels?"

"The language of . . . no, I can't say as I am."

"It's the latest thing according to the magazines. Gentlemen send secret messages to their ladies through jewels. The first letters in the names of the jewels spell out a message."

He frowned.

"For instance, if he wanted to tell her she was dear to him, he might send a piece of jewelry made of a diamond, an emerald, an amethyst, and a ruby. D-e-a-r."

"I see. How intriguing."

Wordlessly she slid the bracelet back along the counter and watched his expression change as recognition dawned. He blinked. "But surely . . . that is, I can't imagine . . . . Who would want to harm you, Miss Browning?"

"That's what I'm trying to find out." She slipped the bracelet back into her bag. "I know I can count upon your complete discretion in this matter."

"Of course. But if you feel you're in danger, why not go to the police?"

"Have you seen the papers of late? The stories about our family?"

He toyed with his jeweler's loupe, not meeting her gaze. "I have."

"If I alert the police, there will be even more speculation."

"I suppose you're right." The jeweler rubbed his chin. "There is one man, name of Ryan. He has a shop in the Yamacraw neighborhood, caters to the Irish who live there. It's mostly inexpensive things—plain wedding bands, paste necklaces for those with pretensions. Hard to imagine anyone of your acquaintance patronizing his shop, but I don't suppose it would hurt to ask." He scribbled an address on the back of a receipt. "Now, you really must excuse me."

Celia took the slip and started for the door.

"Be careful, Miss."

She let herself out of the shop and headed for the carriage. "Home, please, Joseph. I'm exhausted."

"Don't wonder." Joseph opened the door and handed her inside. "You been runnin' faster than the Cassville steam train this whole blessed day."

He climbed into his seat and turned for home.

14

SUTTON HALTED THE RIG AT THE GATE AND JUMPED DOWN to help Celia out, his gloved hands clasping hers. He tethered the horse, and they hurried up the front steps and into the foyer. Overnight the weather had turned colder, and now fires burned in the parlor fireplaces and in Papa's library.

"There the two o' you are." Mrs. Maguire hurried into the foyer, a laden tea tray in her hands. "I expected you half an hour ago." She proffered the tray. "I hope the scones are not stone cold by now."

"I'm sure they'll be delicious anyway," Sutton told her. "Nobody makes afternoon tea quite the way you do, Mrs. Maguire."

She blushed. "You are full o' the blarney, Sutton Mackay, and that's the truth."

He laughed.

"We're sorry to be late," Celia said. "Poseidon threw a shoe, and we had to wait for the groom to come back from exercising Miss Waring's mare. And we hadn't been out to the track in a while. Both the boys needed a good run."

"Both the boys?" The housekeeper shook her head. "You talk about those horses like they're regular people. Well, off with your coats and into the parlor. I don't have time to stand here jibber-jabberin'."

Celia shed her gloves, unbuttoned her cloak, and unwound her scarf. "The bergamot tea smells heavenly, Mrs. Maguire."

The housekeeper preceded them into the parlor and set the tray on the side table beside Celia's chair. "I'll be in the kitchen if you need anything."

"Thank you." Celia lifted the ivory-colored teapot and filled their cups. "Where's Papa?"

"Still in his room. I heard him rattling around in his library at two o'clock this morning. I expect he's still asleep. And don't you go waking him."

"Of course we won't."

"Miss Ivy sent for Joseph and the carriage just after you left this morning. Shopping, I reckon." Mrs. Maguire headed back to the kitchen.

Sutton helped himself to a scone and slathered it with butter and strawberry jam. "Grandmother tells me you have chosen a gown for our big day."

"Yes. I hope you will approve."

"You'd look beautiful in homespun. All I want is for you to marry me." He took a bite, chewed, and swallowed. "Grandmother says I'm a fool for waiting."

"I certainly respect her opinion," Celia said drily.

Sutton laughed. "Me too. And she's right. Whatever happens will happen whether we are married or not. I had a letter from Griffin Rutledge in Charleston last week. He's nearly concluded his deal with the shipbuilders in Liverpool. They're eager to begin construction of my boat as soon as I can secure commitments from the investors."

"I see." She had pushed his trip to England to the back of her mind, not wanting to face the prospect of another long separation. It took weeks for letters to cross the Atlantic, and the silence during his absences was nearly unbearable.

"So I figure we'll sail at the end of January."

Her cup rattled in its saucer. "We?"

"Yes. I understand it's usual for wives to accompany their husbands on such voyages."

"Wives? Wait. Are you saying—"

"I'm saying let's get married right after the new year. That will give us a month to get settled before we sail."

"But my dress isn't close to being finished. And what about the reception?"

"If I remember correctly, it wasn't too long ago that you were suggesting a January wedding."

"Yes, but I—"

"Offer the dressmaker a small bonus for putting a rush on it. I'll bet she finishes in record time." He reached over and cupped her cheek in his hand. "You do want to marry me?"

"Oh, yes." All her life she had dreamed of the perfect wedding day. Coming down the stairs on Papa's arm with friends around to share in the happiness. Tables set with the best china and silver, laden with enough food to feed half of the city. Banks of flowers from their own gardens in every room. Now it would happen sooner than she'd planned. Not many flowers would be blooming in the middle of winter, and some of her friends might not return from their Christmas travels in time to attend. But those were minor disappointments compared to the prospect of waiting months for Sutton's return.

"I was so dreading being apart from you again, and now I won't have to."

He drew her onto his lap and wound a dark curl around his fingers. "You may regret it if we hit bad weather on the crossing. The Atlantic can be brutal in the winter."

"Not as brutal as waiting here, wondering whether you are all right and counting the days till you come home. Oh, I can't wait to tell Papa our news."

"I can't wait until you're mine." He kissed her, and she rested her head on his shoulder, listening to the crackling of the fire in the grate. Safe in Sutton's arms, she could forget about the anonymous messages, the bracelet, the intruder who had shoved her to the ground in the garden. The niggling questions about the past.

"Oh, dear. I am sorry." Ivy stood in the parlor doorway, her arms laden with packages. "I seem to be interrupting at precisely the wrong time."

Celia slid off Sutton's lap and smoothed her hair. "You might have knocked."

"I should have, but I didn't have a hand free." Ivy dumped her parcels onto the settee and peeled off her gloves. "Is there any more tea? I'm half frozen. I do believe it's turned colder since this morning. Maybe we'll have snow, like the storm that came when Uncle David was a boy. He says the snowdrifts were waist high in some places. Wouldn't that be wonderful?"

"But not so wonderful for business," Sutton said. "It's harder to keep the men on the docks when the weather's bad."

"Oh, I didn't think of that." Her voice softened. "Of course I wouldn't wish for anything that would make things more difficult for you."

Celia eyed the half-dozen parcels strewn across the settee. "You bought out the stores."

"Not really. I picked up a few Christmas presents." Ivy grabbed a scone off the tray and made a place for herself on the settee. "I saw a darling little cameo brooch in Loyer's window and couldn't resist getting it for Mrs. Maguire." She laughed. "That one purchase put me in the mood for shopping, and the next thing I knew, I had bought all this."

She nibbled the scone and dusted off her fingers. "I got something for you, Sutton."

"Well, don't tell me now." An amused smile played on his lips. "I like to be surprised on Christmas."

"Oh, this isn't for Christmas. It's something I ran across that put me in mind of you." She sifted through the packages and handed him one. "Open it."

He shifted in his chair. "You're very kind, but really, you shouldn't have. You made that lovely scarf for my homecoming and that was quite enough."

"Please. I insist."

He tore away the brown wrapping paper and lifted the lid on a small box. "A compass. Very useful indeed. Thank you."

"I thought you could use it when you sail to England," Ivy said, "and it might put you in mind of me. Of all of us, really. All of us who will be waiting here at home for you."

Sutton set the compass aside. "Actually there will be one less person waiting for me. Celia and I have just this moment decided to wed in January. She will be going to England with me."

Sutton smiled into Celia's eyes, and his look warmed her heart. How had she been so lucky to have this man fall in love with her?

Ivy frowned. "You're getting married in the dead of winter? What will our friends say?"

Celia laughed. "I hope they will say congratulations."

"It's true that January is not the ideal time for a society wedding, nor for a honeymoon voyage," Sutton said. "But Celia and I don't want to be apart any longer."

Ivy fell back against the settee. "But, Celia, what about your dress? And—you simply can't get married so soon!"

"Of course we can." Sutton grinned. "All we need is a ring and a minister."

Ivy got to her feet. "I think you're both being very selfish. Uncle David will be terribly disappointed."

"Papa will be happy that I'm happy." Celia clasped Sutton's hand. "And all I want is to marry Sutton Mackay."

Ivy huffed out a noisy breath. "Well, all I can say is that this is surely a surprise."

Sutton rose and held out his hand to Celia. "Speaking of surprises, can you take another one today, darling?"

"That depends. Is it a good one or a bad one?"

"A good one, I hope."

"Then by all means tell me."

"Remember the night of our engagement, when I told you I was working on another surprise?"

She nodded, thinking again of the bracelet. "I thought once I had guessed what it was, but I was mistaken."

"Come with me."

He crossed the foyer and went through the French doors and into the terrace, Celia and Ivy trailing in his wake. He crossed the garden to the toolshed, ducked inside, and emerged with a golden-haired, roly-poly puppy tucked under his arm.

Celia gave a little cry of delight and held out her arms. "Is she mine?"

"She's a he. But yes, he's yours." Sutton handed her the pup, who looked up at Celia with adoring brown eyes and licked her face.

Sutton laughed. "He loves you already."

"Everybody loves Celia." Ivy reached over to scratch the puppy's ears.

Celia cradled the warm little body in her arms. "We should get him out of this cold."

They started back along the garden path toward the house.

"How did you get him here without my knowing?" Celia asked Sutton.

"I brought the little fellow over this morning, and Joseph

agreed to look after him for me." Sutton smiled down at the pup. "He's a good boy. Aren't you?"

The dog's tail thumped against Celia's arm. She nuzzled his face, taking in the warm, milky puppy smell. "He's beautiful."

"I remembered your letter about old Jack dying last year—how heartbroken you were over losing him. So I thought it was time you got a new companion. And I like the idea of your having someone around to protect you when I can't be here."

"I thought I never wanted another dog after Jack. But now I'm so happy to have this little baby." Celia stroked the puppy, and he snuggled against her and closed his eyes. "I'll have to think of a name for him."

As they continued along the path, her skirt snagged on a low bush. She bent to free it and spotted a palm-size remnant of white fabric beneath the thick leaves. She retrieved it, thinking she had torn her petticoat without realizing it. Or perhaps Mrs. Maguire had. If it belonged to the housekeeper, Mrs. Maguire would insist on patching the tear. She didn't believe in wasting perfectly serviceable linens any more than she believed in wasting lard and flour. Or words. Celia tucked the bit of cloth in to her pocket, and they returned to the house.

Ivy gathered her purchases. "I should take these things up to my room. Good-bye, Sutton."

"Miss Ivy." Sutton inclined his head. "Thank you again for the compass. I'm sure Celia and I will find it useful on our trip."

Ivy shrugged. "It was nothing. Just a foolish impulse."

"It was a most thoughtful impulse, and I appreciate—"

"Saints in a sock!" Papa had appeared at the top of the stairs and now stood peering over the railing. "Is that a dog?"

Celia laughed. "Yes, Papa. He's a present from Sutton. Isn't he beautiful?"

The puppy stirred and yipped a greeting.

Papa came down the stairs, a broad smile on his face. "This

house has been too quiet since Jack passed. But I hadn't the heart to replace the old boy."

Sutton shook Papa's hand by way of greeting. "I saw this pup when he was just a few days old, but I had to wait until he was old enough to leave his mama and his littermates. I've been bursting ever since to surprise Celia."

"Well, it's a cracking good surprise. I'm delighted with the little fellow." Papa stroked the puppy's white belly. "What will you name him, Celia?"

"I don't know yet. But Papa, Sutton and I have something to tell you."

"Oh?"

She told him about their wedding plans.

"Are you sure, my dear?" he asked, his voice laced with concern. "You get only one chance to have a wedding, you know."

"That's what I told her, but she won't listen to me," Ivy said. "Excuse me. I must get these things upstairs." Ivy whirled away and hurried up the stairs.

"Christmas is still six weeks away," Celia told her father. "And the *Carolina* isn't scheduled to sail until the end of January. We have enough time."

"And you are willing to cross the Atlantic in winter?"

"To be with Sutton. Yes."

"In that case, I'll stop by the church and speak to Mr. Clark. And see that Mrs. Maguire is informed so she can prepare."

"Father suggested the Pulaski Hotel would be a good place for the reception," Sutton said. "Less work for Mrs. Maguire."

Celia exhaled a shaky breath. Suppose the rest of the hotel staff were as inhospitable as the waiter had been? She still burned with humiliation when she remembered the haughty look on his face and the way he had steered her and Mrs. Mackay to the worst table, out of sight of the other diners.

But she wasn't about to let that waiter—or anyone else—beat her. No matter what it took, she would find the truth. Only then could she begin her life with Sutton free from the ghosts of her family's troubled past.

~

Celia exited the carriage and pushed through the gate of the Female Asylum. The lacy veil of last night's frost still lay across the lawn, glittering in the pale sunlight. Smoke spiraled from the building's twin chimneys, filling the air with the scent of burning oak. She rang the bell and was soon admitted to Mrs. Clayton's cheerful parlor.

"Miss Browning." The older woman rose to greet her. "I'm delighted to see you. It has been a while since you were here."

"Yes. I'm glad Ivy was able to come in my stead. From what she tells me, Louisa seems to prefer her company to mine anyway."

"Oh, I don't know about that. Do come in and warm yourself. I've tea if you like."

"Yes, please." Celia took a seat near the fire and removed her gloves.

Mrs. Clayton poured and passed her a steaming cup. Celia added milk from the blue pitcher and took a sip of the bergamot-infused brew.

"Caroline Manigault was here yesterday." Mrs. Clayton stirred sugar into her tea. "She tells me you and Mr. Mackay are to marry early next year."

"Yes. We decided it only last Saturday." Celia smiled. "News travels fast."

"In Savannah? It surely does. Especially bad news, I'm sorry to say."

"I hope you've had none here, Mrs. Clayton."

"Unfortunately, we have. And Louisa is a part of it, I'm afraid."

"What happened?"

"Friday night week before last, when news of that riot got out, some of the girls slipped out and went downtown to witness the disturbance for themselves. Louisa among them."

"But how did they know? The situation seemed to develop spontaneously."

"Far from it. That Irish drayman, Mr. Gleason, was one of the ones behind it. The girls are forbidden to socialize with the deliverymen, but that one has a bit of a silver tongue. I'm not surprised he turned their heads with all his noble-sounding talk."

"I'm sure it was disconcerting to find some of your charges missing, but I suppose we can't really blame them. The same kind of thing happened when I was away at school." Celia smiled. "For young, impressionable girls who find themselves far away from all that is familiar, such adventures are simply too tempting to resist."

"Yes, well. The real difficulty is that one of the girls didn't come back."

"Louisa is gone?"

"Louisa came back. It's Sylvie Kelly that's gone for good. She ran off with that no-good Gleason." The director shook her head. "Not a brain in her head, that one. And this could not have come at a worse time."

Celia raised her brows. "The board of managers?"

Mrs. Clayton sighed. "Two of the members were here yesterday. And of course they insisted Sylvie's behavior is further proof that training for anything other than domestic service is a waste of time and money."

The clock chimed, and Mrs. Clayton rose. "I must speak to Miss Ransom before the next class commences. You will find Louisa in her room—confined there until the end of this week for breaking house rules."

Celia finished her tea and headed up the stairs.

Louisa lay curled beneath a blue wool blanket, fists tucked beneath her chin, eyes closed. But Celia had a feeling it was all a pose and that Louisa had done her best to eavesdrop on her conversation with Mrs. Clayton.

"Louisa? Are you awake?"

The girl stretched and yawned and opened her eyes. "Might as well sleep till Christmas. There is nothing to do here in the Female Jail."

Celia hid a smile. "I heard about your adventure. Was it worth it?"

"It sure was." Louisa sat up and threw off the blanket. "I saw some things I been wanting to see ever since I got off Captain Stevens's boat. The Pulaski Hotel for one—fanciest place I ever saw. But I didn't get to see the inside. You ever been there?"

"Yes."

"Is it fancy inside too? Gold mirrors and such?"

"People say it's the nicest hotel in town."

"Saw the train come in, too, right before the riot started. Sylvie said it come clear from Marietta. But I don't know nothin' about that place. Ain't never been there." The girl shrugged. "Saw the city market—more food than I ever laid eyes on in one place. Then me and Sylvie started out counting the stores, but we stopped after we got to twenty. Savannah's bigger'n I thought."

"Well, I'm happy that you satisfied your curiosity, but if you want to stay on here, you'll have to follow the rules. And that means no sneaking out at night."

Another shrug.

Celia opened her bag and took out a slender volume. "I brought you something new to read—if you've finished with the book I left last time."

Louisa slid off the narrow cot and opened the small

clothespress in the corner. Standing on tiptoe, she retrieved the book from the top shelf and thrust the copy of *Indiana* into Celia's hand.

"What did you think of it?" Celia asked.

"Didn't read it. I guess I'm not very smart when it comes to reading."

"I think we simply haven't found you the right kind of books yet. Miss Lorens tells me you've done a fine job with *Ravenscliffe.*"

"I guess so. I like Miss Lorens. She's like me."

"Really? In what way?"

"Her mama died too."

"I'm sorry. I didn't know about your mother. You must miss her."

"Not really. She died in my baby time."

"I see. I was very young when my mother died, but I do have some memories of her."

Louisa's eyes widened. "You and your cousin both got no mama?"

"That's right. But we have my papa, who looks after us, and a wonderful housekeeper who makes the best benne seed cookies in all of Georgia. And I'm getting married soon, so I will have my husband's family too."

Louisa chewed a fingernail. "Miss Lorens told me you are . . . betrothed."

Celia smiled. "Well, shall we read for a while?"

"I'm not in the mood. Besides, I have to go to the privy."

Celia released an exasperated sigh. "Perhaps we should agree that this arrangement is not working, Louisa. Another tutor might be better for you."

"Suit yourself."

"I'll speak to Mrs. Clayton on the way out."

But Mrs. Clayton was not in the parlor, nor in her office. Celia let herself out and climbed into the carriage. She hated to admit defeat, but there was no use fooling herself. She had not made much progress with the headstrong runaway. Better to concentrate her efforts on fund-raising. There was little else she could do for Louisa.

15

It took nearly a week to devise a plan to visit the jeweler in Yamacraw. Celia could hardly ask Joseph to take her. The driver was usually the soul of discretion, but in this case Celia couldn't be sure he wouldn't tell Papa of her strange request. And Papa, of course, would forbid her to visit the bustling, gritty neighborhood on the northern edge of town.

The place was notorious for its drinking establishments and brothels frequented by sailors and dock workers, railroad workers, and draymen. Free blacks, poor whites, and slaves who were permitted to live apart from their masters crowded into squalid shanties and wooden tenements along the river. Celia had never seen it for herself, of course, but Mr. Thompson often complained in his newspaper editorials that the entire neighborhood was a blight upon Savannah.

On Friday morning, after finishing the invitations to her fund-raising reception for the Female Asylum, Celia asked Joseph to drive her to the Ten Broeck Racing Course, where she spent an hour riding Zeus. After their run, when Finn had returned Zeus to his stall and was brushing him down, Celia lingered. She leaned against the half-door and turned up her collar against the cold wind. "Busy day here today?"

"No, Miss. Not 'specially. I took Poseidon out for a while this morning like Mr. Mackay asked me to. And Miss Waring sent word she don't intend to ride today." Finn blew on his hands to warm them. "I reckon it's a mite too cold for the likes o' her."

"Would you consider driving me to Indian Street? I'm happy to pay you for your time."

He picked up a rag and began polishing her saddle, a frown creasing his brow. "Indian Street? Ain't that up in Yamacraw?"

"Yes. I have some business there."

"But that fancy carriage of yours will be warmer and more comfortable than my ratty old buggy."

"Undoubtedly. But the reason for my trip is . . . private. I can't ask my driver to take me. I'd be so grateful if you could help me out. It won't take more than an hour. And I'm happy to pay you for your time."

"No need for that." Finn studied her face. "Yamacraw surely ain't no place for the likes o' you, Miss. But if you're bound and determined to go—"

"I am."

"All right."

Fifteen minutes later she was bundled up in Finn's buggy, an old blanket tucked around her knees, her face hidden by her wide-brimmed hat. The buggy bounced along the rutted road, the slate-colored river flashing through the trees, autumn leaves fluttering against the azure sky. As they drew near the Irish neighborhood, the rattle of wagons and the shouts of draymen and sailors assaulted her ears. The air grew thick with smoke and the stench of open sewers and boiling cabbage.

Celia covered her nose with her handkerchief and breathed through her mouth as she peered around her. The shanties and the dirt streets all looked the same. How would she ever find the jeweler? She had been wrong to come here. She would have to think of another plan.

Just as Celia decided to ask Finn to turn around, he guided the buggy onto Indian Street. A skinny dog ran into the road, barking furiously. Finn snapped his whip and the dog retreated, running toward the river.

"Here we are, Miss."

Smoke curled from the chimneys, giving off the odors of grease, ashes, and roasting sweet potatoes. Though it was barely past noon, groups of men, black and white, gathered near the drinking establishments. Two women in fancy dresses and plumed hats strolled past to the sound of whistles and catcalls. Ragged children kicked a stick along the unpaved street lined with horses, wagons, and buggies. A young man in a brown tweed coat lifted his hat and stared at them as they rolled past.

Spotting the jeweler's sign in a dirty window, Celia said to Finn, "Stop here." The groom halted the rig near the door, and she hurried inside.

The shop was barely large enough to accommodate the scratched wooden counter, upon which rested two small glass cases displaying rings, earbobs, and necklaces. The entire place smelled of unwashed bodies, rancid food, and tobacco.

Celia leaned against the counter. "Mr. Ryan?"

"That's me. Help you, Miss?" The jeweler, an imposing man with a ruddy complexion and a shock of white hair, set aside his pipe and hooked his spectacles over his ears.

Celia took the bracelet from her bag and laid it on the counter. "Someone told me you might have made this."

Mr. Ryan studied the bracelet. Held it up to the light. "'Tis my handiwork, to be sure." He shook his head. "Too bad I wasn't able to use real jewels instead o' paste, but 'tis the intent behind the gift that's the important thing."

"That's true."

"Don't be too hard on the lad what gave it to ye. When it comes to matters of the heart, we do the best we can."

"So it was a young man who ordered it?"

"Aye. Paid in advance too. He was a shy one. Hardly more than a boy, that one. Didn't want to give his name. Just told me where to send the bracelet when it was finished."

"I see." Celia tried to control the quaver in her voice. Now that she was getting somewhere, she realized that solving this mystery had become about much more than proving Leo Channing wrong. More even than figuring out who was out to harm her, though that was a nagging worry. She wanted to know the truth about her past—the whole truth, before her marriage to Sutton. There would be children one day. She wanted them to grow up without the nagging questions and the empty spaces that were part and parcel of her own childhood.

And yet she feared the very answers she was seeking. She had developed an attachment to the story of her own life as she knew it, and a part of her didn't want that story challenged. What if, in solving the mystery of the bracelet, she discovered things she didn't want to know? Things that might alter her feelings for those she loved most? *You can't unring a bell,* Papa often reminded her.

Mr. Ryan handed her the bracelet. "I hope you enjoy the bauble, even though it ain't real. 'Cept for the diamonds the boy brought in with him."

Obviously the jeweler hadn't heard of the language of the jewels either and saw nothing sinister in the arrangement of the stones.

Celia tucked the bracelet away. "I wonder—do you happen to have the address he provided?"

"I imagine I've got it here somewhere, but my customers depend on me to keep their secrets. They may be poor, but they fall in love same as the fancy gentlemen and the lady mucks living in the mansions down from here." Mr. Ryan tapped his chest. "The feelin' inside here is just the same, whether you're a pauper or a prince."

"I suppose you're right."

"'Tis not so unusual for a man to keep secret the name of his beloved. Or to want something special for her birthday, without her finding out ahead of time." He peered at her over the top of his spectacles. "Back in Waterford, my old man had a sayin': Melodious is the closed mouth. I try to remember that."

"You came from Waterford."

"Long time ago, Miss. I came to Savannah more'n thirty years ago—aboard a ship loaded with Paddies and Bridgets, as they say."

"I have a dear friend from Waterford. She's been here a long time too. Tell me, do you make barmbrack for All Hallows' Eve?"

His whole face lit up. "Barmbrack—haven't thought of it for years. I loved that cake when I was a lad. Loved me colcannon too."

Celia nodded at the mention of the mashed potatoes with cabbage and butter that Mrs. Maguire made on All Hallows' Eve. "Mrs.—that is, my Irish friend, still makes it every year."

She waited, hoping the conversation and the mention of home would change the jeweler's mind. But when he offered nothing more than a benign smile, she left the shop and returned to Finn O'Grady's waiting buggy.

What young man could have commissioned the bracelet? Besides Sutton, she knew of no admirers apart from her father's clerk. Given the bracelet's poor quality, she doubted now that it was the expression of Mr. Shaw's infatuation. But Mr. Ryan's refusal to provide the delivery address put her at another dead end.

"Ready, Miss?" Finn handed her into the buggy.

The door to the jewelry store opened and Mr. Ryan hurried out, a piece of paper in his hand. "Wait!"

He hurried across the street, scattering another group of hollow-eyed children, and handed her the paper. "I don't know why I'm doin' this, goin' against my own rules, but—"

Celia read the address scribbled on the gray paper, and hope soared again. "Thank you, Mr. Ryan."

"See you keep it to yourself. I got to keep me customers' trust, ye know."

"I will. Thank you again."

"Back to the stables, Miss Browning?" the groom asked as Mr. Ryan returned to his shop.

Celia checked the watch she wore on a chain around her neck. "Yes, please. Joseph will be returning to the track to drive me home."

Finn glanced at her. "Looks like you got what you came for."

"What?"

"That piece of paper. You're holdin' onto it for dear life."

Celia tucked the paper away and tried to focus on the passing scenery. But she could hardly wait to visit the address on Liberty Street.

Dressed in a deep purple frock, Ivy swept into Celia's room, her cloak draped over her arm. "Aren't you ready yet, Cousin? The lecture starts in less than an hour and you know how crowded it will be."

"In a minute." Celia finished pinning her hair and turned from the mirror. Normally she enjoyed the readings, lectures, exhibits, and concerts at the Chatham Literary and Art Society, but this afternoon she was too nervous to think of sitting through a talk about the writings of Miss Jane Austen. She was counting on the large crowd and the celebrity of the lecturer to hold Ivy's attention while she, Celia, slipped away. The address Mr. Ryan had provided was only a short walk from the lecture hall. With any luck, she would be back before the program ended and Ivy discovered her absence.

"I wish Uncle David were coming with us." Ivy picked up a book from Celia's night table and put it down again. "I fear he's working too hard these days."

"I agree. He needs a diversion, but Papa is not one for the writings of a romantic like Miss Austen." Celia picked up her cloak and reticule. Her puppy scampered from beneath her writing table, his little rump in the air, his tail moving back and forth like a metronome. She smiled and bent to scratch his ears. "No, Maxwell, you cannot come with me. But I promise we'll walk in the garden when I get back."

The puppy grabbed a shawl from the back of her chair and dragged it across the floor. She chased him until she cornered him. He yipped and looked up at her, his eyes bright, as if his antics might persuade her to change her mind. She took the shawl away from him and hung it in the clothespress. "I must go now. You behave yourself."

Ivy rolled her eyes. "I'm sure he understood every word and will behave perfectly in our absence."

"He understands more than you think." Celia tossed the puppy a scrap of old linen to play with before following Ivy down the curving staircase to the foyer.

The door to Papa's study was ajar. He was bent over his books. A wispy wreath of smoke from his pipe curled toward the ceiling.

"We're off to the Austen lecture, Papa."

He nodded and waved one hand without looking up.

"Don't work too long. Promise?"

He grunted and looked up at her, his blue eyes alight with love. "Stop fussing over me, Celia. I'm all right."

"You should rest this afternoon." She stepped into the room. "You're far too busy these days."

He set down his pen. "I might say the same for you, my dear. I hardly see you anymore."

"Oh, I know it. Between wedding plans and organizing my reception for the Female Asylum and spending time with Zeus and Maxwell, I have hardly a moment to myself."

"How goes the fund-raising?"

"Better than I expected, given that some on the board of managers oppose any efforts to equip the girls for anything except sweeping floors and polishing silver. Most of the ladies I've talked to have pledged generous sums, and I expect a reasonable turnout for the reception, despite the crowded calendar this time of year."

"Celia!" Ivy shouted from the foyer. "Come away this instant, or I shall leave without you."

"Your cousin sounds perturbed." Papa turned back to his ledgers. "You'd better go."

Celia followed Ivy out the door and into the waiting carriage. Soon they joined a line of other conveyances slowly making their way toward the society's lecture hall. Ivy fussed with her hair and fidgeted in her seat. "Now we're going to be late. I hate being late."

"We've plenty of time. You know these things never begin promptly."

"This one will. Nobody would dare keep Dr. Sharp waiting."

Ivy had been enamored with Dr. Elizabeth Sharp since reading an article about her in the *Home Journal* magazine. Not only was Dr. Sharp a leading scholar of English literature, she had also traveled all over the world and was a poet in her own right. Some said her visit to Savannah was the most important literary event since Mr. Thackeray's tours years earlier.

At last the carriage came to a halt. Joseph helped Celia and Ivy out of the carriage, and they joined the swarm of ladies and a few well-dressed gentlemen pressing toward the door. When they entered, Celia saw that the lecture hall was already half full. Mrs. Lawton and Mrs. Gordon were sitting together in the second row, the brims of their hats touching as they talked.

Celia looked around, hoping to find Sutton's mother similarly engaged. As the time of her wedding approached, Celia was growing even more fond of Mrs. Mackay. She'd rather not be forced into making an excuse for choosing to sit apart from her future mother-in-law.

At last she saw Cornelia, dressed in a cobalt-blue dress and matching hat and conversing with Mrs. Stiles. She seemed to have no idea Celia was even there. Good. It would be easier to sneak away if she was never spotted in the first place.

Celia and Ivy found seats near the back. Celia hung back for a moment to allow two other women to occupy the seats between hers and Ivy's. Ivy sent her a questioning look, and Celia responded with a slight shrug. She waited impatiently as the gas sconces along the walls were dimmed, leaving the lectern at the front of the room bathed in light.

The president of the society took the stage to make the introduction. Then Dr. Sharp, dressed in a suit of deep violet trimmed in black lace, rose from her chair behind the lectern and acknowledged the applause. She took her time putting on her spectacles and opening her notes. "It is a truth universally acknowledged that a single man in possession of a good fortune must be in want of a wife."

Celia smiled at the opening line from *Pride and Prejudice* and listened raptly as Dr. Sharp began her lecture. She hated to leave what promised to be a lively discussion, but she had to know the identity of the young man who had sent her the bracelet. She waited until Dr. Sharp reached the end of a longer passage, when another burst of applause masked the sounds of her departure from the lecture hall.

Outside she spotted her carriage waiting in a long line of conveyances. Joseph, pipe in hand, was deep in conversation with a group of fellow carriage drivers. She checked the address Mr. Ryan had given her, though it had fairly burned itself into her brain, and set off on foot for Liberty Street.

Situated across from the old cemetery, the white clapboard house was plain and small. A deep porch wrapped around three sides. Dark-green paint peeled from the shutters of narrow windows flanking the door. A crack in the fanlight above the entry fractured the late afternoon sunlight spilling across the porch. Celia crossed a patch of lawn bordered by pride-of-India trees. Mounting the steps, she lifted the brass door knocker and let it fall.

Presently a woman who seemed neither old nor young opened the door. "What is it?"

"I'm sorry to arrive unannounced. I've come to speak to a young man who sent a gift to me a while back and didn't reveal his name. I was told he lives here."

"Whoever told you that told you wrong," the woman said. "I've had only one boarder the past few months, and he is clear on the far side of young."

Celia checked the paper the jeweler had given her. Unless he had made a mistake, this was the right house. The woman stood back and began to close the door.

"Wait." Celia glanced around. "Perhaps I was given the wrong address after all. Do you know, is there anyone nearby who might have sent a—"

"What's the trouble, Mrs. Adams?"

The voice was unmistakable. Celia froze as a man appeared in the narrow entry hall, one finger marking his place in his book. Finally she said, "Mr. Channing."

The reporter stared at her in genuine surprise. "Miss Browning. I thought you didn't want anything to do with me. And I must say the feeling is mutual. You cost me my job, and now you're disturbing my Saturday afternoon with Mr. Shakespeare."

"I didn't expect to find you here."

Mrs. Adams looked first at Celia and then at Mr. Channing. "Seems you two know each other, so I'll leave you to your bibble-babble. I've got a pie in the oven, and it's about to burn."

As his landlady hurried away, Leo Channing swept one arm toward the parlor. "I believe the polite thing to do is to invite you inside."

"No, thank you. I haven't much time, and this won't take long."

He leaned against the door frame and clutched his leather-bound book to his chest. "I'm all ears."

"Someone sent a bracelet to my house. Anonymously. And then I found out—"

"You're complaining?" He laughed. "Girls like you live for the admiration of men. But I can assure you, as much as I wanted to interview you, I am not the one who sent it."

"I know that. As I was saying before you interrupted, I have learned that a young man ordered it and asked that it be sent to this address. I came here today to find out who he is and why he sent it."

"Indeed." Leo Channing's eyes lowered to half mast. It was like being observed by a coiled cobra. She took a step back, causing the wooden porch to creak.

"I might know something," he said. "But I want something in return."

"I told you before. I was a child when the accidents occurred. I remember very little. I don't know anything that has not already been reported, and even if—"

"Yes, I know all that. Even if you did know, you wouldn't say anything to sully your precious family name. Or jeopardize your marriage to the dashing Mr. Mackay."

"That's right."

"Did you ever find the diary?"

"I never heard of it. I have no evidence it ever existed. But if I should find it, I wouldn't give it to you. Nor divulge its contents."

"Of course not."

"I thought you'd have left Savannah by now. You did say you have family waiting in Baltimore, and since you're no longer at the newspaper—"

"I was able to come up with the funds to stay on here a while longer. I haven't given up on writing a book about the house of love and grief."

"Well, nobody will read it since it will have absolutely no relationship to the truth."

"If you are so sure of that, then why go to such lengths to stop me?"

She sighed and glanced down the street. Dr. Sharp's lecture would end soon. And there was no point in continuing this conversation.

"I'm sorry to have disturbed your reading." She turned on her heel.

"Wait." He came out onto the porch and leaned against a railing. "You might not believe this, but despite your appalling naïveté, I can't help admiring you, Miss Browning. Such loyalty to your father—and to your dear cousin. But are you certain it's warranted?"

"What do you mean?"

"Never mind." He seemed to be enjoying this little torment. Like a cat with a mouse.

"I must go."

"Without finding out what I know about the bracelet? Come on. Be a good sport. As a sign of good faith, I'll go first."

Though she couldn't imagine what bit of information he

would demand in return and where she would get it, she waited, both hands clutching her reticule.

"Shortly after the masquerade party you threw for your intended, I received an anonymous note at the newspaper office. I was asked to provide an address where a gift—I assume now it was your bracelet—could be delivered to me. It was such a curious request that I agreed. I left my reply at the newspaper office, and it was picked up while I was in the archives, reading up on your family."

And stealing the copies of the paper in the bargain. "What about the man who came to retrieve the bracelet from you?"

"I never saw him. When the package arrived here, I took it to the office like I was asked to do, and it was picked up while I was trying to track down Charlie Lamar. I wanted to talk to Lamar before he sailed the *Wanderer* for Africa, but I never could get hold of him." Channing shook his head. "Somehow the big stories always get away from me."

Celia released an exasperated sigh. All this planning, all this time wasted, and she was no closer to learning the identity of the man who had sent the bracelet. "Well, whoever he is, he certainly went to a lot of trouble to keep from being discovered."

Mr. Channing rubbed his unshaven chin. "That's why I agreed to the plan. I was mighty curious as to why someone would single out a stranger like me to trust with a piece of valuable jewelry."

"So you opened the package."

He shrugged. "My reporter's curiosity got the better of me. What puzzles me is how he knew I wouldn't simply abscond with it."

"The jeweler who made the bracelet told me it isn't valuable. I suppose whoever ordered it felt he had little to lose if you didn't keep your promise."

"I thought it might turn into a story I could use for the paper, but in the end it seems it was only the pitiful tale of some fellow who was too shy and too poor to court you properly. As if any other suitor would have half a chance with Sutton Mackay in the picture."

Celia hadn't encouraged any man's attentions. All her life she had cared for no one but Sutton, and everyone in Savannah knew it. The other young men of her acquaintance were old family friends with sweethearts of their own or gentlemen she met in the course of shopping and paying social calls. Mr. Loyer at the jewelry store downtown was old enough to be her father. Lucius Harland owned the bookstore she frequented, but he cared for nothing save books. Miles Frost was a year Celia's senior and, like Sutton, a Harvard graduate and a member of the Chatham Artillery. When they were younger, she and Miles had engaged in a bit of harmless flirtation, but it had never been serious—and now, according to Alicia Thayer, Miles was seriously courting Mary Quarterman.

That left Papa's clerk, Elliott Shaw. Celia hadn't seen him since refusing his gift the night of the masquerade. Certainly he had embarrassed them both that night. Even so, it didn't seem likely that Mr. Shaw would risk his livelihood in pursuit of the impossible.

Leo Channing squinted into the distance. "If I were you, I'd forget all about that cheap little bauble and stop trying to ferret the poor fellow out. At least leave him with his dignity."

Celia nodded. She wouldn't tell him about the hidden message in the jewels or the cryptic note written on the packaging. To do so would only increase his curiosity.

"I must go." She brushed past him, heading for the street. She would have to hurry now, to make it back to the lecture hall before the reception ended and Ivy noticed her absence.

"You're forgetting something."

Celia sighed. "I told you, I don't know anything that hasn't been mentioned in the papers."

"Surely you know the name of the woman who died in your carriage house. I was intrigued to discover that, in all the newspaper accounts of the event, her name was never mentioned."

"Mr. Channing. For the last time, I don't know her name."

He leaned against the porch railing. "For some reason, I believe you. But you still owe me, and I always collect what's coming to me."

He grasped her arm as she turned away. "Find that diary."

"Let go." She wrenched her arm free.

"Find the diary, and you'll find the name. I'll be waiting."

16

Joseph halted the carriage outside the Mackays' house. Earlier in the day a chilly rain had fallen, and now a brisk wind guttered the gas lamps flanking the entrance. Papa opened the carriage door and helped Celia out. He offered her his arm, and in the gathering dusk they passed through the wrought-iron gate and mounted the steps to the front door.

Mrs. Johns, the Mackays' housekeeper, answered the bell and ushered them into the foyer. "Good evening, Miss Browning. Mr. Browning."

"Mrs. Johns." Papa helped Celia remove her dark-green cloak, then removed his hat and scarf and shrugged out of his coat.

The housekeeper draped the garments over her arm and nodded toward the parlor. "The Mackays are waiting for you."

Burke and Cornelia Mackay rose in welcome as Celia and her father crossed the foyer and entered the parlor where a cozy fire burned in the grate.

"My dear." Sutton's father planted a cool kiss on Celia's brow. "I haven't seen you in a long while, but Sutton keeps me apprised of your plans. I'm grateful to you for settling that boy down."

Celia smiled. "It's my pleasure, sir."

He laughed and shook Papa's hand. "David. I'm glad you could come. It's been too long since we enjoyed an evening together."

"Yes," Papa said. "I've been looking forward to it."

"Ivy isn't joining us this evening?" Mrs. Mackay asked.

"She has a terrible cough," Celia said. "She spent entirely too much time out in the damp this week, I expect. She sends her regrets."

"That's too bad. I hate to think of her spending the evening alone."

"She has some books from the circulating library to keep her company. And Maxwell, of course."

Mrs. Mackay smiled. "Maxwell is a darling. Sutton brought him by for introductions before he took him to you. But please, sit down." She motioned them to chairs before the fire. "Sutton's upstairs, waiting to escort his grandmother down. She isn't as steady on her feet these days, and we worry she might fall. Though we don't tell her that."

Papa settled himself before the fire and sniffed the air appreciatively. "Something smells good, Cornelia."

"I had Mrs. Johns make your favorites. Roast beef and all the trimmings. And a pecan pie for dessert."

Celia saw a look of concern flicker across Papa's face and understood what he was thinking: after all of Burke Mackay's business reversals and the loss of his ship and cargo, could he really afford to entertain at all? Perhaps the sale of his farm had been finalized. Or perhaps the new investor in Mackay Shipping had already come through with an infusion of cash.

"Tell me, Celia," Mrs. Mackay began. "What did you think of Dr. Sharp's lecture last week? There was such a crowd I didn't have a chance to speak to you during the reception."

Celia stared into the flickering fire. She didn't want to lie to Sutton's mother nor upset her father. And she could hardly admit to spending half an hour on Leo Channing's front porch, trying to solve the mystery of the bracelet. "I thought beginning with the opening from *Pride and Prejudice* was inspired," she said finally. "But I confess I stepped outside for a bit and missed a part of it."

"I don't blame you," Mrs. Mackay said. "We were packed in so closely I could barely draw a breath. I could have used some fresh air myself."

Celia was saved from further discussion by the sound of Caroline Manigault's musical laughter. Arm in arm, Sutton and his grandmother descended the staircase, apparently enjoying themselves immensely. Celia rose with her father and the Mackays as Sutton led Mrs. Manigault into the parlor. In his dove-gray tailored jacket and trousers, a white shirt, and a deep-red cravat, Sutton reminded Celia of an illustration in one of her magazines. Surely she was about to marry the most handsome man in all of Georgia.

"Caroline." Papa greeted Mrs. Manigault with a warm smile and a slight bow. "You're looking very well."

She cocked her head and studied his face. "Thank you, David. I'm as well as can be expected at my age. But I'm worried about you. I heard Dr. Dearing paid you a call."

"I appreciate your concern, but it was nothing." Papa smiled at her before turning to Sutton. "How are you my, boy? I missed seeing you at the club this week."

"In fine fettle, thanks." Sutton's gray eyes shone. "Our new brig has arrived from Charleston. Mr. Rutledge came over with her, just to be sure she arrived without mishap."

"I'm relieved to hear that, son." Mrs. Mackay stood on tiptoe to kiss Sutton's cheek. "I was afraid it might not arrive in time for this year's shipping season."

Mrs. Johns appeared in the doorway. "Mrs. Mackay? Dinner is ready."

Mrs. Mackay inclined her head to her guests. "Shall we go in?"

Mr. Mackay offered his arm to his wife. Celia linked her arm through her father's. Sutton and Mrs. Manigault followed.

"Mr. Rutledge was as good as his word," Mr. Mackay said as they crossed the foyer and entered the candlelit dining room. "We're lucky to have him as our partner."

"Yes, we are, Father. The partnership provides some stability for us while we recover from the loss of the *Electra*." Sutton paused while he pulled out his grandmother's chair and helped her settle. "But make no mistake. Griffin Rutledge will benefit just as handsomely from our connections to the foreign markets and to my connections to investors in Liverpool."

"Sutton Burke Mackay." Mrs. Mackay addressed her son from her place at the head of the dining table. "I don't want to hear a single word this evening about that blockade-boat scheme of yours."

"Of course not, Mother," he said gravely. "Tell me, what did you do today?"

The small talk continued while Mrs. Johns moved around the table serving the beef, potatoes, and cinnamon-infused carrots. She poured glasses of Madeira from the Mackays' cellar, then quietly withdrew. Celia gave herself over to the enjoyment of Mrs. Johns' excellent cooking and to the pleasant hum of conversation around the table. For a while it was possible to forget the bracelet and Leo Channing and the debt she owed him.

Papa and Mr. Mackay discussed the new opportunities for foreign commerce arising from Japan's agreement to open more ports to American ships and to allow Americans to live there.

"Well, I'm sure I wouldn't want to live in such a strange place halfway around the world," Mrs. Mackay said. "Imagine not being able to speak a word of Japanese nor understand anything anyone said. How could you buy food in the markets? How could you order a new hat?"

"Now that," Sutton said, pointing his fork at his mother, "would be a disaster of gigantic proportions."

"Tease me all you want, Sutton, but I am much too old and set in my ways to even think of going off to someplace like Japan."

"I think a trip to the Far East would be quite wonderful," Mrs. Manigault said. "I've always wanted to see some place more exotic than London and Paris."

"Tell you what, Grandmother," Sutton said. "The first time one of our vessels sets sail for those climes, you'll be aboard."

Mr. Mackay lifted the decanter to refill his glass, the heavy crystal reflecting the light. "Between the opportunities in Japan and that new transatlantic cable system, the whole world is opening up to shipping concerns like ours."

Mrs. Manigault frowned. "But didn't I read somewhere that the cable broke? President Buchanan was terribly disappointed. I'm sure Queen Victoria must be no less so." She shook her head. "Such a promising new invention."

"The cable will be repaired, Grandmother," Sutton said.

"So it will, son." Mr. Mackay took a sip of his wine. "And in another five years, ten at the most, the sky will be the limit. We should see our profits double. Perhaps even triple."

"If we can stay out of war," Papa said. "But I don't intend to mar this evening with talk of that problem."

"You're quite right, David," Mrs. Manigault said brightly. "No sense in borrowing trouble, I always say. Did anyone else see the story in the papers about those gold prospectors in Colorado? They say there are fifty thousand people looking for gold around Denver, and the town is growing like a weed. The paper says Denver is planning on building a theater and a circulating library too."

"Maybe so, Mama," Mrs. Mackay said. "But Denver will never rival Savannah." She smiled at each of them in turn. "There is no place on earth quite like Savannah."

Mr. Mackay caught Celia's eye. "You've been awfully quiet this evening, my dear."

"I'm enjoying the conversation," Celia said. Evenings like this, with those she loved most gathered at table, reminded her that, despite old misfortunes and present worries, she was among the lucky ones.

Mrs. Johns came in to clear the table and serve the pie and coffee. When dinner was over, they returned to the parlor. Mr. Mackay tended the fire and poured brandy for the gentlemen.

"Thank you, Father, but I'll pass." Sutton held up his hand, palm out, and smiled at Celia, who occupied the settee next to Mrs. Manigault. "I'd like to take Celia down to the waterfront and show her our new ship."

"But Sutton, it's the middle of the night," his mother said. "It's too dark to see very much."

"It isn't that late. The streetlamps are on, and the gaslights along the row are burning. This ship represents the future to Celia and me. I'd love for her to see it."

"Celia, kindly talk some sense into your intended," Mr. Mackay said, but the twinkle in his dark eyes told her he knew his cause was lost.

Celia rose and kissed both Mackays and Sutton's grandmother, then clasped Papa's hand. "You will forgive us for not staying longer?"

Papa nodded. "Take our carriage if you wish. But don't forget to come back for me at a decent hour."

Mrs. Manigault waved one mottled hand. "Go on, child. We are all old, but not too old to remember what it's like to be in love and with an entire lifetime to look forward to. Just be sure to bundle up. It will be cold down on the river this time of night."

Mrs. Johns retrieved Celia's cloak, and Sutton helped her into it. They left the house and, moments later, Joseph turned the carriage toward the river.

Sutton leaned forward and clasped Celia's hand, the heat of his palm radiating through the fabric of her glove. "Wait until you see my new ship. She's sleek as an otter and bigger by a third than the *Electra,* so we can move the same amount of cargo in fewer trips. Despite our earlier losses, we ought to make a modest profit this season."

"But won't a larger ship mean hiring more men to load and sail her?"

"Yes, but Mackay Shipping has always paid a fair wage, and there are plenty of men who need work. We can offset the higher labor costs by getting our shipments out in greater quantities. And if I can find new customers in Japan, we'll make even more."

He squeezed her hand and she squeezed back, thrilled to see him so excited about the new ship and the future.

"And how is the pup?" Sutton grinned. "You still like him?"

"Oh, Sutton, he's wonderful. We all love him. Mrs. Maguire complains about his muddy paws and all the table scraps he's eating, but I think she secretly loves him too. Even Ivy has taken to him, though she would never admit it."

"I was surprised your cousin wasn't at dinner this evening. Mother told me Ivy was invited."

"She has a cough, but I think mostly she didn't want to attend without an escort." Celia sighed as the carriage neared Commerce Row. "I do feel terrible that her romances never seem to lead anywhere."

"Well, it has been my observation that any reasonably attractive woman who wants to wed can find someone suitable. Perhaps your cousin is more in love with the idea of love than with the realities of it."

The carriage drew to a stop. Sutton got out and offered Celia his hand. She stepped onto the street. Gaslights illuminated the buildings along the waterfront. Light shimmered on the dark water, hanging like orange globes in the darkness. Ships rocked gently at their moorings. Beyond the wharf, the river was a gray, vaporous fog.

Sutton called up to Joseph, "We won't be long."

"Take your time, Mr. Mackay," the driver said, taking out his pipe. "I ain't in no hurry this evening."

Sutton took Celia's arm, and they walked the short distance to the pier where a sleek brigantine rested at anchor.

"There she is." Sutton's voice was soft in the darkness. "I know you can't see too much, but what do you think?"

"I can see enough to know she's a beautiful ship." Celia tucked her arm through his. "I'm happy for you. And for your father."

Sutton nodded. "The loss of the *Electra* hit him hard. She was the first ship he purchased when he started Mackay Shipping. When she went down, she took a part of our family's history with her."

Two men, obviously into their cups, made their way along the waterfront. One of them called out a drunken greeting as they passed. Sutton drew Celia closer to his side, and they started back along the pier toward the shuttered buildings lining the waterfront. "When I was away at Harvard some of my Northern classmates teased me for making so much of my heritage. They didn't understand how important tradition and our family ties are to Southerners. How important it is to guard the honor and respect our ancestors built, one generation at a time."

Celia's worries came rushing back. Leo Channing was bent on writing a book that might well destroy the very honor and respect her own family enjoyed. She had to find the diary he had spoken of, if in fact it existed, and hope it would put the rumors about her aunt and the unnamed laundress to rest once and for all. The sooner the better.

". . . if you have no objection." Sutton had stopped walking and was standing near the entrance to Mackay Shipping, smiling down at her.

"Sorry. What?"

"I said I'd like us to take this boat to England instead of the *Carolina*. And I want to name her the *Celia B.* Though you won't be Celia B. for much longer."

"I'm honored. But isn't it bad luck to change the name of a ship?"

"I don't believe in superstitions."

She laughed. "You once believed in haints."

"Nah. I just needed some reason to get you into that boat with me. I—"

The sound of breaking glass made them both jump.

"Wait for me in the carriage," Sutton said. "It's probably nothing more than those two drunks getting into mischief, but I'd better check."

Though reluctant to leave Sutton, Celia started for the carriage, her rapid steps sounding hollow on the wooden pier. Joseph was bundled into his coat on the driver's seat, the glow from his pipe a tiny spark in the darkness. She turned. Sutton had already disappeared around the corner. But reflected in the window of a cotton factor's office, she saw a dark figure that seemed to be staring right at her, his image wavering like a flame. She blinked and looked again, her eyes straining against the dim light. The figure had disappeared.

Once again, Celia had the feeling she was being followed, and she had had enough. She spun on her heel and retraced her steps.

"Miss Celia?" Joseph called out. "Where in world you goin'? Where's Mr. Sutton gone to?"

Celia hurried along the wharf. All was quiet except for the sighing and creaking of the ships straining in their moorings. The cotton factor's office was dark and locked up tight. Where was

Sutton? Behind the building a group of rough-looking men had gathered beneath a gaslight and were passing around a bottle of spirits. One of their number slumped against the wooden stairs, his head falling onto his chest.

Then someone bumped into her with such force that she nearly lost her balance. She gasped. "Sutton?"

"Not quite."

Celia looked up and into the eyes of Elliott Shaw.

17

"FIND THE DIARY AND YOU'LL FIND THE NAME."

Celia woke and bolted from her bed, shaking and drenched in sweat. The memory of her last conversation with Leo Channing and her unexpected encounter with Elliott Shaw sent a chill through her, making her head pound.

Mr. Shaw had apologized for frightening her. He had worked late on Saturday evening, finishing a report Papa wanted, and had just happened upon her as she turned the corner. His explanation seemed logical enough, but somehow she hadn't quite believed him. Moments later, Sutton had returned and Mr. Shaw had taken his leave, disappearing into the wispy fog.

Now Celia slid her arms into the sleeves of her dressing gown and parted the curtains. A gray skein of clouds shrouded the sky, and a hard rain pelted the windows, drowning out the street sounds below.

She splashed her face with water and pinned her hair, in no hurry to get dressed. None of her friends would come calling on such a disagreeable morning.

Maxwell rose from his place at the foot of her bed and emitted a frantic yelp, his tail beating the air. She sighed. The thing about puppies was that they had to be taken out of doors regardless of the weather.

She slapped her thigh. "Come on, then."

The puppy scampered down the staircase and spun in circles as he waited for her to reach the kitchen door. She opened the door and sent him out into the rain, watching through the window as he sniffed and circled before disappearing into a tangle of jessamine. A moment later he returned, making muddy paw prints on the floor.

"You're finally awake, I see." Mrs. Maguire came into the kitchen carrying a stack of laundry. She pulled out a towel and handed it to Celia.

Celia wrapped the wriggling puppy in the towel and cleaned his paws. "Yes. Sutton and I exercised the horses after church yesterday, and Zeus fairly wore me out. I'm sorry to be so late this morning."

"Lose an hour in the mornin' and you'll be lookin' for it all day." Mrs. Maguire set a plate of scraps on the floor, and Maxwell fell on his breakfast like a prisoner at a last meal.

Celia laughed and stroked his damp head. "Slow down, boy. Nobody is out to steal your food."

Mrs. Maguire pointed a finger at Celia. "Now, I'll thank you to get that wet dog out of my kitchen. I've got three loaves of bread in the oven, and I don't need the likes o' him underfoot while I'm tending to 'em."

"But he won't be underfoot. See." Maxwell had polished off the last of his meal, curled into a corner, and was fast asleep, his little golden head resting on his front paws.

Mrs. Maguire retrieved the plate and shook her head. "Why on earth Mr. Mackay thought we needed a dog in this house is a mystery for the ages."

"Well, just look at him," Celia said. "He's adorable. And he's such wonderful company."

"Humph." The housekeeper turned toward the kitchen. "I expect you're wantin' some breakfast too."

"Yes, please." Celia followed Mrs. Maguire into the kitchen and perched on a chair drawn up to a tall counter that ran the length of the stone wall. Heat from the stove warmed the room, and the smell of baking bread permeated the air. "Is Ivy awake?"

"Still sleeping off that cough, I reckon." Mrs. Maguire filled a china plate with biscuits, sausage, and eggs and slid it onto the counter. "Dr. Dearing sent over a tonic for her last evening." The housekeeper laid out a place setting of heavy silver—knife, fork, and spoon placed just so atop a heavy white napkin. "Your *da* took the last of the coffee out to Joseph this morning, but I can make more."

"Thank you, but I don't want any." Celia bit into a biscuit and watched Mrs. Maguire go about her work. The housekeeper's practiced movements and the comforting smells coming from the stove seemed to invite the sharing of confidences. During Morning Prayer yesterday, Celia had decided to ask Mrs. Maguire about Aunt Eugenia's death and the alleged diary. If she could think of a way to broach the subject that would not arouse the older woman's suspicions. On those rare occasions when the subject of those long-ago incidents arose, Mrs. Maguire was as guarded and noncommittal as Papa.

Celia no longer knew how many of her memories were hard facts and how many were stories she'd imagined to keep from losing all sense of her own history. Perhaps in her girlhood it was better not to have known what really happened in those sad and mysterious weeks just after her eighth birthday. Even now, Papa deflected her occasional questions, apparently trying to protect her. But she was a grown woman, about to be married. She no longer wished to be protected. She wanted the truth, even if the truth rearranged everything she thought she knew.

She finished her breakfast and pushed her plate aside. Through the open doorway she saw Maxwell lying on his side, fast asleep. The rain continued dripping off the eaves and beading the windows, but inside the kitchen the air was warm and still.

"Mrs. Maguire? At church yesterday, Mrs. Cates remarked that my hat was very similar in color to one my mother once wore."

"Humph." Mrs. Maguire picked up her kitchen knife and began peeling apples.

"Papa says robin's-egg blue was Mother's favorite color. Did you know that?"

"She did wear a lot of blue back in the day. But I always thought lavender was her best shade. It more nearly matched her eyes."

"Papa says my eyes are violet."

"Lavender, violet, it's all the same." An apple peel fell in a single spiral into Mrs. Maguire's lap.

"I remember once when I was very small, Aunt Eugenia came to visit and brought Mama some purple silk she'd bought in Charleston."

"I wouldn't know about that. I don't remember."

"What do you remember about the two of them? Were they close? Did they like the same things?"

Mrs. Maguire's hands stilled, and she pursed her lips as if the questions called to memory something she'd rather not discuss. But at last she said, "They loved each other, sure. But Miss Eugenia's keepin' the slaves your grandfather gave her never did set well with Miss Francesca. She and your da have always been opposed to the idea of owning other people."

The housekeeper picked up another apple. "When Miss Eugenia married Mr. Lorens and he took over the plantation on St. Simons, she and Miss Francesca had quite a set-to over it. Miss Francesca wasn't happy about a near stranger gettin' his hands on Butler property. But all that is water under the bridge. I don't see why you want to bring it up now."

"After dinner the other night Sutton was speaking of how important family history and tradition are. I've always felt like a big part of my history is missing. But I can't ask Papa and risk upsetting him. You know what the doctor said."

"I do, and that's another reason why you ought to let sleepin' dogs lie. Just go on with your wedding plans and be happy with Sutton Mackay. Leave the past where it belongs. Anyway, I'm not the one you ought to be askin.'"

"There is no one else to ask, Mrs. Maguire."

The housekeeper rose and dumped an apron full of apple peelings into the pail beside the door. She peered into the oven to check on the bread.

"Do you remember when Aunt Eugenia and Ivy arrived here, just before the accidents?"

"Of course I do." The oven door slapped shut. "Woke up half of Madison Square when that carriage rolled up to the door in the middle of the night and Miss Eugenia come running up the steps ringing the bell and screaming like the divil himself was after her." Mrs. Maguire sprinkled flour onto her marble pastry slab and began rolling out a piecrust. "'Course it wasn't the divil. 'Twas only Mr. Lorens. But some say the two was one and the same."

Celia nodded. Ivy had hinted at some kind of strife between her mother and father, but still this news put a dent in Celia's image of the Brownings as one harmonious family. "I was only eight, but I remember feeling scared for Aunt Eugenia and for Ivy."

Thunder rumbled as Mrs. Maguire removed the bread from the oven and slid the pie in. "Miss Ivy was the tougher o' the two, if you ask me." Celia recalled those first few days after their arrival, when Ivy and Aunt Eugenia had occupied the bright, airy room across the hall from her own. Confused and frightened by her aunt's tears, Celia had gone about her activities on tiptoe. But Ivy had seemed detached, retreating far beyond the reach of anyone.

Sometimes she seemed to be there still—all these years later—in a world of her own making.

Where had Uncle Magnus been during this time? Celia frowned, trying to remember. She recalled so little about him. But even to one of her tender years, he seemed more charming than attractive, with his butter-colored hair and eyes so pale they seemed nearly colorless. Certainly he was not nearly as handsome as Papa. He was foreign born and without connections or property. It made no sense why Eugenia Butler, who had plenty of both, had chosen him over other suitors. Perhaps it was true that a woman in love abandons all reason.

Another memory surfaced. For her sixth birthday, Uncle Magnus had brought Ivy and Aunt Eugenia to Savannah for the celebration. She remembered his love of jokes and stories and how Aunt Eugenia, who seemed serious and a little sad, had refused to dance with him and frowned when he got too boisterous.

She couldn't recall another single instance of his presence in the house—until he'd followed Aunt Eugenia and Ivy here.

"I remember that Aunt Eugenia spent a lot of time sitting in our garden," Celia said. "One day she made crowns of magnolia leaves for Ivy and me. I cried when the leaves shriveled on mine and I had to throw it out."

Mrs. Maguire fetched her broom and began sweeping, her movements quick and full of purpose.

"Do you remember that, Mrs. Maguire?"

"I do not." Swish-swish went the broom. "And *nither* do I see the purpose of all this talk. Half the morning's gone and here you sit, still in your dressing gown."

"Well, I can hardly pay social calls in this weather." Celia glanced out the window. "I hope the weather improves by tomorrow. Mrs. Foyle is already cross with me because I asked her to finish my dress sooner than planned. I don't dare cancel my fitting."

Mrs. Maguire's expression softened. "No, it won't do to delay completin' your weddin' dress. Your da is sure looking forward to the festivities. Just this mornin' he asked me about your cake. But that's a job better suited to Mrs. Hemphill at the bakery."

"I suppose. May I ask one more question?"

Mrs. Maguire leaned on her broom and sighed. "You'll ask it no matter what I say, so go ahead. But I am not promisin' to answer."

"Aunt Eugenia was here for several weeks before the accident. I was so young I can't remember—what did she do with herself all day? I can't imagine she would have gone visiting or that my mother's friends would have visited her. Not after the ruckus Uncle Magnus caused when she left him and came here."

"She kept mostly to herself, she and Ivy. They slept like the dead for the first few days. Then your papa sent for the doctor, and he gave Miss Eugenia some kind of tonic that perked her up. After that she did seem to prefer the garden. Seemed like every time I called her for dinner, she was sitting on the bench beneath the magnolias with her writing box on her lap."

"She had a writing box? What did it look like?"

"Oh, child, I didn't pay that much attention. Your aunt's arrival set this whole household on its ear. I had my hands full taking care of you and your da, and keeping an eye on your cousin. Miss Ivy was a handful back then." She paused. "Now that I think about it, I remember that box was made out of a reddish-colored wood. Rosewood, maybe. With a lid that closed to make a writing desk. Not so different from your own, best as I can recollect."

"What happened to it after—"

"I don't know. Maybe Miss Ivy has it."

"Maybe I have what?" Ivy stepped into the kitchen, Maxwell at her heels. She was dressed, her hair pinned into a perfect cascade of blond curls, but her skin looked pale and dry. Faint blue half-moons bloomed beneath her eyes.

"Your mother's writing box," Mrs. Maguire said before Celia could say anything.

"Writing box?" Ivy frowned and shook her head. "I don't remember a writing box." She eyed the bread cooling on the counter. "That smells wonderful, Mrs. Maguire. May I have some?"

Without waiting for an answer, Ivy found the bread knife and sliced into the loaf. Maxwell stationed himself at her feet, sat on his haunches, and stared at her until she picked off a piece and tossed it to him. "There, you little beggar. Now go away. I'm famished."

Through the window, Celia saw a carriage turning onto the street, flaps buttoned tight against the cold rain. Moments later, the bell rang. Mrs. Maguire sent Celia a pointed look. "Didn't I tell you to get dressed? Now there's someone at the door, and look at you."

Ivy brushed crumbs from her fingers. "I'll answer it."

"Niver you mind." Mrs. Maguire dusted off her fingers and patted her hair into place. "I'll attend to it. Just keep that dog away from the door."

Celia scooped Maxwell into her arms. Mrs. Maguire hurried to the door and soon returned, a puzzled expression in her eyes.

"Who is it?" Celia asked.

"Wasn't nobody there. They left this on the doorstep. It's addressed to you."

Celia set Maxwell on his feet and took the envelope from Mrs. Maguire. It was spattered with rain, and the inked address had started to run. She tore it open and silently scanned the single line. "An oak is often split by a wedge from its own branch."

"What is it?" Ivy helped herself to another slice of bread. "An invitation of some sort?"

"It's nothing important." Celia tucked the letter into her pocket. "You are so right, Mrs. Maguire. I have dawdled long enough. I must get dressed. Come along, Maxwell."

Celia and the dog hurried up the stairs. She dressed quickly and sat down to reread the note, the puppy curled contentedly in her lap. She thought of the other cryptic messages that had arrived at the house since last month, words both chilling and strangely familiar.

"Foul deeds will rise . . ."

"Foul whisperings are abroad. Unnatural deeds do breed unnatural troubles."

And now, *"An oak is often split by a wedge from its own branch."*

The words hinted at betrayal. Leo Channing had once suggested that Papa and Ivy were not to be trusted, but that was ridiculous. Papa would never do anything foul, and Ivy was practically her sister, even if they were no more compatible than oil and water.

The diary. If Celia found the diary, maybe she would solve the mystery and discharge her obligation to Mr. Channing without causing her family harm. And maybe she would find some clue as to who had sent the bracelet and why.

But the two might not even be connected. Maybe Leo Channing was right, and the bracelet was from some shy admirer who had no inkling of the message hidden in the jewels. But instinct told Celia the bracelet meant more. And she still couldn't shake the sense that someone was watching her. Waiting.

Wishing her harm.

Find the diary and you'll find the name. Celia gently pushed Maxwell off her lap and stood. She hurried along the upper gallery to the end of the hall where a narrow door led to the attic.

The door opened easily, and she stepped into the musty space. Light from a cobwebbed window high on the wall cast shadows over the jumbled contents of the room. Her heart sped up as she moved farther into the small space and realized there was no other means of exit. She propped the door open with an empty valise and waited for her eyes to adjust to the gloom.

The rain beat onto the roof with a sound like cannon fire. The air was thick with dust. Celia stifled a sneeze and sorted through a stack of books that smelled of mold. On a broken chair sat a box of faded newspaper clippings and three old ledgers from the Butler plantations on St. Simons. An old camphine lamp. A leather trunk with a rusted lock looked promising, but it was empty. In the corner, an oil portrait of Aunt Eugenia wearing a blue silk gown rested in a broken gilt frame next to a stack of watercolor pictures. Celia recognized her own garden in the paintings—the wrought-iron bench that sat beneath the magnolias, the pride-of-India trees, the riot of pink roses climbing a painted wooden trellis.

She lifted the painting of the roses toward the fall of gray light coming through the rain-smeared window and saw the initials in the corner. FBB. Her mother's work, then. She couldn't remember seeing her mother at an easel, but a faded memory surfaced as she studied the picture. A spring morning in the garden with her mother, the bees gathering in the jessamine, the air heavy with the smells of wet earth and the river. Her mother's enchanting laughter and the sense that the garden was their own private world, a magical place filled with beauty and wonder.

Setting aside the painting, Celia moved farther into the attic. Here was another trunk, the key still in the lock. It opened easily to reveal more of her mother's things—a small black velvet box containing a single garnet earbob, a packet of letters bound with a faded pink ribbon, a slim book of poetry inscribed by the author, a well-worn copy of *The Book of Common Prayer.* Celia ran her fingers over each item, imagining them in her mother's hands.

The light in the attic faded as the storm intensified. She put everything back into the trunk and poked around in the corners of the room. But there was no sign of a rosewood writing box, no sign of a diary. Perhaps Uncle Magnus had taken them when he left. Perhaps Ivy had them after all and had simply forgotten about them after all these years.

She was retracing her steps, stepping carefully around a couple of hatboxes and a wreath made of silk ribbons, when the attic door slammed shut. She jumped, then shuddered. She distinctly remembered propping open the door. She made her way to the door. The knob wouldn't turn. She was drawn back in time to that day in the garden shed. Panic swept over her like a rogue wave, stealing her breath.

Now she pounded the door with both fists, but the sound of the storm drowned the sound of her voice. "Let me out! Mrs. Maguire! Help!"

Celia sank to the floor. They couldn't hear her. She tried to think. What time was it now? Surely it was near noon, and Mrs. Maguire would miss her when she didn't show up for lunch. Or else Ivy would eventually notice her absence. At the very worst, they would look for her this evening when Papa came home and Celia was absent from supper. All she had to do was remain calm. Breathe.

Minutes passed. An hour. The storm subsided. She pounded on the door again and fought the rising fear that all the air was being sucked from the room. The walls seem to press in around her. Rationally it made sense to simply sit and wait for rescue, but fear compelled her to look for another way out.

She ran her palms along the wooden walls, and eventually her hands closed around a metal doorknob. A tiny door, perhaps only three feet high, swung open. She bent and stepped forward into a void, her foot twisting painfully as it landed on the narrow stair. She started down, keeping one hand on the wall for balance. Reaching the bottom step, she looked around for the door that would take her into the main house and safety. But there was no door, just a narrow passageway that seemed to lead away from the house and toward the garden.

Surely this passageway eventually led to the outside. Celia felt her way along the narrow space and tried not to remember that here there was even less air to breathe. All she had to do was keep putting one foot in front of the other.

At last a shaft of light fell across her darkened path, and she rushed toward it. She pushed through another door, the planks grayed and thick with cobwebs. Realization dawned as she looked around. She was in the carriage house.

After the death of the laundress, Papa had sent their carriages to the livery and locked the doors to this place. There was nothing here now except odds and ends—a wooden table with a splintered leg, a stack of rusted tin buckets, a coil of rotted rope. The windows—one of them broken—were too high up to allow her to climb out, but at least there was light. And she could breathe.

The wind rattled the loose glass in the broken window pane. She couldn't explain it exactly, but she felt a strong presence here, an ineffable sadness mixed with a fierce anger that seemed to shimmer like a live thing in the pearlescent light.

A sudden movement in the rafters caught her eye and she looked up. A sparrow had flown in through the broken window and was desperately seeking a way out. She watched the bird circling in confusion until it rested on a rafter near the center of the building.

Her breath caught.

Hanging from the rafter were the remains of a noose, the ends of the rope frayed and gray, moving ever so slightly in the stale, damp air.

18

OUTSIDE: MAXWELL'S FRANTIC BARKING. CELIA RUSHED TO the wide front doors of the carriage house and pounded them with her fists. "Maxwell! Come! Here, boy!"

The puppy scratched at the doors. She knelt on the floor and pressed her face to crack between the doors. "Maxwell, here I am!"

"Maxwell." Ivy's voice. "Get back here."

But the puppy kept up his barking and scratching. Soon footsteps sounded on the path.

"Ivy!" Celia yelled. "Open the door and let me out of here!"

"Miss Celia?" Mrs. Maguire's voice came through the door. "What in the name of all that is holy are you doin' in there?"

"Never mind. Just let me out, please."

"I can't remove all these boards, and besides, I don't have the key. You'll have to go back the way you came."

Back through the long, dark passageway, up the steep hidden staircase, across the gloomy attic to the door. She shivered. "Then go inside and open the attic door."

"What were you doing in the attic?"

"Mrs. Maguire, please take Maxwell inside before he gets a chill and do as I ask."

"Come on, Maxie," Ivy said, her voice muffled. "Don't worry, Cousin. I've got him."

Footsteps receded. Celia left the carriage house, retracing her steps as quickly as she dared. By the time she returned to the attic, Mrs. Maguire had reached the second floor and stood at the opened door, the keys in her hands.

"My faith, girl! You look like you've seen a ghost," the housekeeper said.

"I was frightened. I've always been afraid of being locked in, ever since the time Ivy—"

"Then you ought not have been poking around in there."

"I propped the door open."

"With this?" Mrs Maguire picked up the valise and tossed it into the attic with more force than necessary. "No wonder. 'Tisn't heavy enough to keep the door from blowing shut when there's a draft downstairs."

"But—"

"Are you all right, Celia?" Ivy appeared at the top of the stairs, a damp but joyful Maxwell at her heels.

"I'm all right now." Celia lifted Maxwell. The weight of the warm puppy calmed her frazzled nerves. She briefly buried her face in his damp hair. "I could use some tea, though."

"I'll see to it." Mrs. Maguire closed the door once more, locked it carefully, and started for the kitchen. "I'll bring it to the parlor when it's ready."

Ivy looped her arm through Celia's. "You gave us quite a turn, disappearing like that."

"It wasn't my idea," Celia said as they started down the staircase to the parlor. "Ivy, did you know there's a passageway between here and the carriage house?"

"I . . . no. Is that why you were in the carriage house? How strange."

Celia nodded. "I found it accidentally when I was looking for another way out of the attic."

They reached the foyer and entered the parlor. The curtains were drawn against the late November chill. The fire in the grate had burned to coals that gleamed like rubies. Celia plopped down on the settee, settled Maxwell at her feet, and resumed her train of thought. "I can't imagine a use for such a passageway. It's narrow and dark, and certainly it's—"

"I'll bet even Uncle David doesn't know about it." Ivy fluffed her skirts and folded her hands in her lap. "But I wouldn't advise you to ask. It might upset him. You know how he is. He'd want to investigate every nook and cranny, and that elf-size door is hardly—"

"Here we are." Mrs. Maguire bustled in with the tea tray. She busied herself pouring, then pointed to the small plate of benne seed cookies. "I made those for Mr. Mackay, but he hasn't shown himself here much lately, so you might as well have 'em."

Celia picked up her teacup. "Sutton's been busy since the new ship arrived from Charleston. Did I tell you he's decided to name her for me?"

"I'm not surprised," Mrs. Maguire said. "The boy is besotted with you. It wouldn't surprise me if he named his carriage, his house, and everything else he owns after you."

The front door opened and Papa came in, his hat and cloak dripping rain. Maxwell lifted his head, considered whether or not to bestir himself, and went back to sleep. Celia rose and went into the foyer to greet her father, her heart warming at the sight of his gentle smile.

"You're home early, Papa."

He handed her his hat, and she set it on the hall tree. "A section of the track washed out north of here and delayed the train from Marietta. It's too wet to load cotton anyway, so I sent the men home for the day." He glanced toward the parlor. "Is there tea?"

"Yes, you're just in time."

Celia took his arm as they returned to the parlor. "Aside from the delayed shipment, how are things on Commerce Row?"

"Perking along. This morning I went over the books with Elliott Shaw. Barring any disasters, we should have a record profit this season." He paused. "There is one bit of news. Mr. Shaw has given his notice. He intends to leave by the end of the month. He's going back to his sister's in Cassville."

"But why? I realize his sister has been ill recently. But Mr. Shaw has been your clerk forever."

"I asked that very question and he said, 'Ask your daughter.'" Papa removed his coat and shook it out. "Has something happened that I ought to know about?"

"Mr. Shaw turned up uninvited at the masquerade ball with a gift for me, which naturally I refused."

"I see."

"And then he showed up on the waterfront the night Sutton and I went to see the new ship. He said he'd been working late on some report you wanted. But I'm not sure I believe him. I—"

"Mr. Browning." Mrs. Maguire placed a brimming teacup on the small table next to Papa's chair. "I've made your tea the way you like it, and there are cookies on the tray. But I can make something more substantial if you like."

"This will be plenty, Mrs. Maguire. I had lunch at the club and ate more than I should have." He picked up a cookie. "Besides, I don't want to spoil my appetite for whatever you are planning for dinner this evening."

Mrs. Maguire's eyes widened. "Oh, my faith! In all the excitement I forgot all about my pork roast and cabbage. If I don't get them in the pot soon, you won't have any dinner till midnight."

The housekeeper hurried out. Papa looked from Celia to Ivy. "Excitement? What happened?"

"Nothing really," Celia said quickly. "I was up in the attic, and the wind blew the door closed. Ivy and Mrs. Maguire rescued me."

Papa helped himself to more tea. "I've been meaning to clean out that attic, but somehow I never get around to it. What were you doing up there?"

"Just poking around," Celia said. "The weather was too disagreeable for visiting or for walking Maxwell in the park." She smiled at him and shrugged. "A girl can read only so many books on a day like this."

He laughed. "I suppose that's true."

"I found some of mother's watercolors. Would you mind if I had them framed? I might like to have them in my dressing room when Sutton and I are married and living on our own."

"Of course, darling. Take whatever you want. I'd forgotten how fond your mother was of painting. She never wanted me to see her work, though."

Maxwell woke, stretched, and padded across the room to nudge Papa's hand with his nose. "Hello, my man." Papa stroked the puppy's head. "Ivy? You've been quiet. What did you do today, apart from rescuing your cousin from the attic?"

"I had a letter from a school friend. Leticia Hopewell. She's living in New York now and has invited me to visit. I'm thinking of going."

"Not before Celia's wedding, surely."

Ivy's eyes went bright with sudden tears, but she managed a smile. "No, of course not, Uncle David. Not before then."

He finished his tea and got to his feet. "If you ladies will excuse me, I think I'll lie down for a while before dinner. It isn't often I get a chance to come home early for a rest."

He kissed Celia's cheek. "You could do with a rest, too, my dear. You're very pale. Are you quite sure you're all right?"

"I had a bad dream last night, that's all. But a nap sounds

like a good idea." She picked up Maxwell and turned to her cousin. "What about you, Ivy?"

"I want to finish my tea and write a letter to Leticia. I'll see you at dinner." She smiled. "Let's hope Mrs. Maguire has the roast in the pot by now."

Celia followed her father up the curving staircase. At the top of the stairs they parted, and she went into her room and closed the door.

She removed her dress and lay down on the bed. She closed her eyes but she couldn't shake the awful image of the frayed noose in the carriage house. She'd always thought the death of the laundress had been an accident. But how did a person accidently die by hanging?

She didn't believe that, any more than she believed that a sudden draft had caused the attic door to slam shut. Even if it had, it wouldn't have locked all by itself. Mrs. Maguire had had to open it with a key.

Her eyes flew open, and she sat upright in bed as another realization dawned. Ivy had claimed not to know about the secret passageway leading to the carriage house, yet she had perfectly described the door that led to the stairs adjoining it.

Ivy could have locked the door, but surely she was past such childish mischief. And it was unthinkable that Mrs. Maguire would have locked her in.

Or was it?

Maxwell jumped onto the bed and licked her face. Celia tucked him beneath her arm and tried to think. But the harder she worked to understand the puzzle of the bracelet, the strange anonymous messages, the diary, and the attic and how they all fit together, the more confused and afraid she became.

"Miss Browning, will you kindly hold still." The dressmaker scowled as Celia shifted from one foot to the other.

Celia returned the woman's frown. How could the pinning of a single sleeve take so much time? Mrs. Foyle might be the most sought-after modiste in Savannah, but she was slower than the hands on a schoolroom clock. "Are you almost finished?"

Mrs. Foyle spoke around a mouthful of pins. "Not too much longer."

She pinched the fabric at Celia's waist. "You've lost weight since our last fitting."

"Too many things on my mind these days. They have stolen my appetite."

The dressmaker pinned the waist and held up a length of lace that would eventually be attached to the gown's voluminous overskirt. "With your wedding only weeks away, I'm sure I don't wonder at it. But you'll want to keep some flesh on those bones between now and then if you don't want to look like a refugee on your wedding day."

Mrs. Foyle stood back to admire her work. "That's all for today. Please bring your mother's veil as soon as you can so I can adjust the length for you."

"I'm sorry," Celia said. "I meant to bring it sooner, but it slipped my mind." She ducked behind the screen in the corner of the dress shop and changed into her simple violet and cream day dress. She had done her best to emulate the best qualities her mother was said to possess: graciousness, discretion, charity, piety. But the compounding mysteries surrounding the bracelet, the diary, and the anonymous notes, coupled with the incident in the attic, had stretched her self-control to the limit.

Never had she felt so alone. She couldn't burden her father or Sutton with her worries; they had troubles of their own. Mrs. Maguire seemed to get angry whenever Celia brought up the subject of her aunt and the laundress. And both Mrs. Maguire and Ivy, for whatever reason, had lied to her yesterday. Clearly, Celia was on her own.

Celia finished doing up her buttons, retrieved her hat and cloak, and headed for the door just as Ivy rushed in, her light-blue eyes shining. "Thank goodness I've caught you. I was afraid you might have gone by now."

"We've just finished her fitting," Mrs. Foyle said. She waved them out the door.

On the sidewalk, Ivy took Celia's arm. "I've a tremendous favor to ask. I've just come from the circulating library, and there's wonderful news. The Georgia Historical Society has invited Mr. Thoreau to Savannah, and it's rumored he will accept. Mr. Truesdale at the library has asked me to help plan the occasion. He has called a meeting for noon today, and now I haven't the time to read with Louisa. She's doing so well lately that I hate to disappoint her."

Two gentlemen approaching on the street tipped their hats as they passed. Celia dipped her head in return. "And you'd like me to go in your place."

"Would you? After all, I took your turn when you went shopping with Mrs. Mackay."

They reached the carriage where Joseph waited to drive them home. Celia sighed. Working with Louisa was a trial, and yesterday's events had left mistrust and anger simmering in Celia's heart like soup on a fire. But Ivy was right. Celia did owe her the favor.

Joseph jumped off the carriage and opened the door. "Going home, Misses?"

Celia sighed again. "Take me to the Female Asylum, please, Joseph. And then deliver my cousin to the library. I shall be ready to return home at noon."

"All right, Miss." The carriage driver helped the cousins inside and closed the door. "You two surely must be the mos' busy ladies in all of Savannah."

Minutes later they drew up at the asylum. Ivy leaned forward to place a hand on Celia's arm. "Be patient with Louisa. I know she can be stubborn and prickly, but she's really a lovely girl when you get to know her. And we must remember that she has had no one except Mrs. Clayton and Miss Ransom to guide her."

The carriage rocked as Joseph got down to open the door.

"There's a Christmas tea at the library a week from Saturday," Ivy went on. "Mr. Truesdale and Miss Bole are soliciting donations to purchase more books for our collection. I told him he could count on us to help."

"I'm sure it will be wonderful, and of course I want to support the library. But you should not have spoken for me. I already have plans."

"Here we are, Miss Celia." Joseph opened the door and offered her his hand.

"Sutton and I are planning an outing on that day." Celia couldn't stop the smile spreading across her face. Sutton had been so busy the past two weeks that they'd barely seen each other.

"An outing?" Ivy frowned. "In the middle of December?"

"It shouldn't be *that* cold," Celia said as Joseph helped her out of the carriage. "And you know what they say: Love warms the hands as well as the heart."

Celia waved to Ivy, ran lightly up the steps to the asylum, and rang the bell. Red-haired Annie Wilcox answered the door, a beribboned bonnet in her hands.

"Hello, Annie," Celia said. "You're working on a new hat, I see."

"Yes'm. It's meant to be a Christmas present for Mrs. Clayton's sister." Annie stepped back to allow Celia into the hallway. "I've been working on it every chance I get."

Celia smiled. "But not neglecting your reading and writing, I hope."

"Oh, no. Miss Ransom would have a conniption fit if I was to stop my reading and such. Do you know I am the only girl in here who can work out long division?"

"You have a fine mind, Annie. I won't be surprised if you become a very famous businesswoman one day." Celia looked around. "I must go. I'm here to read with Louisa."

"Louisa? Then you'd better come into the parlor, Miss Browning. I'll fetch Mrs. Clayton."

19

Kneeling next to Ivy in the Brownings' usual pew, Celia closed her eyes and murmured a prayer for her father, who had not felt well enough to attend church. Celia had left him propped on his pillows with his books and a breakfast tray. He tried to make light of his weakened condition, but his pallor and the circles beneath his eyes told a different story. Yesterday Dr. Dearing had called to check on what he called Papa's "pleural effusions" and to leave a bottle of Sydenham's laudanum. The powerful concoction was made of opium mixed with saffron, bruised cinnamon and cloves, and a pint of sherry wine. Nothing could stop the deterioration of Papa's heart, but at least the laudanum would keep him more comfortable.

In the pew to Celia's left, an olive-skinned child squirmed in her seat and fussed with the ribbons on her hat, reminding Celia of Louisa. According to Mrs. Clayton, the girl had disappeared sometime on Tuesday evening, apparently by climbing out the window onto the roof and then down a magnolia tree to the ground. Though Louisa had been difficult and not particularly interested in her studies, Celia couldn't help feeling a sense of loss and more than a little curiosity. Why had she left the comfort and safely of the asylum? Perhaps she'd grown tired of rules and schedules and had left in search of more freedom and adventure.

Mrs. Clayton had reported Louisa's disappearance to the police. Maybe they'd found her by now. Or maybe the girl was stowed away on Captain Stevens's boat, headed for home—wherever that was. Celia prayed that Louisa was safe and that the girl might one day find her place in the world. For now, there was nothing more that the ladies of Savannah could do for one lost girl. There were so many others needing guidance and encouragement.

Last night's fund-raising reception, which Celia had hosted at the Chatham Literary and Arts Society, had been mostly a success. Lucy Chase and her mother had declined Celia's invitation without giving an excuse, as had one or two others. Still, the room had filled with ladies, who enjoyed an assortment of iced cakes, fruits, cookies, and candies while they chatted and discreetly deposited checks into a large glass bowl in the middle of the refreshments table. By the end of the evening, Celia had collected enough to purchase the piano, with enough left for the sewing machine when it became available. The remainder would be added to the building fund. Surely such a show of support for the asylum would silence Mrs. Clayton's critics on the board of managers and allow her work to continue.

The chiming of bells signaled the end of the service.

"The grace of our Lord Jesus Christ and the love of God and the fellowship of the Holy Ghost be with us all evermore," the rector intoned. "Amen."

The crowd stirred, gathering cloaks and shawls, hats and gloves and small children. Ivy stood on tiptoe and looked around. "There are the Mackays, but I don't see Sutton."

"He came in late. He's on the back pew." Celia drew on her gloves. "What do you want with him anyway?"

"I bought him a Christmas present."

Celia frowned as her cousin continued, "Oh, I know I've already given him a couple of things since he got home, but I just keep finding little things I know he will enjoy, and I can't resist." Ivy stepped into the aisle. "I hope I can catch him before he leaves."

Celia caught Ivy's arm. "I wish you wouldn't."

Ivy's eyes widened, and she gave a short laugh. "Surely you're not jealous."

Just then Sarah Lawton crossed the aisle and nodded to Celia, her magnificent necklace—the one with the jewels that spelled *adored*—glittering in the light. Celia returned the older woman's nod and pressed into the aisle behind Ivy.

"Of course I'm not jealous," Celia murmured. She nodded to Mrs. Stiles as the older woman preceded them to the door.

"Then what's the matter?" Ivy whispered. "Sutton will be family soon—practically a brother to me. I don't see the harm in—"

"It's embarrassing to him," Celia said. "First you knit him that red scarf, and then you gave him the compass, and now you have another present. It's too much, Ivy. Even for an almost-brother, it simply isn't appropriate."

Ivy's eyes flashed. "So the two of you have been gossiping about me?"

"Not at all. Sutton mentioned that your generosity is a bit overwhelming. That's all."

They reached the yard where parishioners milled about, chatting, waiting for carriages and rigs to be brought around. Ivy spotted Sutton talking with another man and lifted her hand in a little wave. "Let's let Sutton tell me himself."

"Celia." Mrs. Mackay wove through the knot of worshipers and, reaching Celia, planted a kiss on her cheek. "You look lovely this morning, my dear. Hello, Ivy."

"Mrs. Mackay." Ivy bobbed her head, then glanced over her shoulder. "If you'll excuse me, I was just about to speak to that charming son of yours."

"Ask him not to tarry. I want to get home as soon as possible." Mrs. Mackay smiled at Celia. "My shoes are pinching my toes."

Celia watched Ivy making a beeline for Sutton, sympathy for her cousin warring with her growing irritation at Ivy's boldness. Sutton was too much a gentleman to speak ill to anyone, let alone a member of the family. But Ivy's behavior was becoming an embarrassment.

"How is your father?" Mrs. Mackay burrowed into her cloak. "I noticed his absence this morning. Somehow church feels incomplete without him."

Celia recounted the details of the physician's latest visit. "Dr. Dearing says the laudanum will help, but it's important not to upset him. And he must rest, which is the difficulty. Papa loves to be in the middle of everything that happens on Commerce Row. So we—"

"There you are!" Alicia Thayer made her way to Celia's side, a saucy grin on her face. "I was hoping to catch you this morning. Good morning, Mrs. Mackay." Alicia smiled at Sutton's mother. "Wasn't Celia's fund-raising reception last night just wonderful?"

Without waiting for a reply, Alicia opened her reticule and handed Celia a check. "This is for the asylum."

"Thank you, but you've contributed already."

"Oh, this one isn't from me. It's from the Philadelphia cousins. I wrote to them all about the Female Asylum and our plans to expand the girls' training beyond preparing them for domestic duties." Alicia laughed. "My Yankee kin support emancipation in all its forms." She gave Celia a quick embrace. "I must go. Mother is waiting. And the Quartermans are coming for lunch. But I'll see you soon."

Celia waved to her friend and tucked the check into her reticule just as the Mackays' carriage drew up. Sutton handed his mother into the carriage and waited while she arranged her silk skirts. "Father and I will be along in a moment. He wants to speak to Mr. Waring."

"Well, don't be long, Sutton. Mrs. Johns will have Sunday dinner ready soon, and you know how she fusses when she thinks the food is getting cold." Mrs. Mackay waved a gloved hand at Celia. "Good-bye, my dear."

Sutton knocked on the carriage to signal the driver and then turned to Celia. "Good morning, my love."

Celia returned his smile but couldn't help teasing him. "You were late to church, Sutton Mackay. Late night last night?"

"Yes, a wild night of wine, women, and song. There was much dancing." He clasped her hand and twirled her around, his expression one of amused mischief.

"A wild night, was it? I thought you looked a bit bleary-eyed when I spotted you last night on my way home from that drinking establishment I so love to frequent."

They broke into laughter just as Ivy joined them. "What's so funny?"

"I'm having a delightful time teasing Celia." Sutton smiled at Ivy. "But she gives as good as she gets. One of the many reasons I can't wait to marry her."

Sutton nodded to an older couple just emerging from the church. "There's Mrs. Boles from the circulating library. Mother told me you're helping with the fund-raising to bring Mr. Thoreau to Savannah."

"Yes," Ivy said. "We're holding a tea this coming Saturday. I invited Celia, but she said the two of you already have plans."

"We do." Sutton squeezed Celia's hand. "We're taking a picnic over to Screven's Landing, where we went the first night we met."

"Oh? I have never been there. It's too bad I can't come along. I'd enjoy seeing where my dearest cousin first fell in love."

"There's not much to see." Sutton caught his father's eye and waved him over. "Just an old road through the rice fields and a couple of abandoned shacks. But it's special to Celia and me."

"Oh, I'm sure it is," Ivy said as the Brownings' carriage rounded the corner and stopped before them.

Sutton helped Celia and Ivy inside and closed the carriage door. He leaned in to speak to Celia. "The inspections of the *Celia B* went very well. She's tight as a drum and ready to go. Father and I are going to Charleston on Wednesday. While I'm there I want to talk to Griffin Rutledge about the plans for the boat. But I'll be home early enough on Friday to go riding if you like."

At Sutton's mention of his plans for building the blockade-runner, the joy went out of the day for Celia. The specter of secession and war reignited her deepest fears and reminded her of the uncertainties of her future. But she forced a smile. "I'd love to go riding."

"I should be back by two o'clock. I'll send word to Finn O'Grady to have the horses tacked up and ready to go."

"All right."

"And then on Saturday we'll head for Screven's Landing. If this mild weather holds." Sutton stepped back as Joseph spoke to the horse and the carriage began to move.

Ivy stared out the window as the carriage turned onto Bull Street.

"You didn't give Sutton another present?" Celia said.

"As a matter of fact, I didn't."

"Thank you, Ivy. Sutton truly appreciates your generosity, but I think it's better not to—"

With a rattle of harness, the carriage came to a stop at their gate.

"I didn't give him the present," Ivy said again as they left the carriage and mounted the steps to the front door. "I almost did, but then I thought of something even better."

The afternoon weather was exceedingly fine for December, and after a morning at his desk in the study, Papa had called for Joseph and had taken the carriage to Commerce Row. Watching from her window as her father slowly made his way down the steps and through the gate to the street, Celia stifled the impulse to go after him. Still, according to Dr. Dearing, some people with Papa's condition lived for a long while, and it was important for her father to keep his spirits up. Perhaps it was better for Papa to stay busy and feel useful than to be treated as a complete invalid.

This morning he had included her in his perusing of the company's ledgers. Despite last year's financial crisis that had affected the entire country, Browning Shipping was having its best year ever. But Papa was not pleased that Elliott Shaw, in his haste to quit Commerce Row, had left without preparing last month's bills for the factors who handled the transport of their clients' cotton, lumber, and pitch. One day soon Papa would need someone to replace Mr. Shaw, someone who could work with Celia and with the lawyers and bankers who would act as trustees for Browning Shipping when the company passed to her. A development she didn't like to consider.

Celia heard Mrs. Maguire's footsteps on the stairs. She opened the door and stepped into the hallway in time to see the housekeeper unlocking the door to the attic. Celia darted back into her room, then slowly peeked out the doorway.

A few moments later, Mrs. Maguire came out carrying a bundle wrapped in burlap. Celia watched as the older woman locked the attic door, descended the staircase, and turned toward the kitchen. Leaving Maxwell asleep on the foot of her bed, she followed Mrs. Maguire. By the time Celia reached the kitchen, the housekeeper had disposed of the bundle and was hurriedly scooping flour into the yellow crockery bowl she used for baking bread.

"Mrs. Maguire."

The housekeeper started, one flour-dusted hand clapped to her heart. "Miss Celia, you scared the life out o' me. You ought not to sneak up on folks like that."

"Sorry." Celia perched on a stool next to the wooden counter and scanned the room, but there was no sign of the mysterious bundle. "Where's Ivy?"

"Gone to another meetin' about that big to-do they're plannin' for the library. She said not to expect her till late. There's a dinner at the hotel for the committee members." Mrs. Maguire busied herself mixing flour, soda, and salt. At last she looked up. "You're not going to the asylum today?"

Celia shook her head. "I usually go on Wednesdays, but not anymore. My pupil absconded last week."

"Pardon?"

"She ran away. Mrs. Clayton has no idea where the girl went."

"My faith. She just up and left, after everything you and Miss Ivy have done for her?" Mrs. Maguire dusted the bread dough with flour and covered it with a towel. "Sure and I don't understand it."

Celia nodded absently, her eyes still searching the kitchen. What had the housekeeper taken from the attic? And what had she done with it?

Mrs. Maguire wiped the counter and set the teakettle on to boil. "No need to wait around in here. I'll bring your tea to the parlor when it's ready."

"Oh, I don't mind waiting here."

"Don't you have something to do?" Mrs. Maguire took down the tea caddy and measured tea into the warmed pot.

"Not really."

"*Nivertheless*, I wish you'd give me some room, girl. You're givin' me the jitters. Have you taken that dog o' yours—"

Maxwell raced into the room and launched himself into Celia's arms, wriggling and wagging his tail. Seconds later he leapt to the floor and ran to the kitchen door.

"Better take him into the garden before he makes a mess to clean up," Mrs. Maguire said.

Celia slid off the stool. "Come on, sweet boy. I'll take you out."

She opened the door and followed Maxwell into the garden. He raced around, sniffing at every bush and blade of grass on his way to the back gate. While he explored, Celia pushed through the rosebushes and jessamine and rounded the corner to the small kitchen window. She cupped her hands to the glass and peered into the kitchen just in time to see the housekeeper remove the burlap bundle from the cupboard behind the stove.

She spun away from the window, her heart hammering. What was Mrs. Maguire hiding?

"Maxwell!" She clapped her hands, and the puppy bounded toward her. She picked him up and returned to the kitchen as Mrs. Maguire emerged with the tea tray. Celia followed the older woman to the parlor and waited while the tea was poured. Mrs. Maguire returned to the kitchen with a comment about checking on the bread, but Celia scarcely heard her. She settled Maxwell at her feet and spooned sugar into her tea, her mind whirling.

The more she tried to unravel the mysteries of her own house, the more tangled it all became.

20

CELIA LAY AWAKE, LISTENING FOR THE CLICK OF THE KITCHEN door latch, the signal that Mrs. Maguire had finished her work and retired to her room by way of the servants' staircase.

Papa and Ivy had gone to their rooms early. Surely by now they were deeply asleep. Leaving Maxwell to his puppy dreams, Celia rose and drew on a dressing gown. She lit the lamp, and, when the flame steadied, opened her bedroom door.

The house was quiet. Pale light from the gas lamps along the street filtered through the fanlight, illuminating the entry hall. She closed the door to her bedroom and hurried along the gallery, her bare toes sinking into the thick carpets covering the wooden floors. She descended the staircase, crossed the cold marble floor of the entry hall, headed past the parlor where the last orange embers from the evening's fire still glowed faintly in the darkness.

In the kitchen, she set her lamp on the counter and crossed to the wooden cupboard behind the stove where Mrs. Maguire kept tins of coffee and tea, assorted spices, and bins of flour.

Outside a dog barked and she froze, hoping the sound wouldn't wake Maxwell. He was still a puppy, but his sharp bark was loud enough to wake half of Savannah. The barking ceased, and she eased open a drawer that held an assortment of knives and serving spoons, then another drawer filled with dish towels. At last, beneath the stack of linens, she felt the solid object beneath the rough burlap.

The writing box was rectangular in shape, the rosewood highly polished as if the box were new. Celia carried it to the table and turned up the wick in the lamp. She lifted the small brass latch of the box and opened the lid. Inside were several velvet-lined compartments meant to hold nibs and pencils, bottles of ink, and writing paper. Tucked away in the back was a small book bound in red leather. She drew it out and held it up to the light.

Celia's ears rang. She had never believed a single word Leo Channing said, but somehow he had known about this diary. Perhaps he had told the truth when he said people in Savannah knew things they would never divulge, at least to her.

"Find the diary, and you'll find the name." Even now the memory of his words was like a cold hand gripping her heart.

Celia perched on the stool and opened the journal. The first few pages had been ripped out, leaving a ragged edge. Some of the remaining pages were puckered, and the ink was splotched and faded as if the diary had been left in the rain—or dampened by tears.

> *May 23.* Eleven years ago, on this date in the year 1832, I joined my fortunes to those of Magnus Lorens, and for ten of those eleven I lived in as perfect a bliss as was possible, given my terrible loss and the secret I am forced to bear. But of late laughter and affection have been replaced by silence and indifference, and he will not say the cause. He insists that my emotions are those of an overwrought woman, and that his ardent feelings have not changed. I do not believe him. Minty and Octavia sick today. Picked six quarts of strawberries.

July 21. Visitors arrived this evening. I was nearly ready to retire, as there is little to do in the country in the evenings, but just before twilight a carriage turned off the main road and came up the avenue to the house. And oh, what a joy to see my friends the Reids from Atherton Hall. Isabella brought squash, beans, and cucumbers from her garden as well as new trimmings for my summer hat, which I had requested she purchase for me on her next trip to town. I sent Octavia down to the slave street to fetch Molly, who is far and away the best cook on St. Simons, and asked her to prepare a late supper for us. Afterwards I took the ladies into the parlor, and we stayed up until midnight playing endless hands of smoot and catching up on all the news. I felt terrible for Mr. Reid, who as the lone gentleman in our party had to content himself with a quick walk around the house and a cheroot on the porch, as my husband did not appear until long after I had settled my guests into their rooms and they were fast asleep.

Footsteps on the servants' staircase set Celia's heart to racing. She extinguished the lamp and crouched behind the stove, scarcely daring to breathe, praying Mrs. Maguire would not find her here. Someone moved across the room, and when her eyes adjusted to the darkness she saw Papa rummaging in the bread box. A few moments later he left the kitchen and padded down the hallway, his footfalls growing softer, then louder, as he moved from the carpeted hallway to the marble foyer and up the curving staircase to his bedroom.

Celia was glad he was hungry enough to want to eat at midnight, but worried that the laudanum had confused him so that he had used the servants' staircase. And in the dark. She held her breath until she heard his door close, then waited a moment longer before relighting the lamp and returning to the diary.

July 22 . Rain. Ivy is restless and refuses to stand still to be measured for a new dress. Bought ten yards of barish delaine and the same of pink calico in Savannah. All the talk in town was of Joseph Smith and his assertion that divine revelation has sanctioned the practice of polygamy. It is very convenient for him and his male followers, but what of the women? Molly made an excellent roasted turnip soup for dinner, but my husband did not appear at table to partake of it.

July 23. During Morning Prayer today I made my own private petition, praying mightily for Mr. Lorens, and was quite overcome with shekinah. Perhaps God has heard my pleading, and these present troubles will soon resolve themselves.

Shekinah. Celia puzzled over the unfamiliar word and made a note to look it up later. The diary contained only a few more entries, and she intended to finish reading before Mrs. Maguire appeared to start the fire for making breakfast.

August 3. Mr. Lorens came in today in an exceedingly jovial mood. He returned from a week in Savannah bringing gifts of a breast pin and a length of purple lace for me and new books for Ivy. She does not seem very much overjoyed with them but of course is glad of any attention from her absentee father. It is so rare these days. Sometimes I fear he suspects what I cannot say.

August 8. Isabella Reid and Tessie Wright called here this morning, Mrs. W still in mourning dress for the child lost to the fever last summer, a boy just a year old. Mrs. Reid brought an article clipped from the *Southern Woman's Magazine* which asserts that it is the duty of all Southern women to support the continuation of our system of free whites and black slaves. I pretended to agree, for to disagree would be social suicide. But I have become a silent abolitionist. Slavery degrades the white man as surely as it degrades the Negro.

Molly served brandied peaches for dessert tonight. Mr. Lorens was much pleased.

August 11. Men demand their wives' fidelity as their due but feel free to indulge their own passions without restraint.

August 12. Ivy was sick all night. The news spread quickly through the slave street. This morning Scipio, Quash, and Liddy appeared on the front porch, expressions grave, and inquiring after the health of the little miss. Liddy and Scipio are especially concerned that our lands remain in our family's hands. Scipio fears if I have no heirs, this place will be sold and them along with it, and he and Liddy do not wish to be separated. He was much relieved when I told him Ivy has improved. I saw no reason to tell him that my husband has wrested my lands from my control, sold off parcels without my consent, and I am powerless to stop him.

August 14. My suspicions are confirmed. I am betrayed beneath my own roof, and by someone I knew and trusted. Tessie Wright called here this morning only too eager to share the news. Septima is about to give birth and has quit the island. This is a small blessing, for had she remained, I would have had to remove her myself. I cannot bear Tessie's righteous hypocrisy. She knows very well who fathered every mulatto child on this island but pretends that those beneath her own roof are the product of some conjurer's spell. As for the mulattoes themselves, they are quite proud of their mixed parentage, seeing it as an advantage to their own prospects. Oh, what a hateful thing slavery is.

August 15. What a liar my husband has become. He has cleaved my heart in two, and yet he acts as if he is the very soul of virtue, worthy of my respect. What a reprobate! How is it possible that I still love him?

August 17. When I think of my husband as I first knew him, a handsome young Swede newly arrived aboard a Danish brig from Copenhagen by way of Havana, so full of fun and charm, so attentive to my thoughts and feelings and eager to assuage my unrelenting grief, I can scarcely credit that he is the same man who has taken no note of his marriage vows and looks upon me now with such indifference.

September 3. Septima has returned to St. Simons without her misbegotten child. My husband is heedless of my humiliation and anger, my outrage that he should consider her my equal. I refuse to pretend that his slave wife does not exist. I cannot bear another moment in this house. Ivy and I leave immediately for Savannah. I know not what will happen after that.

September 9. Arrived three nights ago at the house of my late sister's husband in Savannah, only to discover that Mr. Lorens had somehow discovered my plan and followed me here. He seeks some compromise by which I will return to St. Simons to resume my duties as plantation mistress and allow him to keep his harlot. Even if I could countenance such an outrage, I cannot allow my daughter to be exposed to such an arrangement. I sent my husband away. I do not wish to see his face ever again.

September 12. This morning as I sat on the sunny little balcony off my bedroom, contemplating the garden and my own future, I spotted a carriage carrying my husband and his concubine, heading down Bull Street. I will admit to her singular beauty. Her hair is long and straight, her skin is somewhere between olive and cream, her eyes a mossy green. It is clear she has won his heart, but Savannah is my city. My home. I will not cede it to the likes of her. One of us must go.

One of us must go.

Outside, a milk wagon clattered down the darkened street. Celia set the diary aside as a memory of that September morning surfaced. Celia and Ivy were in the garden pretending to be ballerinas. Celia remembered the feel of the warm sun on her bare head, the scent of jessamine and roses, the whisper of her skirts in the late summer grass as she turned. Then the sound of applause. She looked up to see Aunt Eugenia on the balcony, her auburn hair in a messy plait over her shoulder, her writing box lying on her chair.

Aunt Eugenia gathered the hem of her dressing gown and climbed onto the balcony's narrow wooden rail.

"Mama!" Ivy yelled. "What are you doing?"

"Don't worry, sugar, your mama's as nimble as a cat." Aunt Eugenia smiled down at the two girls. "Do you know that from up here you can see nearly all of Madison Square? I never realized that before."

"Mama, please get down before you fall and break your neck." Ivy crossed the garden and stood directly below the balcony, staring up at her mother. "Please. You're scaring me."

"Life's a scary proposition. Best learn to deal with it."

Then Mrs. Maguire, her ample figure bathed in sharp-angled sunlight, appeared in the open doorway. Celia was too far away to hear the conversation, but not too far away to see her aunt's shoulders stiffen before she followed the housekeeper inside.

Minutes later, Mrs. Maguire had summoned Celia and Ivy from the garden and given them sandwiches and cake in the kitchen.

Now Celia tried to recall what had happened next. Perhaps she had been sent to her room for a nap. Or perhaps she had blocked out a memory too painful to retain. The next thing she remembered was the sound of voices—Aunt Eugenia's and that of another woman. Had her aunt summoned Septima in order to deliver an ultimatum as the diary suggested? Had the laundress arrived with Uncle Magnus in hopes of effecting the compromise he wanted?

She remembered only the sounds of voices raised in anger and the sounds of running feet along the gallery.

A thud. A piercing scream. And then silence.

Shekinah. From the Hebrew word meaning "to dwell." The manifestation of the presence of God. Divine presence.

Celia returned the dictionary to the shelf and stared out the window. Rain had fallen all night and now a wet, gray mantle blanketed the city. Even if Sutton's boat from Charleston arrived on time, the Ten Broeck track was now too wet to exercise the horses. Zeus and Poseidon would have to wait for fairer weather.

Though she was glad of any opportunity to spend time with Sutton, perhaps it was just as well the weather had not cooperated. Today she was too unsettled to enjoy anything. Her thoughts turned again to her Aunt Eugenia's death and its aftermath.

What did she know for certain about that day? Only that Aunt Eugenia had fallen from her bedroom balcony and died. But what had caused the fall in the first place? Had Aunt Eugenia, crazed with jealous grief, and burdened by the weight of her unnamed dark secret, climbed onto the railing and deliberately jumped to her death, or had she meant only to frighten her husband with the threat of suicide?

Had she been pushed off the railing? And if so, who had done it? The laundress? Or Uncle Magnus, wishing to be free of his wife? Some people in Savannah certainly thought Magnus had killed Eugenia. The fact that he had left town so abruptly, disappearing without a trace, gave added credence to this view.

And then two weeks later, Septima had been found dead. Celia shivered at the memory of the remnants of the noose she'd seen in the boarded-up carriage house. Clearly, the woman had not succumbed to some sudden malady as Papa and Mrs. Maguire claimed.

Celia stoked the fire in the study, orange sparks popping and flying up. She couldn't imagine Uncle Magnus killing his own wife. And Septima had just as strong a reason for murder. With Aunt Eugenia out of the picture, Uncle Magnus would have been free to install the laundress as mistress of the plantation and name her child as his heir.

Celia felt a rush of rage at that thought. The Butler land belonged to her family, not to a black-hearted foreigner who had come to Savannah with little more than the clothes on his back and charmed his way into a young woman's tender affections, only to betray her in the most egregious manner—at a time when Aunt Eugenia was in the throes of some private grief.

"Miss Celia?" Mrs. Maguire stepped into the room. "Your father is awake and wishes a word with you."

"Thank you. I'll go right up."

She climbed the stairs and went first to change out of her dressing gown and tidy her hair. In the hallway she nearly collided with Ivy, who had emerged from Papa's room carrying a towel-draped tray that gave off scents of sausage, warm bread, and cinnamon.

"Celia," Ivy said. "There you are. Uncle David just finished his breakfast and wants you."

"Yes, so Mrs. Maguire said." Celia indicated the silver tray. "She would have taken care of that."

"Oh, I know, but I wanted to speak to Uncle David anyway, and I thought I'd save Mrs. Maguire another trip up the stairs." Ivy grinned. "She's not as young as she used to be, you know."

Ivy headed down the stairs. Celia went along the gallery to Papa's room and knocked on the door.

"Come in." He was propped on his pillows, hands folded over the pale-blue counterpane. The curtains were open to the watery light and the rain dribbling down the glass. A fire crackled in the grate.

"Good morning, Papa." She bent to kiss his forehead. "You sent for me?"

"Yes, darling." He motioned with one hand. "Pull up that chair."

She settled herself on the small needlepoint chair, noting with dismay how pale and fragile he looked. Perhaps he'd spent part of last night prowling in the kitchen again. "Did you sleep well, Papa?"

"I'm afraid not. Here lately it seems the laudanum isn't working very well." He frowned. "Might as well be drinking sarsaparilla for all the good it's doing."

"You should ask Dr. Dearing whether there's something else you could try."

"Tincture of opium is the remedy of last resort. If it won't help me, nothing can." Papa rolled onto his side to lift a water glass from the side table and drank deeply.

When he finished, she took the glass from him, set it on the table, and fluffed his pillows. "What did you want to see me about, Papa?"

"I've been thinking about your mother and about dear Eugenia. One good marriage, one bad one. Even women of means are at the mercy of the men they marry. I don't wish that to happen to you, my dear. I couldn't bear it."

She gaped at him. "Sutton loves me, Papa. I would trust him with my life. Besides, he has money of his own. He isn't anything like Uncle—"

"I want you to have this." Papa opened the drawer in the side table and withdrew a large envelope.

She opened it. "Ten thousand dollars?"

"Don't put it in the bank. Put it away in some secret place. If trouble comes and things shouldn't work out the way you hoped—"

"Thank you, Papa, but you mustn't worry. It isn't good for you. Sutton and I will look out for each other, no matter what."

He nodded. "He's a good man. A noble man. I've no cause to doubt his intentions or his affection for you. But circumstances can change us, darling." He waved one hand. "Should Georgia secede, should war come—"

"It won't."

"If war comes, both of you will be sorely tested. Such a crisis can strain even the strongest of marital ties." He took another sip of water. "Don't invest that money in government bonds. If the South loses the war, the bonds won't be worth anything. You'd be penniless, and I cannot bear the thought of my only child living in dire poverty. Ten thousand isn't a fortune, but it's enough for you to start over if necessary." His eyes held hers. "Promise me you will set this money aside and tend it carefully."

"All right, I promise, but you're worrying needlessly. Sutton and I are going to have the most beautiful wedding Savannah has ever seen, and when we get back from England, we'll settle down right here. The politics will get sorted out, and we will go on just as before. You'll see."

Celia's rosy prediction seemed to set his mind at ease. He smiled then, and the light came back into his eyes. "Speaking of weddings, how are the preparations coming?"

"Mrs. Maguire and Mrs. Hemphill are planning the most elaborate wedding cake you ever saw," Celia said, relieved at the change of subject. "My gown is almost finished, and oh, Papa, it's delicious." She went on to describe the billowing satin skirt, the pagoda sleeves, the delicate lace. "And Mrs. Foyle shortened Mama's veil for me. I picked it up just last week."

"What a vision your mother was in that veil." He sat up straighter in the bed. "Try it on for me. Let me see how it looks on you."

"Now?"

"Certainly. Why not?" He glanced out the window. "The rain is letting up and I must leave soon to get to Commerce Row. I've a meeting this afternoon with a new cotton factor who wants to do some business before the season ends. And Burke Mackay is sending over a young man to replace Mr. Shaw."

"Are you sure you're up to it, Papa? Perhaps you should stay home today and try to sleep."

"I'll feel better taking charge of business than lying here worrying about a future I can't control."

"All right. I'll be right back."

She tucked the envelope under her arm and returned to her room for the veil, but the unexpected gift and Papa's reasons for giving it had cast a pall over her happiness. She didn't want to believe that anything could change the way she and Sutton felt about each other. Or that war—if it came—could so radically alter her world.

She shook the veil from its muslin nest and draped it over her head, arranging the delicate lace across her shoulders, and returned to Papa's room.

A tender smile erased the years from his face. "If I didn't know better, I'd swear it was Francesca standing there. She would be so proud of you, darling."

Tears welled in her eyes. "Thank you, Papa. I hope so."

"The one regret of my life is that she was taken from us before you had a chance to know her well. To appreciate her many virtues." He cleared his throat. "I suppose I haven't taught you very much about being a woman."

"But you have taught me everything about being human."

"Well." He wiped his eyes. "I'd better get to work. Now that Mr. Shaw has left us, I seem always to be behind."

She fingered her veil. "I looked over our ledgers last week as you asked. We're doing well."

"We've been lucky this season. Good cotton crops, no bad storms at sea. Everyone on Commerce Row will make money this year—even the Mackays, thank God." He threw back the covers. "Enough dawdling. You must excuse me now. Time's a-wasting."

Celia returned to her room and put the veil away. The door to Ivy's room across the hall stood ajar, revealing a jumble of dresses, shawls, and hatboxes on the unmade bed. In the middle of it all sat Maxwell calmly demolishing one of Ivy's delicate kid gloves.

"Maxwell, no!" Celia chased him down and took the mangled glove from his mouth. "Now look what you've done!"

He sat on his haunches and cocked his head, and she couldn't help but laugh. "Now we shall have to buy Ivy a new pair. Come on, you little thief. Let's go outside."

She patted her thigh, and he raced ahead of her down the stairs. She let him into the garden, then peered into the parlor, expecting to find Ivy. But the room was deserted, the morning fire nearly out.

A moment later the puppy scratched on the door, and she went to let him in. Celia took his towel from its peg beside the kitchen door and dried him off before giving him a bite of bacon left from breakfast. He gobbled it and waited for more.

"Sorry, sweet boy. That's all." She held up both hands, palms out, and Maxwell headed for his favorite napping spot next to the warm kitchen hearth.

Mrs. Maguire came in with an armload of wood for the cookstove and dumped it into the wood box. She dusted off her hands and filled the teapot. "Is your da up and about?"

"Yes, but I wish he'd stay home. He hasn't been sleeping well lately, and the weather today is so disagreeable."

"So 'tis." Mrs. Maguire took two cups from the cupboard and set them on a tray. "I thought I heard him prowling around down here last night, and not for the first time, either."

Celia avoided the housekeeper's steely expression. It wouldn't do for Mrs. Maguire to suspect her, even though the diary had already given up all the information it was going to. The missing pages nagged at her, begged to be found, but Celia's search had turned up nothing. "Papa told me the laudanum isn't working very well. He won't talk to the doctor, but somebody should."

Mrs. Maguire measured tea leaves into the pot. "'Tis surely a worrisome situation, but your da is a grown man, and capable of looking after himself. He won't take kindly to your interfering."

"But I can't bear to think he's suffering if there might be another medicine—"

"Laudanum's the most powerful tonic there is, as far as I can tell. And the truth is, the longer a person takes it, the more the body gets used to it. Eventually Mr. Browning will have to take larger doses to ease his pains." Mrs. Maguire paused to pour hot water onto the tea leaves. "Leastways that's how it was with me poor sister back in the Waterford days."

"I never knew you had a sister."

"'Twas a very long time ago now, but I miss her to this day.

Talkin' about her still makes me weep, so I try not to." The housekeeper turned away. "Now where on earth did I leave my sugar tongs?"

The doorbell sounded, rousing Maxwell from his nap. Mrs. Maguire patted her hair and retied her apron. "You sit tight, Miss Celia. I'll see who it is."

But Celia followed the housekeeper along the long, narrow hallway, stopping just inside the parlor door.

A moment later, Mrs. Maguire returned. "A visitor for Miss Ivy, shy about givin' me her name. I told her Miss Ivy's gone out for the day. So now she wants to see you."

"I can't imagine who would venture out on a day like this."

Mrs Maguire nodded. "Looks like a drowned rat, she does. I'd best bring the tea in. And some cake too—from the looks of her she hasn't eaten for a while."

The housekeeper hurried away and in a moment returned with the visitor. "Miss Celia, here she is."

Mrs. Maguire turned to rekindle the fire in the grate. The caller removed her hooded cape and stood dripping water onto the carpet.

"Louisa? Heavens above. Where on earth have you been?"

"I'll get the tea." Mrs. Maguire headed for the kitchen.

Celia took Louisa's cloak to the hall tree and motioned the girl to a chair before the fire. "Do you realize Mrs. Clayton has been frantic to find you? Why did you run away from the asylum? Does she know you are safe?"

"She knows. I went by there this morning and told her I won't be living there no more." Louisa pushed her damp curls off her face and warmed her hands before the fire. "I got me a job and a room at the boardinghouse on Broad Street."

"A job? Doing what?"

"Fancy needlework for the linen shop down from the hotel.

Embroidering monograms on sheets and pillowcases and such. Mrs. Foyle at the dress shop said she didn't have no room for people like me."

"I see." Celia paused while Mrs. Maguire delivered the tea tray.

The housekeeper eyed the girl warily. "Is everything all right, Miss Browning?"

"Fine. Thank you, Mrs. Maguire."

Mrs. Maguire withdrew. Celia filled a plate with slices of cake and poured tea into a delicate ivory cup. "Here you are, Louisa."

The girl picked up the cake with her fingers and devoured it in three bites, washing it down with gulps of tea. "Sure tastes better'n anything we get at the Female Asylum. I purely got sick of nothin' for breakfast 'cept grits and eggs."

"Nevertheless, it was thoughtless of you to leave there without telling anyone, after everything Mrs. Clayton has done to help you. She could have turned you in to the police. Captain Stevens could have as well. You've repaid their kindness by running away—not once, but twice. At least."

The girl lifted one shoulder and let it fall. "Can I have some more cake?"

Celia placed another slice of cake on the girl's plate. Louisa consumed it at a more leisurely pace as she surveyed the parlor. She wiped her fingers on her napkin and crumpled it into her plate. "I always wondered how this house looked. It's even fancier than I thought."

Celia sipped her tea and gathered her patience. "Why do you want to see my cousin?"

The girl opened her drawstring bag and withdrew a thin volume of poetry. "I wanted to return this."

"Thank you. I'll see that she gets it. I'm happy that you thought to return it."

Another small shrug. "I didn't like it enough to keep it. I

couldn't understand a single word of it. Why don't poets say what they mean in plain old words 'stead of fancying it up so nobody can make heads or tails of it?"

The girl lifted her hem and extended her feet toward the fire. "My toes are freezing."

Celia noticed a ragged hole in the hem of the girl's petticoat. Recognition dawned. Frowning, she set down her cup. "How did you get that tear in your petticoat?"

"What tear?"

"Louisa. The night of the riot I went to investigate a noise in the garden and discovered a prowler hiding near the carriage house. That prowler shoved me into the dirt and got away. Later I found a piece of torn fabric there. It matches your petticoat."

"Must be dozens of petticoats just like mine in Savannah."

"Not with the same fine needlework as yours. I saw your work when we first met at the asylum. So maybe you ought to tell me why you were sneaking around here in the middle of the night. Or if you prefer, we can go down to the police barracks, and you can tell them."

Louisa dropped her gaze. "I wanted to see the carriage house, but it's all boarded up."

"Yes, we stopped using it many years ago. I can't imagine why it would have any interest for you."

Louisa lifted her head, her blue eyes defiant. "I didn't mean to scare you that night, and I didn't mean to hurt you. I only wanted to see the place where my mother died."

21

Afternoon sunlight glinted on the river. Whitecaps stirred by a light breeze lapped against the boat as Sutton rowed toward Screven's Ferry Landing. A morning storm had delayed their departure, but at last the skies had cleared, promising a fine day. Celia, tucked into the stern of the sturdy little craft and snuggled beneath a woolen blanket, scarcely stopped for breath as the story of Louisa's visit poured out of her. Sutton's return from Charleston the previous week had been delayed, and Celia hadn't wanted to tell anyone else about Louisa's startling claim.

"How do you know the girl is telling the truth?" Sutton asked.

"She knew Septima's name, which I didn't know myself until I found Aunt Eugenia's diary. Somehow Louisa found out her mother had died in our carriage house. Aunt Eugenia's diary mentioned that my uncle's mistress had a child. It's hard to tell Louisa's age exactly, but with the dates in the diary—it's not out of the question."

Sutton let out a low whistle.

"Septima left St. Simons just before her baby was born and returned shortly afterward. When Aunt Eugenia found out about the affair, she left St. Simons, and Uncle Magnus followed her here. Apparently Septima followed them to Savannah—or else my uncle provided a place for her to live in the city. Aunt Eugenia mentions that he was absent from the island quite a lot, and she mentions seeing the two of them riding in a carriage together in Savannah."

"How in the world did Louisa know it was your family who was involved?"

"After Septima's death, my uncle disappeared. Friends of Septima's living on St. Simons raised Louisa. When they finally told her as much as they knew of the story, she stowed away on Captain Stevens's boat and came here to Savannah to find out the rest for herself."

Celia watched a wood duck flapping along the water's surface. "It was just a coincidence that Mrs. Clayton asked Ivy and me to help Louisa catch up on her reading."

They approached the landing. Celia steadied herself as the boat scraped the sandy bottom.

Sutton rested the oars in the locks but made no move to go ashore. "You haven't told Ivy she has a half sister?"

"Not yet."

"How do you know Louisa won't spill the beans?"

"I told her I wouldn't mention to the police that I caught her trespassing on my property if she would wait and let me tell Ivy in my own way. You know how flighty Ivy can be when she's upset, and I don't want her worrying Papa. He has not been sleeping well lately, and there is no need to make matters worse by bringing up this entire sordid episode."

Sutton released a noisy breath. "What a story. It is unsavory, but darling, it has nothing to do with you. Magnus Lorens is not your blood kin, and even if he were, no one could hold you or your father accountable for his sins."

"I know. And I will tell Ivy soon. But I want our wedding to be perfect and not marred by fresh gossip. If word gets out that Ivy and Louisa are half sisters—"

"Don't worry." He smiled into her eyes. "Our wedding will be perfect. You'll see."

"I hope so, for Papa's sake as well as ours."

"So do I. But the weather is fine, and we have the afternoon to ourselves. Just for today, let's put everything else out of our minds and enjoy it." Sutton secured the boat to the rotted wooden pilings and helped Celia out, then reached for the picnic hamper Mrs. Maguire had packed.

The area was much as Celia remembered it—flat and overgrown, veined with narrow paths leading into the woods and the rice fields beyond. She studied the trunks of the old trees, wondering which one bore the marks of Sutton's pocketknife. Together they started up a narrow footpath that disappeared into the old forest. The wind stirred the Spanish moss draping the gnarled oaks. The brown leaves trembled with the shadows of a pair of jays.

After a few moments Sutton stopped and pointed. "It must be right around here somewhere."

Celia looked past his shoulder to a massive oak whose branches spread across the path and over the water. "Is that it?"

He grinned. "I think so."

They picked their way through the undergrowth and stopped beneath the tree. "There's your initial, Celia. And here's mine."

He set down their basket and ran his fingers over the carvings. "I can't believe they're still here."

"It seems so long ago," she said. "But I remember everything about that night. I was half scared and half thrilled to be out here with you, alone in the dark. It seemed very grown-up and very adventurous."

He laughed. "I was the one who was scared. I was dying to impress you, and after that old woman showed up and then got hurt, I figured you'd never speak to me again."

"I knew it was an accident." She smiled up at him. "I've never doubted your good intentions, your good heart. It's one of the things I love most about you."

"Really?" Sutton folded his arms and leaned against the tree, clearly enjoying her compliment. "What else do you find irresistible? My amazing business acumen? My skill on the dance floor? My devastating good looks?"

She tilted her head and pretended to consider. "No, all in all, I'd have to say it's your incredible modesty."

He threw back his head and laughed, and she joined in.

He lifted her off her feet and twirled her around. "Celia Francesca Browning, I do love you quite beyond all reason."

He bent his head to kiss her, and she was lost in the moment, all her troubles forgotten. All she felt was Sutton—his warmth, his touch, his tenderness, and his strength.

They drew apart. A wave of emotion pulled at her like an undertow. She watched the play of sun and shadow on his face, and suddenly he looked as he had as a young boy with the sun on his shoulders, intent upon the steamers and schooners in the harbor, one hand shading his eyes against the brittle light reflecting off the river. Despite the difficulties of an Atlantic crossing in winter, Celia was impatient to begin their voyage to England, to share his love of ships and the sea.

He retrieved their basket and took her hand. "Hungry?"

"A little." She chafed her arms. "A bit chilly as well. I'm glad Mrs. Maguire insisted we bring an extra blanket."

"Let's find a spot to build a fire and warm up that coffee you brought."

Hand in hand they retraced their steps along the tangled footpath. Sutton told her about the shipment of lumber he was readying for transport to Jamaica and about some improvements he was making to the *Celia B.* She told him about the Christmas preparations taking place at home and the gifts she had purchased for her father and Ivy.

"Nothing for me?" he teased when she paused for breath.

"Of course I've bought you a present, but I don't want to talk about it. You're too good at guessing, and I want you to be surprised."

He grinned. "So long as Ivy doesn't surprise me with more gifts. I never know what to make of her."

Celia jammed her hands into her pockets. "Sometimes I don't either. She has always set so much store by presents. Once, Ivy told Papa she wanted a doll she had seen in a shop window downtown. It was beautiful and shockingly expensive. But it was Ivy's birthday, so Papa bought it for her. Aunt Eugenia had been dead for less than a year, and I suppose he thought the doll would comfort her somehow."

They walked for some time, discussing this and that, Sutton's occasional laughter ringing through the trees. Celia paused while Sutton lifted a fallen branch from the path, then returned to the subject of her cousin and their difficult kinship. "One year when my birthday came around, Papa gave me a blown-glass carousel with six white horses that pranced when you pressed a button to start music playing."

The memory slowed her steps along the narrow path. "It was the most enchanting thing I'd ever seen. Papa said my mother had purchased it in Paris before I was born. I kept it beside my bed and played with it every night just before going to sleep. It was like keeping a little part of her with me." Sutton placed an arm around her shoulders to draw her closer, but he didn't interrupt. "One day I found Ivy in my room, playing with the carousel. I yelled at her to put it down, that it was mine. And the next thing I knew it was on the floor, broken into a million pieces."

Celia paused, surprised at the anger she felt even now. "Of

course Ivy claimed it was an accident. Mrs. Maguire took her side and told me I had to forgive Ivy because she was an orphan."

A thorn caught at her skirt as they passed, and she yanked it free. "It was that way for most of our childhood. Even though Ivy is older, I was always the one expected to forgive and forget." Celia shrugged. "She would never admit it, but she's envious that I'm younger and marrying first."

They continued along the path until they reached a clearing near the river's edge. Sutton set the basket down. "Maybe she'll meet someone at our Christmas party next Friday."

"Your mother told me she's invited half of Savannah."

Sutton laughed. "It's not much of an exaggeration. Mrs. Johns has been baking all week. If half the city shows up at my house, there has to be at least one acceptable bachelor in the lot." He looked around. "Wait here. I'll get some wood for the fire. I won't be long."

Celia watched him disappear into the trees. To her left, the river shimmered beneath the pale winter sun. A squirrel darted across the clearing and scampered up a tree. She spread the tablecloth on the ground, then set out their plates and cups. The jar of coffee Mrs. Maguire had sent was still warm in her hands, but already the winter afternoon was waning. The wind was rising, bringing a chill from the river.

She heard a noise behind her and turned to look over her shoulder, certain she'd heard someone breathing. But that was impossible. Hardly anyone came out here these days. Unless the old woman who lived here all those years ago was still around.

A twig snapped. An icicle of fear pricked her heart. Something was alive in the silence, and she was suddenly afraid. She scrambled to her feet. "Who's there?"

A moment later she heard footsteps on the forest floor and let out a relieved sigh. "Sutton?"

"No. Not Sutton." Ivy emerged from the shadows and crossed into the clearing, a picnic basket over her arm.

Celia frowned. "You scared the life out of me!"

"Sorry."

"What are you doing here? I thought you were busy at the circulating library today."

"Oh, they can do without me. Mr. Truesdale and Mrs. Boles have everything under control, so I decided to join your outing." Ivy nodded toward her basket. "I hope you don't mind."

"I do mind. This is the first time Sutton and I have had an afternoon to ourselves since he got home. I wish you wouldn't spoil it." Celia looked around the clearing. "How did you get here anyway?"

"My *sister* rowed me over. Technically, my half sister, but I guess a half is better than nothing."

Celia gaped at her. "How did you find out?"

"Louisa told me."

"She promised not to."

Ivy's blue eyes flashed. "How could you be so selfish as to keep that kind of news from me?"

"I intended to tell you, once I figured out what Louisa wants."

"What she wants?"

"Don't you think she will want an inheritance of some sort? Now that she knows she's related to us, she won't be content to stitch monograms in a linen shop."

"You're wrong about Louisa. She only wants a family, and I'm all she's got." Ivy shifted her basket to her other arm. "However, since my father sold off everything years ago, we do need money. Surely Uncle David can afford to give Louisa and me the same ten thousand he's given you. And don't bother to deny it. I heard the whole conversation."

"Eavesdropping doesn't become you, Ivy. And no, I won't hear of Papa's giving her a dime. He is not responsible for Uncle

Magnus's sins, and I will not have him upset over this. A shock like this might well kill him."

Ivy's expression went hard. For the first time in their lives, Celia saw real hate in her cousin's eyes. "It isn't only the money you want," Celia said.

"You're right. It isn't." Ivy scanned the clearing. "Where is Sutton anyway?"

"He'll be right back, and he will not be pleased to find you here." Celia struggled to soften her tone. "I suspect you have developed tender feelings for him. But you cannot make someone love you if he doesn't. And you can't buy love with knitted scarves or a compass."

"I know that."

"Well then?"

"I heard that sob story you told Sutton just now—about the stupid broken carousel." Ivy fiddled with the cover of her basket as she spoke. "I suppose in some way I've always wanted whatever you had. And you've always had your heart's desires."

"But I—"

Celia froze as Ivy reached into the basket and brought out a pistol.

"Ivy. What are you doing?" Her mouth was dry, her heart beat wildly. "Put that thing down before somebody gets hurt."

"I believe that's the general intention."

Celia licked her lips. "You may be many things, but you are not a killer."

Ivy gave a short laugh. "How can you be so sure?"

"What are you talking about?" Celia felt faint. Had Ivy harmed Sutton? Surely Celia would have heard the shot.

"Oh, don't worry. I would never harm Sutton. I was talking about the woman in the carriage house. Louisa's mother. Only I didn't know that then, of course."

"You didn't kill Septima. She hanged herself. I saw the remnants of the noose myself."

Ivy slowly shook her head. "I was playing in the garden that day, and when it started raining, I ran into the carriage house. Septima was standing on a table with the noose already around her neck. The table was about to collapse beneath her. One leg had already splintered. I could see she was scared to move. And for a minute, I thought of calling my papa to come get her down. But then I thought of how she was the reason Mama died and Papa was so angry all the time and drinking too much, and his drinking was making Uncle David mad at us.

"I walked over to the table. She looked down and said, 'Help me.' But I didn't. I kicked the table away. There was an awful sound, and then it was all over."

"Dear God in heaven." Celia eyed the weapon. Ivy seemed to have forgotten it.

Ivy shrugged. "Papa found me in the carriage house and realized what had happened. I remember there was some sort of commotion on the street, people milling about, and we went back through the tunnel to the attic so that nobody would see us leaving the carriage house."

"So that's how you knew about the little door. Though you claimed otherwise."

Ivy ignored that. "He knew if he left Savannah immediately, everyone would blame him for her death. So he disappeared—to spare me. To give me a chance at a decent life. And then Mr. Channing showed up here last September, asking questions. And you started poking around, looking into the story. I tried to scare you, to make you stop, but—"

"Wait a minute. You are the one who sent those anonymous notes?"

"No, Mr. Channing did that. But don't blame him. He was trying to help me."

"Because?"

"He thought I knew more than I did. I fooled him too."

"The bracelet?"

Ivy smiled. "Now that was my idea. I figured if you were worried that someone wanted you dead, you might leave Savannah."

"And then you would have Sutton all for yourself?"

Ivy shrugged again.

Celia shook her head. "How could someone as smart as you hatch such a childish—?"

"I'm back, my love." Sutton strode into the clearing, his arms full of firewood.

Ivy swung around and leveled the gun at his chest. "Hello, my darling."

Sutton went ashen. He tossed the firewood onto the ground. "Ivy? What's going on here?"

"I've come to claim what is mine."

"What on earth are you talking about?"

"Well, you're not mine yet, but you will be."

"You intend to shoot me?"

"Only if Celia refuses to cooperate."

Ivy drew a brown bottle from the basket. Celia gaped at it. "That's Papa's laudanum."

"Yes, it is. And you, my *treasured* cousin, are going to drink it all."

"Ivy, you don't want to do this." Sutton moved toward her, but she lifted the pistol again. "Stay back."

Turning to Celia, Ivy said, "Suicide by laudanum is not that uncommon. But don't worry; it's a painless way to go. Much better than death by hanging, I can assure you."

"Nobody will believe I took my own life," Celia said. "Not with my wedding coming up."

"They'll believe it when I explain that you found Sutton and me here and became distraught when you found out he loves me and not you."

"That's ridiculous," Sutton said. "Ivy, you're not thinking straight. What makes you think I'd ever go along with that?"

"I know it's a shock, Sutton, the idea of marrying me, but I have many good qualities that you will come to appreciate by and by," Ivy said. "You have to give me a chance."

Celia felt tears building behind her eyes. How had her cousin become so unhinged and yet managed to appear so normal? Were there clues Celia had missed along the way?

Ivy waved the pistol. "You will drink the laudanum, Cousin. Or I will shoot him through the heart. Then neither of us will have him."

"Ivy, please listen to me. This is—"

"The Bible says there is no greater love than to lay down your life for a friend. Do you love Sutton enough to die for him?"

Sutton's eyes sought Celia's. Her pulse thrummed in her ears as if she'd fallen from her horse and was lying on the hard ground. Winded and terrified that any sudden movement might break her in two.

"Yes, Ivy. I love him that much."

"Of course you do." Ivy shoved the bottle into Celia's hands. "Now, drink."

22

"NO!" SUTTON KNOCKED THE BOTTLE FROM CELIA'S HAND and stepped in front of Ivy, the barrel of the gun pressing against his chest. "Go ahead. My life for hers."

They stood there in tableau for what seemed hours until Ivy slowly lowered the weapon. Tears ran down her cheeks.

"That's what I thought." Sutton took the gun from her hand and studied it. "This belongs to Mr. Browning."

Stunned, Celia watched the contents of the medicine bottle soaking into the ground. Black spots danced before her eyes. She sank to her knees and felt Sutton's arms go around her.

"You're all right, darling. Just keep breathing."

"I can't believe she was going to shoot you."

"This weapon is a relic—an old dueling pistol. I doubt it would have fired even if Ivy had been brave enough to pull the trigger."

Now Celia recognized the weapon as one of the pair Papa kept on display in his study.

Sutton kept one eye on Ivy, who had collapsed into a heap on the ground, her rose-colored gown billowing up around her. "Mr. Browning showed me the pistols once when we were discussing weapons for the Chatham Artillery."

Dimly Celia heard Ivy's plaintive voice. "All I wanted was to be normal. To have a home and family of my own. But I never had a chance. Not a single chance in life."

"It was a terrible misfortune," Sutton said, "losing your parents at such a tender age. But the Brownings gave you every chance. And this ill-conceived scheme is how you sought to repay them?"

"Opportunity." Ivy looked up at them, her expression so full of pain that Celia had to look away. "But not love. In all those years, you'd think someone could manage to love me."

Despite everything, Celia felt a rush of sympathy for her cousin, and deep regret that she hadn't seen before what seemed so clear now: Ivy's barbed remarks and sarcasm, her brittle laughter and blithe chatter, hid a heart broken by longing and loneliness.

"Ivy," Celia said. "Papa and I do love you. Perhaps we didn't express it in so many words, but haven't we provided for your every need? Encouraged you to socialize with our friends? Papa would have settled a sum on you had you accepted that marriage proposal. But—"

"Mr. Carlisle didn't care for me—not in the way I wanted. And I didn't love him either." Ivy pulled a handkerchief from her sleeve and mopped her face. "I couldn't even attract a poor Irish drayman! And now it's too late to marry anyone." She turned her red-rimmed eyes on Sutton. "I suppose now you'll turn me over to the police."

"If Celia weren't involved, I certainly would," Sutton said. "I don't take kindly to armed threats. But I won't subject Celia or her father to the difficulties of a prosecution."

"Prosecution?" Ivy got to her feet. "You said yourself the gun wouldn't fire."

"That's hardly the point, is it?" Sutton drew Celia closer to his side. "Feeling better, darling?"

Celia couldn't stop shaking. "A little."

Sutton opened the jar of coffee and poured some into a cup. "Drink this."

It was bitter and cold, but it cleared her head. Celia drank it all and set down the cup. Sutton helped her to her feet and stood with one arm around her shoulder. "Let's go home."

"What about me?" Ivy asked, her voice suddenly panicked. "Louisa borrowed a boat and rowed me over here, but I told her I'd be coming back with you."

"A grave miscalculation," Sutton said.

"You can't leave me here. It's getting cold, and it will be dark soon. I could die from the cold. Or from a snakebite." Ivy's eyes were like a child's—fearful and brimming with tears. "But maybe that would be best for everyone."

Sutton let out an exasperated sigh. "No need for such histrionics. We'll take you back with us. But you'll have to find another place to stay. Celia can't possibly trust you now."

Ivy shook her head. "I can't leave Madison Square. I have no inheritance of my own. Nothing except what Uncle David provides."

Sutton bent to gather their things and tucked the empty laudanum bottle into the basket along with the pistol. "Perhaps you can stay with your newfound sister until arrangements are made for you to leave Savannah."

Ivy lifted her chin, suddenly defiant. "If I do leave town, it will be on my own terms."

Celia reached for her cousin's hand, but Ivy jerked away with a ferocity Celia had never before seen. Clearly Ivy's state of mind had worsened, her moods swinging wildly. If only Celia had seen it coming. Now however, despite her sympathy for Ivy, she had to think of her father. "I can't have you upsetting Papa. If you don't leave at once, I will file a complaint with the police." Her voice shook. "I'll tell them everything."

Ivy laughed. "No you won't. You care too much about your precious reputation. Nothing must be allowed to sully the noble Browning name and scandalize your high-society friends. That's why you were so desperate to silence Mr. Channing."

"You're right. I am afraid of losing our good name and the respect of our friends. I don't want the past to cast a shadow over my marriage and over the lives of our children." Celia squeezed Sutton's hand and met her cousin's watery stare. "But I can't worry about how people will talk. Not now. I can't allow you to stay on at our house, stealing my father's medicine, listening at the keyhole to our private conversations, and plotting another ridiculous scheme to come between Sutton and me."

Sutton stuffed the tablecloth into the picnic basket. "We ought to get going. Dark comes early this time of year." He handed Ivy the basket in which she'd hidden the dueling pistol. "You first."

Ivy tossed her curls and spun away, heading along the narrow footpath toward the landing and the waiting boat. Sutton stowed both baskets and handed Ivy into the stern. "Sit there. Don't move."

"Goodness, Sutton, you don't have to be so mean."

He ignored her and seated Celia, then pushed the boat into the water.

A flock of birds exploded from the undergrowth, their cries breaking the strained silence. Celia looked to the west, where the sunset was fading to a luminous gold, streaks of apricot and lavender draining into the deep indigo of the coming winter's night. She felt another tab of pity for her cousin. But Ivy had made her choices. Now she would live with the consequences.

They neared the Broad Street dock, and Sutton feathered the oars, waiting for a small sloop, its sails furled, to tie up at the wharf. Then he brought their boat in, tied up, and helped Celia and Ivy onto the wooden pier. Wordlessly they walked the short distance to the livery, where they retrieved Sutton's horse and rig.

The gaslights were just coming on as the horse trotted along the sandy streets. Lamplight glowed in the windows of houses along Drayton Street, and wreaths of greenery decorated the doors of Celia's neighbors on Madison Square. Christmas was her favorite time of year, but the events of the day had stolen her joy and the happy anticipation of the holiday.

Sutton guided the horse onto Harris Street and stopped his rig at the Brownings' gate. The windows in the parlor and in Papa's study glowed with soft light. Smoke from the twin fireplaces spiraled into the darkness.

Finally Sutton said to Ivy, "I've a ship leaving for Havana Monday morning. I'll see to passage for you. And your sister, if she wants to go."

"Havana? What on earth will I do there?"

"That's up to you. Perhaps you can find work as a lady's companion or in one of the shops along the waterfront. Eventually you might earn enough to pay for passage to Copenhagen and then on to Sweden. If I were a wagering man, I'd bet you'll find your father there."

"But I can't possibly be ready to leave so soon. And anyway, I've lived here since I was a child. What will Uncle David say?"

"He'd say plenty if he knew what you'd done today," Sutton said. "For his sake, we'll tell him you've decided to set out upon a grand adventure. No doubt he'll be disappointed that you won't be here for our wedding. But it's kinder to let him think you chose to leave than to have him know you were willing to murder his only daughter in order to get what you wanted."

"But Sutton, you can't send me to Cuba where I don't know anyone. I don't speak their language. I've never worked at anything other than volunteering at the Female Asylum and the circulating library."

Despite Ivy's crazed scheming, Celia felt responsible for her.

They had grown up together, attended school together. Ivy was ill-prepared to make her own way in the world, and she was, after all, blood kin. In her desperate bid to belong, Ivy had become someone Celia no longer knew. But Celia couldn't turn her cousin out, alone and penniless. "I'll give you some cash to tide you over. I won't let you starve."

Ivy brightened. "You will? You'll give me the ten thousand?"

"Not ten thousand. But enough."

Sutton got out of the rig and helped the women alight. "The *Percival* leaves Savannah on Monday's morning tide," he told Ivy. "I'll send word to the captain to expect you."

He took both Celia's gloved hands in his. "I'll stay here tonight. In the parlor. To keep an eye on things. You'll be safe, my love."

"Thank you." Celia stood on tiptoe and kissed his cheek. "I love you, Sutton Mackay."

"Oh, for heaven's sake, spare me," Ivy said. "It's cold out here. I'm going in."

She turned on her heel and climbed the steps to the door. Celia, saddened and completely bewildered, stared after her.

The smell of biscuits and frying bacon teased Celia awake. She sat up in bed. Maxwell, seeing that his mistress was up, vaulted onto the counterpane and licked her face.

She kissed the top of his warm little head and wondered where the *Percival* was this morning. Together, she and Ivy had told Papa the story they'd devised—that Ivy wanted to see a different part of the world. Papa had been surprised but too weak to ask many questions.

Once Ivy accepted the reality of the situation, she'd made short work of packing up her dresses and shawls, gloves and parasols and walking shoes. By eight o'clock Monday morning, her trunks and hatboxes, her books and her black silk umbrella were stacked in the hallway ready to go.

Mrs. Maguire plodded upstairs with Aunt Eugenia's writing box. "This belonged to your mother. She would have wanted you to have it." Neither she nor Celia said anything about the diary.

It was the only time Ivy shed a tear. She thanked the housekeeper, made room in her trunk for the items, and went downstairs to wait for the carriage.

Presently, Joseph arrived, having already collected Louisa from the boardinghouse. While Joseph loaded Ivy's belongings, Louisa leaned forward and peered out the carriage window, her expression unreadable.

Celia pressed a roll of bills into her cousin's hand. "Sutton says almost everything is inexpensive in Havana. This should last the two of you for a while if you're not extravagant."

Ivy dropped the money into her reticule and squared her shoulders. "Well," she said. "We're off."

She had climbed into the carriage, arranged her skirts, and waived gaily, as if she were on her way to make morning calls. And Celia had stood at the gate, watching, until the carriage was out of sight. Pages of her past, a complicated tangle of love and grief and obligation, had been torn away as surely as had the pages of her aunt's red diary.

Now Ivy's room across the hall was empty, and the entire house seemed too quiet. Celia threw back her covers and padded across the room to tend the fire. She shucked off her nightclothes, shivering in the early-morning chill, and dressed quickly.

Mrs. Maguire tapped on her door. "Miss Celia, your breakfast is getting cold."

"I'm coming."

Celia followed Maxwell and the housekeeper down the stairs.

She let the puppy into the garden and filled her plate in the kitchen. She climbed onto the stool and dug in. The biscuits were light as a cloud, the bacon thick and crisp, the grits warm and sweetened with maple syrup. It was her favorite meal from childhood. She regarded the housekeeper fondly. Undoubtedly this repast was Mrs. Maguire's attempt to comfort her in the wake of Ivy's sudden departure.

Mrs. Maguire poured herself a cup of coffee and leaned against the wooden counter. "How are you feelin' this mornin', my girl?"

"All right." Celia buttered a biscuit and spooned on a blob of strawberry jam. "It's quiet upstairs with only Papa and me."

"Humph. It'll be even quieter here when you are married and off on your own."

"Once we're back from England, Sutton and I will be here so often you'll grow quite weary of us. You'll see."

"I can't imagine that."

Mrs. Maguire studied Celia over the rim of her cup, her expression so intent that Celia began to squirm. "Are you goin' to tell me what really happened between you and Miss Ivy? It must have been something awful bad. I don't believe for one minute she just up and decided to go see the world. Miss Ivy is not the adventurin' kind."

Celia's appetite fled. She set down her butter knife. "Mrs. Maguire, do you believe some houses are cursed?"

"Cursed? By my faith, child, what kind of blather is that?"

The emotions Celia had fought so hard to control bubbled to the surface. "When that reporter, Leo Channing, wrote his first article for the paper last fall, he called our home the house of love and grief. He said the house was cursed because of what happened to my mother and then to Aunt Eugenia and the laundress. I didn't believe it then. But now that Ivy has—well, it seems that every woman who lives here comes to grief."

"What on earth are you talkin' about? I niver heard of such nonsense."

Celia had no doubt that whatever she told the housekeeper would never be repeated. Mrs. Maguire had been both mother and servant, confidante and friend. She was the very soul of discretion, the only one to whom Celia could unburden herself. It was true that the housekeeper had not been completely forthcoming, but surely she'd had her reasons.

"Ivy got the strange notion that she could force Sutton into marrying her."

Celia poured more coffee and told Mrs. Maguire the entire story—the anonymous notes, the bracelet, the trip to Screven's Landing, and everything that had happened there. But she saw no reason to share Ivy's confession about her role in the death in the carriage house. "Ivy was jealous of me when we were children, but I never realized she hated me."

Mrs. Maguire sank into her chair by the window. "By all the saints, I niver would've thought Miss Ivy could do such a thing. She's always been a moody one and high strung, but to think she's capable of stealing Mr. Browning's medicine and his pistol and doin' away with her own kin . . . I just can't countenance it, that's all." She sighed. "On the other hand I guess I know how she felt. Fear is a powerful feelin', Miss Celia."

"Fear? Ivy had a very secure life here. She had nothing to be afraid of."

"Until you started askin' questions about how Miss Eugenia died and what happened in the carriage house."

Celia didn't try to hide her surprise. "You know what she did?"

Mrs. Maguire drained her cup. "What do you suppose people fear most in the world?"

Celia shrugged. "Death, I suppose."

"No, darlin'. They fear loss. Miss Ivy lost her mother and then her father. Then you became engaged to Sutton, and Mr. Browning got sick. That poor girl was about to lose you and the uncle who provided for her. I can imagine her lyin' awake and worryin' about what would happen to her then. She needed a husband to make her feel safe, and Sutton was the only good man she knew."

"That was her own fault. She never wanted to go to dances or to meet any of the boys in our circle. Besides, I'm sure Papa made provisions for her in his will." Celia's coffee had gone cold. She poured a fresh cup. "You still haven't answered my question."

A carriage drew up at the gate. Mrs. Maguire peered out the window. "Here's the doctor."

Celia left the kitchen and met Dr. Dearing at the door. He set his medical bag down and removed his coat and hat. "How is your father today?"

"I'm worried. He hasn't been to Commerce Row since Monday, and you know how much he loves being there."

Dr. Dearing nodded.

"We're going to need a new supply of laudanum," Celia said. "The bottle you left last time got broken."

"I see. When was this?"

"Last Saturday. I went to your office on Monday to get more, but you were out."

They started up the curving staircase together. "I was over on St. Simons," the doctor said, "tending to the Couper twins. Just got back this morning. I came as soon as I received your message."

Celia led him down the hall to her father's room and tapped on the door.

"Leave us for a few moments," the doctor said. "I'll be down to speak with you as soon as I finish my examination."

Celia returned to the parlor to wait. Mrs. Maguire had stoked the fire in the black-marble fireplace and filled a silver tray with the tea things and a plate of the cookies she'd baked for Christmas.

Celia alternately sat and paced and peered out the window. What was taking the doctor so long?

Finally he came down and joined her in the parlor. He refused her offer of refreshments and perched on the edge of the chair nearest the fire.

Celia found herself near tears. "How is he?"

"Well, palpations and percussion of the chest indicate that the dropsy has worsened." He cleared his throat. "That is, the fluid accumulating throughout his body has increased. This is not unexpected in such cases."

"But he will be all right? At least for a while longer?"

"Your father's condition seems to be developing more rapidly than I'd hoped, but the course of hypertrophy is unpredictable. As I said when he first became ill, he might linger in this slow decline, or his heart may give out suddenly." The doctor's expression softened. "You must prepare yourself, my dear. Only God knows when the end will come, but I cannot help thinking it will be fairly soon."

She nodded. None of this was news, of course, and the doctor had done his best to soften the blow, but the impending loss was enough to break her heart in two. Strangely, she found herself missing Ivy's presence.

"I've given him a new tincture of laudanum, which will allow him to rest more comfortably," the doctor continued. "I would suggest he refrain from eating ham and bacon. Anything salty will make him retain more fluids. Other than that, you can only keep him calm, keep his spirits up."

The doctor took off his spectacles and polished them on the sleeve of his jacket. "Despite his condition he seems quite excited about Christmas and about your wedding. Let him celebrate as much as he wants to." He retrieved his hat and coat. "I wish I could offer more encouraging news, but in cases like this it's better to be prepared."

"Thank you for coming, Dr. Dearing."

"No trouble. I'll be by after Christmas to check on him, but of course send for me anytime if you need me."

"I will."

She remained calm and composed as she saw him out. Then the tears came.

23

Every window of the Mackays' mansion glowed with golden candlelight. Wreaths of evergreens and mistletoe decorated the curved wrought-iron staircase leading to the front door, lending the entire house a festive air.

Joseph helped Papa out of the carriage. Celia looped her arm through his. "Are you warm enough, Papa?"

His blue eyes twinkled. "I am, and please do not start clucking over me like a mother hen. I intend to enjoy myself tonight without reminders of my infirmities."

"I'm glad you felt well enough to come out tonight. And aren't I lucky to be escorted by the handsomest man in Savannah."

He laughed and patted her arm as they made their way up the stairs to the front door. Behind them came the sounds of prancing hooves and jingling harness as other carriages arrived for the Mackays' Christmas Eve party.

The Mackays' housekeeper opened the door and beamed at Celia and her father. "There you are, Mr. Browning. It surely does my heart good to see you up and about, sir."

"Thank you." Papa handed her his hat and unbuttoned his coat. "It's good to be among friends on such a beautiful night. There's something special about Savannah at Christmas, don't you think, Mrs. Johns?"

The housekeeper bobbed her head, stepped behind him to greet the Greens and the Sorrels, and waited while greetings were exchanged. Then she directed everyone to the library, where a cheerful fire blazed in the grate and candlelight danced against the pale green walls.

"David. And Celia." Mr. Mackay bowed to Celia, shook Papa's hand, and directed him to a chair near the fire before turning to the other guests. Celia arranged her skirts and nodded to the other ladies, who were busy chatting with Mrs. Mackay.

Sutton's mother excused herself, crossed the room, and bent to embrace Celia. "You look lovely, my dear. Despite recent events, I do hope you have a wonderful Christmas."

"You too." Celia squeezed Cornelia's hands and made room for the older woman on the embroidered settee. Though she loved every room of the Mackays' house, this one was her favorite because it held the most reminders of Sutton's boyhood. She glanced at his framed charcoal sketches of the great herons on St. Simons, wings spread as they circled the marshes. The medals he had won at school, the jumble of mementos from the Mackay family trips to Europe that spilled from shelves flanking the fireplace.

"Has my son seen you in that dress?" Mrs. Mackay asked.

Celia shook her head. "It's new. Mrs. Foyle received a shipment from Paris a few weeks ago, and I saw this one when I went for my final gown fitting. The color is called ashes of roses."

"Well, it's very becoming."

"It was an extravagance, but when I bought it, I thought I could wear it during our wedding trip abroad. But now—"

"Celia." Sutton made his way across the crowded library and bent to kiss her cheek. "I must go back upstairs in a moment to get

Grandmother, but she insisted I not keep you waiting any longer." His eyes shone with admiration and affection. "New gown?"

She nodded and blinked back sudden tears.

He frowned. "You don't like it? I think it's quite fetching."

"Thank you. I—"

"You're still upset about what happened last week."

Mrs. Mackay murmured, "Sutton told us about it. I'm so sorry for all of it, but I hope you won't dwell on it, my dear. Don't let it spoil your Christmas Eve."

Celia saw her father watching her from across the room and forced a smile. "I won't. Papa has so looked forward to this evening."

"I'm sorry not to have invited more young people. I'm sure you would have enjoyed seeing Alicia Thayer. And Mary Quarterman. But I trimmed the guest list so as not to tire your father overmuch."

"That was very thoughtful." Celia looked around the room at the faces of her father's oldest friends—the Greens and the Sorrels, the Lawtons, the Stileses, and the Dicksons. She had known them all her life. And tonight, not one of them had asked after Ivy. She was grateful for their discretion.

"Perhaps it's just as well you didn't invite Mary," Celia said. "She's mostly kept her distance all season. Last Sunday at church, she brushed past me without a single word."

"Because of that silly business with that newspaperman?" Cornelia shook her head. "Anyone who pays the slightest attention to him does not deserve your friendship. But perhaps Mary was simply preoccupied. Mrs. Dickson told me the Quartermans are entertaining cousins from the North for Christmas, and apparently the Northern folk have some very strange notions about us."

Sutton raised a brow. "Such as?"

"They think we're all slaveholders and not fit for the company of enlightened abolitionists such as themselves. Mrs. Dickson said they were astonished to learn that slaveholders are in the minority almost everywhere in the South."

"Alicia Thayer's kin in Philadelphia told her the same thing," Celia said. "If you ask me, despite their air of superiority, the Northerners seem shockingly ill-informed."

Sutton grinned. "Well said. Excuse me, ladies. I must get Grandmother before Mrs. Johns sounds the dinner gong."

He left the library and returned a bit later with Mrs. Manigault, who looked regal in a cranberry-hued gown trimmed with black lace. The gentlemen rose as she entered the room. Mrs. Manigault took her time greeting each guest, her melodious voice warm with welcome, the suite of diamonds she'd donned for the occasion glittering in the candlelight.

"Mrs. Mackay?" Mrs. Johns said from the doorway. "Dinner is ready."

"Thank you." Mrs. Mackay nodded to her guests. "Ladies and gentlemen, shall we go in?"

Mr. Mackay escorted his wife. Sutton followed with his grandmother, and Celia went in on her father's arm. The rest of the guests entered the sumptuous dining room, exclaiming over the table draped in heavy white damask and set with the Mackays' best bone china. A blazing candelabra and deep red roses in silver bowls reflected the candlelight.

Two uniformed serving girls brought in each course—soup, oysters, roast capon, and a platter of root vegetables. While they ate, Mr. Stiles regaled the guests with a tale of the baseball game he'd attended in New York in the summer. "I don't believe I've ever heard a more lively crowd," he said, gesturing with his oyster fork. "My ears rang for the better part of an hour after the game ended."

"I heard that more than a thousand people were in attendance," Mrs. Lawton said. "Imagine that many people willing to pay fifty cents to watch a bunch of rowdy men hit a ball with a wooden club. I'm sure I would not find such a game appealing in the least."

"It was quite exciting," Mr. Stiles said. "The team from Brooklyn got eighteen hits and still lost to the New York All Stars." He paused while one of the serving girls refilled his glass. "I won't be surprised if baseball becomes the most popular sport in the entire country one of these days."

"It will never surpass the reading of a good book as entertainment, Mr. Stiles," Mrs. Manigault said. "For us women especially there is nothing more delightful than the prospect of a new book." She looked around the table, her eyes bright with curiosity. "Has anyone else read *The Courtship of Miles Standish*?"

Mr. Green shook his head. "Can't say as I have, Miss Caroline. I never was one for Mr. Longfellow's writings. I'm afraid I don't find them very entertaining."

Mr. Sorrel's dark eyes glinted with amusement. "You're very much in the minority then, Charles. Just last week, I read in the paper that Mr. Longfellow sold over three hundred thousand copies of his works last year."

Mr. Mackay turned to Papa. "You're awfully quiet tonight, David."

Celia tensed at the thought that Papa might be feeling worse, but he lifted a brow and smiled at their host. "I'm enjoying the discussion. I've never seen a baseball game. It sounds like fun."

Papa caught Mr. Green's eye. "I saw a whole army of men over on Macon Street last week. Working on your house, I suppose."

"Yes, but progress is slow. I don't imagine it will be finished for another year or two." Mr. Green picked up his fork and speared a bit of potato. "I want the best of everything, and perfection takes time."

Sutton winked at Celia. Everyone in Savannah knew the story of Mr. Green's arrival from England when he was just a boy. With hardly a cent to his name, he'd taken a job as a clerk and eventually gone into the cotton-exporting business with Mr. Low. Now he was among the richest men in Savannah. The house he was building on Macon Street would be the fanciest and most expensive on Madison Square.

Mrs. Johns and the serving girls came in with dessert—iced fruitcakes decorated with tiny spun-sugar snowflakes, an English trifle in a tall crystal bowl, and coffee and hot chocolate in gleaming silver pots. While they enjoyed the "afters," Mrs. Stiles and Mrs. Lawton spoke of plans to expand the Savannah Club and to organize a series of fishing trips to Isle of Hope once spring arrived.

"I do hope our young newlyweds will have returned from their travels by then." Mrs. Lawton fingered her jeweled necklace and smiled at Celia. "Our little excursions won't be the same without you, my dear."

Suddenly Celia found it hard to breathe. She pushed away from the table and got to her feet. The gentlemen rose with her.

"Celia, are you all right?" Papa asked.

"I'm fine. I need a breath of air is all."

"It is rather warm in here, Cornelia," Mrs. Manigault said. "Since everyone has finished, why don't we adjourn to the library and leave the men to their cigars?"

Sutton rounded the table, and took Celia's arm. "Come on. I'll walk you out for a moment."

Celia let him lead her out of the dining room and through the entry foyer to the door. On the way out, Sutton snagged her cloak from the hall tree, and when they reached the front steps he helped her into it. "Take some deep breaths, darling."

She filled her lungs and stared at the flickering gaslights lining the street, the row of waiting carriages, the elegant houses dressed in their holiday finery. Christmas was supposed to be a time of joy and celebration, but all she felt was the beginning of grief. "Papa is dying."

They sat down on the steps. Sutton drew her close and released a gusty sigh. "I know it. I've watched him weaken over these past weeks down on the Row, struggling to pretend nothing is wrong. I hate that there is nothing I can do for him. For you."

"Oh, Sutton, I waited so long for you to come home so we could begin our life together. But I can't marry and sail for England—not with him in this condition. I can't leave him to die without me."

"Of course not."

"Then you agree we'll have to postpone everything until . . ."

"I'm willing to wait, but I think we should ask your father what he wants."

She shook her head. "He will tell me to go to England. He will put my happiness ahead of his own. He always has."

"That's what the best of fathers do."

Tears ran down her face. "How can I possibly live without him? For most of my life he has been both mother and father to me."

Sutton fished a handkerchief from his pocket and handed it over.

She sniffed and wiped her eyes. "Maybe Leo Channing is right. Maybe our house is cursed."

"You don't believe that."

"After everything that happened with Ivy, I don't know what to believe anymore. About anything."

"Believe this." Taking her face in his hands, he planted a reverent kiss on her lips. She clung to him, a swell of feeling—powerful and bittersweet—stopping further words.

"Whatever comes, we'll get through it together," he said. "However long it takes, one day you will be my wife. The beautiful, young Mrs. Mackay."

His voice cracked, and in the lambent light she saw the shine of tears in his eyes. Then he smiled and touched the tip of his finger to her nose. "You must marry me now. There is no turning back since you accepted my proposal in front of dozens of witnesses. And since I've already named my best ship after you."

The front door opened, and Mr. Mackay stepped onto the porch. "Is everything all right, son?"

"We're fine, Father," Sutton said. "We'll be there in a minute."

Sutton drew her to her feet and they returned to the party.

Celia prepared a breakfast tray and took it into the library, where Papa had spent the night asleep on the settee. Though he had enjoyed the Mackays' party, the effort had tired him so thoroughly that he couldn't mount the stairs to his own bed nor attend this morning's Christmas service at St. John's. Mrs. Maguire had offered to stay, but Celia insisted she keep her plans to join her friends for church and a late luncheon afterward. Sutton would call in the afternoon. For now, she was alone with her father.

Papa sat up and threw off the coverlet. He rubbed a hand over his stubbled chin. "I must look worse than a stevedore after a three-day bender."

"Not quite that bad." Celia grinned and set the tray on the small table next to the settee. She added wood to the fire in the fireplace, then poured his tea. "Mrs. Maguire is off to meet her friends for church, but she made grits this morning. I made toast and eggs and brought the orange marmalade you like."

He frowned. "No ham or bacon? Not even on Christmas Day?"

"You know what Dr. Dearing said. No salt."

"Bah." He picked up his spoon and ate a bite of grits. "Might as well be eating paper."

He glanced up at her. "Aren't you having breakfast?"

"I'm not hungry. I ate too much at the Mackays' last night."

"Nice try, but I'm your father. I can see when something is worrying you."

"Of course I'm worried, Papa. I hate seeing you so tired and pale."

He sipped his tea, his hand trembling as he set down his cup. "Worrying won't change a thing, darling. Nobody lives forever, and honestly, I'd rather know my days are at an end, so I can make the most of each one."

She nodded and swallowed the painful lump in her throat.

"At least have some tea with me." He gestured toward the china pot. "I hate to eat alone."

"All right." She started toward the kitchen for a cup, just as Maxwell scampered down the stairs. He made a quick detour into the parlor to greet Papa, then followed Celia to the kitchen door, his golden tail fanning the air. She let him out and joined Papa in the library.

Papa spread marmalade on his toast. "Maxwell is certainly a charming little fellow."

She smiled and poured tea into her cup. "Yes. A worthy successor to Jack. When he died, I thought I could never love another dog in the same way, but Maxwell has won my heart."

"What will you do with the dog when you and Sutton leave for England next month?"

"That won't pose a problem because we're postponing our wedding."

"On my account?" Papa shook his head. "That won't do at all, Celia. I appreciate the sentiment, but I can't permit you to postpone your plans because you're waiting for my demise. Sutton has the right idea about building a ship capable of avoiding a Yankee blockade. The sooner he gets started, the better."

"But we don't know for certain that we'll have to fight. And I'd never forgive myself if I left Savannah and came back to find that you had . . . that you were . . ."

"It's a necessary end. It will come when it will come." His expression softened. "As much as I love Savannah, I've always wanted to see the high country. One of these days I reckon I will."

Celia could stop her tears no longer.

Papa set aside his tray and drew her onto the settee. When her sobs finally subsided, he released her and patted her hair. "Enough weeping. It's Christmas."

She pressed the heels of her hands to her eyes. "I don't feel much like celebrating."

"Well, that's too bad because I do. Your presents are in my room, beneath the extra blankets in the clothespress. Go get them, please. And no peeking."

Just then Maxwell barked. Celia let him in and went up to her room to get the gifts she'd bought for Papa and Sutton. In his room she found two packages addressed to her—one heavy, the other light. She carried everything into the parlor.

Papa had moved to his favorite chair by the fire. He smiled when she and Maxwell came in.

She handed him a wrapped package. "You go first."

He tore away the paper to reveal Mr. Wood's book about gold fever in California. "I've been meaning to read this ever since it was published. It will afford many happy hours before the fire this winter."

Her other gift to him was a new muffler made of the finest wool in a blue that matched his eyes. He set it aside and watched as she unwrapped a travel journal bound in dark-blue leather, her initials stamped in gold on the cover. "It's beautiful, Papa. Thank you. Wherever did you find it?"

He smiled. "I ordered it from a store in Charleston. I expect you to fill every page with the details of your trip. It will be something to pass along to your grandchildren one day. Now open the other one."

She unwrapped the heavier package and gave a little gasp of pleasure at the sight of four of her mother's small paintings mounted in matching gilt frames. "These are the pictures I found in the attic."

"Yes. I wanted you to have them for the home you'll share with Sutton. A little piece of this house to take along with you."

She felt a sudden stab of sorrow at the thought of leaving her childhood home. What would happen to this house when Papa was no longer alive?

"I'm leaving the house in trust for you," he said, as if reading her thoughts, "so it will stay in the Browning family. Ivy will need a home when she's done with her grand adventures. But your place will be with Sutton, wherever that turns out to be."

She embraced him and planted a kiss on his head. "I do love you, Papa."

"I suspected as much." He got to his feet. "Could you help me up the stairs? I want to make myself presentable before Sutton arrives."

She wrapped an arm around his waist and helped him up to his room. She brought hot water and towels and his shaving things. While he cleaned up, she took his breakfast tray to the kitchen, tidied the library, and rekindled the fire.

In all of the chaos surrounding Ivy's hurried departure, there had been little time for decorating the house for Christmas, not that she felt like celebrating. But remembering Dr. Dearing's words, she took half a dozen candles and the silver candlesticks from the dining room and arranged them on the mantel in the library. She filled a crystal bowl with cinnamon sticks and oranges, ordered weeks ago for Christmas, and set it on the side table near Papa's chair, then carefully unwrapped her mother's collection of porcelain angels kept in a special box in the parlor.

She arranged the angels on the mahogany side table that had been her mother's.

"It's lovely, Celia. Very festive." Papa came in looking as if he were dressed for a day on Commerce Row and plopped into his chair. The French mantel clock chimed the hour. "What time is Sutton due?"

"Early afternoon—after church and luncheon with his parents." She passed a hand over her hair. "I should go up and get ready. Do you need anything?"

"Not a thing. I'm going to sit here with my new book and enjoy the fire." Maxwell trotted in and sat down beside Papa's chair, his tail thumping the floor. "You go ahead. Take your time. Maxwell will keep me company."

Upstairs Celia bathed and stepped into a forest-green velvet dress trimmed in white lace. What a strange Christmas this was without the big parties her father always hosted, without Ivy running in and out, as excited and expectant as a child. One year the Brownings had spent the holiday on a Waccamaw River rice plantation belonging to Papa's friend Mr. Fraser. The celebration had continued for days with card games, candy pulling, and fireworks. While Celia and Ivy played the piano and sang with the other ladies, Papa and the men had gone hunting. The following year, Papa had hosted the Frasers in Savannah with Christmas dinner for a hundred guests.

Now the house was silent. Celia brushed her hair and thought of Ivy. She imagined her cousin stepping off the *Percival* in Havana, surrounded by strangers speaking a strange tongue. At least Ivy had Louisa for company. Would they make a life in Cuba or undertake a voyage to Sweden to look for Uncle Magnus? Who knew whether he was even alive?

Celia fastened her shoes and, with a final glance in the mirror, went back downstairs. Papa had fallen asleep, his new book open on his lap. Maxwell was curled up before the fire, one paw covering his nose.

She took a chair opposite her father and in the flickering candlelight watched the slow rise and fall of his chest, trying to memorize the sound of his breath, the shape of his hands, the contours of his face.

24

LONG SHADOWS FELL ACROSS THE SQUARE AS SUTTON DREW up at the gate. Leaving her book on her chair, Celia met him at the door. Without waiting to remove his coat and gloves, he folded her into his arms.

"Sorry to be so late. Mr. Lawton caught me after church with a thousand questions about the *Celia B*, and of course that made me late for Mother's Christmas luncheon." He released her and unbuttoned his coat. "How is your—hello, Maxwell."

The puppy had heard the door and now raced along the gallery, barking.

Celia whirled around. "Quiet, Maxwell!" The dog sat, and she turned back to Sutton. "Papa's doing as well as expected. He slept for most of the afternoon."

Sutton hung his coat and hat, and they went into the library.

"Sutton!" Papa rose unsteadily to shake his hand. "Happy Christmas, my boy."

"Thank you, sir. Did we wake you?"

Papa shook his head. "Not really. I was dozing, but I heard your rig coming along the street. I've been inside all day. Tell me, what kind of weather have we today?"

Sutton warmed his hands before the fire. "It's chilly, but I don't mind. The cold weather makes it seem more like Christmas, don't you think?"

"I do. I love the climate here in Savannah, but I wouldn't mind a good snowfall now and then." Papa dropped heavily into his chair. "Celia and I have been talking about your upcoming trip to Liverpool. I'm glad you and Mr. Rutledge are thinking ahead to the time when a blockade-runner might just save the South."

"I hope it won't come to that, but I'm ready to serve Georgia in whatever way becomes necessary." Sutton glanced at Celia. "However, last night Celia and I decided to postpone the Liverpool trip for a while. Griffin Rutledge knows the plan nearly as well as I do. And there is plenty to do here, getting Mackay Shipping back on its—"

Sutton paused as Papa took a deep breath and winced, eyes rounded in surprise. "What's the matter, Mr. Browning? Are you all right?"

"I'm . . . not quite sure. Celia, would you bring a glass of water?"

"Of course. You're in pain, Papa. You need the laudanum."

Celia ran up to his room for the medicine and a glass of water and returned to the library. She measured the tincture into the glass and handed it to her father.

"Not just yet. Once I take it, I'll fall asleep and miss everything."

Sutton frowned. "Perhaps you should lie down, sir."

"In a little while. I want to hear the rest of your plans."

"I was saying that Griff Rutledge can stand in for me in Liverpool. As soon as the Atlantic cable is repaired, I can keep informed of things from here. And Celia and I will be here to look after you."

Papa frowned. "Who knows when that cable will be fully restored? Besides, Mrs. Maguire will see to me."

"I'm not leaving you, Papa," Celia said. "That's final."

He closed his eyes, his face contorted, and took a few shallow breaths. "What day is this?"

"Saturday, Papa. Christmas Day, remember?"

"Do you suppose there's a . . . rule against holding a wedding on Christmas?"

"A—what do you mean?"

Papa reached for her hand. "Something has shifted inside me. I felt it just now. I can't explain how I know, but I have a feeling that my time has grown shorter than I thought. And I don't want to go and miss your wedding."

Celia's mind spun wildly. The wedding was set for late January. Mrs. Hemphill had been engaged to bake a cake for the reception they'd planned. Invitations were due back from the engravers next week. Her trousseau was not nearly complete. She and Sutton had not even discussed where they would live. "But—"

"We have all we need," Papa said. "A beautiful bride, a willing groom, and the rector of St. John's just down the street."

Celia looked at Sutton, a hundred questions in her eyes.

"If Celia is willing, I'm ready," Sutton said. "I would like to change my clothes and collect my parents. And Grandmother. She has been looking forward to the wedding more than anyone. Except me."

Celia knelt beside her father's chair. "If it will make you happy, Papa, of course I'm willing."

Sutton rose. "I'll get my family and send for the rector."

Celia walked with him to the door. "This isn't at all what we planned, but it feels like the right thing to do."

"Yes." He kissed her forehead. "I won't be long."

Celia returned to the library and peeked in. Papa, hands folded across his middle, was already asleep before the fire. The clock chimed as she ascended the stairs to her room, a hundred emotions roiling in her chest.

She loved Sutton with all her heart. And she did want Papa to witness her marriage vows, but everything was happening too fast. The most important day of her life was being compressed into something that, years from now, she would have trouble remembering.

Every woman dreamed of the receptions and parties, the happy anticipation leading up to the ceremony itself, and the dinner afterward where there would be toasts and laughter and a few tears too. If she was totally honest, she had to admit she'd also counted on the wedding as a test of whether Leo Channing's newspaper stories had done any permanent damage to the Browning name.

In her room, she removed her dress and took her wedding gown from the clothespress. She arranged the skirt and the lace veil across her bed, wishing her mother could be here to share her happiness, to whisper the kind of last-minute advice that only a mother could give. She closed her eyes and tried to summon Francesca's face. But so many years had passed that even the few memories she'd tried to hold onto had faded. All she had now were stories. Where would she and Sutton spend their first night as husband and wife? Here? At the Mackays'? Perhaps it was better to be prepared for anything. She packed a few things from her incomplete trousseau—a deep purple day dress, a new dressing gown, her stockings and corset and delicate embroidered underthings.

By the time she was finished it was past four o'clock. She sat at the dressing table and gathered her hair into a fall of curls anchored in place with two jet combs. She dabbed perfume onto each wrist, added a bit of rice powder to her nose and some clear pomade to her lips.

"Celia?"

She opened the door to find Mrs. Manigault standing there, her eyes bright with tears. "Oh, my dear, may I come in?"

Celia stepped aside and fell into the older woman's powder-scented embrace.

"There now, it's all right." Mrs. Manigault patted Celia's shoulder. "I don't blame you for those tears, but you don't want to go downstairs with your eyes all swollen."

Celia pulled away and gulped air. "No, I suppose not."

Mrs. Manigault crossed the room, poured water into the basin, and handed Celia a wet cloth. "Here. Bathe your eyes, and then we'll see about getting you buttoned into that gown."

Celia pressed the cool compress to her eyes and a few minutes later stepped into the gown. The older woman's fingers were surprisingly nimble at the buttons. Soon Celia was dressed and standing before the cheval glass adjusting her mother's veil.

Mrs. Manigault smiled into the mirror. "Sutton will never forget the way you look just now. Even when you are my age, in his eyes you will look just the same."

"A lovely thought anyway." Celia turned from the mirror to place a kiss on the woman's cheek. "Thank you for helping me to dress. I was wondering how I'd manage all those buttons."

"Mrs. Maguire arrived just after we did and offered to come up, but I asked for the honor for myself."

"I'm glad you did."

"This hurried-up wedding is not what you wanted. But just now this house is filled with those who love you most and long only for your happiness. And isn't that the purpose of a ceremony anyway? To send two people off on a new life together, surrounded by love?"

"Of course. But you know Savannah. As soon as word of this gets out, people will start speculating on the reasons behind it."

"True. Some will be unable to refrain from questioning the timing. But one thing I've learned in my long life is that people are not nearly as interested in others as they are in themselves.

Soon enough they will return to their own little dramas. And you and my handsome grandson will be the brightest young couple in town." Mrs. Manigault patted Celia's hand. "Now you wait here, and I'll go see whether your father is ready."

"Has the rector arrived yet?"

"Sutton reports that Mr. Clark is away for the rest of the day visiting his family, but his assistant, Mr. Soames, is here."

Celia suppressed a sigh. She had known the rector ever since his arrival at St. John's. He had dined in her home on occasion. He and Papa were friends. Mr. Soames was new. A stranger.

"Now don't fret," Mrs. Manigault said. "Mr. Soames is just as qualified as Mr. Clark to read the marriage ceremony, and he is the very soul of kindness."

Celia nodded. "Please be careful on the stairs."

"Sutton is stationed in the foyer, waiting to assist me on the way down." Mrs. Manigault kissed Celia's cheek. "Be happy, Celia. Be kind to my grandson. He loves you so."

Celia swallowed the hard lump in her throat. "I will do my best."

"Mrs. Maguire will let you know when to come down."

Waiting for her cue, Celia closed her eyes and prayed for peace. For her father. For her future with Sutton. "Make me a worthy wife, pleasing to you and to Sutton."

"Miss Celia?" Mrs. Maguire bustled in, her face pink, eyes bright. "If this turn of events don't take the rag right off the bush, I'm sure I don't know what would! Gettin' married on Christmas!"

"I'm just as surprised as you, but it's what Papa wants."

"I know it. And judgin' from the way he looks just now, I'd say you made the wise decision. I just wish I'd had some warning, so I could have made a decent wedding supper."

"There are only us and the Mackays. And Mr. Soames, if he wants to stay. Whatever we have will be all right."

"But Mrs. Hemphill was so excited about baking that fancy wedding cake we ordered."

"We'll serve it at a reception later on, if Papa is up to it."

Mrs. Maguire sniffed, and the tears rolled down her wrinkled cheeks. "Oh, my Celia. I've looked after you all your life. Made plenty o' mistakes with you, I am sure. But I've done my best by you. And now, in the twinkling o' my eye, 'tis all over."

"I've no complaints, Mrs. Maguire." Celia regarded the housekeeper with deep affection. "Or very few anyway."

Mrs. Maguire turned away and tightened the straps on Celia's small leather trunk. "At least you're already packed."

"Yes, but I'm not sure where we're to go after the ceremony."

"The Pulaski Hotel, Mr. Mackay says. I'm surprised there was a vacancy, it bein' Christmas." Mrs. Maguire patted Celia's hand. "'Tis a fine place for settin' sail on the seas o' matrimony."

Remembering the waiter's snub when she and Mrs. Mackay had stopped there for lunch last fall, Celia hoped that tonight she might find a warmer welcome.

"Your da is waitin' for you at the bottom o' the stairs. Let me go first so's I don't spoil your big entrance."

Celia reached out to embrace the housekeeper, but Mrs. Maguire shook her head and pulled away. "If I don't get out o' here this very minute, I'll be floodin' the whole place wi' tears."

Celia waited five minutes, opened the door, and stepped into the hall. Her mother's veil fluttered as she passed the Butler and Browning portraits lining the gallery. Below, Papa stood, shoulders back, beaming up at her, and she felt tears welling in her eyes. She lifted the hem of her heavy gown and started down the stairs.

"My dear." Papa's voice when she reached him was barely a whisper. "For a moment it was as if I was seeing your mother again. You are beautiful."

"Thank you."

"I'm the one who should thank you, for changing your plans for me."

He clasped her hands. She felt faint, overcome with love for him and with sorrow for all that would never be. There could be no Christmases with grandchildren on his knee, no summer outings to Isle of Hope, nor a hundred other memories that might have been made if not for his illness. This moment, fragile as a moth's wing, would have to sustain her in the long years ahead. There was so much she wanted to say, but emotion stopped her words. She embraced him, her head resting on his shoulder. A sob caught in her throat. "I love you, Papa."

"I have never doubted that for a single moment. You have been the joy of all my days." He straightened and offered his arm. "Shall we go?"

She took his arm and felt it tremble. They crossed the foyer and entered the library. Mr. Soames was already in place, his back to the fireplace, the prayer book in his hands. Sutton, resplendent in a new gray wool suit, white shirt, and light-blue cravat, stood next to the minister. He caught sight of her, and his face opened with a delight so palpable that she felt a rush of warmth to her face.

Mrs. Mackay and Mrs. Manigault occupied the settee. Mrs. Maguire stood behind them, her careworn hands clasped tightly at her waist. Mr. Mackay and Papa took the two chairs opposite.

Celia noticed that Mrs. Maguire had set out even more candles. Their light reflected in the bowls of oranges and cinnamon decorating the end tables, the flames burning as steadily as her love for the man she was about to marry.

She caught the housekeeper's eye and whispered, "Where's Maxwell?"

"Safe in the garden with a ham bone to bury. Didn't want him whining to go outside in the middle of the I-dos."

"Miss Browning. Mr. Mackay." The young minister began the

marriage service, his voice as solemn as the expression on his face. "Is it your wish, entered into freely and in the spirit of love, to be married?"

"It is." Celia and Sutton spoke as one.

"Then let us begin."

The rest of it happened as in a dream. Celia heard her own voice and Sutton's repeating the timeless vows, but everything seemed far away. As they knelt for the final blessing, she turned her head to look at her father, who was weeping openly, a handkerchief pressed to his eyes.

Then the Mackays surrounded her and Sutton, each of them pressing kisses on her cheek. Mrs. Maguire hurried to the kitchen and soon announced a light supper. Mr. Soames offered his congratulations but made his excuses and left. After the makeshift meal, they returned to the library for coffee, the Mackays keeping up Papa's spirits with memories of the old days and with reports of the goings-on down on Commerce Row.

Darkness fell, and the sound of Christmas revelry on the streets outside filtered into the house. Policemen on horseback patrolled the noisy crowd. Carolers sang. Fireworks popped and whined, sending Maxwell into an excited frenzy at the door. Mrs. Maguire let him in, and he made straight for Celia, his little body trembling with excitement. Celia picked him up and nuzzled his face, oblivious to his dirty paws.

Mrs. Maguire produced a towel and laid it over Celia's gown. "You'll be wanting that dress for your own daughter someday, and it won't do to have it ruined."

Celia set Maxwell at her feet. "Stay there."

The pup obeyed, but he kept one eye trained on her as if he knew something extremely important had happened while he was in the garden.

An hour later, after a second round of coffee and pie, Mr.

Mackay rose. "Cornelia, Caroline, we ought to go home and let David rest. I'm sure the newlyweds are tired too."

"I'm not tired." Sutton winked at Celia, and her face heated.

Mrs. Manigault rose and pinned Sutton with her flinty gaze. "You've married the finest girl in Savannah. I expect you to remember that."

"It isn't likely I'll forget, Grandmother. But you're here to remind me, should I ever be remiss."

"Nobody lives forever," she said tartly, "not even us Manigaults. Now, fetch my wrap please, dear boy. And find my cane. I seem to have misplaced it."

When the Mackays' carriage disappeared into the crowded square, Mrs. Maguire took charge. "Miss Celia and Mr. Mackay, you head on down to the hotel whenever you've a mind to. I'll look after Mr. Browning, see he gets his medicines and such."

"Yes, Celia," Papa said, his expression tender. "You two go on along. I'll be fine."

"We'll be back tomorrow, Papa."

"I'll look forward to it. For now, though, I am worn to a nub. Sutton, could you help me with the stairs? Suddenly I'm weak as water. Too much happy excitement, I expect."

Sutton helped him up the stairs and retrieved Celia's valise from her room. They made the short drive to the Pulaski Hotel, the carriage following slowly behind groups of raucous sailors, excited children, and pink-cheeked carolers.

Sutton lifted Celia from the carriage and escorted her inside. The hotel lobby was dressed for Christmas with crystal bowls of greenery, masses of candles on the fireplace mantel, and a beribboned nosegay of mistletoe suspended above the deserted reception desk.

Sutton rang the little silver bell. Presently the sleepy-eyed night clerk appeared, one suspender falling off his shoulder.

"Oh, yes. Mr. and Mrs . . . Mackay." The clerk nodded. "I have your reservation right here. Oh dear, where did I put that key?"

Sutton let out a long sigh. "Is there a bellman about?"

"Sorry, sir. We're a bit shorthanded tonight. Most of the staff has gone home to celebrate Christmas—what's left of it. Now just a minute. I know I have that key around here somewhere."

Sutton turned to Celia. "I'll bring the bags in. I won't be long."

"All right." Suddenly she was exhausted. She took a chair by the window and watched the noisy celebration, the crowds pulsing along Bryan Street. It was a wonder any of the hotel guests could sleep with the incessant popping of fireworks, the shrieking of policemen's whistles, and the rumbling of carriages.

"Here it is." The desk clerk held up the room key. "I knew I'd find it. Now where is your mister?"

"Getting our bags." Celia went to the door. What was taking Sutton so long? Cupping her hands, she peered into the darkness. The carriage had disappeared. And so had Sutton.

25

"MA'AM? MA'AM, ARE YOU ALL RIGHT?"

Celia blinked, surprised to find herself in a half-sitting position on the hotel settee, a small wooden stool beneath her feet. "What happened?"

"You fainted, I reckon." The night clerk pressed a glass of sherry into her hands. "This will revive you."

She took one sip and handed it back. "Has my husband returned?"

"Not yet, but I imagine he'll be back in a minute. Most likely he's having a hard time finding someone to look after his horse and carriage. Livery closed up at six o'clock, tight as a clam."

She sat up. "But if that were the case, why wouldn't he have brought our bags in first?"

The clerk shrugged. "I'm sure I don't know."

The door opened and a gray-haired man came in, accompanied by a much younger woman in a tight crimson dress and a feathered hat.

"Excuse me, ma'am," the clerk said. "I need to tend to these customers, but I can give you the key to your room if you want to go on up. It's getting awfully late."

"I'd rather wait here if you don't mind."

"Suit yourself." He returned to the desk.

While the clerk spoke to the man, the woman crossed the lobby and plopped down in a chair next to Celia, sending the scents of whisky, tobacco, and perfume wafting into the air. She smiled at Celia. "Mercy, there's a commotion in the street. People yelling and running ever' which away. Carriages are backed up all the way from here to the waterfront."

Celia looked up. Sutton had been gone a long time, but perhaps the clerk was right and Sutton had merely been delayed by the crowd.

"Policemen are everywhere," the woman went on. "One of the brutes almost ran me down. But lucky for me, that nice gentleman over there came to my rescue."

Undoubtedly, the woman was quite capable of looking after herself, but Celia nodded.

"If you don't mind my sayin' so, that's some fancy dress you're wearing."

Celia was not in the mood for conversation. But she couldn't remain mute either. "Thank you."

"Some special occasion?" the woman asked. "Besides Christmas, I mean."

"My wedding dress. I was married this afternoon."

"Well now, that was not the smartest decision you could have made. From here on out, you'll get one cheap present meant for both Christmas and your anniversary."

"I'm not worried about that."

The woman stood. "Looks like Romeo has finally got us a room. I'll be seein' you."

Celia watched the pair ascend the staircase, the woman's hips swaying beneath her tight gown.

Tamping down her impatience, she got to her feet and went outside. The crowd had thinned, but several conveyances still lined the street. There was no sign of Sutton.

She had turned to go back in when someone slammed into her so hard she nearly fell. Before she could catch her breath, strong arms lifted her off her feet. She caught a whiff of spirits, tobacco, and ashes.

"Who are you? What do you want? Let me go!"

Celia squirmed in the viselike grasp as the kidnapper unceremoniously dumped her into a cramped carriage. Wedged between his dark-clad, hulking form and the door, she couldn't move. The carriage gathered speed as it turned up one street and down the other, bouncing as it hit bumps and holes in the unpaved road.

Her heartbeat thrummed in her ears. Who was this man, and what did he want with her? She had heard of a wedding-night prank called a shivaree. But shivarees were mostly a custom of country people. If this was meant to be a joke, it was not in the least amusing.

Through the small window, Celia caught a glimpse of moonlight lying on the river. They must be near the wharf then. She could find her way back to the hotel from here.

She elbowed the man. "Stop this carriage at once."

He didn't answer.

A moment later the carriage slowed, and the smell of burning timber filled her nose. Now they were surrounded by policemen on horseback and groups of men shouting and running back and forth in the street, dodging carriages and buggies that seemed to be going in all directions. A faint orange glow illuminated the darkness, casting the shapes of the buildings along Commerce Row into sharp relief.

The carriage jerked to a halt. The door opened. The kidnapper jumped out, then reached for her and set her on her feet. "This way."

There was no mistaking that rough voice. In the midst of the surrounding chaos, Celia went still. "Mr. Channing?"

"I'll explain later." He took her arm and made a path through the crowd of men standing on the waterfront. Now she saw flames leaping from one roof to the next and men fighting to control the blaze.

At the far end of the row where a building had partially collapsed, a group of men bent over the still form of someone lying on the ground.

Celia felt her knees give way. "No!"

Shaking off Mr. Channing's arm, she pushed her way to Sutton's side and knelt on the muddy ground. "Someone call a doctor!"

"Celia." Sutton stirred and reached for her hand. "Thank God. I was afraid I wouldn't—"

She was too frightened to cry. "Darling, what happened?"

Mr. Channing reached them and dropped to the ground on Sutton's other side.

"Your husband here tried to rescue one of the men on the bucket brigade, who got trapped beneath a burning timber. Apparently he went in through a busted-out window and then got trapped himself trying to find a way out. The doors were padlocked, and we feared they were doomed. When we finally broke the lock and got them out, he was half conscious and calling for you. He was threatening to walk all the way back to the hotel, so I thought I'd better fetch you."

Celia felt faint. "I'm grateful, but it wasn't necessary to frighten me to death. You might have explained the situation instead of snatching me off the street like that."

Another water wagon rumbled past. Shouts filled the air.

"I apologize. But given the nature of our relationship, I wasn't sure you'd believe me." Leo Channing looked down at Sutton. "How are you, Mackay?"

"My lungs feel like they're on fire."

"You breathed in a lot of smoke." Channing rose. "You need a doctor."

Sutton licked his lips and struggled into a sitting position. "How . . . how is the other fellow?"

Mr. Channing slowly shook his head. "You did everything you could. Stay put. I'll get the carriage."

Moments later the reporter returned and helped them inside. "I've sent for Dr. Dearing. He'll meet us at the hotel."

Sutton leaned heavily against Celia as the carriage rocked along the street. From what Celia could tell, the fire was finally out. The water wagons were lined up along the darkened road, and the policemen were dispersing the last of the crowd.

Celia cradled Sutton's head and let the tears come. Wordlessly, Mr. Channing proffered his handkerchief. When the carriage drew up at the hotel entrance, he ran inside and soon returned with the night clerk and another man. The three of them helped Sutton out of the carriage and carried him inside.

"Let's put him over there," the clerk said. They half carried Sutton across the room and lowered him onto the settee nearest the fireplace.

The crisis transformed the sleepy night clerk into a model of efficiency. He was everywhere at once, summoning a chambermaid to bring a pillow and blanket, fetching a pitcher of water and fresh linens. He turned up the lights in the gas chandelier and stoked the fire in the fireplace.

Dr. Dearing arrived clutching his medical bag, his hat askew and his shirttail hanging out, his expression the very picture of disapproval. "Miss Browning? Is it your father? I specifically told him not to—"

"Over there, Doc." Mr. Channing pointed. "It's Mr. Mackay. The younger Mr. Mackay, that is."

Celia started to follow, but the doctor held up his hand. "Please. I need room."

"But he's my husband."

"I don't care if he's the emperor of China. I still need space to conduct a proper examination." Dr. Dearing gentled his voice. "I know you're worried, but the sooner I can assess his condition, the better for him."

The clerk appeared at her side with a tea tray. "Come along. You can wait in my office." He motioned to Mr. Channing. "You look like you could use a spot of something yourself."

Mr. Channing rubbed his eyes. "You got anything stronger than tea?"

"Go on in with the lady. I'll bring you a whiskey."

Celia was uncomfortable at having to sit with Channing, but she was near collapse, and besides, he had looked after Sutton.

They entered the small office, a cluttered space lit by a couple of guttering lamps. The clerk poured tea for Celia before leaving to get a bottle and a glass for the newspaperman.

"I must keep an eye on the front desk," the clerk said when he returned. "But let me know if you need anything. I'll fetch you as soon as the doctor is done."

He left.

Channing poured his whiskey and took a long sip. "So here we are again."

Celia added sugar to her tea. "I'm grateful to you for taking care of my husband."

He shrugged. "It wouldn't do for you to become a bride and a widow on the same day. And anybody else would have done the same. Mackay was frantic with worry. Said you wouldn't know what had happened to him." Mr. Channing took a sip of the whiskey. "I was enjoying a spot of Christmas cheer at the establishment for the convivially inclined just down the street and heard the commotion. By the time I got to the Row, that lawyers' office on the corner was blazing away."

"Weems and Phelps." The office was just three doors down from Mackay Shipping Company. Celia had passed it many times on her way to Papa's office.

"That's the one. It took the volunteer fire companies some time to assemble, it being Christmas and all, and in the interim, Mr. Mackay and several others formed a bucket brigade to keep the flames from spreading." The reporter finished the whiskey and helped himself to another. "Then he saw the man trapped inside and went in to save him. You know the rest."

Mr. Channing turned the glass in his hands, his gaze so intent that she looked away. "I didn't realize you were married already."

"I didn't realize you were still in Savannah."

"I was going home for Christmas but missed my train." He shifted in his chair. "I got the note you sent. About the laundress. Septima. I was surprised you kept your side of our bargain."

The tea calmed her. "I never thought I'd say this, but I'm glad you told me about my aunt's diary. It shed some light on things, though I still have many unanswered questions." She set down her cup. "And apart from your wanting me to uncover the diary, I don't know why you sent those unsettling anonymous messages."

"I didn't send them to you. They were for your cousin. Except for the last one. I hoped it would warn you."

"*'An oak is often split by a wedge from its own branch.'* But Ivy said—"

"After your cousin spoke to me the first time, I suspected that Ivy knew what happened in the carriage house."

"Why? What did she tell you?"

"Nothing. But a reporter develops a sixth sense about people. I had a feeling your cousin knew more than she would admit. I hoped the notes would convince her that someone else knew the truth, too, and that she would confide in me."

Mr. Channing poured another drink. "I didn't know she'd pretended the messages were for you. I didn't know about the hidden message in the bracelet either. The so-called language of the jewels—or that she was the one who sent it."

Celia's mind reeled. "Wait a minute. You knew Ivy was responsible for the bracelet?"

"Now I do. But the day you came to my boardinghouse, I thought the little bauble was a gift from an anonymous suitor, just as I told you. It was only later that Ivy confided in me and asked for my help with her plan."

"To do harm to Sutton and me."

"Well, to one or the other. She wanted to prevent your marriage somehow. I'm the first to admit I'm no saint, but I wanted no part of her scheme."

Celia frowned. "And you didn't think to warn me? To alert the authorities to a murder plot?" She narrowed her eyes. "Or maybe you hoped she would do it, and then you'd have your big sensational story."

Mr. Channing clapped a hand to his heart. "You wound me, Mrs. Mackay. Any reporter wants a big story, but even I would not want to see you come to harm."

"Then why on earth didn't you tell me?"

"I knew I would not be believed. Your father would have seen it as another attempt to stir up controversy. Ivy would have denied everything, and I had no proof. I would have been the one arrested."

Celia pondered his words. "I suppose that's true."

"Besides, when I told your cousin I wouldn't help her, I got the impression she was giving up on her plan. I didn't think she was brave enough to attempt such a thing on her own."

"I see. But when I called on the jeweler in Yamacraw, he told me a young man commissioned the bracelet. So who—"

"Miss Lorens chose a jeweler in a part of town where she was unknown and unlikely to cross paths with any of your acquaintances. She told me she dressed as a man, in some get-up she made for a costume party. She's tall enough and, if you don't mind my saying so, big-boned enough, to have gotten away with impersonating a man."

"Robin Hood."

"Pardon?"

"The costume she made for my masquerade party last fall. I saw it when I went to her room that night. Dark-brown trousers and a matching tunic. A brown felt hat. Completely nondescript."

"And therefore unlikely to be remembered. Even if a tunic isn't exactly the height of fashion these days." Mr. Channing stroked his chin. "Robin Hood, eh? Taking from the rich to give to the poor. One does have to admire her sense of irony."

Celia slumped in the chair and rubbed her eyes. "I suppose this gives you much more fodder for your book."

He smiled. "Well, I'm not altogether altruistic. A leopard and his spots and so forth. I still have my theories, but even with the name of the laundress, my investigation has hit a dead end. I could write a book filled with conjecture, but as it happens, I'm on the trail of an even bigger story back in Baltimore. Besides, since your cousin has left the country—"

She stared at him. "My word, Mr. Channing. Is there anything you don't know?"

"A journalist is only as good as his ability to cultivate sources. I happen to have a few good ones down on the waterfront. One of them was loading the *Percival* when your driver delivered Ivy and her companion to the wharf." The newspaperman drained his glass. "I can't prove it, but my guess is that her companion was none other than the daughter of—"

The office door opened, and the night clerk came in. "Mrs. Mackay, your husband is asking for you."

Celia shot to her feet. "Please excuse me, Mr. Channing."

The reporter followed her out of the office. She crossed the deserted lobby at a dead run, nearly colliding with Dr. Dearing. He put out a hand to steady her. "No need to rush. He's got a few blisters and he'll need a couple of days for his lungs to clear, but he's going to be just fine."

"Thank God."

The doctor nodded. "Congratulations on your wedding. Your husband told me of your decision to marry earlier than planned. For what it's worth, I think you made the right choice." He took out his watch and snapped it open. "It's later than I thought. I think I'll toddle on home. Oh, and Merry Christmas."

"Merry Christmas to you. And many thanks."

Sutton struggled to his feet as the doctor left, and Celia walked into his embrace.

Leo Channing retrieved his hat from the chair beside the fireplace. "Mrs. Mackay? I'm headed back to Baltimore the day after tomorrow. So I reckon this is good-bye."

He turned his collar up and left the hotel.

The night clerk hurried over and handed Sutton the room key. "I've located your bags and will send them up shortly. I had the chambermaid put some extra linens in your room in case you'd like to wash the rest of that soot off. There's champagne and sweet biscuits if you're wanting a nightcap. Compliments of the Pulaski Hotel."

Sutton wrapped an arm around Celia's waist, and they went up the stairs together. As they entered the room, Celia caught sight of their images in the cheval glass in the corner.

Her hair was disheveled. Her wedding dress was wrinkled, the hem caked with mud. Sutton's fine gray suit was peppered with holes, his white shirt blackened with soot, and a film of gray ash covered his shoes. His eyebrows were singed, his palms raw and blistered and shiny with salve. And she had worried that her wedding day would be less than memorable.

Now that the crisis was past, she was filled with a mixture of profound relief and no small measure of indignation. She folded her arms across her chest. "How did you get mixed up in the fire, Sutton? I was terribly worried. I couldn't imagine where you had gone."

"When I went out to get our bags from the carriage, a couple of sailors were shouting about a fire on the Row. I was afraid the volunteer companies couldn't get there in time, so I organized a few men to fight the fire until they arrived." He passed a hand over his eyes. "I wasn't sure whether our offices, or your father's, were in danger, but I didn't want to take a chance. Not after the losses we suffered this year, to say nothing of your father's ill health."

"You should have told me you were going."

His brows rose. "I paid a boy a dollar to deliver a message to you. I even wrote down your name so he wouldn't forget."

"Well, he never showed up." Celia's voice wobbled. "I sat alone in the lobby all night. In my wedding dress. Until Leo Channing showed up and manhandled me into his carriage." She brushed away sudden tears. "I thought I was being kidnapped. I was scared I've never see you again."

"Ah, darling, I apologize. I'm sorry he frightened you. But we're together now with our whole lives ahead of us, and our offices are all right. I only wish I'd been able to save that poor man." Sutton stood behind her and wrapped both arms around her waist. "You aren't too sorry you married me?"

Despite his injuries and fatigue, his eyes held the glimmer of mischief she'd loved since the first night they met.

"I haven't made up my mind yet."

Sutton turned her around until they were face-to-face. "I hope you decide soon," he said, his voice rough with emotion, "because the suspense is killing me."

Outside, church bells rang.

"Christmas is almost over," he said softly. "I love you, Mrs. Mackay."

"And I love you, Mr. Mackay."

"I'm profoundly relieved to hear it."

Sutton bent his head to kiss her, and with one hand, doused the light.

26

IF THERE WAS ONE THING AT WHICH THE PEOPLE OF SAVANNAH excelled, it was in organizing a parade. The one for Papa's funeral rivaled that of Mayor Wayne the previous June.

Lines of buggies and carriages wound past the house on Madison Square and rolled slowly toward Laurel Grove Cemetery. Hand in hand, Celia and Sutton walked behind her father's hearse, acknowledging the solemn nods and waving handkerchiefs of the crowd lining the parade route. Numbed with cold and grief, Celia moved as if in a trance. Nothing that had happened in these past days seemed real.

Two mornings ago, Celia had left the Mackays for her daily visit to her father's house and arrived to find Mrs. Maguire sitting on the bottom stair weeping into her handkerchief. "He's gone, my girl. Not half an hour ago."

"Was it—?"

"Peaceful? Yes. But then, Mr. Browning niver was one to make a fuss."

"Have you sent for anyone?"

"Not yet. I thought you might want some time alone with 'im."

Celia went back outside to send her driver for Sutton and the undertaker. Then she sat beside her father's bed and wept silently, holding his hand until they arrived. It was typical of him to die the way he'd lived—with a quiet courage and the inborn modesty that was the truest test of nobility. He left the house for the last time just as the sun came up, gilding the winter frost and the old oaks along the square.

News of his passing made the front page of the papers as far away as Charleston and Atlanta. Condolence cards and telegraph messages arrived from the mayor's office, the governor's office, the members of Papa's social clubs, and his business associates on Commerce Row. And now all those people and more had turned out on the streets to offer a final tribute to the man who had contributed so much to the life of the city.

"Are you all right, darling?" Sutton asked as they arrived at the cemetery.

She nodded and reached beneath her black veil to wipe her eyes.

He squeezed her hand, and she felt the warmth of his hand through their gloves. "It will be over soon," he said.

The black hearse, pulled by a magnificent span of four, halted at the cemetery gates. In a cold silence broken only by the rattle of harness and the snuffling and stamping of the horses, pallbearers carried the coffin to the place where Papa was laid to rest among the senators, bishops, and businessmen who had been his companions in life. After the committal, Celia knelt with the rector and Sutton at the grave for a final private good-bye.

Despite her deep love for him and her bottomless sense of loss, she couldn't help feeling a lingering disappointment that he had never told her everything he knew about what had happened in the house on Madison Square. The story still felt unfinished. Incomplete. What family secrets had he taken to the grave? Had the keeping of those secrets changed who he was? Who she was? When was it justifiable to keep secrets from those we love?

Despite her questions, she could not wish Papa back to face more days of agony. He was at peace. In the high country. And as the old hymn promised, she would see him again one day in that bright place above. She rose and stepped away from the raw wound in the earth.

"Miss Browning?"

Celia turned to find a young man with green eyes and a neatly trimmed red-gold beard standing half hidden behind a marble tombstone. His black suit appeared to be new, but it was ill-fitting—the sleeves too long and the shoulders too tight. He held a worn watch cap in his work-roughened hands.

"I'm Mrs. Mackay now."

"Oh. O' course. Beggin' your pardon." He took a step closer. "I was sorry to hear of your da's passin'. People say he did a lot o' good for the town."

"Thank you." Celia frowned. "I don't believe we've met."

He glanced around the cemetery. It was still crowded with black-clad mourners who stood in small groups, murmuring together. "I'm Michael Gleason. I was hopin' to see Miss Lorens."

Celia bristled. "My cousin is abroad. But I doubt she'd care to see you, after you feigned an attraction to her, then asked for money for your political activities."

The Irish drayman blushed. "I admit it looks unseemly. I ought not to have pressed her for money. But I had a good reason for—"

"Yes, I know," Celia said, taken aback by the force of her own anger. "A reason named Sylvie Kelly."

Mr. Gleason shook his head. "Sylvie wasn't the reason. I'm—"

"What then?"

He paused and squared his shoulders, as if gathering himself. "After I met Ivy, I found out we're kin." He crushed his cap in his hands and stared at spot just past Celia's shoulder. "I'm Ivy's brother."

Celia stood in the middle of her old bedroom, surrounded by trunks and hatboxes. Maxwell played among the jumble of dresses, jackets, crinolines, and shoes littering the bed. When he attacked one of her best white kid boots, she rescued it from his mouth and kissed the top of his head. "No you don't, you little scamp."

Celia could barely keep her mind on preparations for her departure. Michael Gleason's startling claim had been keeping her awake at night. Was his story true? Had her aunt destroyed pages from her diary in order to keep the secret? Maybe it was foolish to pursue such questions now, but the Irish drayman's story was too stunning to ignore.

"Spoiled that pup silly, that's what you've done," Mrs. Maguire said, coming in to dump another armload of jackets onto the bed. "I won't be able to do a thing with 'im after you're gone."

"Oh, he'll be a perfect little gentleman." Celia scratched the dog's belly, and he closed his eyes. "Won't you, sweetheart?"

"You see, that's just what I mean. Calling him 'sweetheart' and lettin' him loll about on your bed like he was the king of Siam. Back in County Waterford, people were people and dogs were dogs, and niver were th' two confused."

Celia laughed. "I supposed I have indulged him these last few days. I'm going to miss him terribly. I wish I could take him with us."

"On your honeymoon?" Mrs. Maguire shook her head. "Mr. Mackay might have something to say about that."

"Sutton loves Maxwell as much as I do. He gave him to me, after all. But Maxwell is still growing. The ship would be too confining for him."

"Humph." Mrs. Maguire held up a dark-green velvet jacket. "Will you take this one or leave it behind?"

"I'll take it. Springtime in Paris can be quite chilly." Celia fingered the cuffed sleeves. "I won't have much occasion to wear it, though. I'll be mostly in mourning clothes."

A deep silence settled over them like dust over a vacant room. Celia watched Mrs. Maguire fold more chemises and petticoats into a leather trunk. "May I ask you something?"

"What is it?"

"Why did you try to hide Aunt Eugenia's writing box from me?"

The permanent flush beneath the older woman's pale Irish skin deepened to crimson, but she denied nothing and calmly continued with her folding. "Are you happier now for havin' read that poor woman's diary?"

"Happier?" Celia made a space for herself on her bed and plopped down, Maxwell at her side. "Not really. More unsettled than ever, if you want to know the truth. I wish you would tell me what you know. Surely you remember what happened when Aunt Eugenia and Ivy came here from St. Simons."

"Won't change anything."

"Of course not, but I still want to know. And there's much more to the story. Aunt Eugenia's diary mentioned that she was grief stricken when she first met Uncle Magnus and hinted that she was keeping a secret from him." Celia looked pointedly at the housekeeper. "I think I know now what that secret was."

Mrs. Maguire's hands stilled above the half-filled trunk. "My mam used to say if you don't want flour on your hands, best stay out of the bin."

"Now that Ivy and Papa are gone, I can't see the point of keeping me in the dark."

With a resigned sigh, Mrs. Maguire moved a pile of clothes from the chair near the window. "Sure and 'tis a complicated tale. Heartbreakin' too."

"Even so, why didn't you tell me?"

"You were a child at the time. You didn't need to know such

things. And then, after you grew up—well, 'twasn't my place. I've been in this house for most of my life, but I'm still a servant, and I never forget it. Besides, I thought it would make things worse if that story started goin' around again. What good could come of it?"

"Is that why you locked me in the attic? That was you, wasn't it? Were you trying to frighten me so I'd stop looking?"

"Of course not. I didn't even know you were in there." Another massive sigh. "I passed by on my way to tidyin' up your father's room and saw the door ajar. I thought somebody had left the door open by mistake, so I closed it. 'Twasn't till after you were rescued that I saw the empty valise a-sittin' next to the stair." The housekeeper frowned as Maxwell shook himself awake and turned in circles before climbing into Celia's lap. "Then later on when you asked about Miss Eugenia's writin' box, I figured you wouldn't rest till you found it—and her diary. And then you'd know what a terrible man your uncle was. So I took it from the attic and put it in my kitchen where you found it."

Mrs. Maguire plucked at a loose thread on the pillow. "If you want my opinion, Magnus Lorens never was worth Miss Eugenia's little finger, but there was no talking her out of marryin' him." She pulled her handkerchief from her sleeve and blotted her nose. "We *niver* discussed it, but I suppose she saw his proposal as the best way out."

"Way out? Of what?"

"The day she wed him, she was already with child."

The room spun. Celia blinked. "Go on."

"Well before she met Magnus Lorens, your aunt was in love with someone else, but her parents thought he was all wrong for her. Unsuitable was how they put it. So her mother—your grandmother—took both her and Miss Francesca to Europe and stayed there for a whole year, waitin' for Miss Eugenia to forget all about him."

"But it didn't work." Celia could imagine her aunt's feelings. Even if she were kept apart from Sutton for a thousand years, her heart wouldn't change.

"No, it didn't. And eventually they had to come home. Miss Eugenia continued living at home, pretending she'd let go of her affections for that young man—Sean Gleason, his name was. But one day he showed up on her doorstep with his own sad tale to tell."

Sean Gleason. Celia's stomach clenched. She hadn't wanted to believe Michael Gleason's wild story—a story he'd claimed to have learned at his parish church shortly after Leo Channing began publishing his newspaper articles. A story that linked his family with hers.

Mrs. Maguire stared out the window. "He and Miss Eugenia each thought they'd been forgotten by the other. While she was away, he married, and his wife had a child born too soon and sick as they come. The boy survived, but his mam didn't. So there Sean Gleason was, a-standin' on her veranda, widowed and with a baby to raise. And there was Miss Eugenia, heartsick and as besotted with 'im as ever."

Celia put the pieces of the puzzle together. "So Sean and Aunt Eugenia got married after all?"

The housekeeper shook her head. "That was the plan the two o' them cooked up, all right—to marry in secret and then tell her parents when it would be too late. But before they could do it, Sean got himself killed workin' on the wharf, and he wasn't even cold in the grave when Miss Eugenia realized she was going to be a mother."

Celia took in a shaky breath. So it was true. "Uncle Magnus is not Ivy's father."

"He is not. He knew Sean Gleason from the docks—I think he was working in one of the shipping offices—and I suppose Sean must have told him about Miss Eugenia. Anyway, Mr. Lorens came to pay his condolences, and once he realized her family had money, he started courtin' her. She was frightened and ashamed and afraid to tell her parents the truth. So when Mr. Lorens proposed marriage, she accepted."

"And when Ivy was born she let him think—"

"That she did."

"Does Ivy know?"

"Nobody knows, far's I can tell. Except the dead, o' course."

The dead and Michael Gleason. And the parish gossips. Celia tried to sort out her feelings, but they were in a worse jumble than the clothes littering her bed. At least Michael hadn't turned away from Ivy because he found her undesirable or because she couldn't give him money. Celia felt a wave of sympathy for her cousin and a rush of anger for Michael Gleason. He ought to have explained everything to Ivy, but he'd waited until it was too late. And she had sailed for Cuba feeling more unloved than ever.

"Mrs. Maguire." Celia shifted on her bed, and Maxwell raised his head before returning to his puppy dreams. "You're the one who ripped out those pages?"

"I am. And I'm not sorry for it, either." Mrs. Maguire clasped her hands tightly in her lap. "I should have destroyed the whole thing. I don't know why I didn't. 'Tis all in the past."

"But Ivy deserves to know who her real father is. If it was me, I'd want to know."

"The Gleasons are only poor Irish, like me. Nothin' to brag about."

Celia digested this news. But still she had questions about the day her aunt died. "Aunt Eugenia knew about Uncle Magnus's affair with Septima, and she knew there was a child. But her diary seems to indicate that most of her friends' husbands behaved the same way. Would she have taken her own life over it?"

"She was beside herself the night she and Ivy arrived here

from St. Simons with Mr. Lorens on their heels. But after a few days she seemed better. Reckon she got used to the idea of him takin' up with another. But that's not to say she still wasn't madder than a hornet. I was surprised when she invited that wench into this house."

"She asked Septima here?"

"Miss Eugenia wanted to talk to her. She asked me to make tea and bring it up to her room. I don't know why she didn't want to meet the woman in the parlor, but I did what she asked me to do. That woman arrived all decked out in satin and lace like the Queen o' England herself. Miss Eugenia out came into the upstairs hallway and called for her to come on up."

Mrs. Maguire closed her eyes. "Miss Ivy had been sick the whole night, and I went back to the kitchen to fix her some broth. When it was ready, I took the tray and started up the stairs, and I heard the two of them—Miss Eugenia and that mulatto woman—arguin'. I went on in to tend to Miss Ivy. Then I heard Mr. Lorens running up the stairs, calling for Miss Eugenia.

"I went into the hallway, intending to tell him Miss Ivy was sick and asking for him, but by the time I got to the door, he was already in Miss Eugenia's room. The door was standin' wide open, and I could see all the way through to Miss Eugenia's balcony. The three of them were still fightin'. Mr. Lorens was trying to grab Miss Eugenia by the arm, and she was cryin' and yellin' at him to leave her alone. When he wouldn't leave, she climbed onto the railing. To scare him into going away, I guess. Or to convince him she meant business.

"Miss Ivy came out of her room. I stepped in front of her so she wouldn't see anything. When I looked again, Mr. Lorens was standing right in front of Miss Eugenia. He raised both his arms. The mulatto woman pushed at him and screamed. And then"—Mrs. Maguire shrugged—"Miss Eugenia was no longer there."

Celia went numb. "He killed her?"

"I can't be sure. Maybe it was the other woman that caused Miss Eugenia to lose her balance. Maybe Mr. Lorens meant to take hold of her and pull her to safety. Of course he said it was an accident, and that was the story that appeared in the papers. That woman—Septima—was never named, and that would have been the end of it if she hadn't come back to the carriage house. But she couldn't stay away from your uncle."

"And you never told Papa what you saw?"

"I wasn't certain what I saw. All during the funeral for Miss Eugenia, I prayed about what to do. I didn't want to send an innocent man to jail, even if he was the worst sort o' human being. But if he had pushed Miss Eugenia off that balcony, he needed to pay for his crime." Mrs. Maguire paused and stared out the window. "I spoke to Father O'Brien about it. And I'd made up my mind to tell Mr. Browning what I'd seen and let him decide what was to be done. But then Septima died and Magnus Lorens vanished."

"Ivy thinks he left to protect her."

Mrs. Maguire snorted. "By the time Miss Eugenia died, he had sold off her land and gambled away most o' the proceeds. Your da got wind of it and that's why that rat ran back to where he came from. Good riddance, I say."

Celia let out a low whistle. "No wonder Mr. Channing was intrigued."

"It was the talk of Savannah for a while, but eventually people went back to their own lives and the whole sad thing was forgotten."

"Until Leo Channing showed up." Celia felt as if she'd been gut-punched. How had Papa lived with the violence, the rumors of miscegenation, the multiple tragedies? With the burdensome secrets?

Mrs. Maguire sighed and wiped her eyes, seemingly exhausted

by her tale. "Maybe I should have told you all this when that reporter showed up."

"I wish you had, but I understand why you didn't." Celia paused. "Mr. Channing stirred up all this trouble, and yet he tried to warn me about Ivy."

Mrs. Maguire looked up, a question in her eyes.

"He left a note at the door. 'An oak is often split by a wedge from its own branch.' I didn't understand what it meant then. But he explained everything the night of the fire."

A carriage stopped at the gate. Mrs. Maguire went to the window and lifted the curtain. "There's Miss Thayer."

"Stay put," Celia said. "I'll let her in."

Celia went downstairs, Maxwell at her heels, and opened the door.

"Celia." Alicia came into the foyer, her brown eyes wet with tears. "I'm so sorry I missed the funeral. Mother and I were in Cassville for Grandmother's birthday. We just got home night before last. Are you all right?"

"I'm fine. Packing for England. We leave tomorrow. But I need a rest. How about some tea? You can catch me up on all your news."

"I'd love some tea, but I can't stay. I have a dress fitting at Mrs. Foyle's. Mrs. Mackay"—Alicia broke off and laughed—"the *other* Mrs. Mackay told Mother you and Sutton were leaving soon. I wanted to see you before you left, to wish you all the happiness in the world."

Alicia drew a small package from her bag. "I brought you a present."

Celia unwrapped a soft leather case that opened to reveal a miniature sketchbook and a set of pencils.

"In case you want to make some sketches of your travels," Alicia said. "You always were the best artist in our class at school. Madame LeFleur said so, and she was never one for false praise."

Celia embraced her friend. "I love it. Thank you."

"You're welcome." Alicia clasped Celia's hand. "Mother and I went out to the asylum yesterday and spoke with Mrs. Clayton. While you're gone, we're going to take charge of raising money for the building fund. You've worked too hard to have the plans stalled now."

"That's wonderful news. I called on Mrs. Clayton last week to discuss it, but she was ill. I left a note for her with Annie Wilcox but haven't had a reply."

"Poor Mrs. Clayton had a bad cough for several days, but she seems quite recovered. I told her I was coming by here today. She says to tell you not to worry about the girls, and there will be plenty of work to do when you get home to Savannah." Alicia peered through the window. "I should go. You know how cross Mrs. Foyle gets when you're even a tiny bit late. You will write to me, Celia?"

"Every chance I get. Though the post can be woefully slow across the Atlantic."

"And you will be home by spring?"

"If all goes according to plan. Why?"

"Can you keep a secret?"

Celia sent her friend a wry smile. "With the best of them."

"Porter Quarterman intends to propose marriage on my birthday next month. He has already spoken to my father, though I'm not supposed to know. That's why I'm off to the modiste's for a new dress." Alicia laughed. "Can you believe I'm to be a sister to Mary?" She squeezed Celia's arm. "You simply must be home in time for my wedding."

"Set the date for June. We're sure to be home by then."

"Done!" Alicia paused, her hand on the doorknob. "Well, good-bye, Mrs. Mackay."

"Good-bye. Mrs. Quarterman."

The sound of Alicia's laughter followed Celia all the way back up the stairs. Mrs. Maguire had left the room, leaving trunks half packed and Maxwell still curled into a golden ball on the pillow.

Celia opened the bottom drawer of her dressing table and took out half a dozen new handkerchiefs, a new jar of lip pomade, and several pairs of earbobs to add to the trunk. Her fingers curled around the small box containing the bracelet that had turned her world upside down. She opened the box and held the trinket in her palm, the fake jewels and the two small diamonds glittering in the light.

Would she have been better off not to have discovered her family's secrets? Would knowing them make her different somehow?

You can't unring the bell.

Celia walked to the small basket she kept for disposing of old letters, broken pencils, and faded ribbons and dropped the bracelet inside.

27

Wednesday, January 26, 1859

THE TIDE WAS IN. THE RIVER, DRESSED IN AZURE, MIRRORED a crystalline winter sky. The wharf teemed with dock workers loading the *Celia B* for the journey to England.

Yesterday afternoon Celia's trunks—and Sutton's—had been delivered to the dock and put aboard. All that had remained this morning was the packing of last-minute items—her toiletries and handkerchiefs, pens and writing paper, the new sketchbook, and the travel journal Papa had given her for Christmas.

Now she stood on the pier, one hand shading her eyes, watching Sutton talking with their captain. Sutton had said that if the weather cooperated they might reach Liverpool in six weeks' time. He planned to spend the second week of March visiting the shipbuilders and making financial arrangements with the London bankers for the construction of his blockade-runner. After that she and Sutton would be off on their honeymoon to Paris, Rome, and Venice. They would return to Savannah in late May, in time to attend Alicia's wedding before leaving for a summer in Saratoga.

Celia reached into her pocket for her handkerchief, and her

fingers brushed the envelope that had arrived this morning. She tore it open.

Celia,

We are safely arrived in Havana. Louisa was ill for a good part of the journey but seems recovered now that we are once again on dry land. At present we are at a small hotel near the waterfront, but it is not an acceptable accommodation for the long term. I hesitate to bring this up, but our situation demands that I have whatever funds might be coming to me from Uncle David's estate after he has passed on. Is he still alive? Or sleeping now with the saints? You can send money in care of the Hotel Tropicale.

On the voyage here I had time to read some of my old books. Remember when we were at the academy and struggling to make sense of the plays of Jean Racine? We laughed at his tragic heroines so blinded by love they couldn't see that their affections were not returned, and we wondered how any modern girl could be so lacking in discernment. And yet that is precisely what happened to me. Of course you're right that nobody can make another person love them, but I stood to lose everyone who mattered to me. I had to try.

I see now that it was hopeless. Sutton was never mine to lose.

Halfway through our voyage, our progress was halted for a day when the *Percival* was becalmed. I found myself with even more time than usual on my hands. Louisa was too ill to accompany me onto the deck, so I spent the day alone with my book of Mr. Shakespeare's plays, skipping from comedy to tragedy to sonnets hoping to read something that would soothe my restless spirit. Don't you find, Celia, that he was a genius in his ability to express so perfectly the yearnings of the human heart? . . .

"Celia?" Sutton strode across the wharf and linked her arm through his. "We're almost ready to sail. Shall we go aboard?"

Celia tucked the letter away to finish later and smiled up at her husband. "I'm ready."

Once they were underway, she would write to Ivy and tell her everything. It was just like Ivy to be scheming, planning ahead for her own benefit with little consideration for Celia's own feelings. Still, Ivy was in for a shock. And despite it all, she deserved the truth. Perhaps learning about her parents and about Michael Gleason, who certainly must have seemed like Ivy's last chance at love, would make a difference.

They went up the creaking gangplank, and Sutton showed her the accommodation he'd expanded just for the two of them. Situated amidships to maximize comfort in high seas, the cabin still smelled of new varnish. It was not overly spacious, but it was large enough for a feather bed, a small table and chairs, and a chest of drawers. Rectangular windows brought in the clear January light and framed her view of the wharf and the city beyond.

"This isn't exactly Madison Square, but it will be home until we reach Liverpool," Sutton said. "Do you like it?"

"It's perfect."

He smiled. "I hope you'll still think so when the heavy weather hits. Shall we go up on deck?"

They joined several crew members at the stern of the ship. Standing beside Sutton watching the lacy whitecaps, the lengthening afternoon shadows, the winter light luminous above the river, everything suddenly quiet except for the lapping of water against the wooden pilings, Celia thought again of everything that had happened to her family, of the questions that would never be fully answered.

At times she felt as if the Brownings had been singled out for trouble. But the truth was that sooner or later misfortune visited every house. Grief and loss were the price one paid for being alive. Spending her days wary and afraid would only rob her of the good things life had to offer, of the thousand small pleasures just waiting to be discovered. Her imagination glowed with anticipation of all she and Sutton would share.

The breeze came up, chilling her face. And she felt new again, ready to let go of old worries and resentments and to embrace whatever came next. She didn't want to wake up some morning fifty years from now and realize she'd mired herself in the past and missed out on everything that made life worthwhile.

The sails unfurled and filled. The ship rocked on the gentle pulse of the river, settling between the wind and the tide. In the company of a Danish brig bound for Copenhagen, the *Celia B* moved slowly toward the sea.

Turning, Celia saw that the balconies of the stores and countinghouses along Commerce Row were crowded with people waving hats and handkerchiefs in farewell.

Sutton drew her to his side. "Take one last look, darling. One last look at home."

Celia wrapped both arms around her husband. "As long as I'm with you, Sutton Mackay, I am home."

Author's Note

Dear Readers,

You've probably noticed that in addition to all of the elements you've come to expect from my novels—romance, history, and mystery—*The Bracelet* contains an extra measure of suspense. But the suspense is based on history as well.

On March 27, 1860, Matilda Moxley Sorrel, wife of wealthy Savannah businessman Francis Sorrel, plunged to her death from the second-floor balcony of a house similar to my fictional one. Stories circulated in Savannah that Mrs. Sorrel had taken her life after learning of her husband's liaison with one of the house servants, a girl called Molly who was said to have been found two weeks later, hanged in the carriage house on the property. Though there seems to be no credible evidence for Molly's existence, Mrs. Sorrel's tragic death is a matter of historical record. Today the story of Matilda and Molly has passed into legend and serves as a ghost tale for visitors to Savannah's Sorrel-Weed House.

Though the Brownings and the Mackays are fictional (there was a prominent family of Mackays in Savannah, but none are portrayed here), many of Celia's friends mentioned in the book were actual persons, among them Mrs. Stiles, Mrs. Low, Nellie Kinzie Gordon (mother of Girl Scouts founder Juliette Low), and

Mrs. Lawton. The Savannah Asylum for Orphan Girls was a real place, as was the Pulaski Hotel, the Ten Broeck Race Course, and the Savannah Poor House and Hospital. And there really was a Captain Stevens who owned cargo boats that traveled between Savannah and the sea islands. The story of Charlie Lamar and the slave ship *Wanderer* is also true.

My second inspiration for this novel comes from a Victorian custom in which gentlemen sent hidden messages to their sweethearts through the language of the jewels. A suitor might send a brooch or a bracelet set with jewels, and the first letters in the jewels' names would spell out such endearments as "adored" or "dear." As you saw, Celia Browning received such a gift, but with a less than endearing message. The blending of this custom with the stories of Matilda and Molly resulted in the book you're now holding.

I hope you enjoyed Celia's story. You'll meet her again when my next historical romantic suspense novel is released in 2015. Until then, thank you for choosing *The Bracelet*.

Warmest wishes,
Dorothy

Reading Group Guide

1. Though Celia enjoys her station in life, she also chafes against the expectations of her family and her circle of friends. Ivy, too, is affected by societal norms. What roles do expectations play for each of the characters in this novel? Have you ever felt constrained or inspired by your family's wishes or the norms of your community?
2. The relationship between Ivy and Celia is a complicated one. Which woman do you think understands the other more completely? Why?
3. Celia's home on Madison Square represents very different things to Celia and Ivy. What do you think the house means to each of them?
4. Ivy believes that the Brownings have provided her with opportunity, but not love. Do you agree? Why or why not?
5. Celia decides to pursue the truth about her family's past, even if her discovery proves uncomfortable. How is Celia changed by what she finds out? Have you ever discovered something in your own past that altered your perception of people and events?
6. What is Leo Channing's role in the story? Do you think his

personal circumstances justified his actions? Why or why not?

7. Were Mr. Browning and Mrs. Maguire justified in keeping the family secrets once Celia was an adult? In similar circumstances, would you want to know the details?
8. At her father's funeral, Celia wonders how her father dealt with the secrets he kept. Was there a price he paid for his silence? What do you think?
9. In her diary, Aunt Eugenia states that she has become a secret abolitionist. What were her reasons for this statement? Does the depiction of the antebellum South in this book differ from your assumptions?
10. In what way is the city of Savannah itself a character in the novel?

ACKNOWLEDGMENTS

I'M GRATEFUL TO EVERY MEMBER OF MY PUBLISHING TEAM for their encouragement and enthusiasm for this book. Two years ago, I pitched the idea for *The Bracelet* to my publisher, the amazing Daisy Hutton, who immediately told me to go for it. Thank you, Daisy. My editors, Becky Philpott and Anne Christian Buchanan, always make my work stronger, for which I am very grateful. Kristen Vasgaard, this cover is truly exceptional. Thank you! Thanks as well to my marketing team, my sales teams, and to everyone who works behind the scenes to bring my books to life. Working with you is my great joy.

Thank you to the incomparable Natasha Kern, who read an early draft of this book and made valuable suggestions. Natasha, I'm so glad you're taking this publishing ride with me.

During the writing of this book, I said good-bye to Major, my beloved twelve-year-old golden retriever, who came into my life as a seven-week-old puppy and who gave me joy every day of his life. Though goldens were first bred in the late 1800s, they were not shown until 1908 and were not recognized as an established breed until 1913—too late for Celia's little puppy, Maxwell, to be specifically identified as a golden retriever. But it was my Major who inspired the creation of Maxwell, and in the pages of this book, Major lives on.

To my author friends, whose humor and wisdom delight me every day, and to my family, thank you. I love you all.

About the Author

A native of west Tennessee, Dorothy Love makes her home in the Texas hill country with her husband and their golden retriever. An award-winning author of numerous young adult novels, Dorothy made her adult debut with the Hickory Ridge novels.